THE
BEND
OF LUCK

By PETER and
MARIA HOEY

The Bend of Luck © 2022 Peter Hoey and Maria Hoey

Editor-in-Chief: Chris Staros.

Published by Top Shelf Productions, an imprint of IDW Publishing, a division of Idea and Design Works, LLC. Offices: Top Shelf Productions, c/o Idea & Design Works, LLC, 2765 Truxtun Road, San Diego, CA 92106. Top Shelf Productions®, the Top Shelf logo, Idea and Design Works®, and the IDW logo are registered trademarks of Idea and Design Works, LLC. All Rights Reserved. With the exception of small excerpts of artwork used for review purposes, none of the contents of this publication may be reprinted without the permission of IDW Publishing. IDW Publishing does not read or accept unsolicited submissions of ideas, stories, or artwork.

Visit our online catalog at www.topshelfcomix.com.

ISBN 978-1-60309-509-9

Printed in China

26 25 24 23 22   1 2 3 4 5

CONTENTS

Luck's always to blame.

–*Jean de La Fontaine*

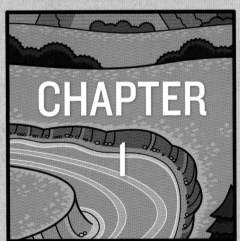

CHAPTER
1

LUCK OCCURS NATURALLY IN THE PHYSICAL WORLD.

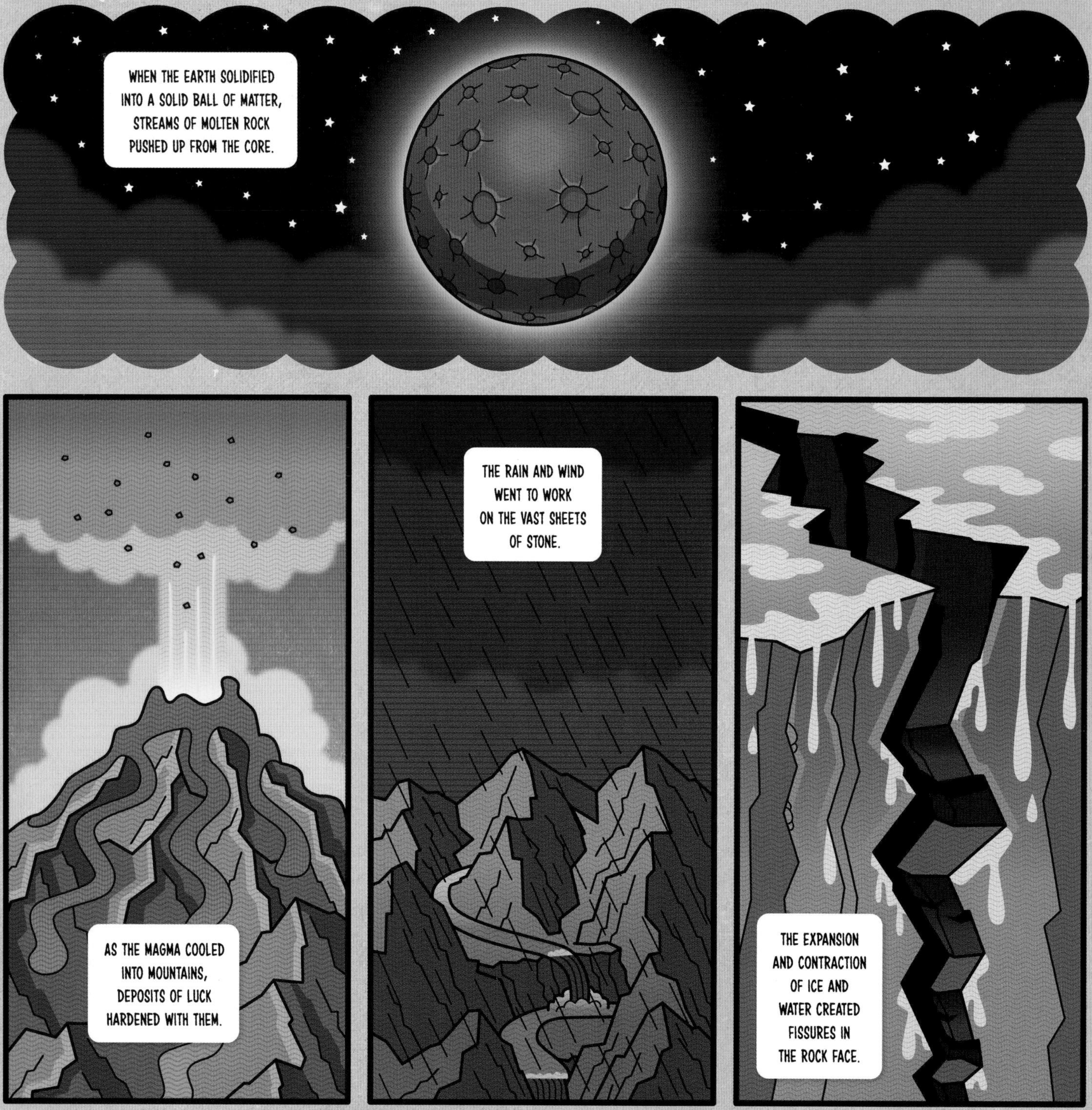
WHEN THE EARTH SOLIDIFIED INTO A SOLID BALL OF MATTER, STREAMS OF MOLTEN ROCK PUSHED UP FROM THE CORE.
AS THE MAGMA COOLED INTO MOUNTAINS, DEPOSITS OF LUCK HARDENED WITH THEM.
THE RAIN AND WIND WENT TO WORK ON THE VAST SHEETS OF STONE.
THE EXPANSION AND CONTRACTION OF ICE AND WATER CREATED FISSURES IN THE ROCK FACE.

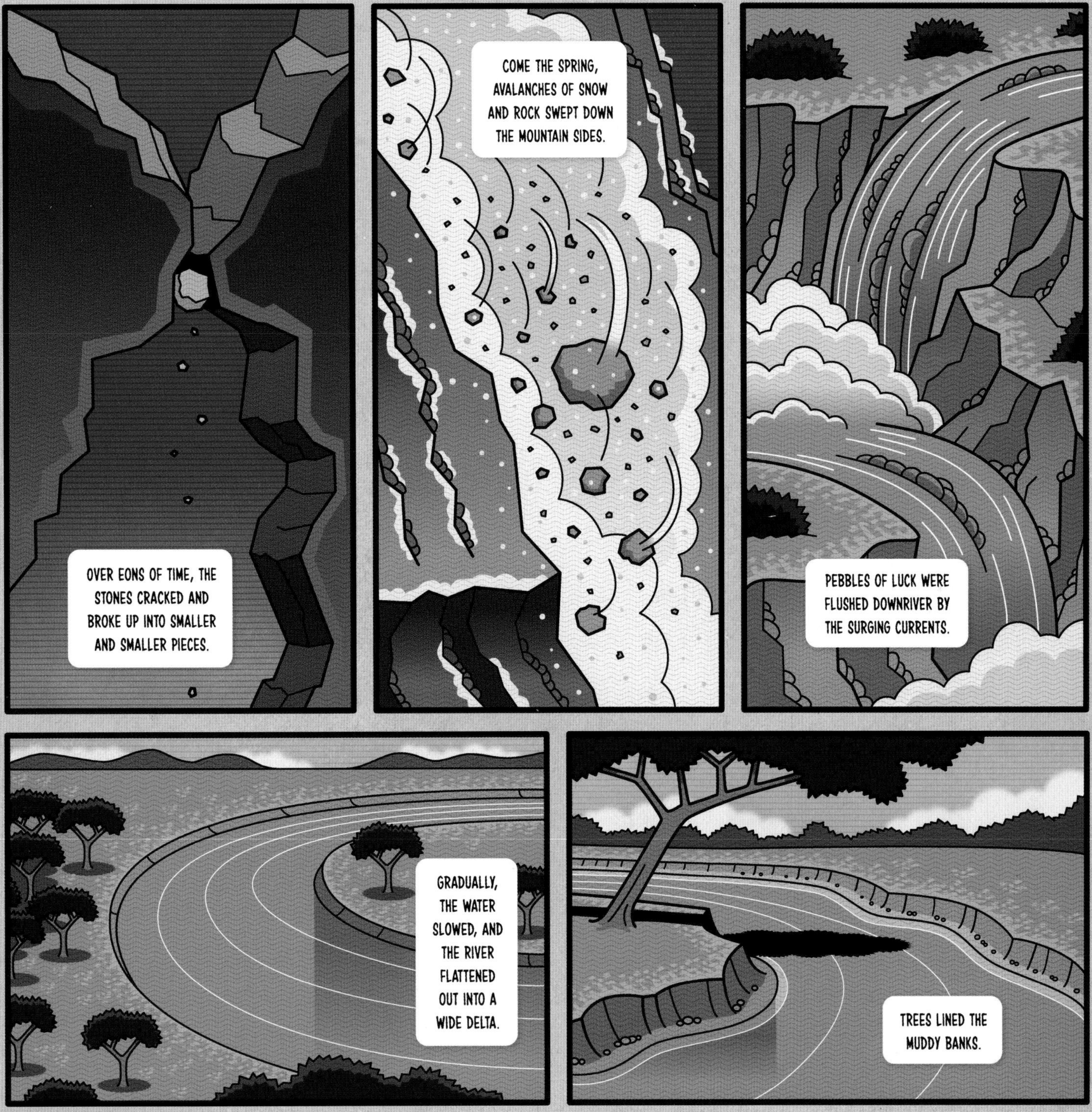
OVER EONS OF TIME, THE STONES CRACKED AND BROKE UP INTO SMALLER AND SMALLER PIECES.
COME THE SPRING, AVALANCHES OF SNOW AND ROCK SWEPT DOWN THE MOUNTAIN SIDES.
PEBBLES OF LUCK WERE FLUSHED DOWNRIVER BY THE SURGING CURRENTS.
GRADUALLY, THE WATER SLOWED, AND THE RIVER FLATTENED OUT INTO A WIDE DELTA.
TREES LINED THE MUDDY BANKS.

BIRDS NESTED IN THE FORESTS.

FISH FILLED THE WATERS.

SMALL STONES OF LUCK CAME TO REST IN A TREE-SHADED POOL.

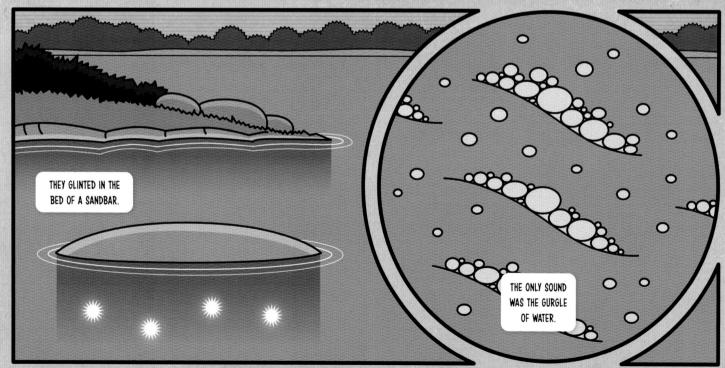

THEY GLINTED IN THE BED OF A SANDBAR.

THE ONLY SOUND WAS THE GURGLE OF WATER.

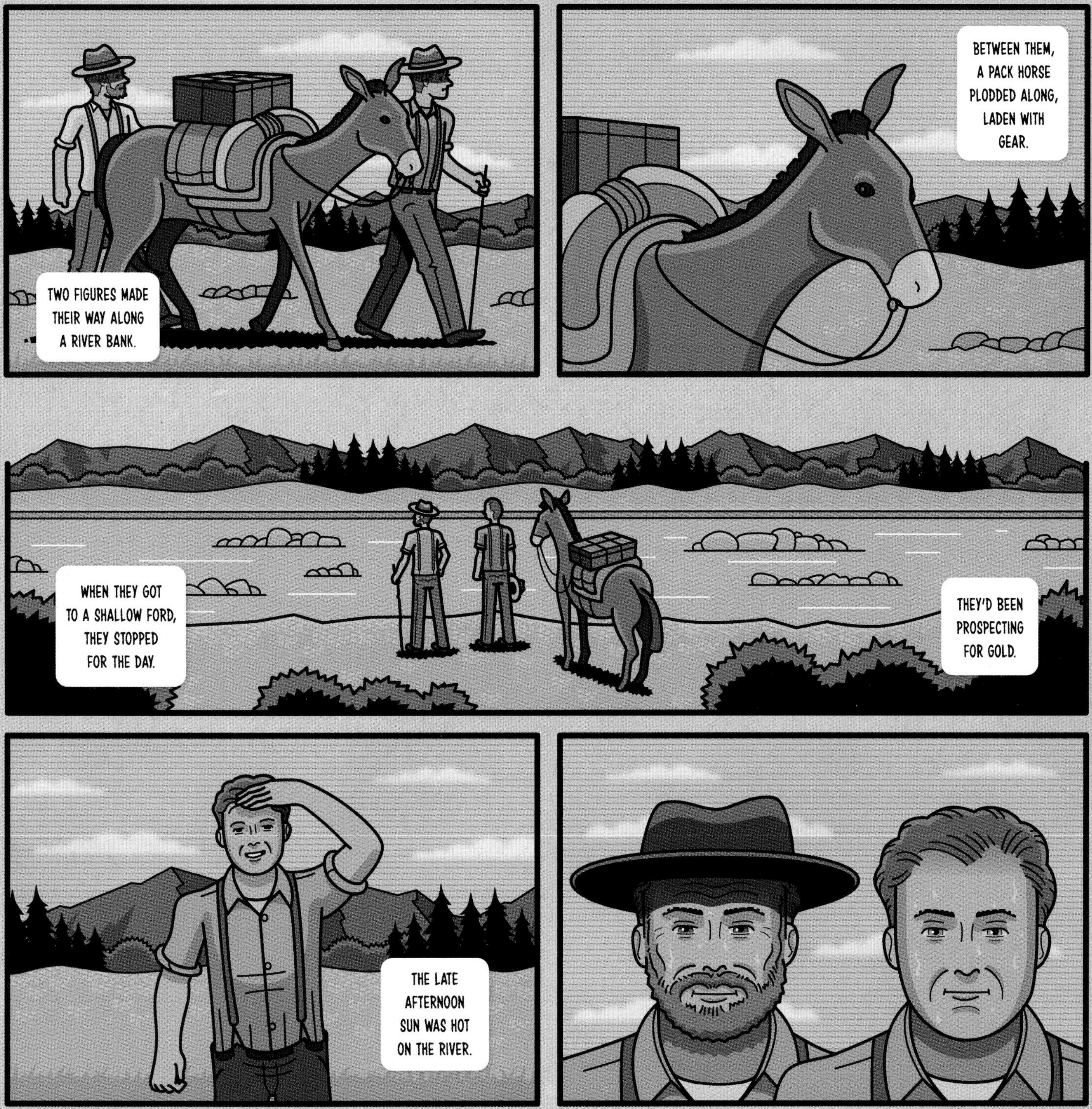
TWO FIGURES MADE THEIR WAY ALONG A RIVER BANK.
BETWEEN THEM, A PACK HORSE PLODDED ALONG, LADEN WITH GEAR.
WHEN THEY GOT TO A SHALLOW FORD, THEY STOPPED FOR THE DAY.
THEY'D BEEN PROSPECTING FOR GOLD.
THE LATE AFTERNOON SUN WAS HOT ON THE RIVER.

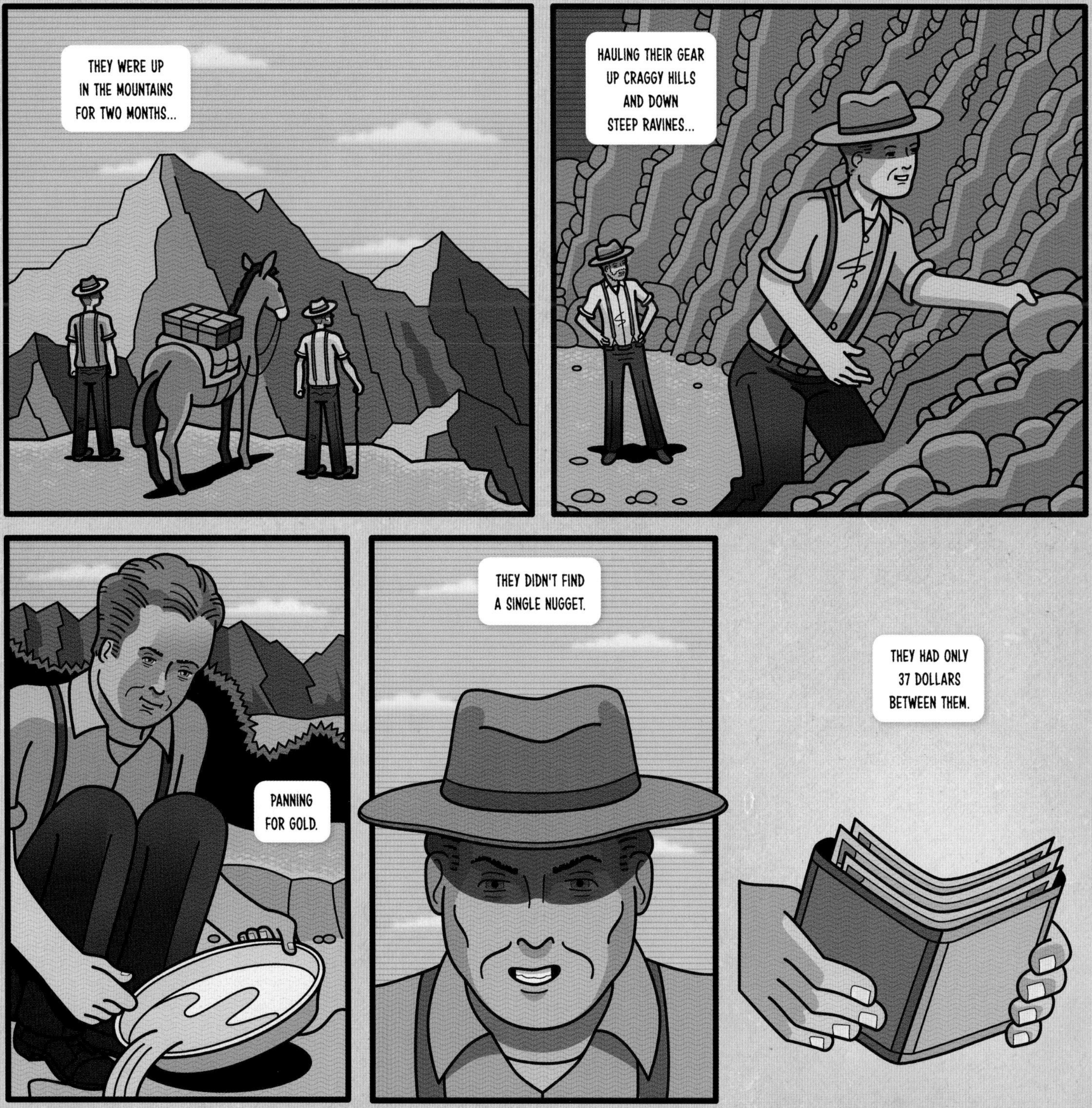
THEY WERE UP IN THE MOUNTAINS FOR TWO MONTHS...
HAULING THEIR GEAR UP CRAGGY HILLS AND DOWN STEEP RAVINES...
PANNING FOR GOLD.
THEY DIDN'T FIND A SINGLE NUGGET.
THEY HAD ONLY 37 DOLLARS BETWEEN THEM.

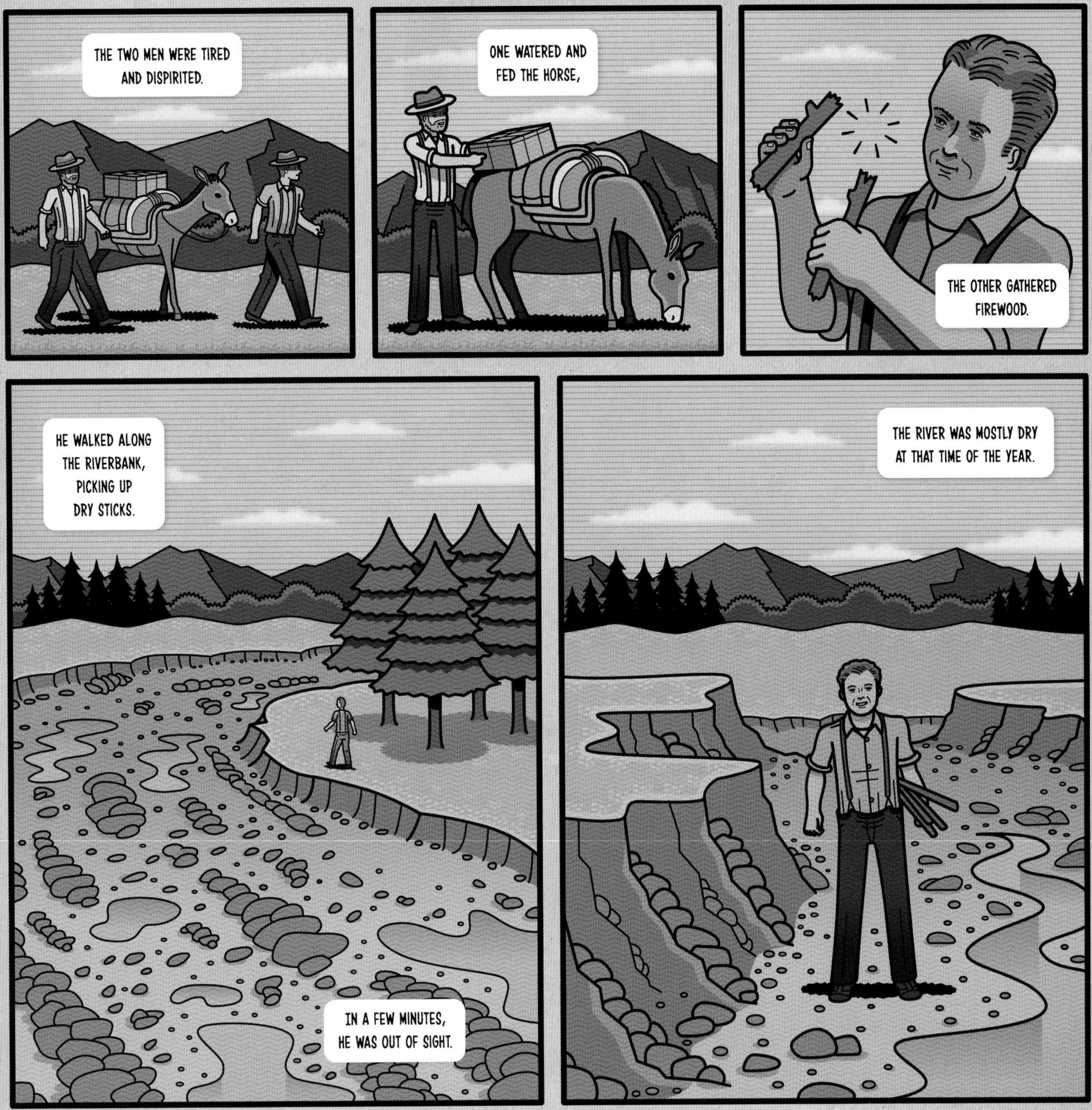
THE TWO MEN WERE TIRED AND DISPIRITED.
ONE WATERED AND FED THE HORSE,
THE OTHER GATHERED FIREWOOD.
HE WALKED ALONG THE RIVERBANK, PICKING UP DRY STICKS.
IN A FEW MINUTES, HE WAS OUT OF SIGHT.
THE RIVER WAS MOSTLY DRY AT THAT TIME OF THE YEAR.

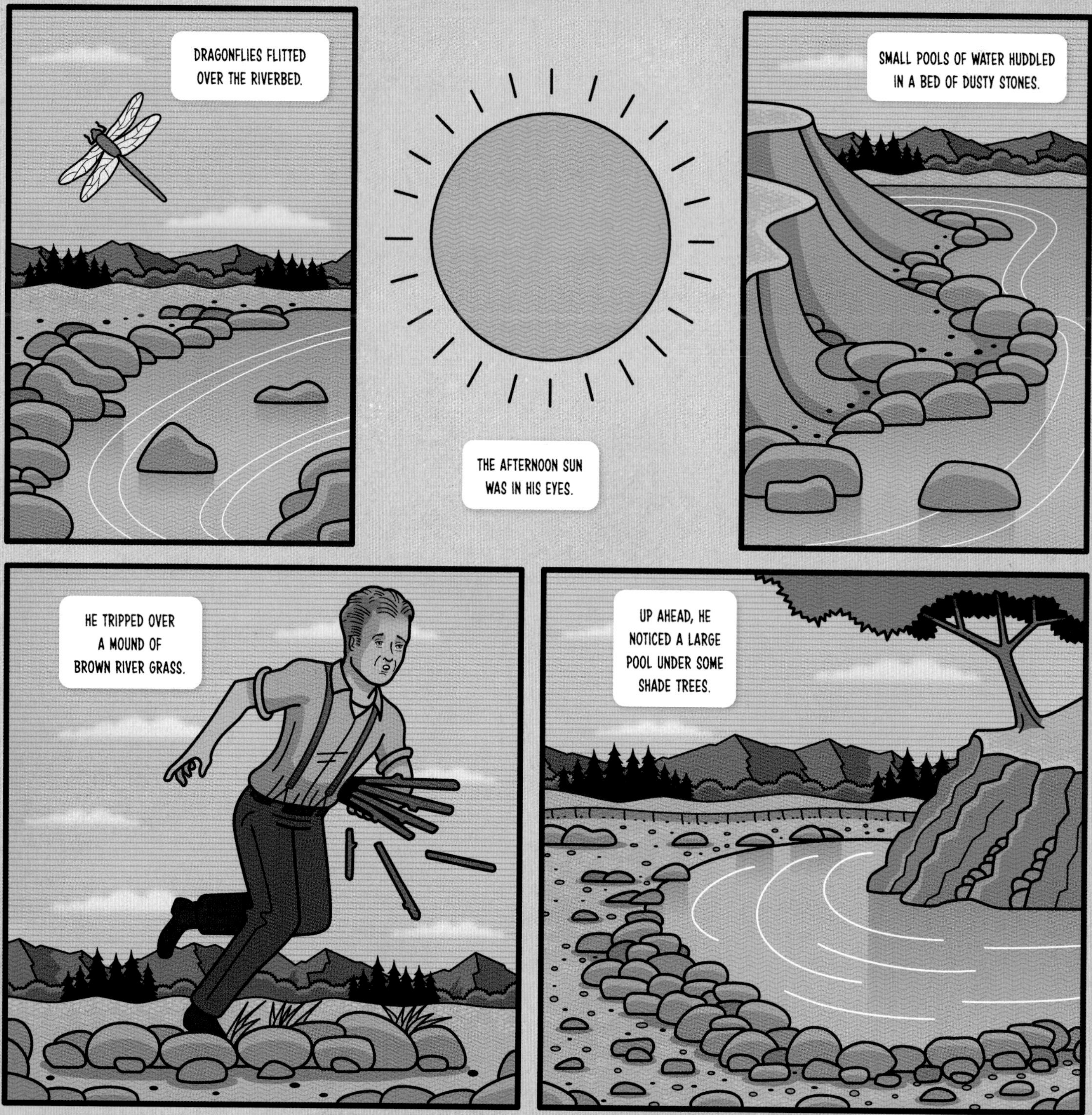
DRAGONFLIES FLITTED OVER THE RIVERBED.
THE AFTERNOON SUN WAS IN HIS EYES.
SMALL POOLS OF WATER HUDDLED IN A BED OF DUSTY STONES.
HE TRIPPED OVER A MOUND OF BROWN RIVER GRASS.
UP AHEAD, HE NOTICED A LARGE POOL UNDER SOME SHADE TREES.

HE DROPPED THE STICKS OF FIREWOOD.

SITTING DOWN ON A LOG, HE UNLACED HIS BOOTS. HE HAD TIME FOR A BATH.

THE SUN SHIMMERED ON THE WATER.

A BREEZE RUSTLED THROUGH THE LEAVES.

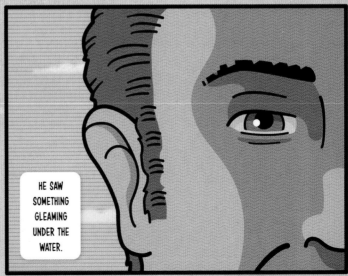

HE SAW SOMETHING GLEAMING UNDER THE WATER.

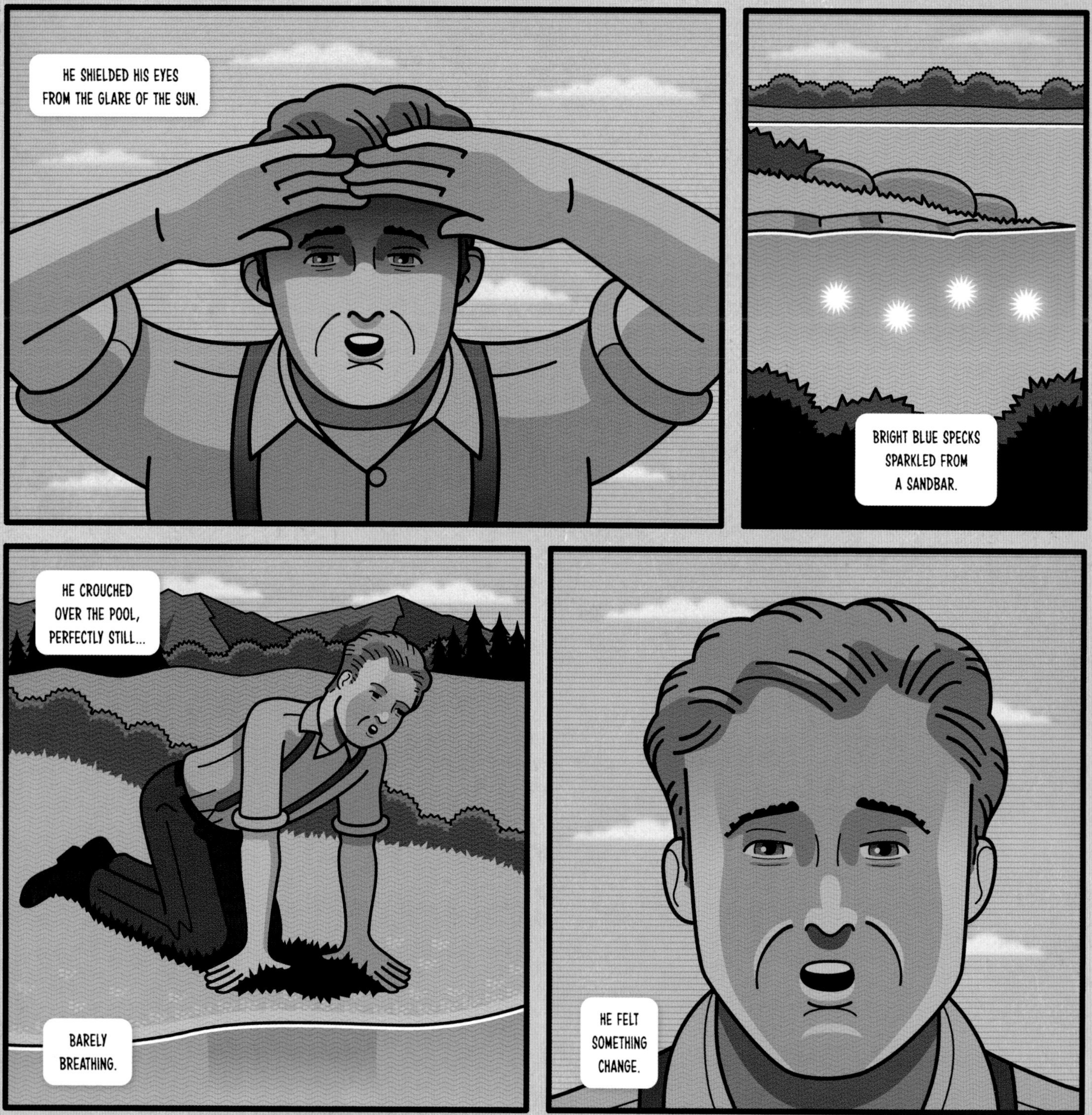
HE SHIELDED HIS EYES FROM THE GLARE OF THE SUN.
BRIGHT BLUE SPECKS SPARKLED FROM A SANDBAR.
HE CROUCHED OVER THE POOL, PERFECTLY STILL...
BARELY BREATHING.
HE FELT SOMETHING CHANGE.

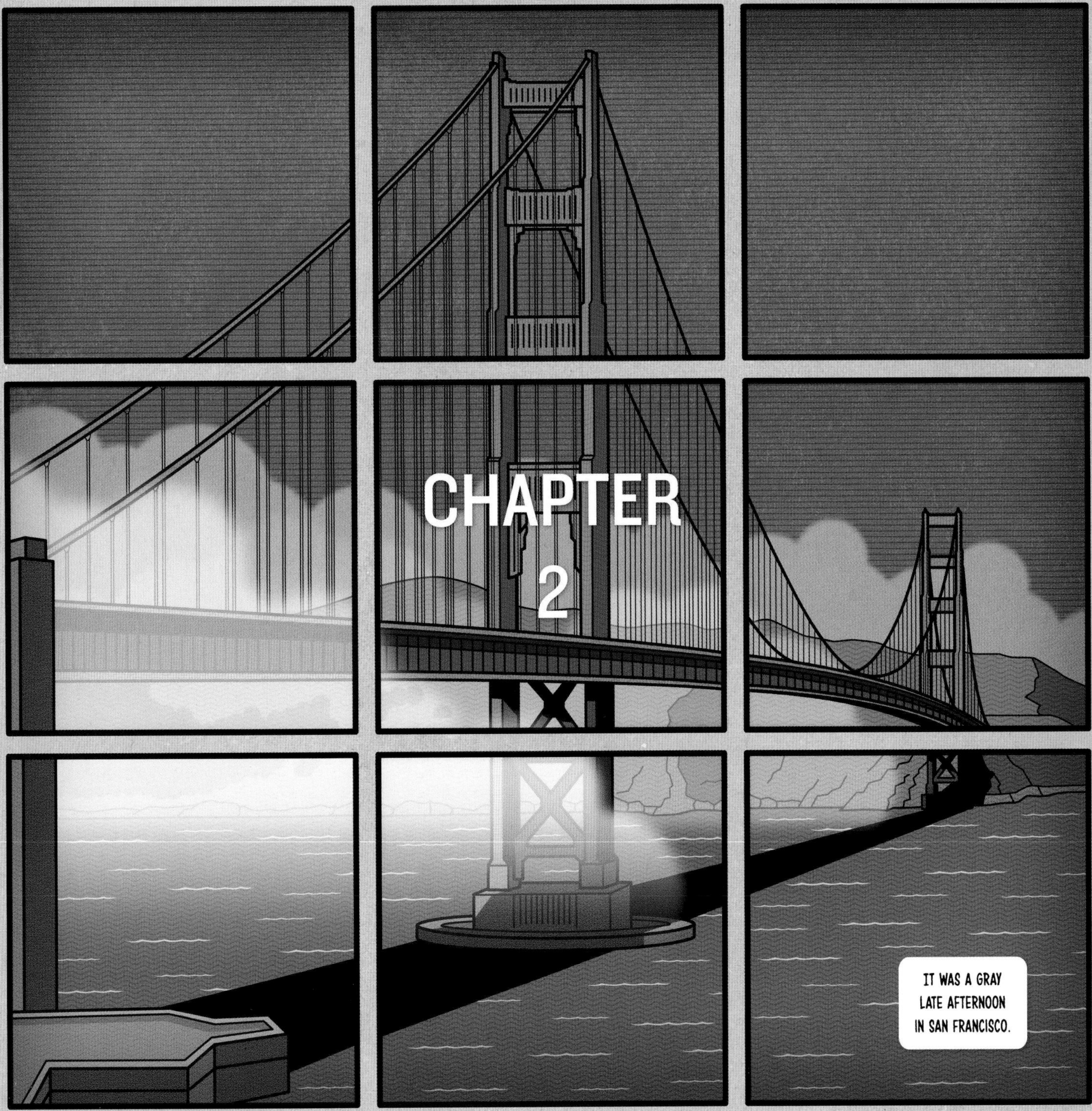
CHAPTER
2
IT WAS A GRAY LATE AFTERNOON IN SAN FRANCISCO.

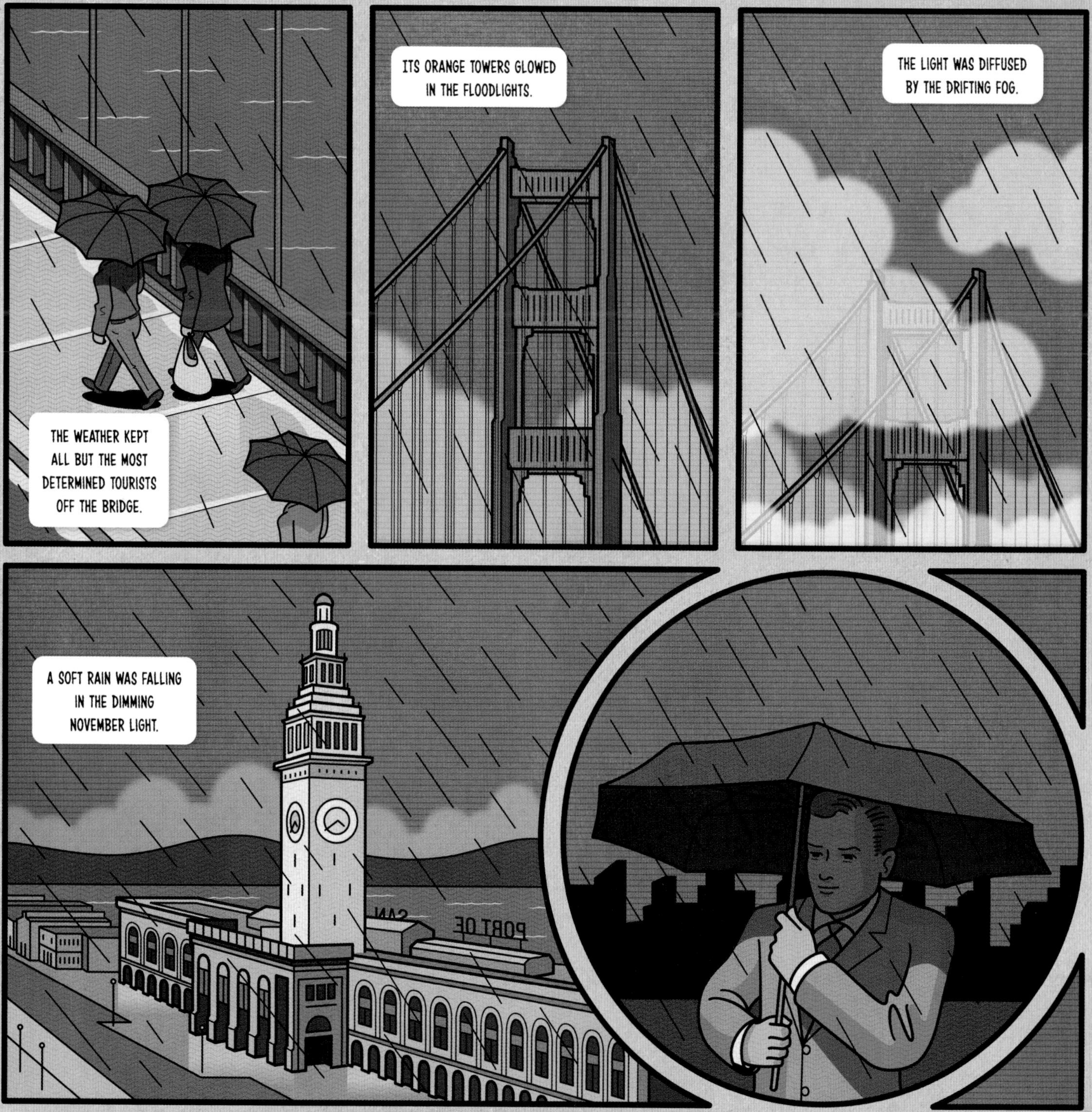
THE WEATHER KEPT ALL BUT THE MOST DETERMINED TOURISTS OFF THE BRIDGE.
ITS ORANGE TOWERS GLOWED IN THE FLOODLIGHTS.
THE LIGHT WAS DIFFUSED BY THE DRIFTING FOG.
A SOFT RAIN WAS FALLING IN THE DIMMING NOVEMBER LIGHT.

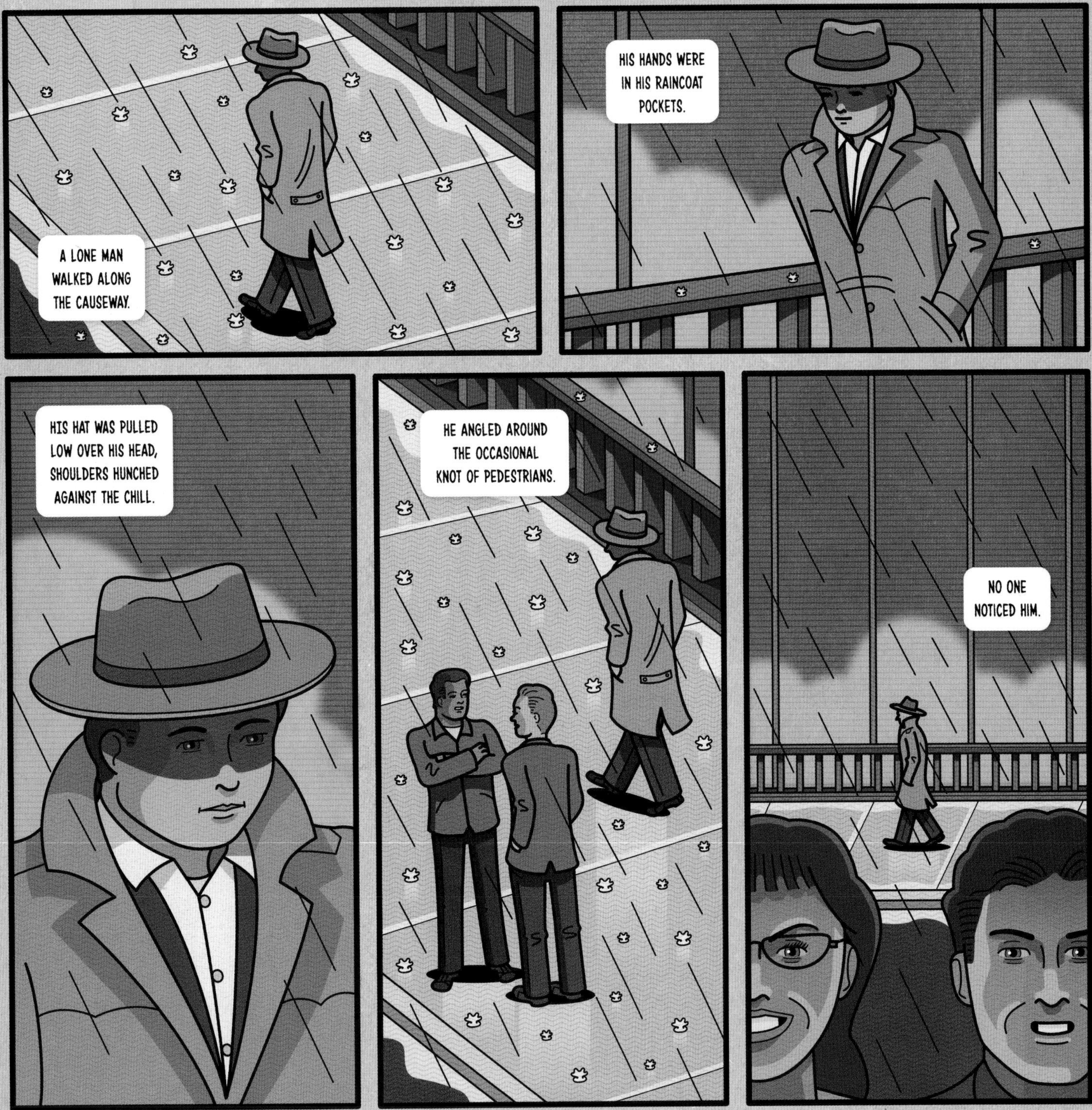
A LONE MAN WALKED ALONG THE CAUSEWAY.
HIS HANDS WERE IN HIS RAINCOAT POCKETS.
HIS HAT WAS PULLED LOW OVER HIS HEAD, SHOULDERS HUNCHED AGAINST THE CHILL.
HE ANGLED AROUND THE OCCASIONAL KNOT OF PEDESTRIANS.
NO ONE NOTICED HIM.

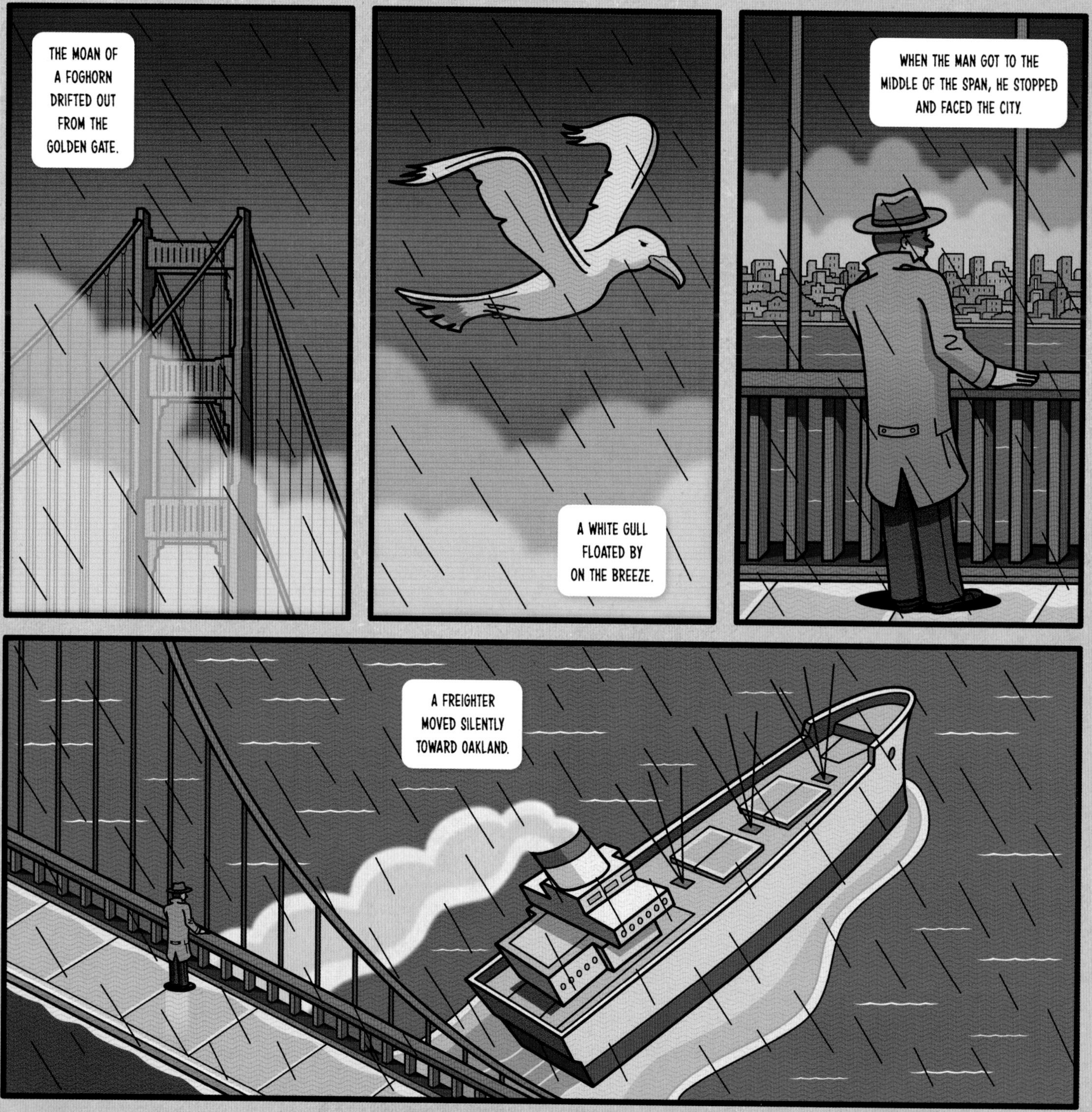
THE MOAN OF A FOGHORN DRIFTED OUT FROM THE GOLDEN GATE.
A WHITE GULL FLOATED BY ON THE BREEZE.
WHEN THE MAN GOT TO THE MIDDLE OF THE SPAN, HE STOPPED AND FACED THE CITY.
A FREIGHTER MOVED SILENTLY TOWARD OAKLAND.

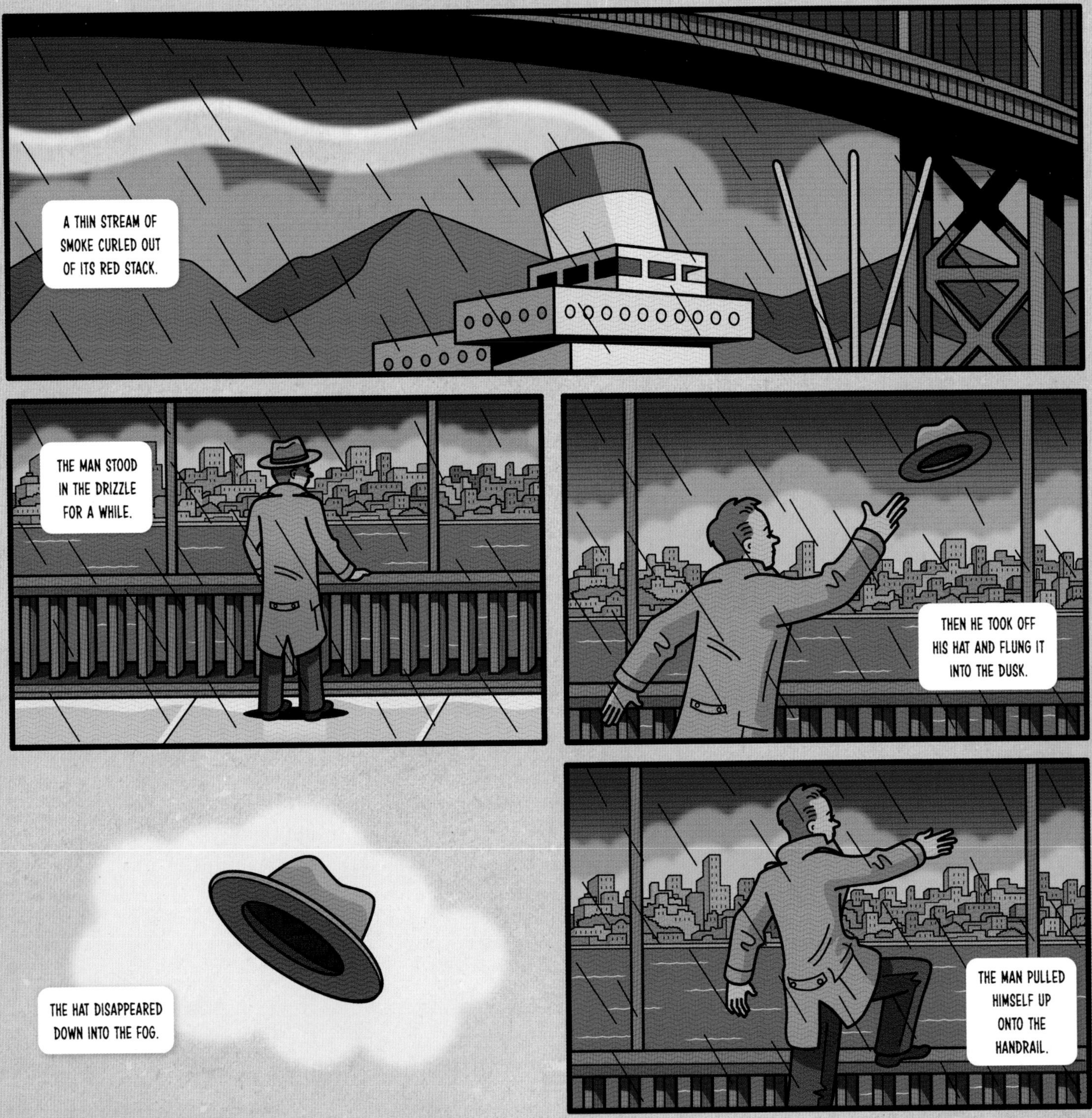
A THIN STREAM OF SMOKE CURLED OUT OF ITS RED STACK.
THE MAN STOOD IN THE DRIZZLE FOR A WHILE.
THEN HE TOOK OFF HIS HAT AND FLUNG IT INTO THE DUSK.
THE HAT DISAPPEARED DOWN INTO THE FOG.
THE MAN PULLED HIMSELF UP ONTO THE HANDRAIL.

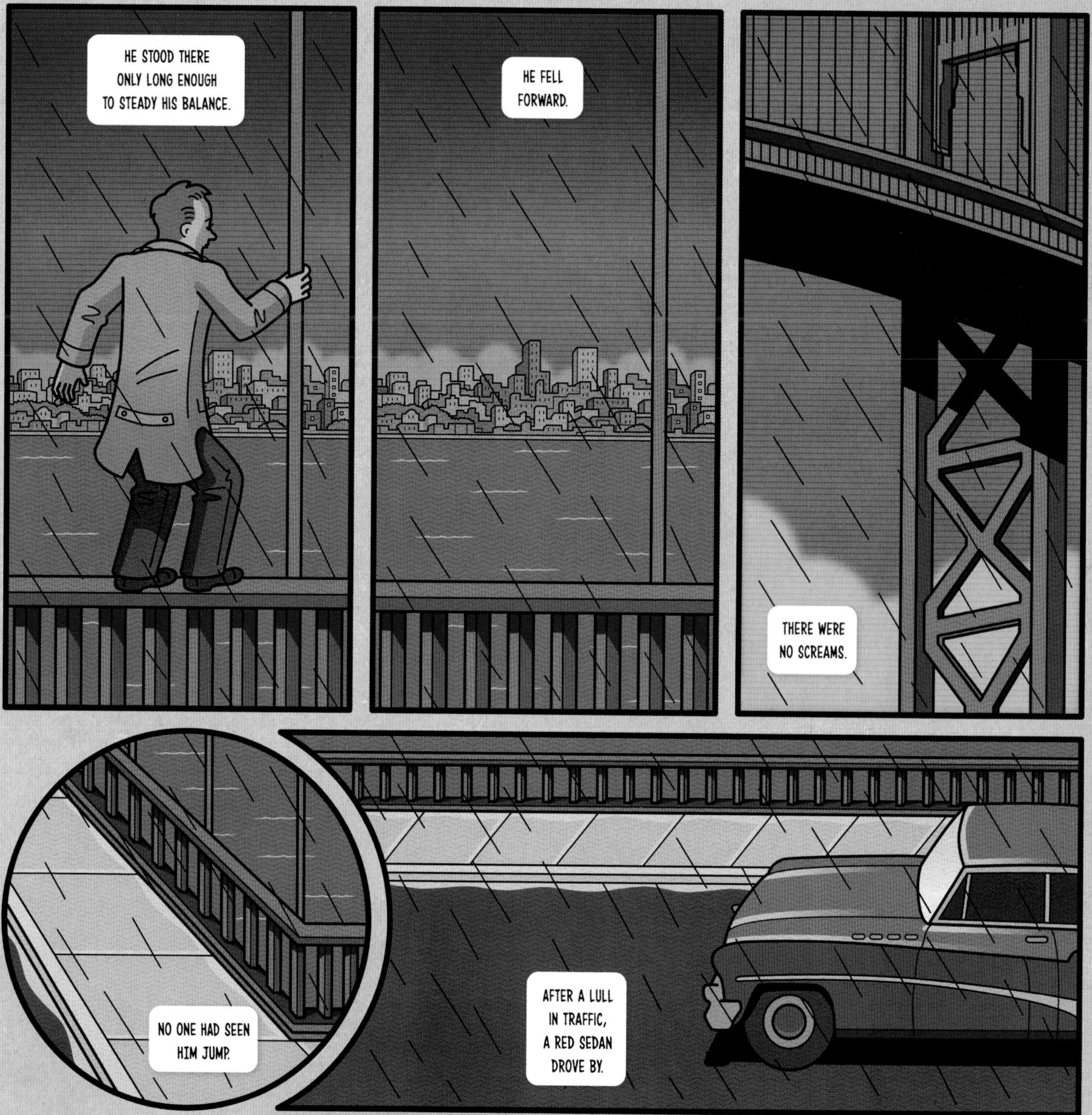
HE STOOD THERE ONLY LONG ENOUGH TO STEADY HIS BALANCE.
HE FELL FORWARD.
THERE WERE NO SCREAMS.
NO ONE HAD SEEN HIM JUMP.
AFTER A LULL IN TRAFFIC, A RED SEDAN DROVE BY.

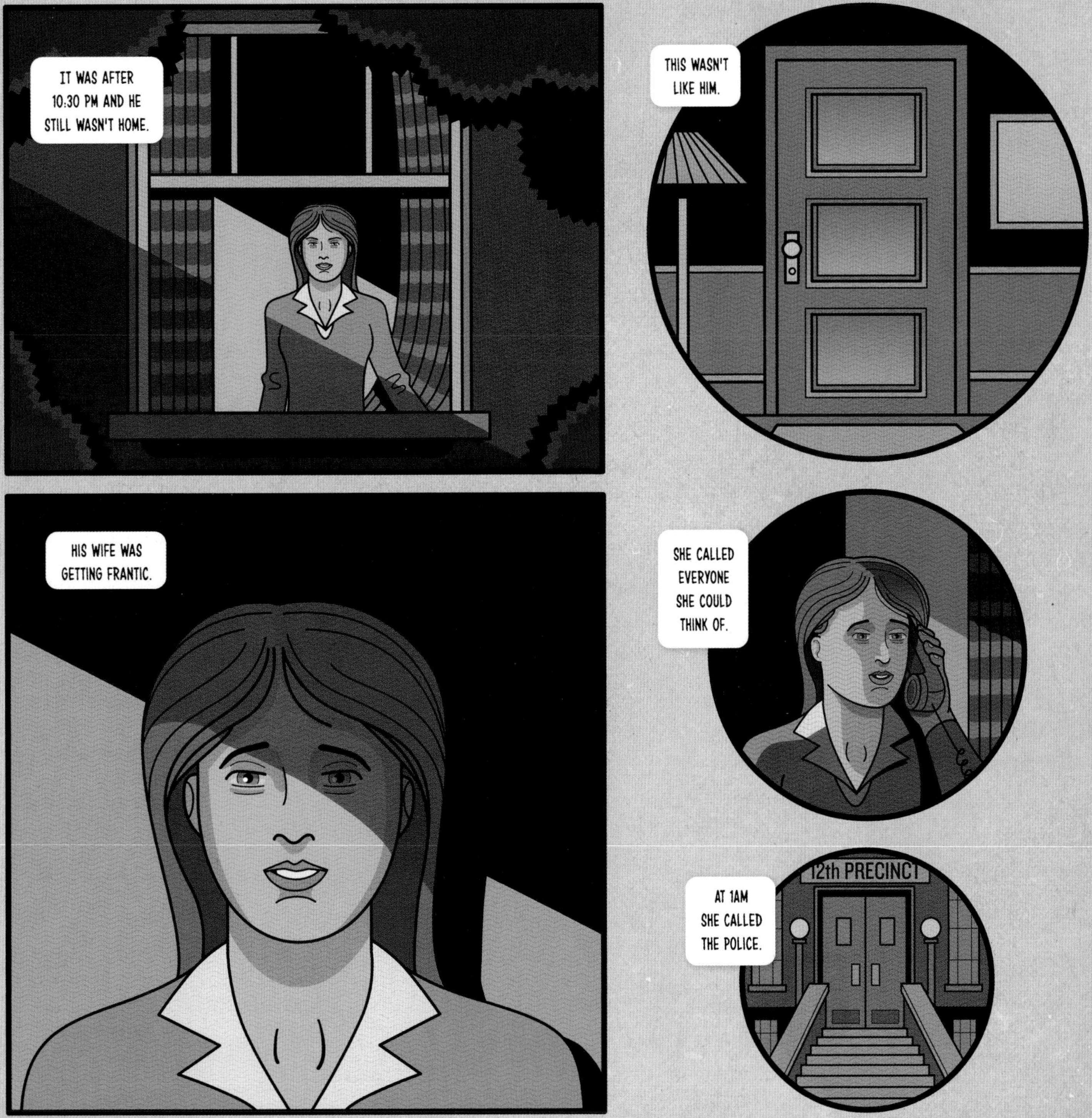
IT WAS AFTER 10:30 PM AND HE STILL WASN'T HOME.
THIS WASN'T LIKE HIM.
HIS WIFE WAS GETTING FRANTIC.
SHE CALLED EVERYONE SHE COULD THINK OF.
12th PRECINCT
AT 1AM SHE CALLED THE POLICE.

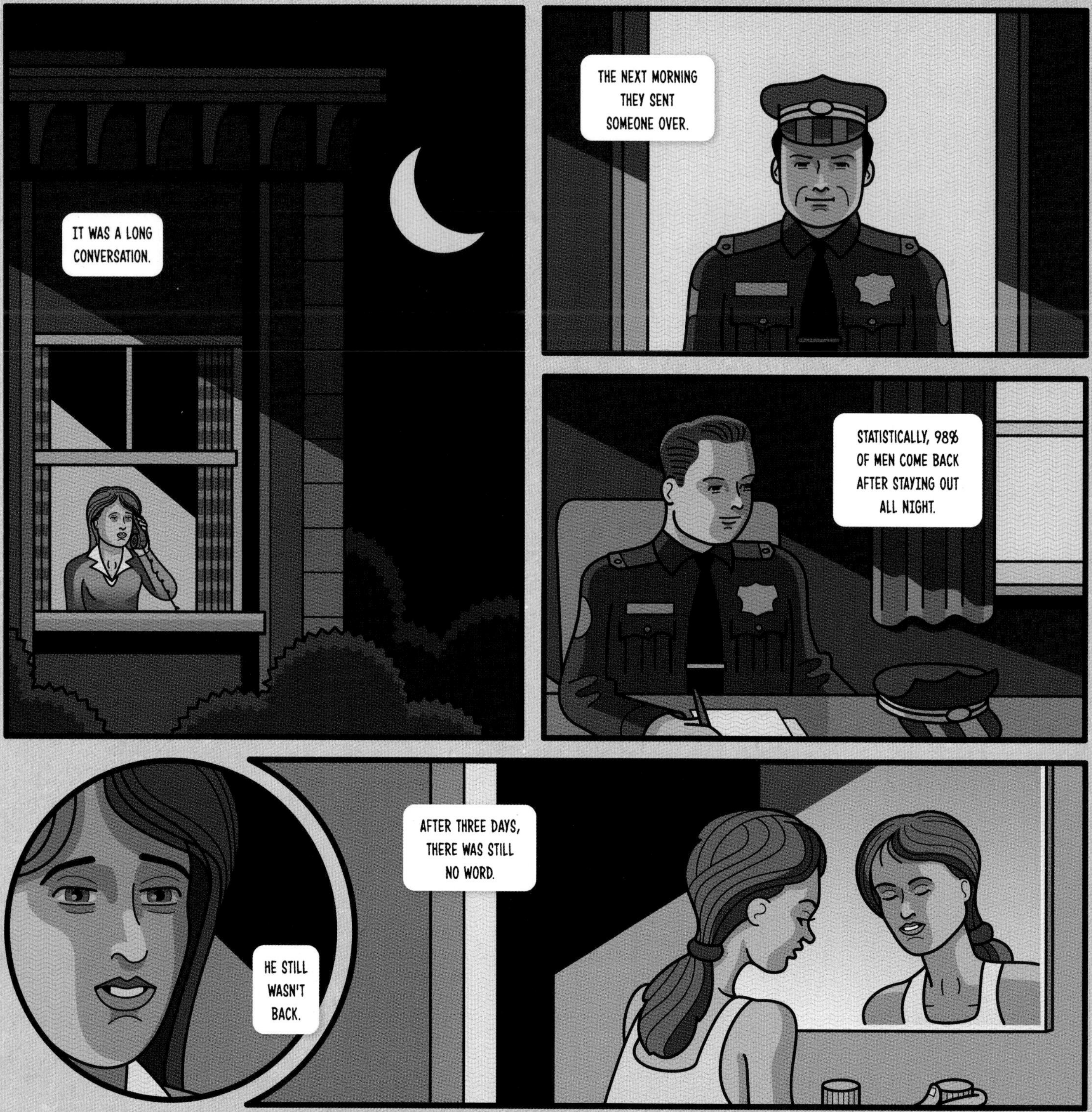
IT WAS A LONG CONVERSATION.
THE NEXT MORNING THEY SENT SOMEONE OVER.
STATISTICALLY, 98% OF MEN COME BACK AFTER STAYING OUT ALL NIGHT.
HE STILL WASN'T BACK.
AFTER THREE DAYS, THERE WAS STILL NO WORD.

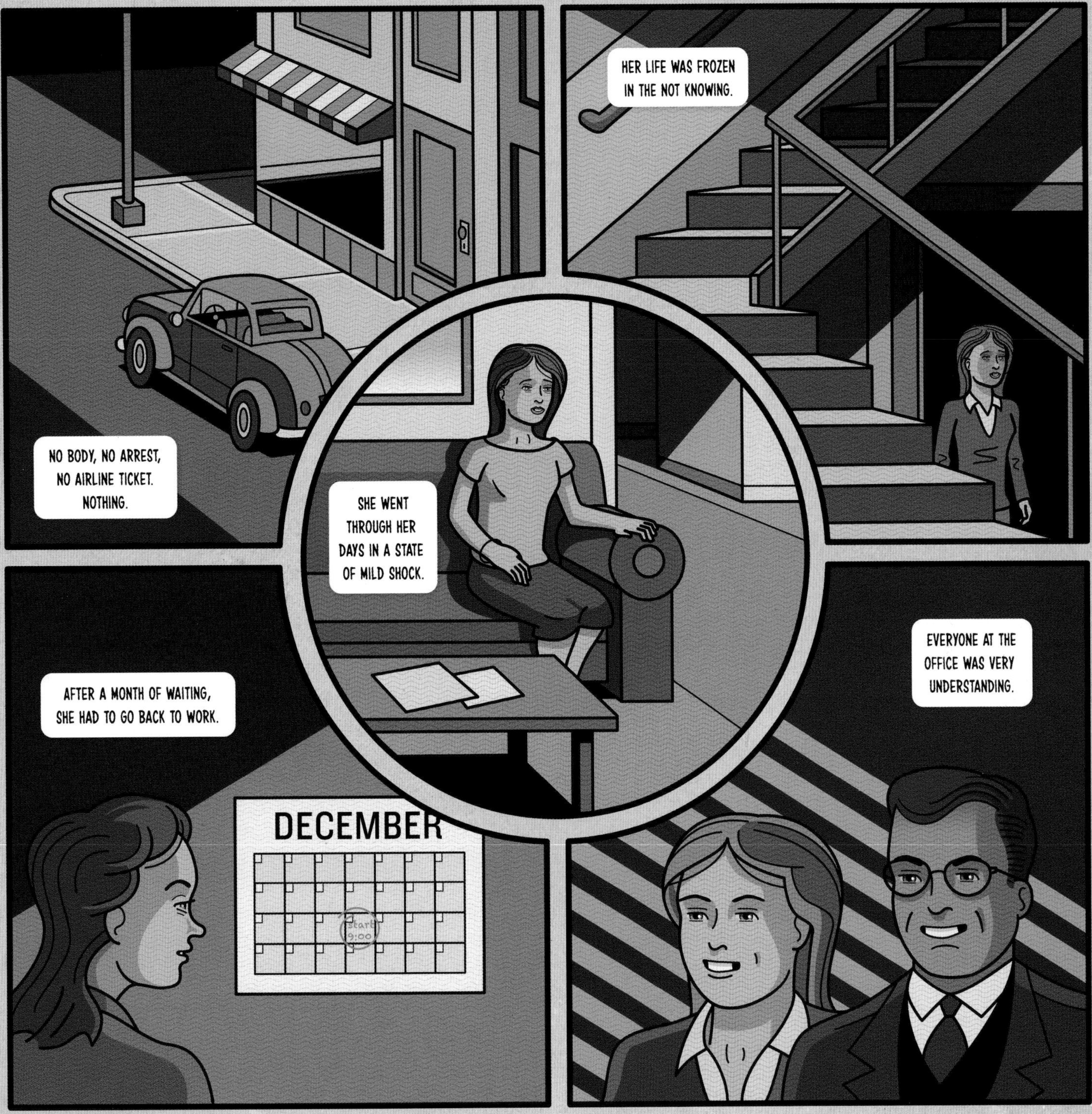
NO BODY, NO ARREST, NO AIRLINE TICKET. NOTHING.
HER LIFE WAS FROZEN IN THE NOT KNOWING.
SHE WENT THROUGH HER DAYS IN A STATE OF MILD SHOCK.
AFTER A MONTH OF WAITING, SHE HAD TO GO BACK TO WORK.
DECEMBER
START 9:00
EVERYONE AT THE OFFICE WAS VERY UNDERSTANDING.

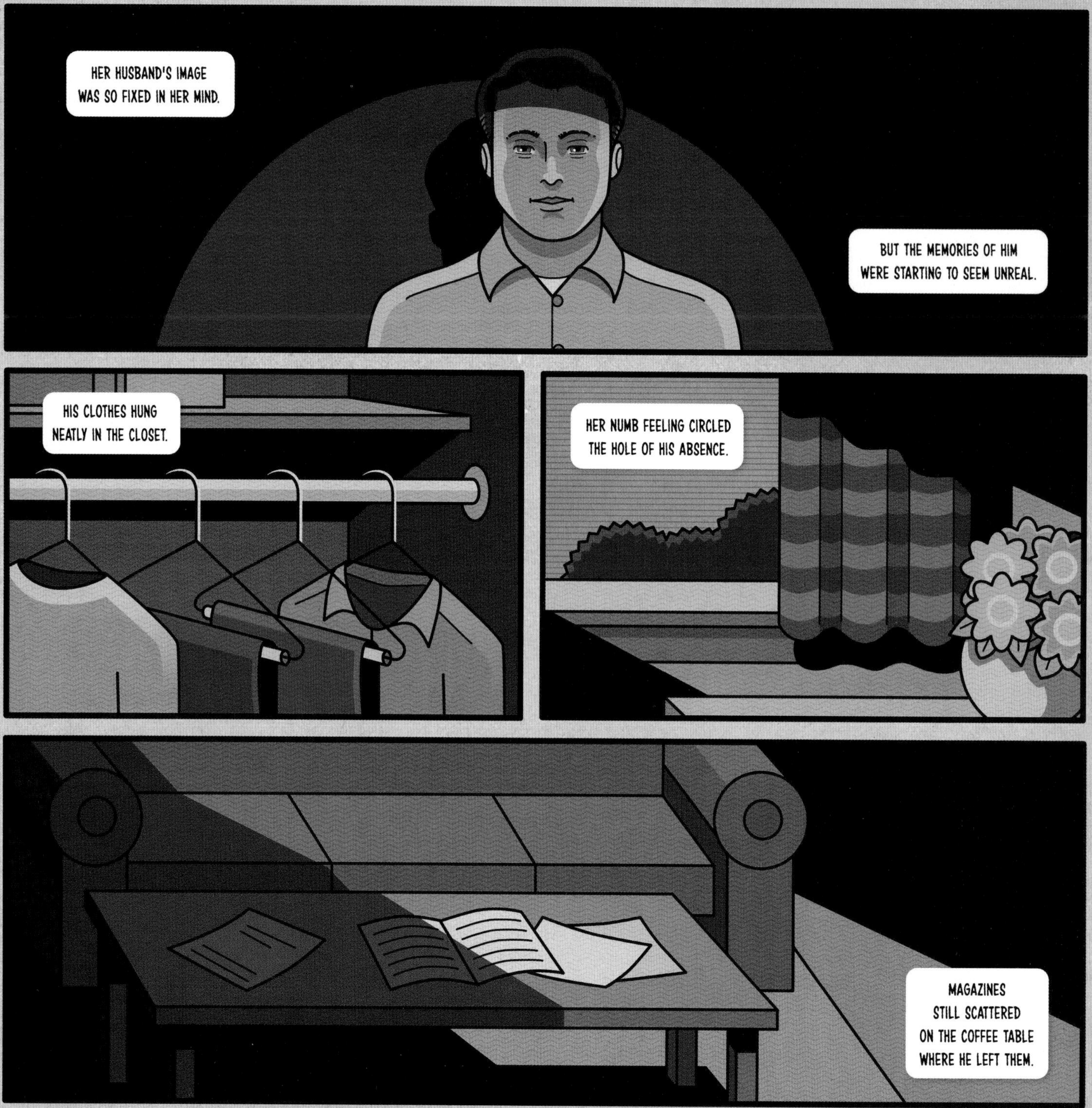
HER HUSBAND'S IMAGE WAS SO FIXED IN HER MIND.
BUT THE MEMORIES OF HIM WERE STARTING TO SEEM UNREAL.
HIS CLOTHES HUNG NEATLY IN THE CLOSET.
HER NUMB FEELING CIRCLED THE HOLE OF HIS ABSENCE.
MAGAZINES STILL SCATTERED ON THE COFFEE TABLE WHERE HE LEFT THEM.

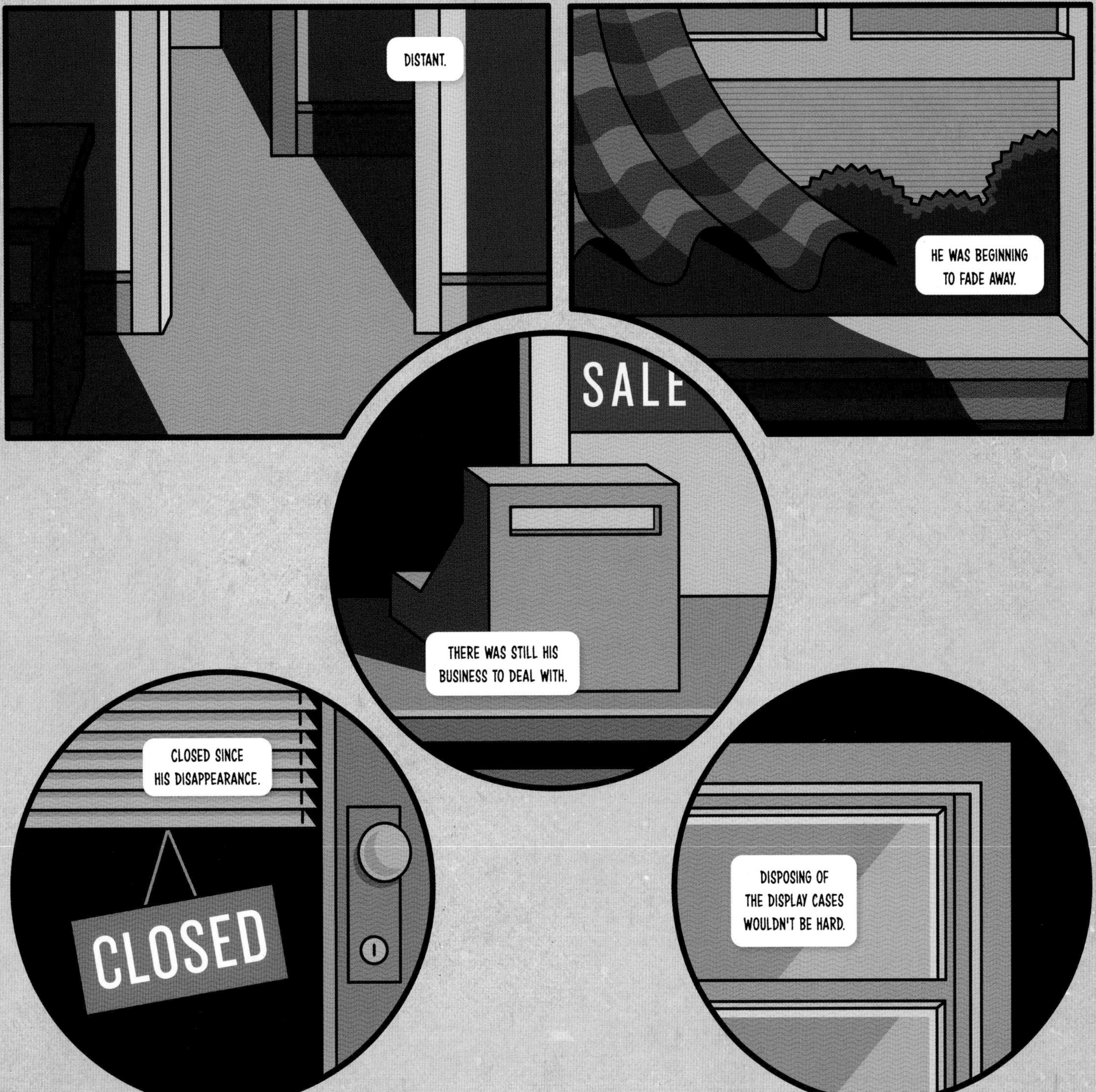
DISTANT.
HE WAS BEGINNING TO FADE AWAY.
SALE
THERE WAS STILL HIS BUSINESS TO DEAL WITH.
CLOSED SINCE HIS DISAPPEARANCE.
CLOSED
DISPOSING OF THE DISPLAY CASES WOULDN'T BE HARD.

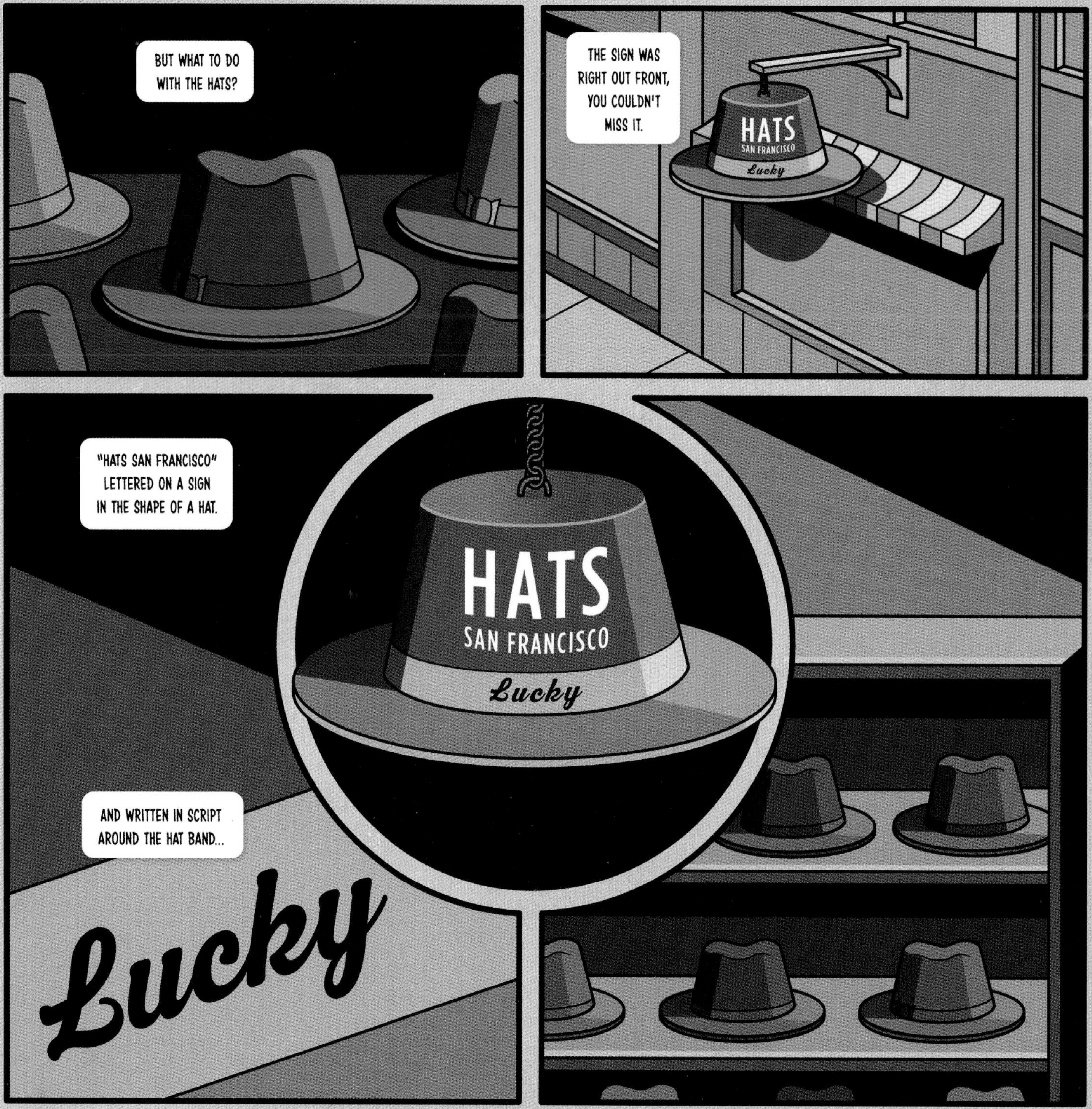

BUT WHAT TO DO WITH THE HATS?
THE SIGN WAS RIGHT OUT FRONT, YOU COULDN'T MISS IT.
HATS
SAN FRANCISCO
Lucky
"HATS SAN FRANCISCO" LETTERED ON A SIGN IN THE SHAPE OF A HAT.
HATS
SAN FRANCISCO
Lucky
AND WRITTEN IN SCRIPT AROUND THE HAT BAND...
Lucky

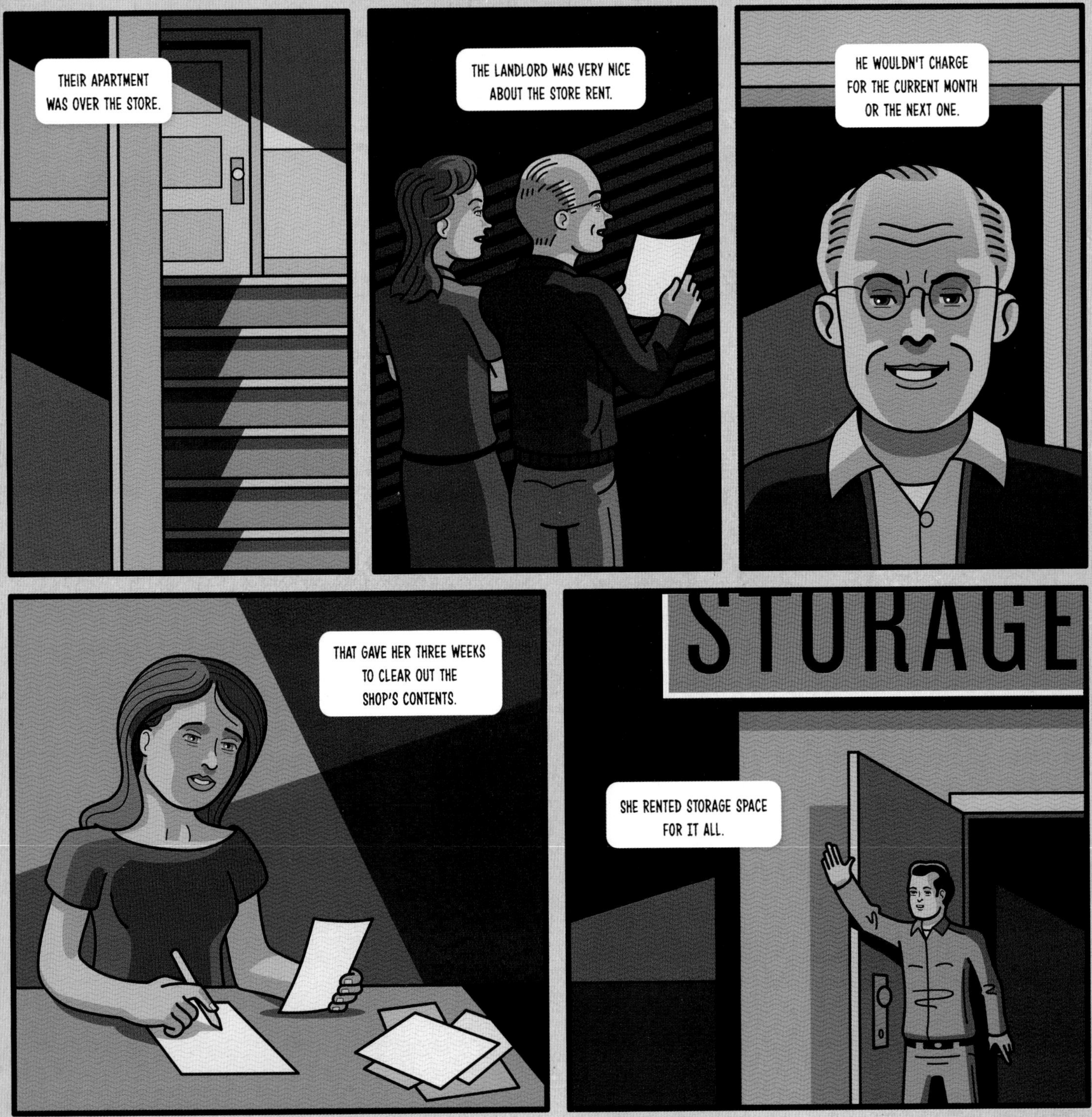
THEIR APARTMENT WAS OVER THE STORE.
THE LANDLORD WAS VERY NICE ABOUT THE STORE RENT.
HE WOULDN'T CHARGE FOR THE CURRENT MONTH OR THE NEXT ONE.
THAT GAVE HER THREE WEEKS TO CLEAR OUT THE SHOP'S CONTENTS.
STORAGE
SHE RENTED STORAGE SPACE FOR IT ALL.

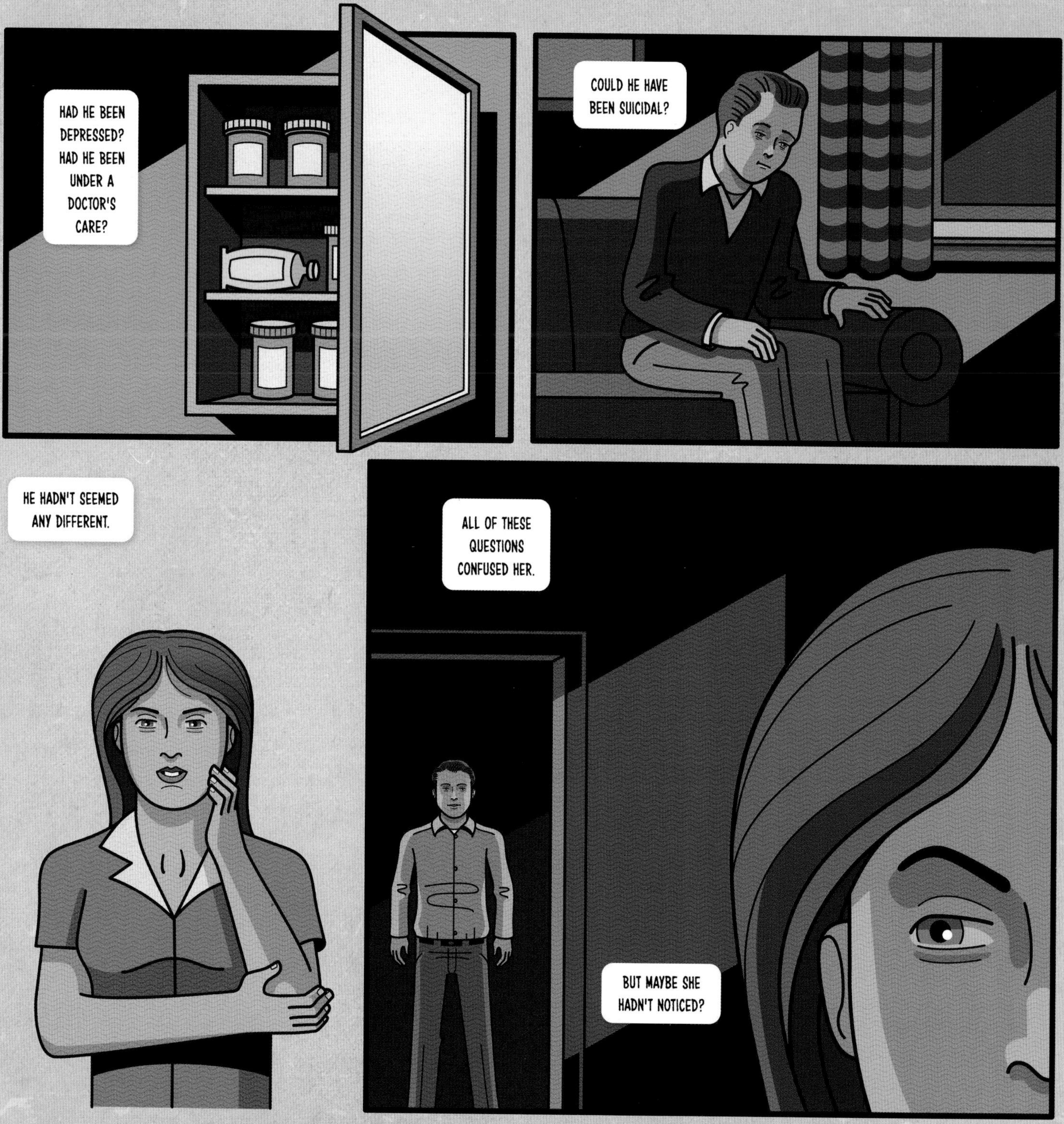
HAD HE BEEN DEPRESSED? HAD HE BEEN UNDER A DOCTOR'S CARE?
COULD HE HAVE BEEN SUICIDAL?
HE HADN'T SEEMED ANY DIFFERENT.
ALL OF THESE QUESTIONS CONFUSED HER.
BUT MAYBE SHE HADN'T NOTICED?

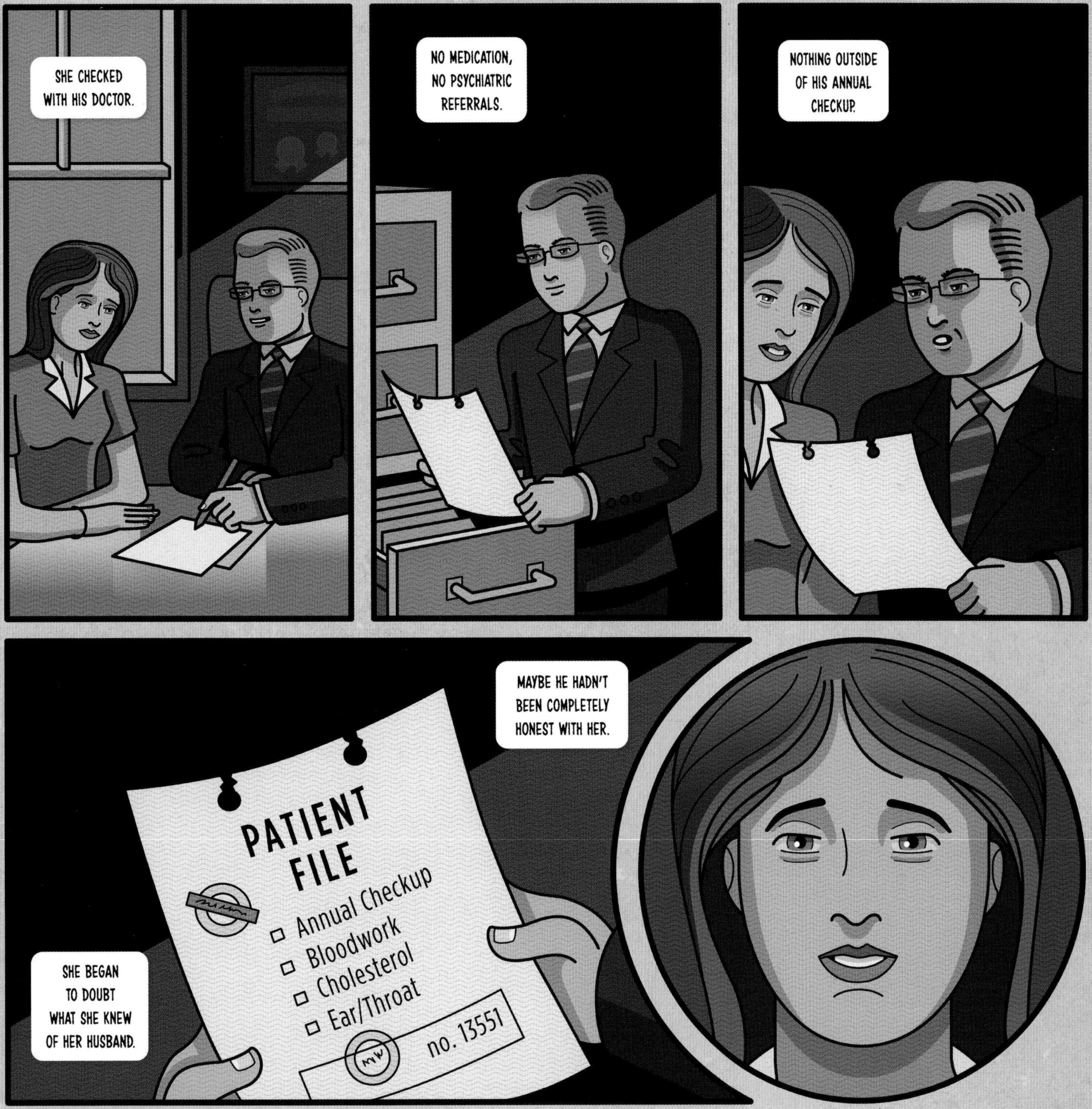
SHE CHECKED WITH HIS DOCTOR.
NO MEDICATION, NO PSYCHIATRIC REFERRALS.
NOTHING OUTSIDE OF HIS ANNUAL CHECKUP.
PATIENT FILE
Annual Checkup
Bloodwork
Cholesterol
Ear/Throat
no. 13551
SHE BEGAN TO DOUBT WHAT SHE KNEW OF HER HUSBAND.
MAYBE HE HADN'T BEEN COMPLETELY HONEST WITH HER.

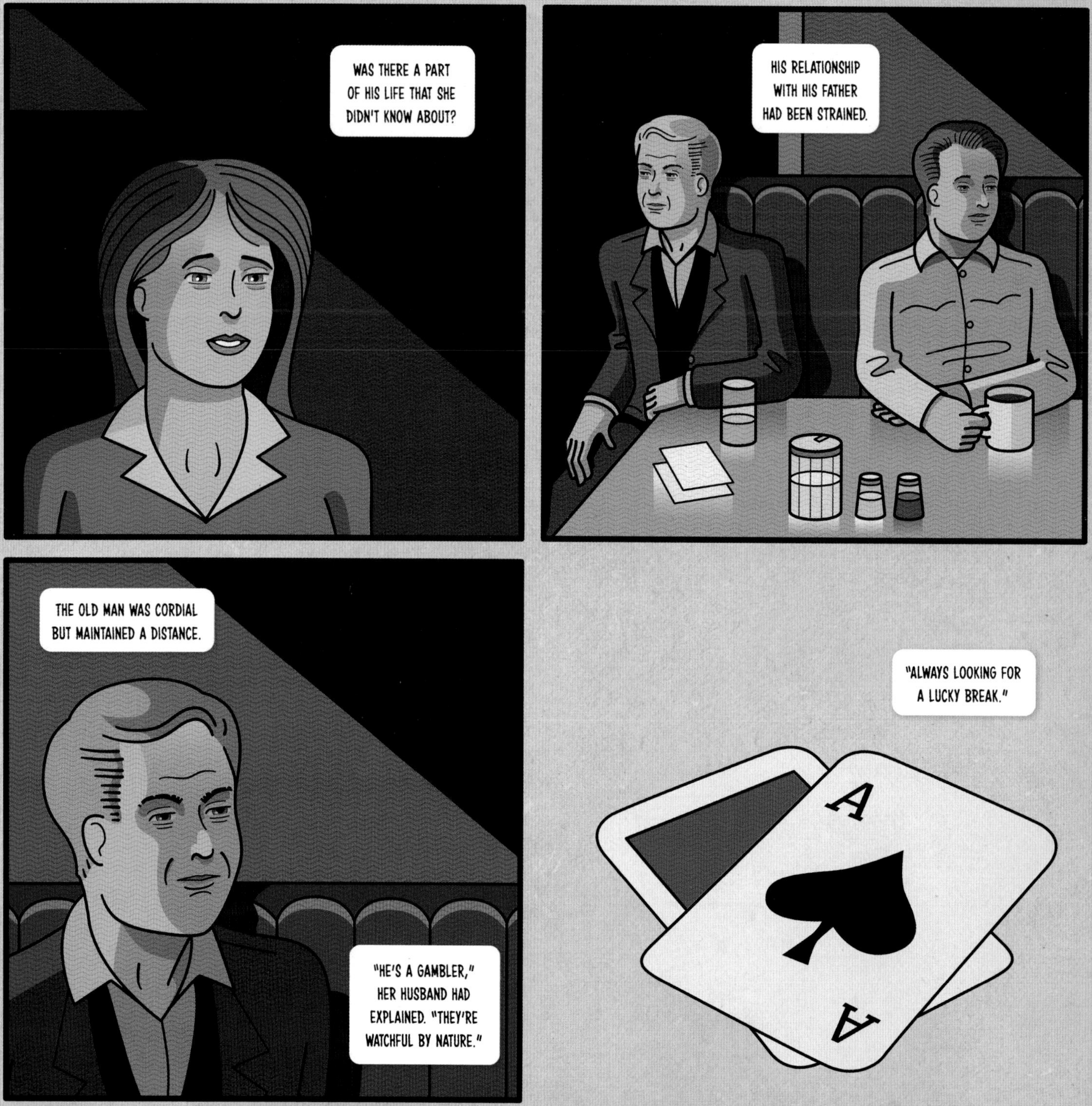
WAS THERE A PART OF HIS LIFE THAT SHE DIDN'T KNOW ABOUT?
HIS RELATIONSHIP WITH HIS FATHER HAD BEEN STRAINED.
THE OLD MAN WAS CORDIAL BUT MAINTAINED A DISTANCE.
"HE'S A GAMBLER," HER HUSBAND HAD EXPLAINED. "THEY'RE WATCHFUL BY NATURE."
"ALWAYS LOOKING FOR A LUCKY BREAK."
A
A

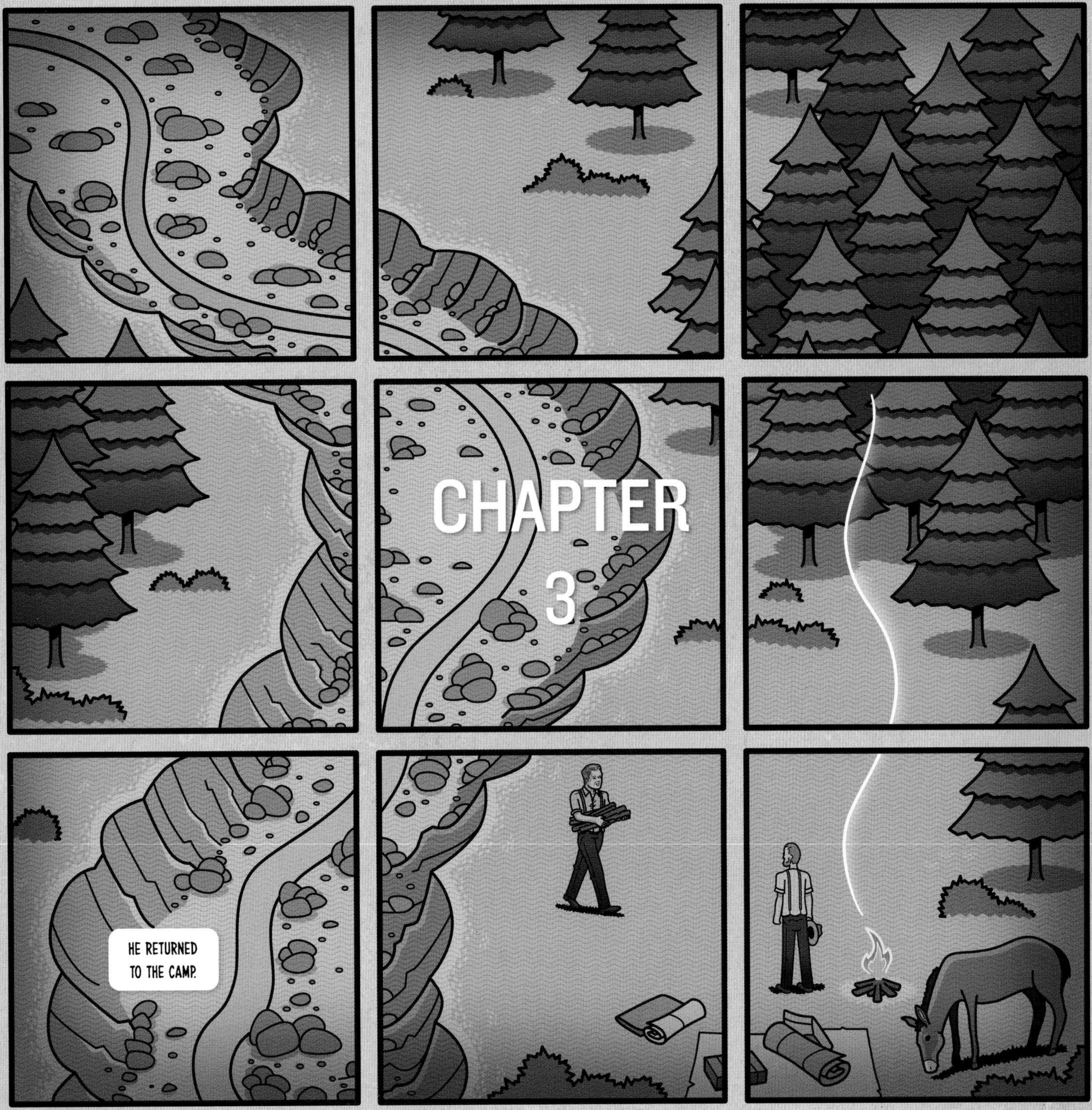
CHAPTER
3
HE RETURNED TO THE CAMP.

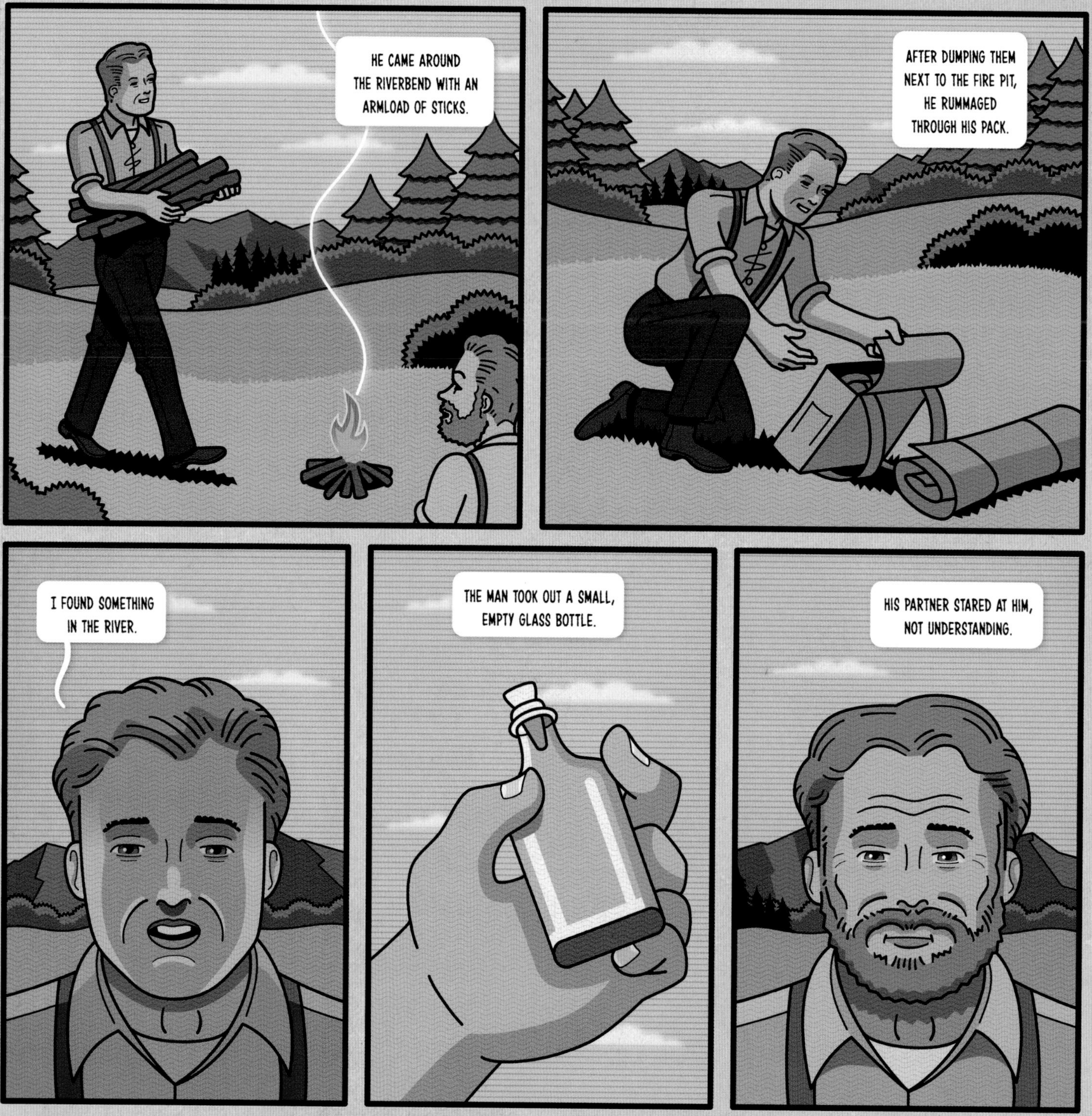
HE CAME AROUND THE RIVERBEND WITH AN ARMLOAD OF STICKS.
AFTER DUMPING THEM NEXT TO THE FIRE PIT, HE RUMMAGED THROUGH HIS PACK.
I FOUND SOMETHING IN THE RIVER.
THE MAN TOOK OUT A SMALL, EMPTY GLASS BOTTLE.
HIS PARTNER STARED AT HIM, NOT UNDERSTANDING.

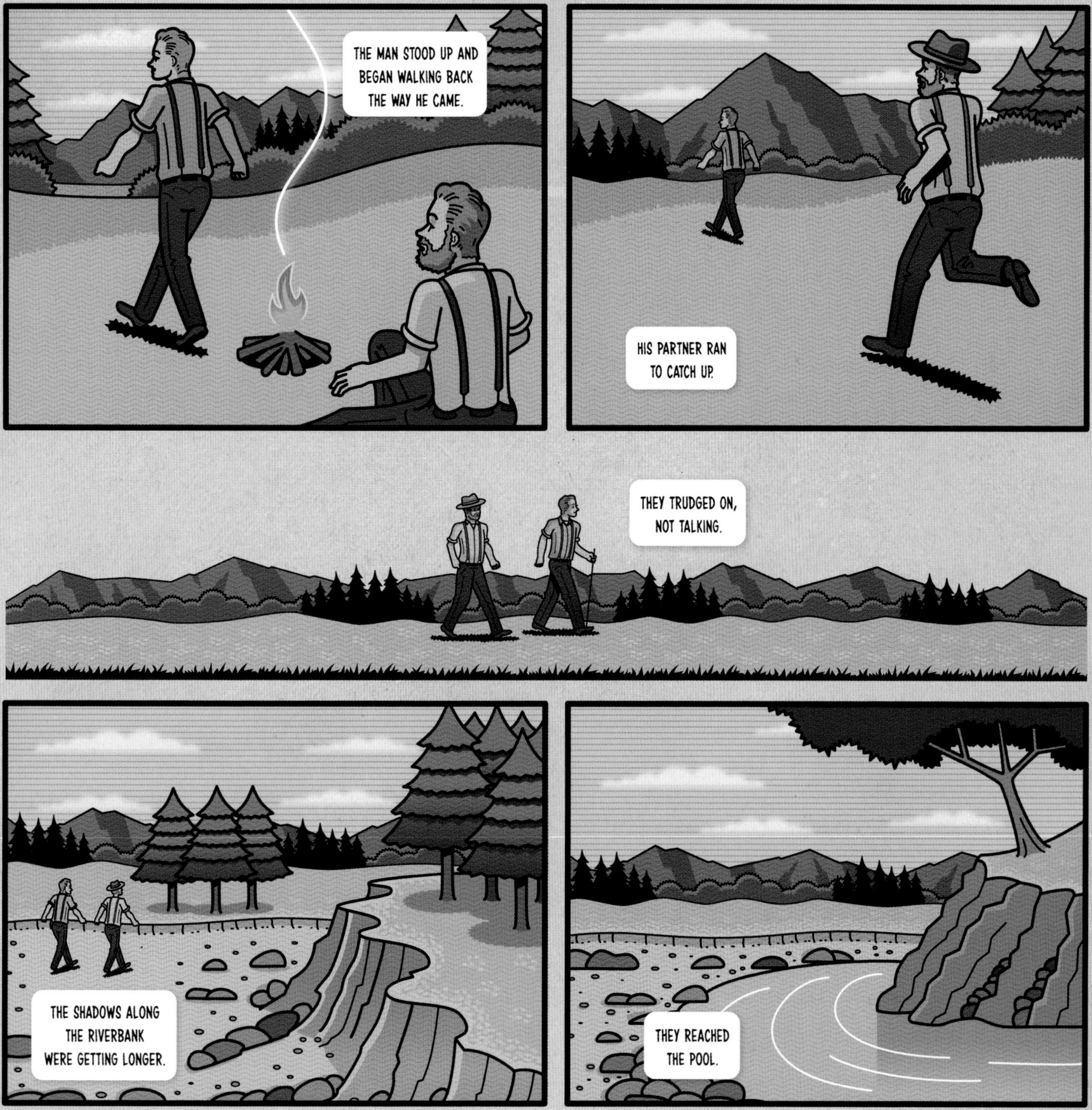
THE MAN STOOD UP AND BEGAN WALKING BACK THE WAY HE CAME.
HIS PARTNER RAN TO CATCH UP.
THEY TRUDGED ON, NOT TALKING.
THE SHADOWS ALONG THE RIVERBANK WERE GETTING LONGER.
THEY REACHED THE POOL.

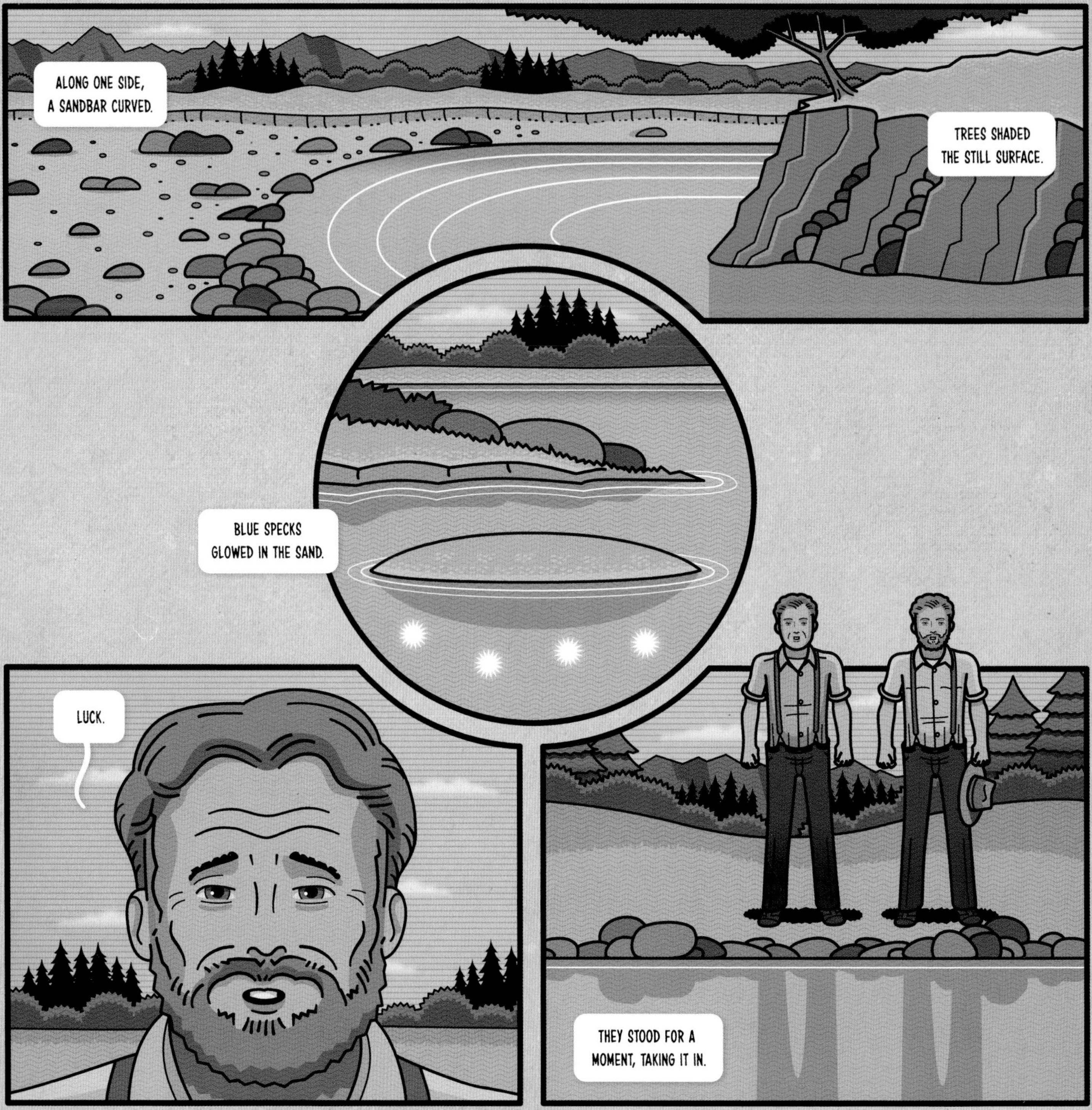
ALONG ONE SIDE, A SANDBAR CURVED.
TREES SHADED THE STILL SURFACE.
BLUE SPECKS GLOWED IN THE SAND.
LUCK.
THEY STOOD FOR A MOMENT, TAKING IT IN.

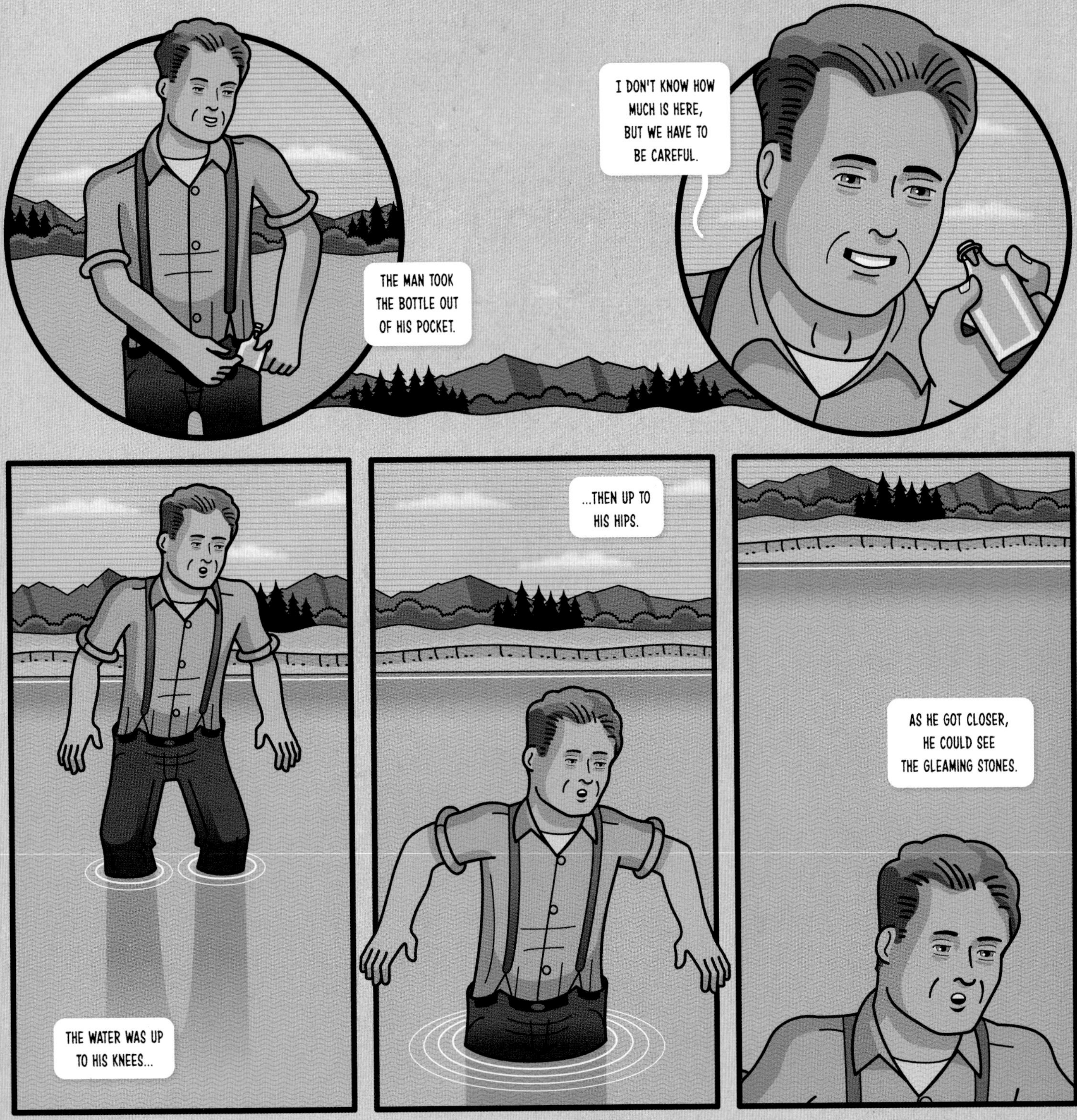
THE MAN TOOK THE BOTTLE OUT OF HIS POCKET.
I DON'T KNOW HOW MUCH IS HERE, BUT WE HAVE TO BE CAREFUL.
THE WATER WAS UP TO HIS KNEES...
...THEN UP TO HIS HIPS.
AS HE GOT CLOSER, HE COULD SEE THE GLEAMING STONES.

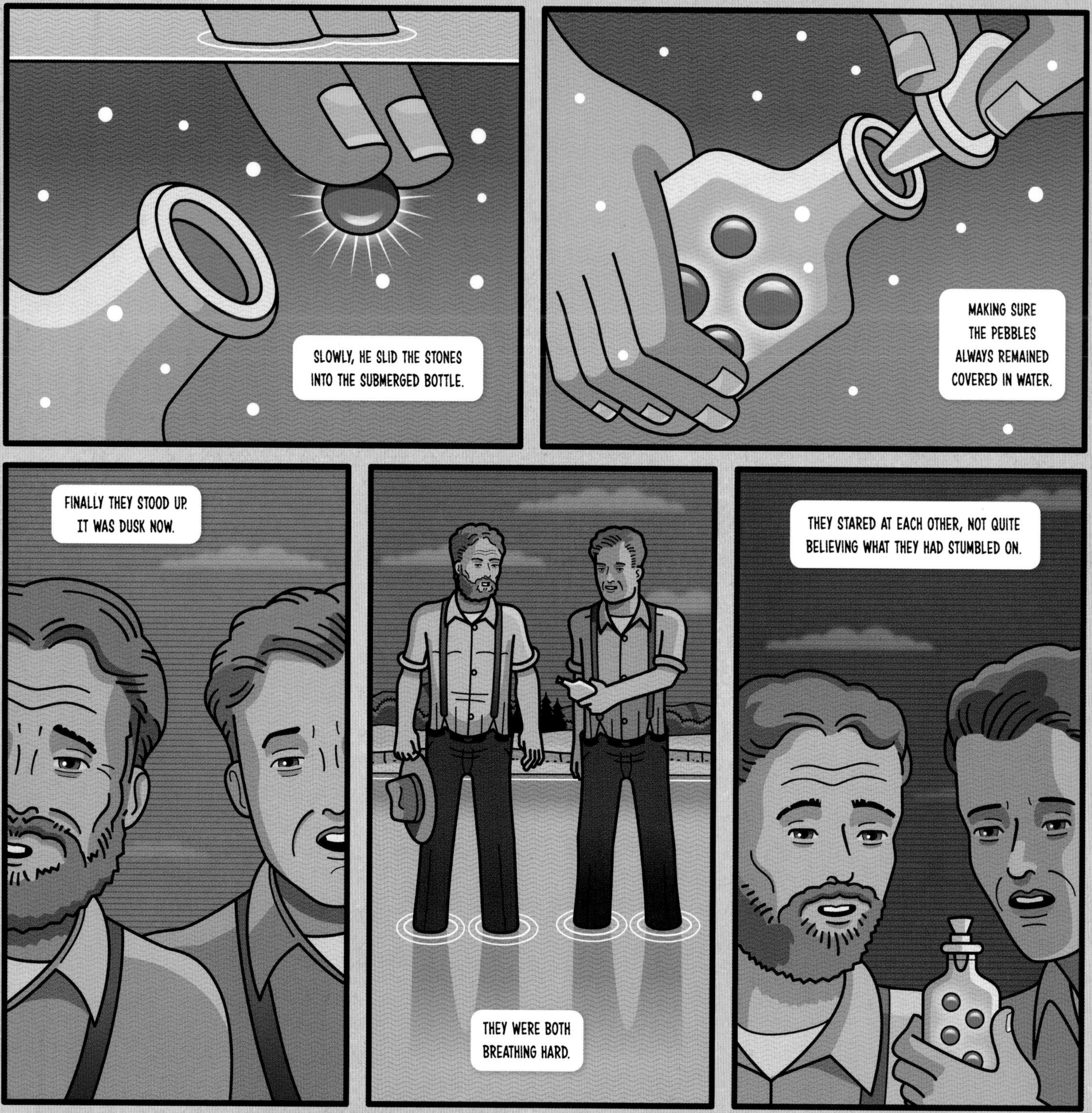
SLOWLY, HE SLID THE STONES INTO THE SUBMERGED BOTTLE.
MAKING SURE THE PEBBLES ALWAYS REMAINED COVERED IN WATER.
FINALLY THEY STOOD UP. IT WAS DUSK NOW.
THEY WERE BOTH BREATHING HARD.
THEY STARED AT EACH OTHER, NOT QUITE BELIEVING WHAT THEY HAD STUMBLED ON.

THE FLICKERING CAMPFIRE LIT UP THEIR FACES.

THE SMALL BOTTLE SAT PERCHED ON A BLANKET BETWEEN THEM.

EVEN SUBMERGED IN CLOUDY RIVER WATER, THE STONES GLEAMED.

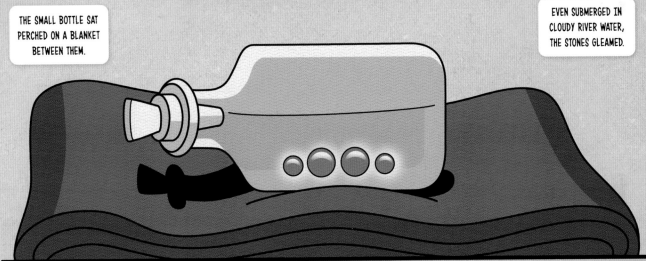

SUNLIGHT WON'T HURT THEM, BUT IF THEY'RE EXPOSED TO AIR, THEY VAPORIZE.

THE OTHER MAN NODDED.

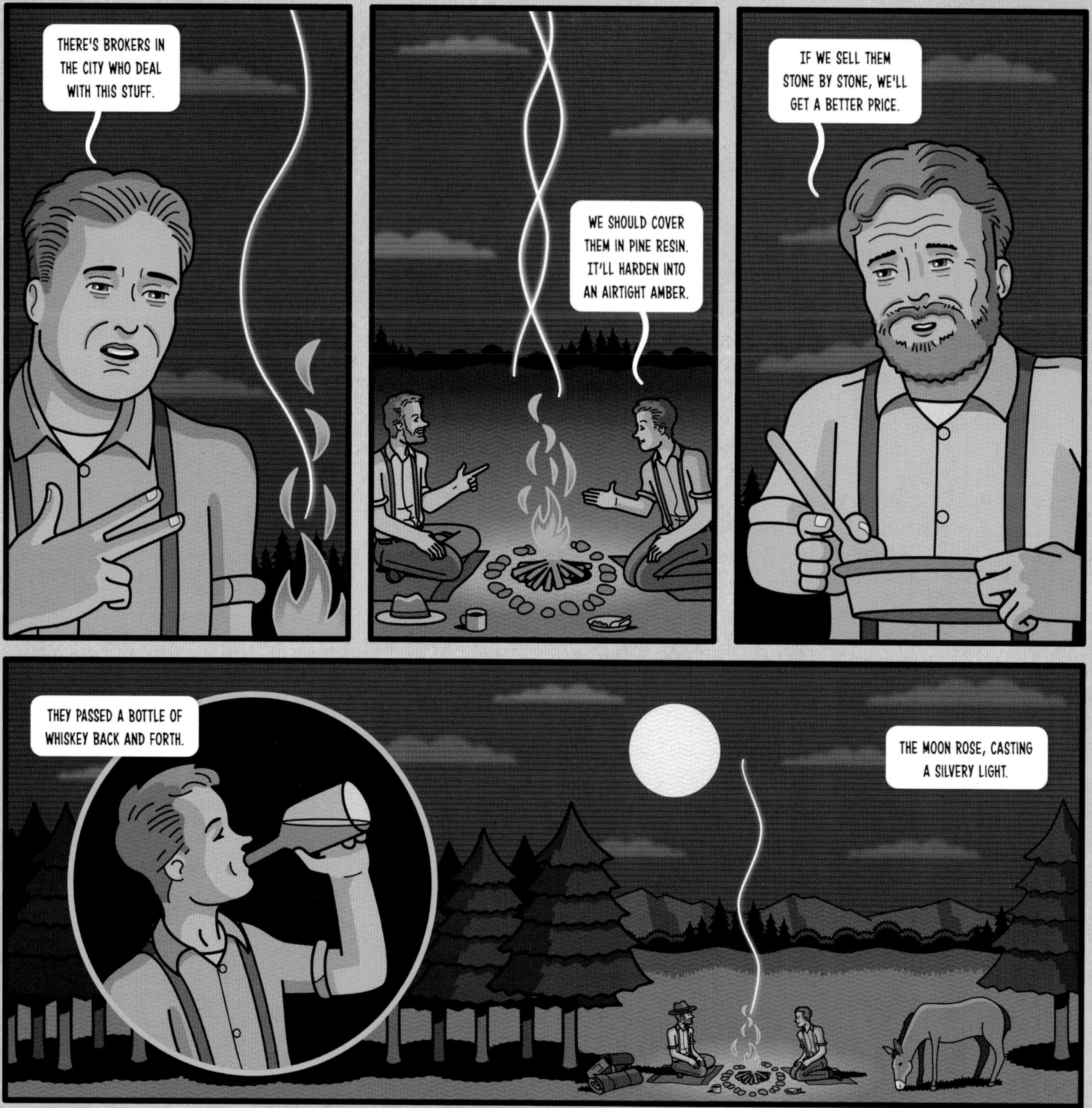
THERE'S BROKERS IN THE CITY WHO DEAL WITH THIS STUFF.
WE SHOULD COVER THEM IN PINE RESIN. IT'LL HARDEN INTO AN AIRTIGHT AMBER.
IF WE SELL THEM STONE BY STONE, WE'LL GET A BETTER PRICE.
THEY PASSED A BOTTLE OF WHISKEY BACK AND FORTH.
THE MOON ROSE, CASTING A SILVERY LIGHT.

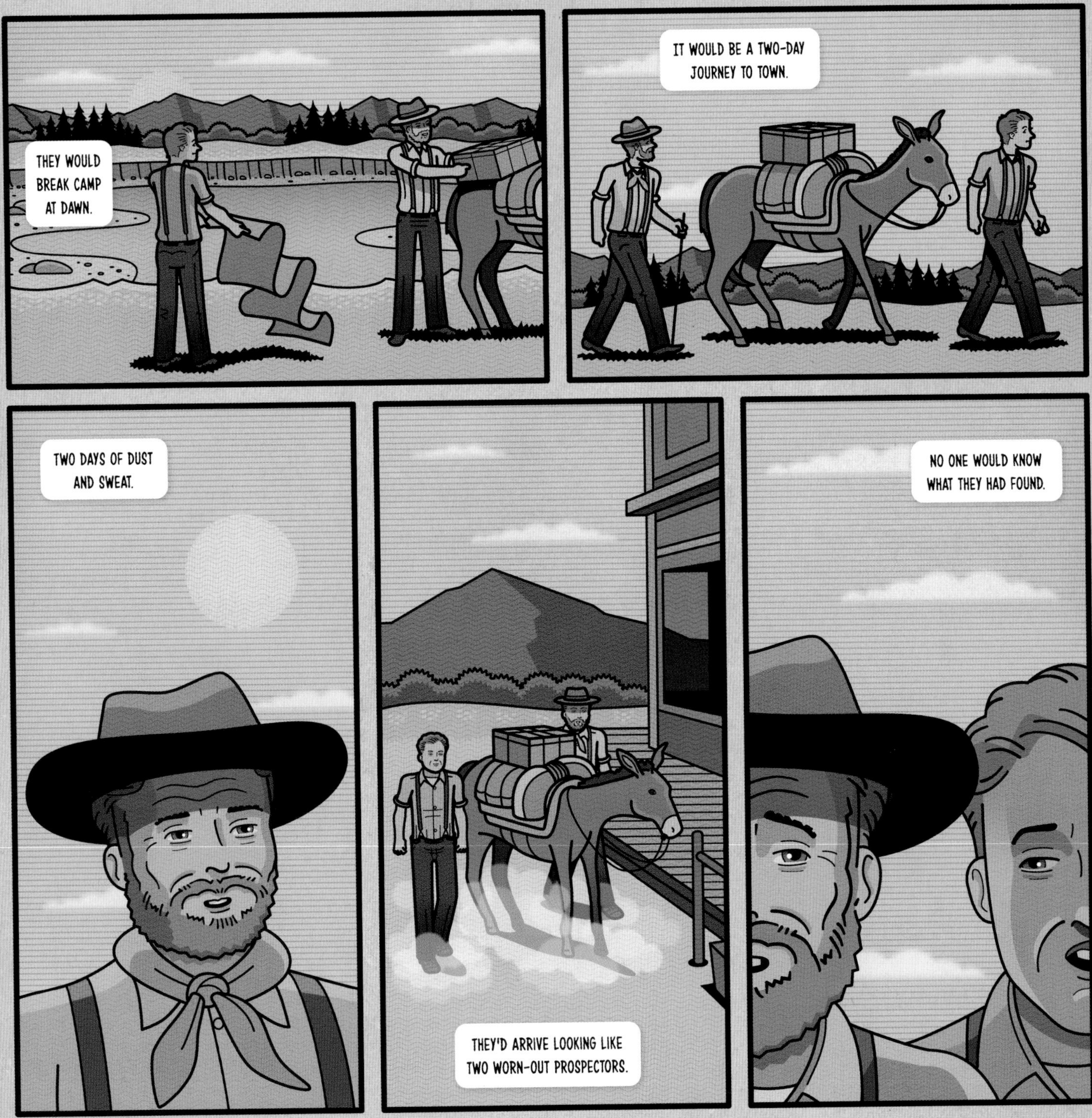
THEY WOULD BREAK CAMP AT DAWN.
IT WOULD BE A TWO-DAY JOURNEY TO TOWN.
TWO DAYS OF DUST AND SWEAT.
THEY'D ARRIVE LOOKING LIKE TWO WORN-OUT PROSPECTORS.
NO ONE WOULD KNOW WHAT THEY HAD FOUND.

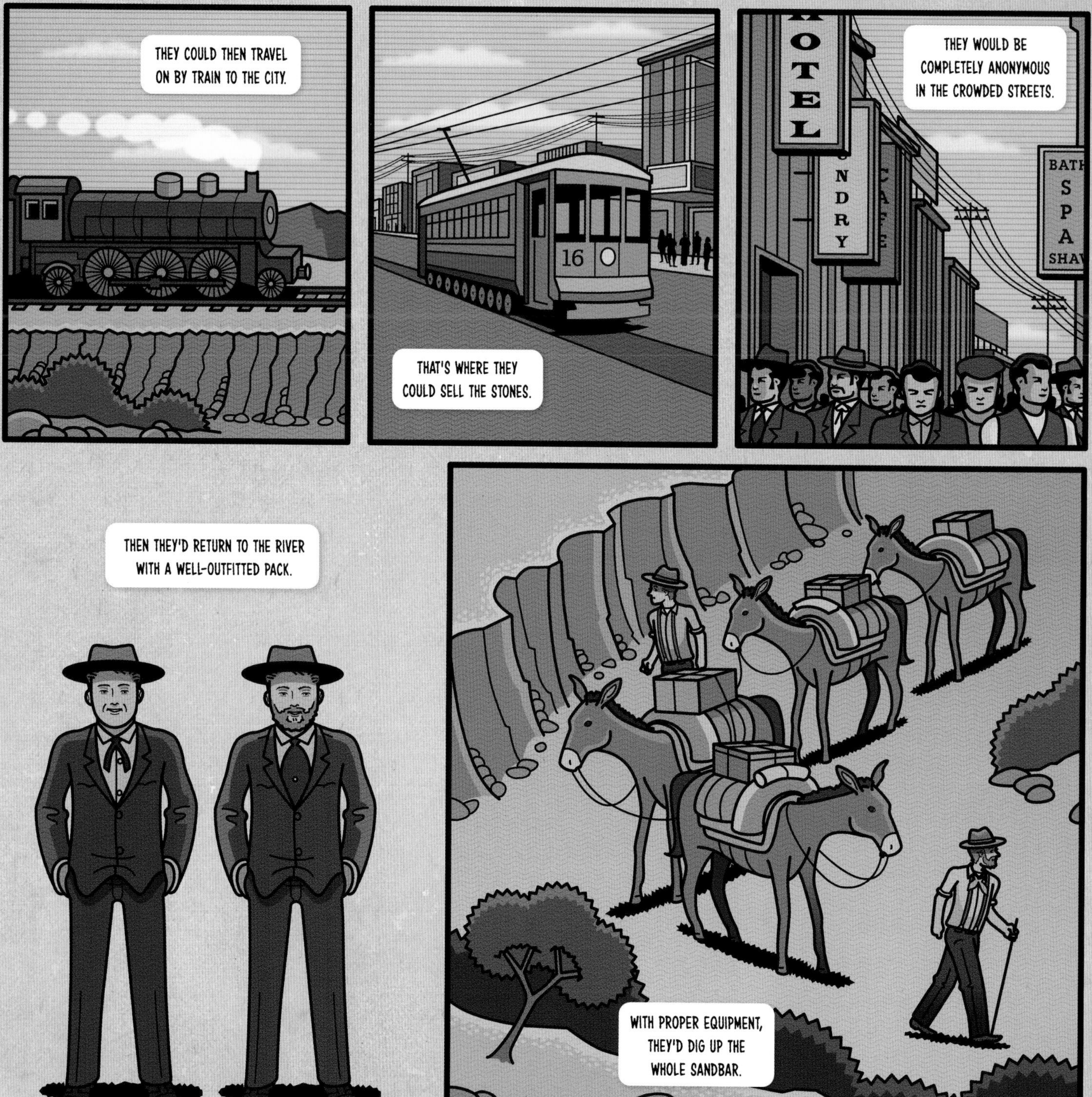
THEY COULD THEN TRAVEL ON BY TRAIN TO THE CITY.
THAT'S WHERE THEY COULD SELL THE STONES.
16
HOTEL
THEY WOULD BE COMPLETELY ANONYMOUS IN THE CROWDED STREETS.
THEN THEY'D RETURN TO THE RIVER WITH A WELL-OUTFITTED PACK.
WITH PROPER EQUIPMENT, THEY'D DIG UP THE WHOLE SANDBAR.

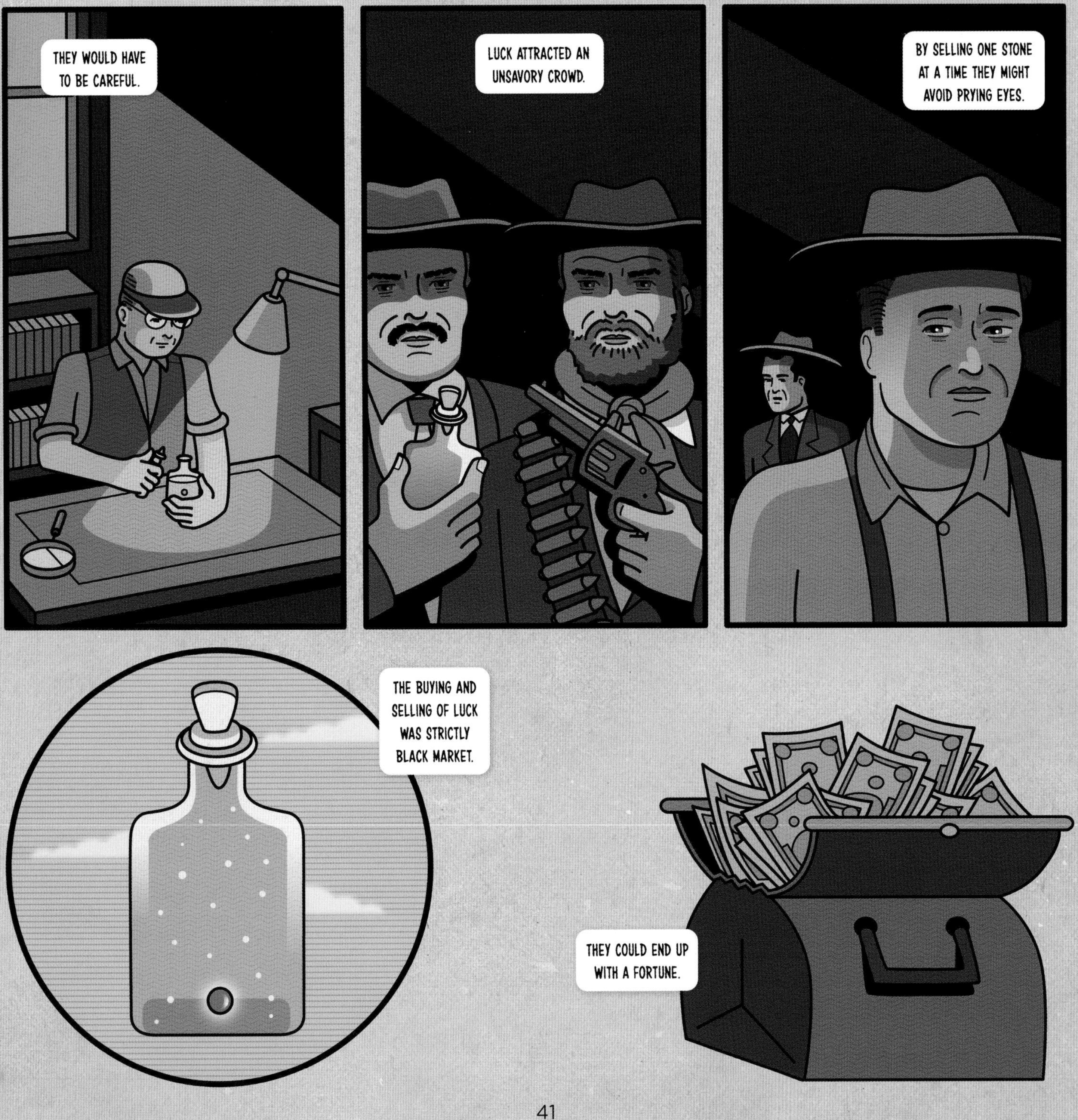
THEY WOULD HAVE TO BE CAREFUL.
LUCK ATTRACTED AN UNSAVORY CROWD.
BY SELLING ONE STONE AT A TIME THEY MIGHT AVOID PRYING EYES.
THE BUYING AND SELLING OF LUCK WAS STRICTLY BLACK MARKET.
THEY COULD END UP WITH A FORTUNE.

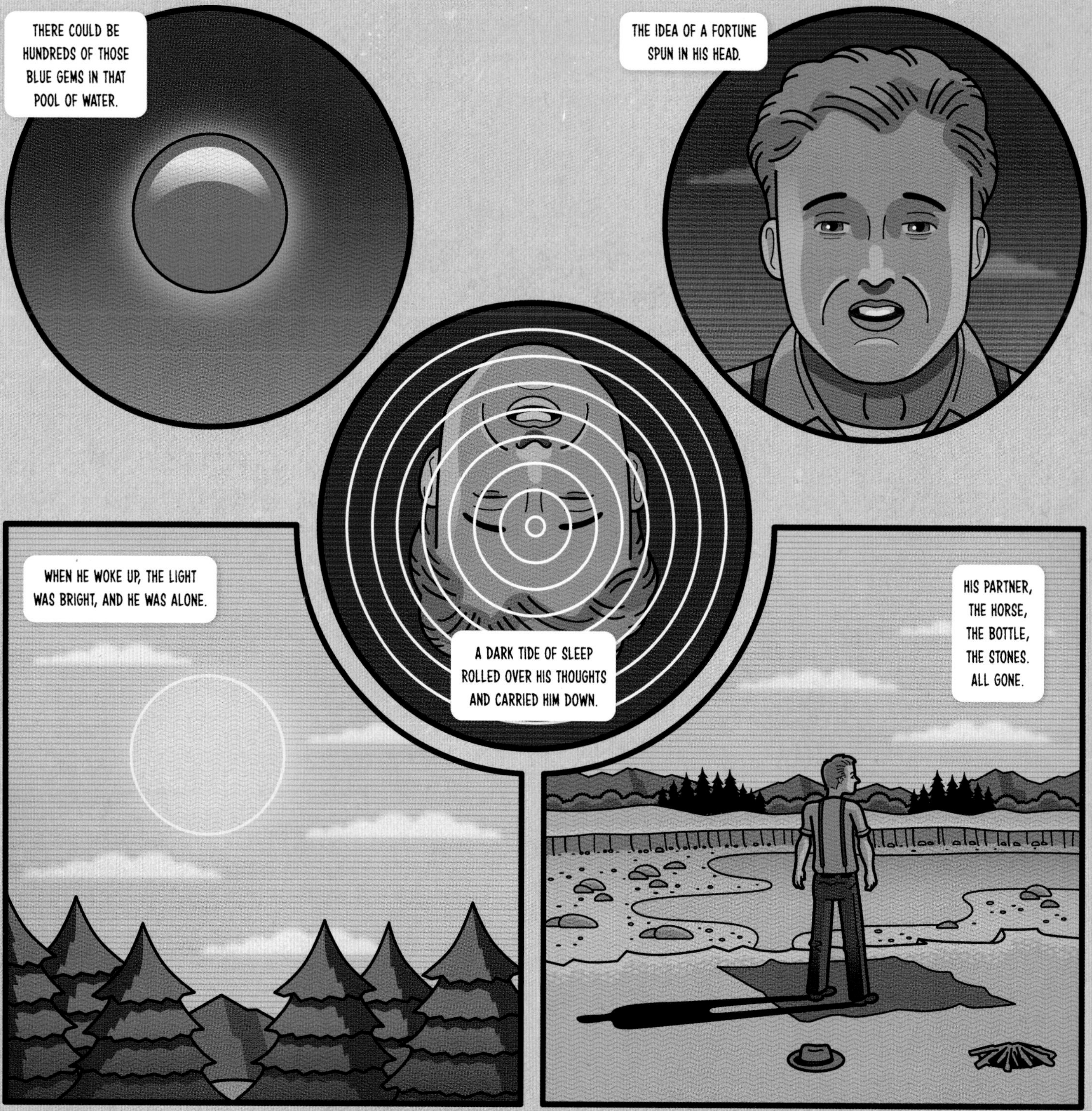
THERE COULD BE HUNDREDS OF THOSE BLUE GEMS IN THAT POOL OF WATER.
THE IDEA OF A FORTUNE SPUN IN HIS HEAD.
A DARK TIDE OF SLEEP ROLLED OVER HIS THOUGHTS AND CARRIED HIM DOWN.
WHEN HE WOKE UP, THE LIGHT WAS BRIGHT, AND HE WAS ALONE.
HIS PARTNER, THE HORSE, THE BOTTLE, THE STONES. ALL GONE.

HATS
SAN FRANCISCO
Lucky
SHE WAS AT THE STORE ALL DAY.
CHAPTER 4

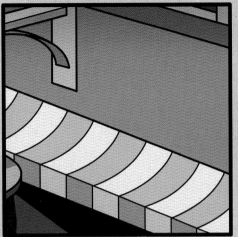

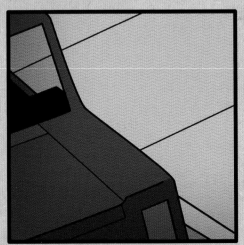

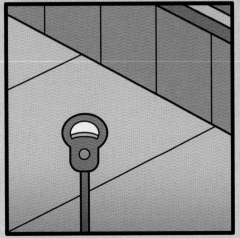

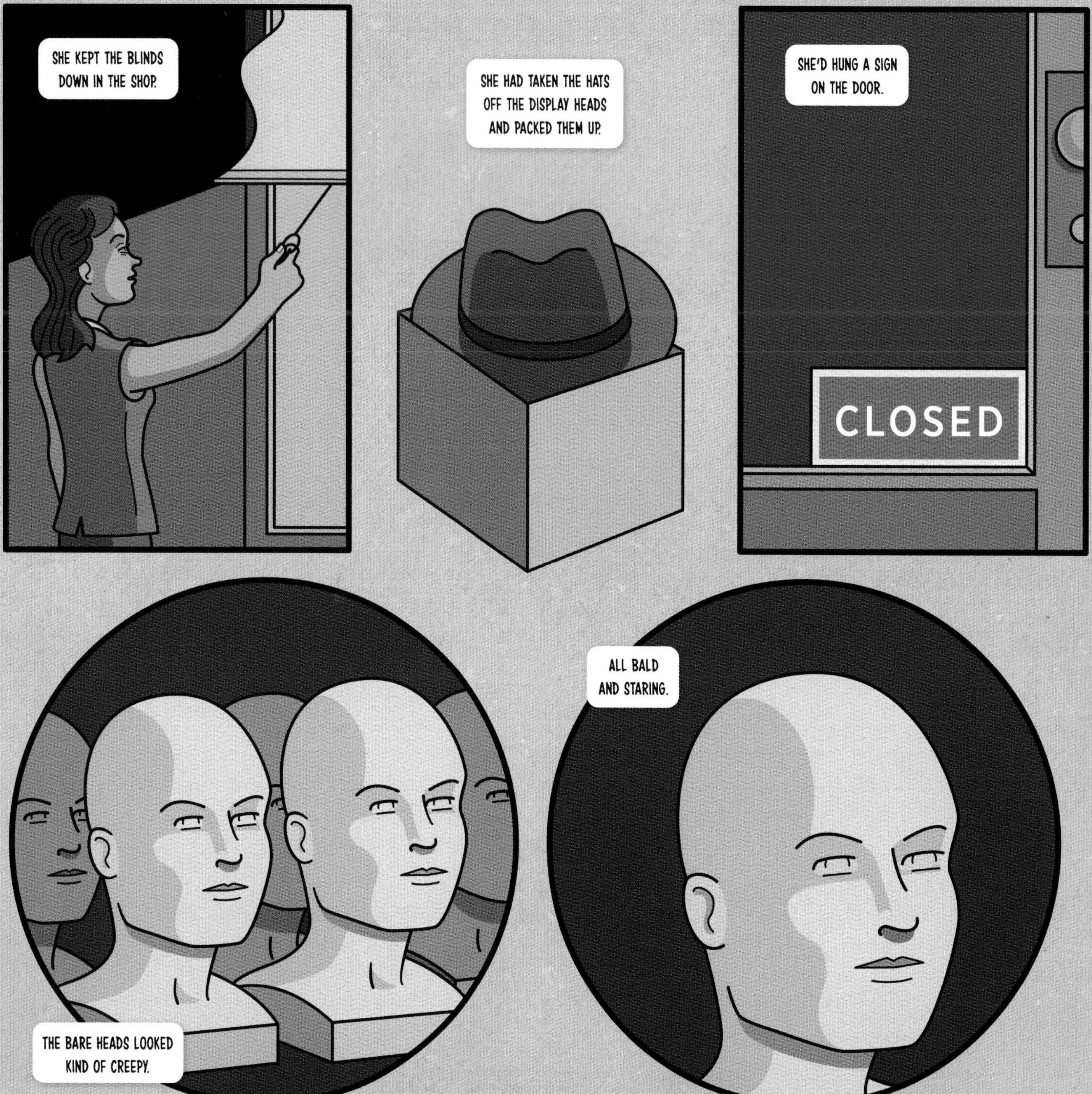
SHE KEPT THE BLINDS DOWN IN THE SHOP.
SHE HAD TAKEN THE HATS OFF THE DISPLAY HEADS AND PACKED THEM UP.
SHE'D HUNG A SIGN ON THE DOOR.
CLOSED
THE BARE HEADS LOOKED KIND OF CREEPY.
ALL BALD AND STARING.

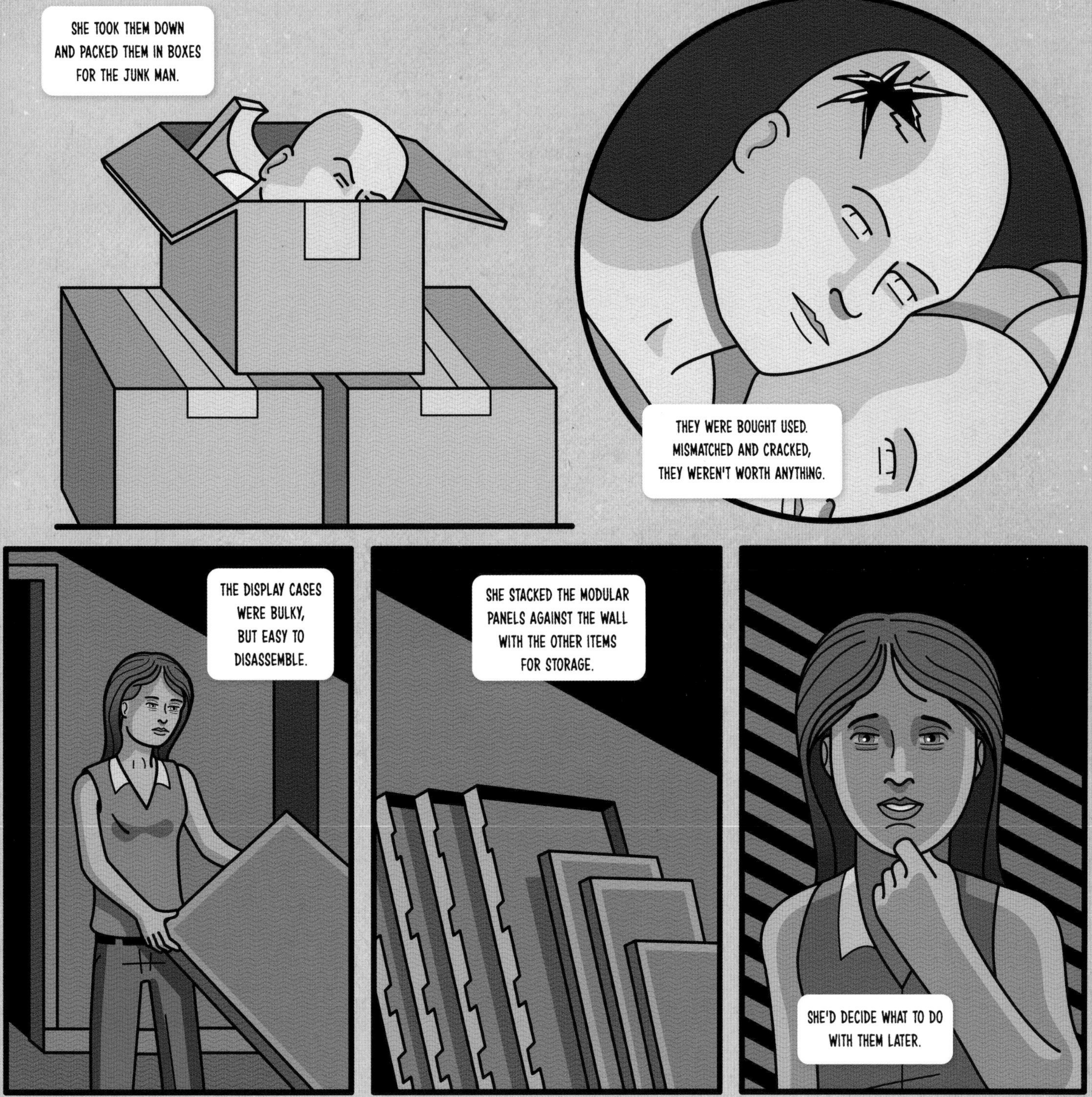
SHE TOOK THEM DOWN AND PACKED THEM IN BOXES FOR THE JUNK MAN.
THEY WERE BOUGHT USED. MISMATCHED AND CRACKED, THEY WEREN'T WORTH ANYTHING.
THE DISPLAY CASES WERE BULKY, BUT EASY TO DISASSEMBLE.
SHE STACKED THE MODULAR PANELS AGAINST THE WALL WITH THE OTHER ITEMS FOR STORAGE.
SHE'D DECIDE WHAT TO DO WITH THEM LATER.

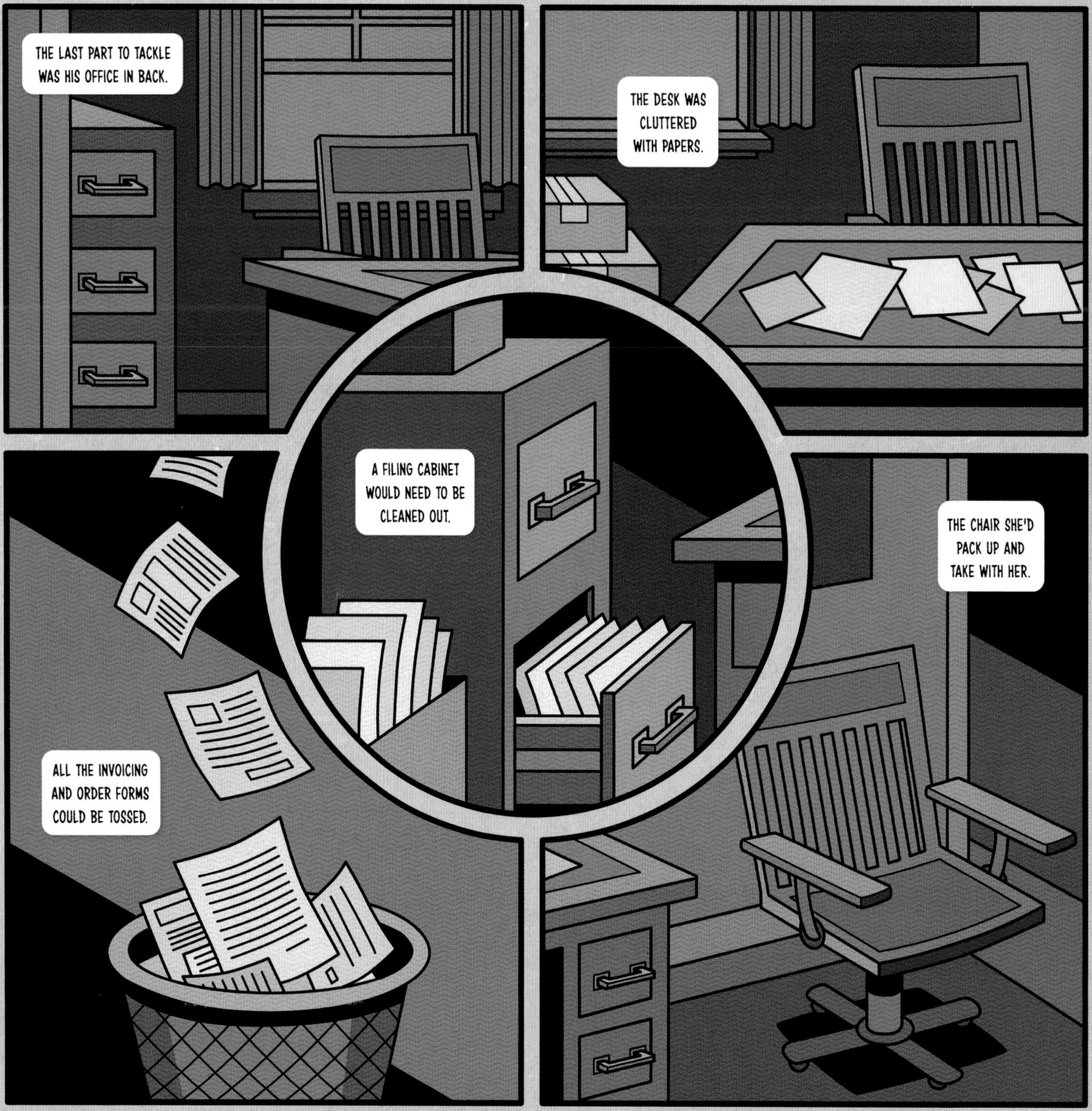
THE LAST PART TO TACKLE WAS HIS OFFICE IN BACK.
THE DESK WAS CLUTTERED WITH PAPERS.
A FILING CABINET WOULD NEED TO BE CLEANED OUT.
ALL THE INVOICING AND ORDER FORMS COULD BE TOSSED.
THE CHAIR SHE'D PACK UP AND TAKE WITH HER.

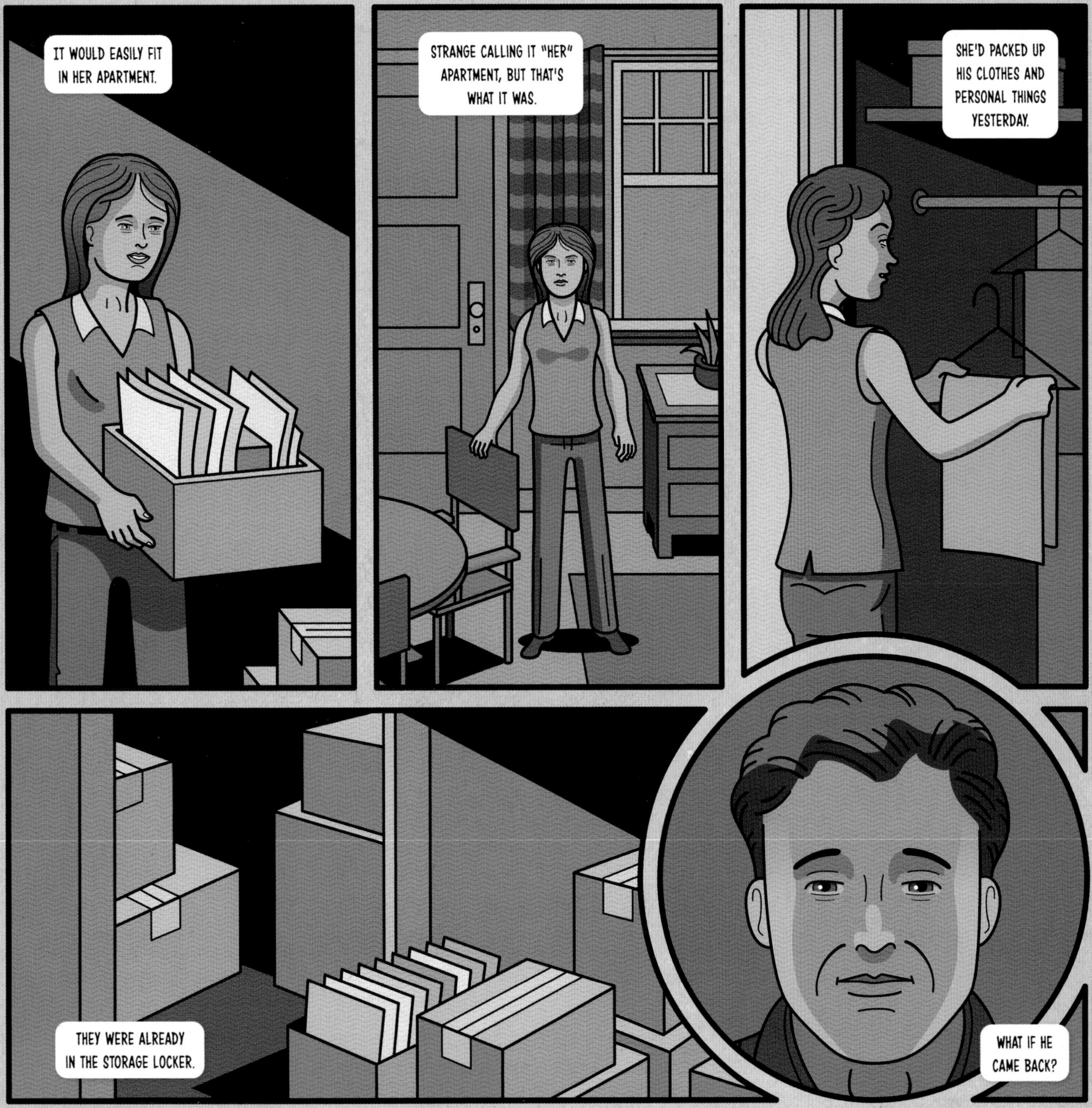
IT WOULD EASILY FIT IN HER APARTMENT.
STRANGE CALLING IT "HER" APARTMENT, BUT THAT'S WHAT IT WAS.
SHE'D PACKED UP HIS CLOTHES AND PERSONAL THINGS YESTERDAY.
THEY WERE ALREADY IN THE STORAGE LOCKER.
WHAT IF HE CAME BACK?

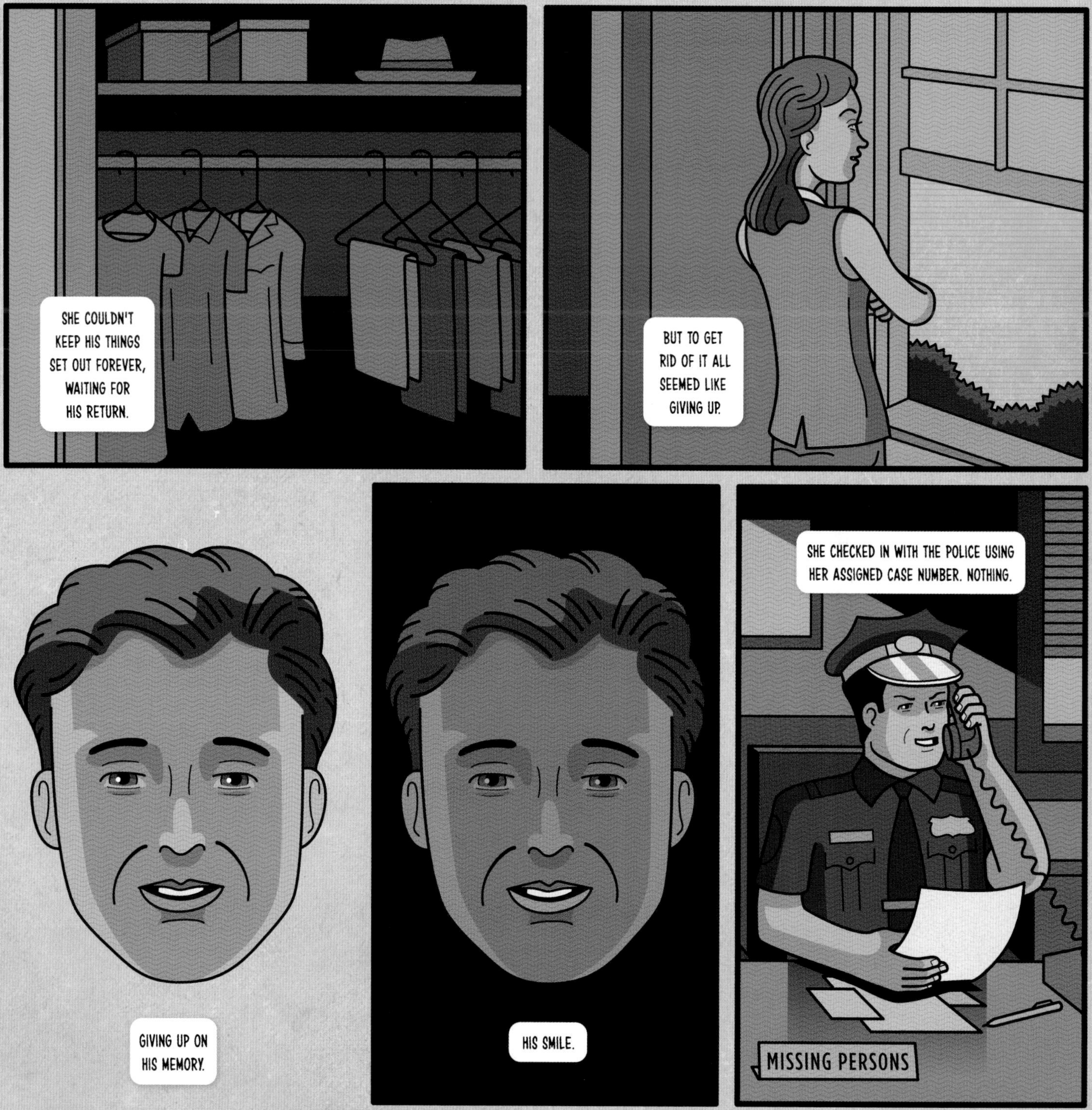
SHE COULDN'T KEEP HIS THINGS SET OUT FOREVER, WAITING FOR HIS RETURN.
BUT TO GET RID OF IT ALL SEEMED LIKE GIVING UP.
GIVING UP ON HIS MEMORY.
HIS SMILE.
SHE CHECKED IN WITH THE POLICE USING HER ASSIGNED CASE NUMBER. NOTHING.
MISSING PERSONS

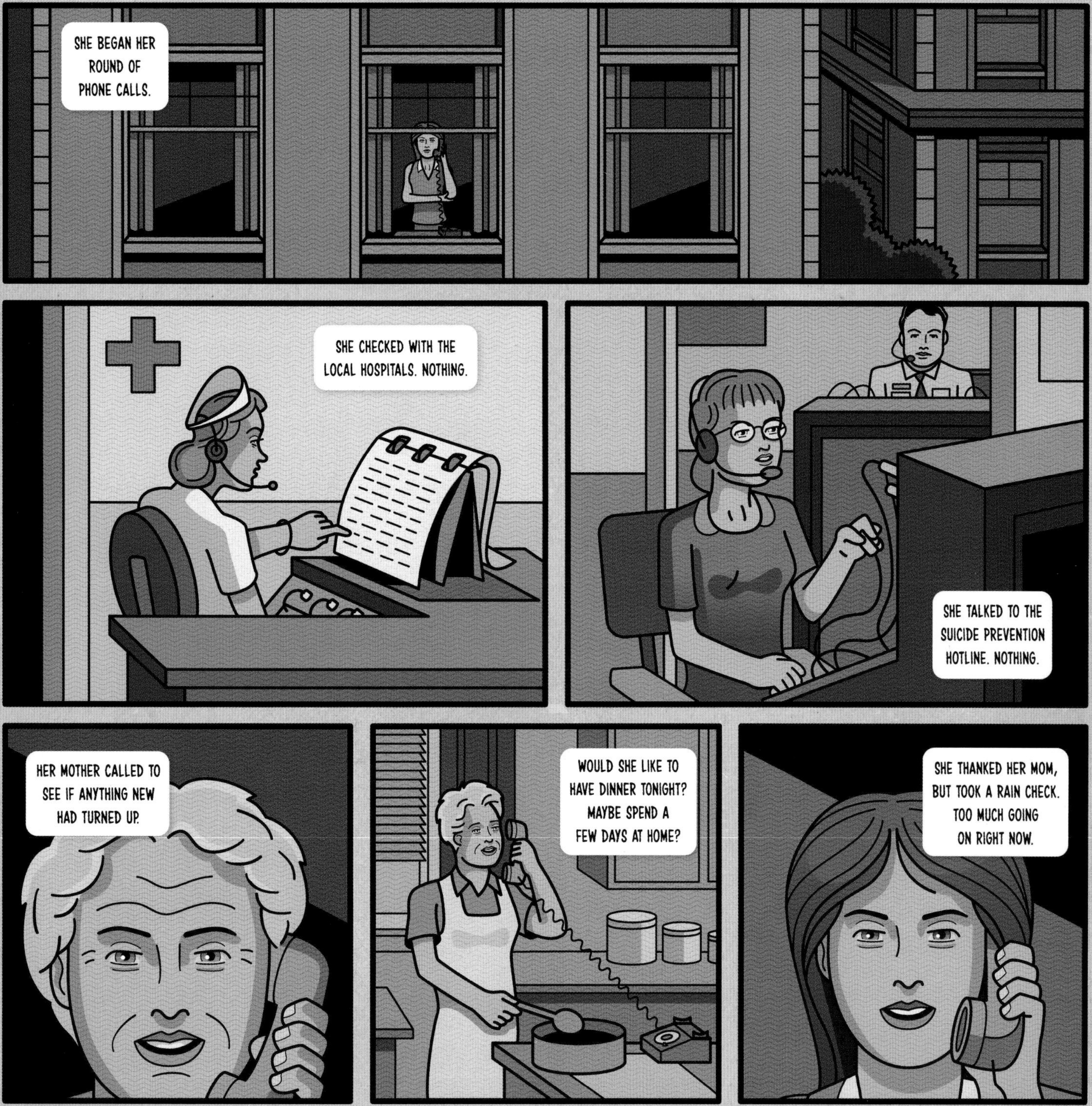
SHE BEGAN HER ROUND OF PHONE CALLS.
SHE CHECKED WITH THE LOCAL HOSPITALS. NOTHING.
SHE TALKED TO THE SUICIDE PREVENTION HOTLINE. NOTHING.
HER MOTHER CALLED TO SEE IF ANYTHING NEW HAD TURNED UP.
WOULD SHE LIKE TO HAVE DINNER TONIGHT? MAYBE SPEND A FEW DAYS AT HOME?
SHE THANKED HER MOM, BUT TOOK A RAIN CHECK. TOO MUCH GOING ON RIGHT NOW.

WHEN SHE STOOD IN HIS STUDIO SHE COULD FEEL HIS PRESENCE.

A JACKET, STILL HANGING ON THE BACK OF A CHAIR.

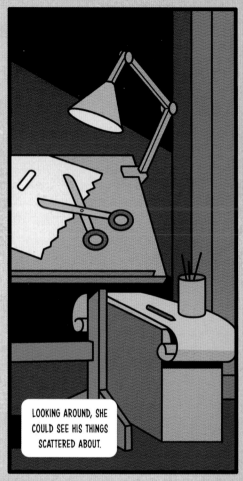

LOOKING AROUND, SHE COULD SEE HIS THINGS SCATTERED ABOUT.

HIS DESK COVERED WITH NOTES AND INVOICES.

ALL WRITTEN IN HIS NEARLY ILLEGIBLE SCRAWL.

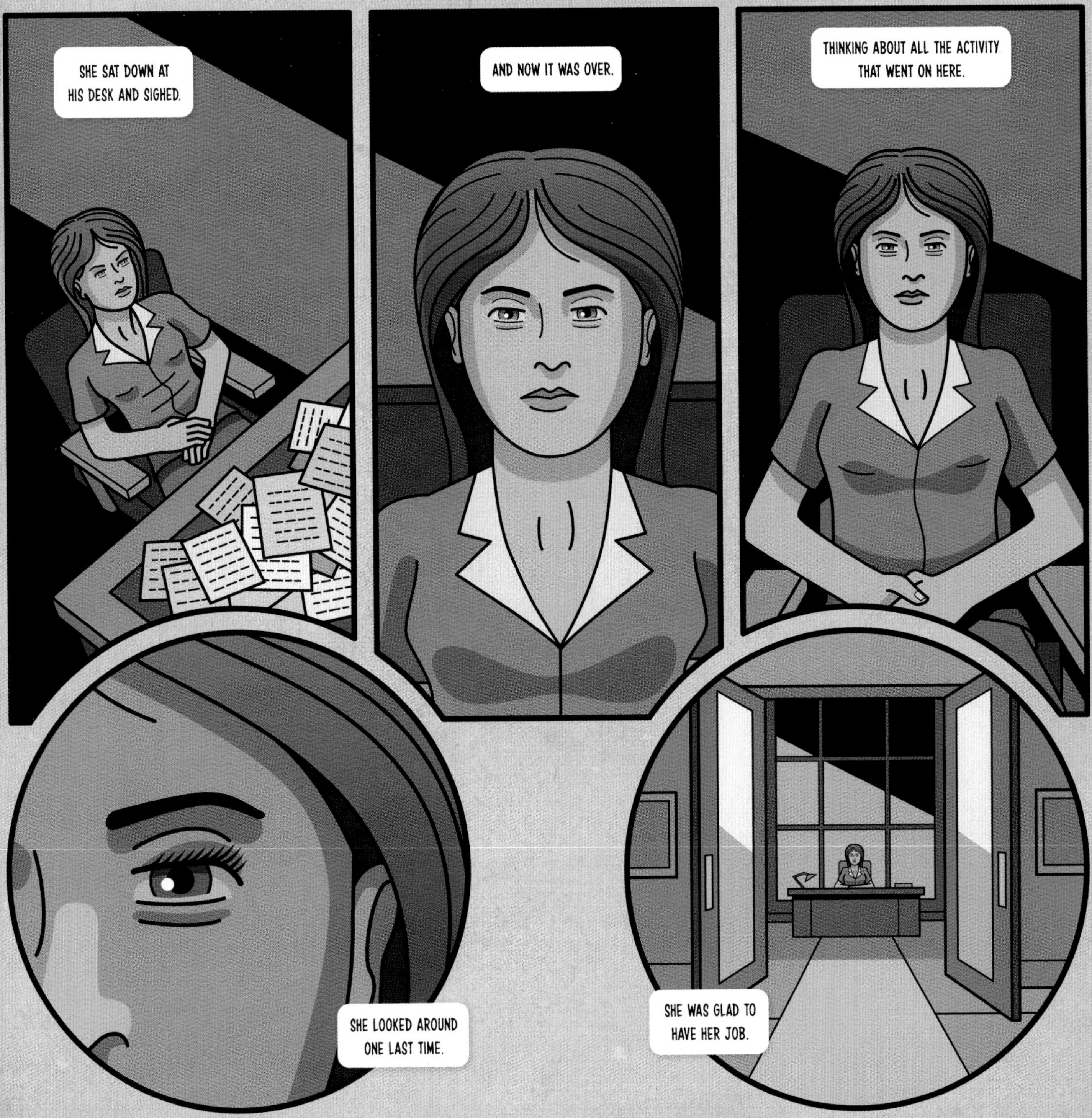
SHE SAT DOWN AT HIS DESK AND SIGHED.
AND NOW IT WAS OVER.
THINKING ABOUT ALL THE ACTIVITY THAT WENT ON HERE.
SHE LOOKED AROUND ONE LAST TIME.
SHE WAS GLAD TO HAVE HER JOB.

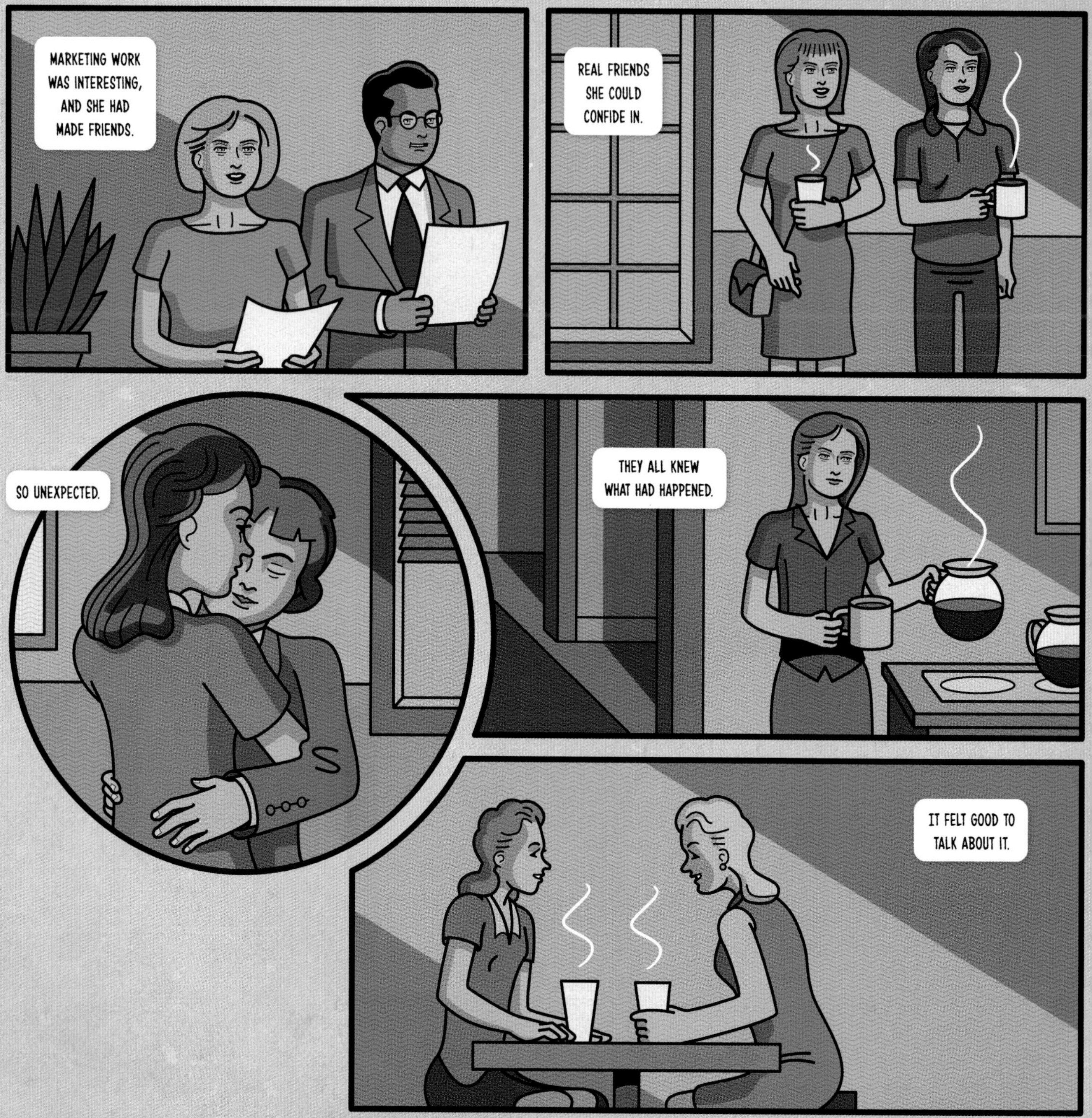
MARKETING WORK WAS INTERESTING, AND SHE HAD MADE FRIENDS.
REAL FRIENDS SHE COULD CONFIDE IN.
SO UNEXPECTED.
THEY ALL KNEW WHAT HAD HAPPENED.
IT FELT GOOD TO TALK ABOUT IT.

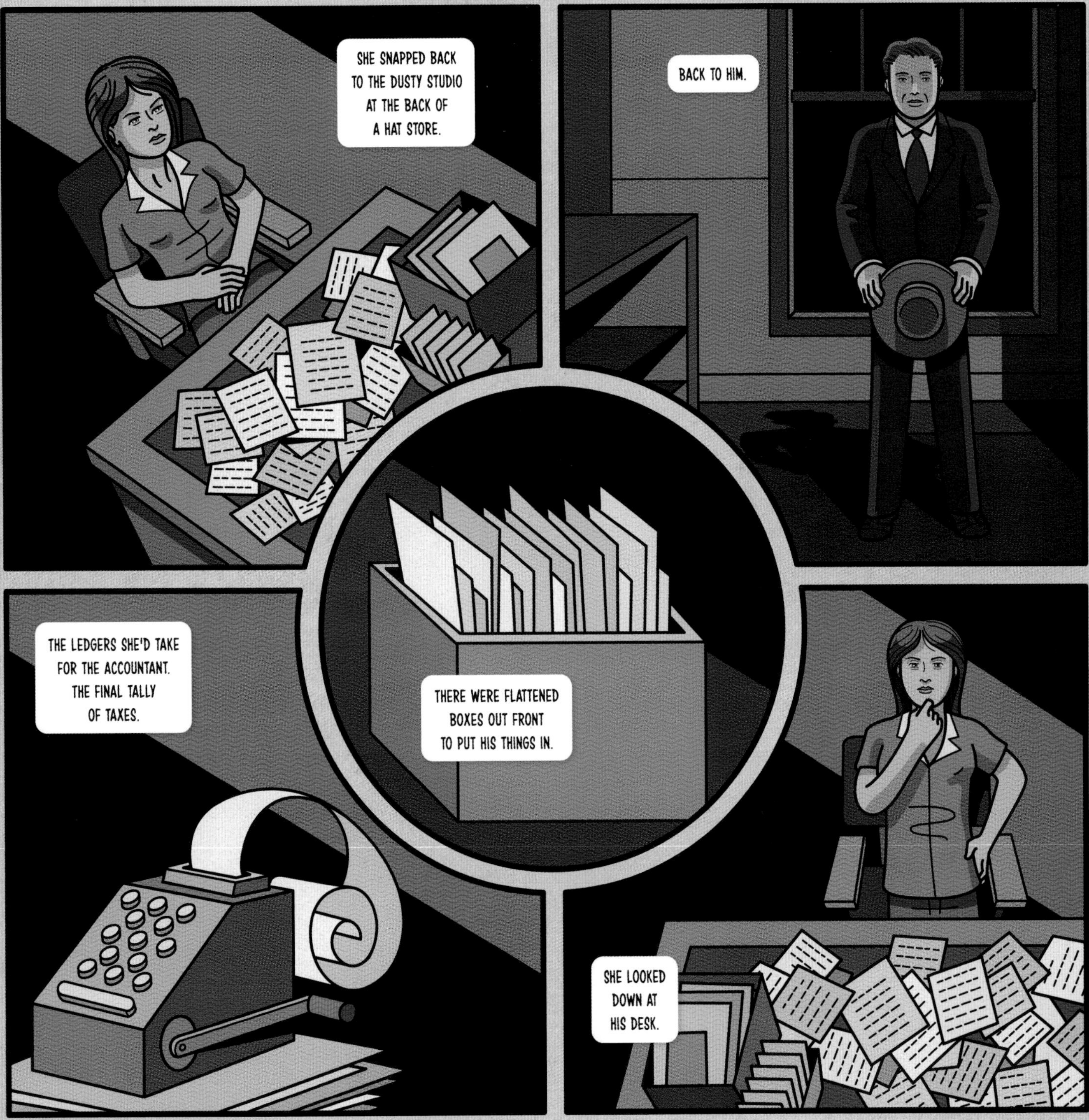
SHE SNAPPED BACK TO THE DUSTY STUDIO AT THE BACK OF A HAT STORE.
BACK TO HIM.
THERE WERE FLATTENED BOXES OUT FRONT TO PUT HIS THINGS IN.
THE LEDGERS SHE'D TAKE FOR THE ACCOUNTANT. THE FINAL TALLY OF TAXES.
SHE LOOKED DOWN AT HIS DESK.

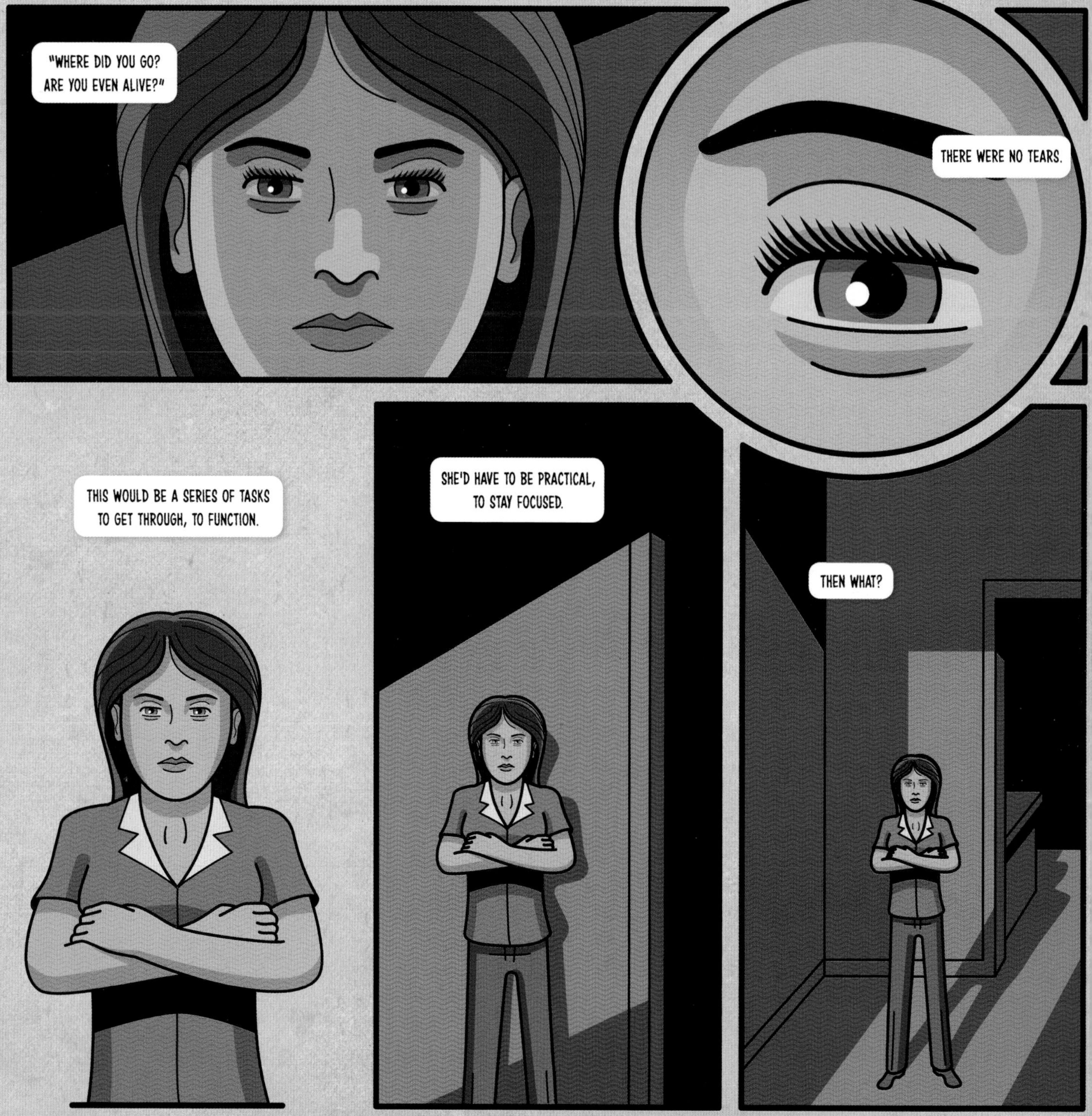
"WHERE DID YOU GO?
ARE YOU EVEN ALIVE?"
THERE WERE NO TEARS.
THIS WOULD BE A SERIES OF TASKS
TO GET THROUGH, TO FUNCTION.
SHE'D HAVE TO BE PRACTICAL,
TO STAY FOCUSED.
THEN WHAT?

CHAPTER
5

IT WAS WARM THAT MORNING, WITH A LOW FOG ON THE WATER.

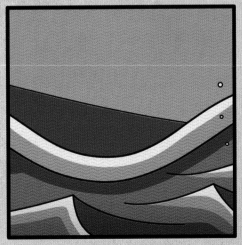

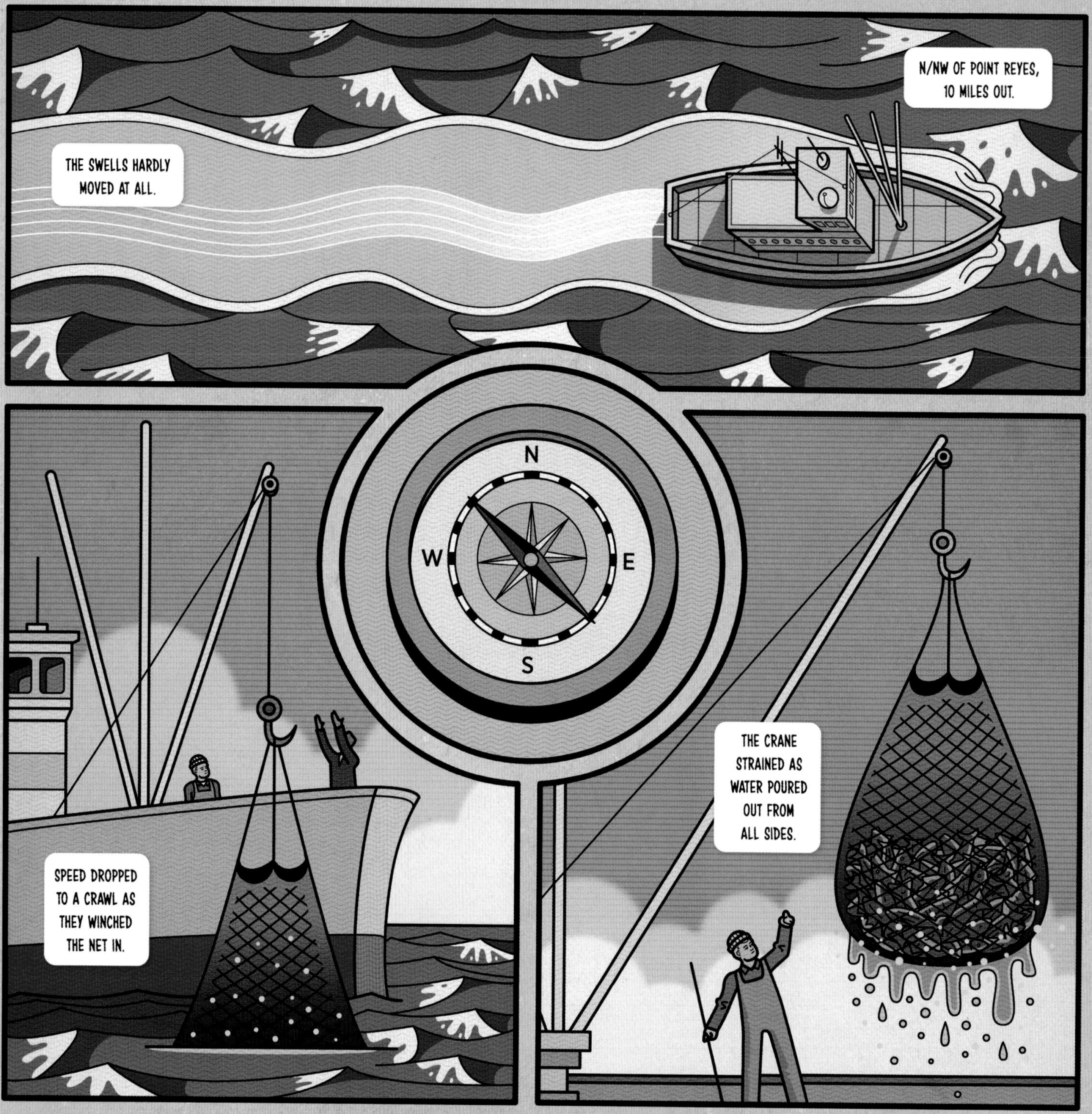

N/NW OF POINT REYES, 10 MILES OUT.
THE SWELLS HARDLY MOVED AT ALL.
N
W
E
S
SPEED DROPPED TO A CRAWL AS THEY WINCHED THE NET IN.
THE CRANE STRAINED AS WATER POURED OUT FROM ALL SIDES.

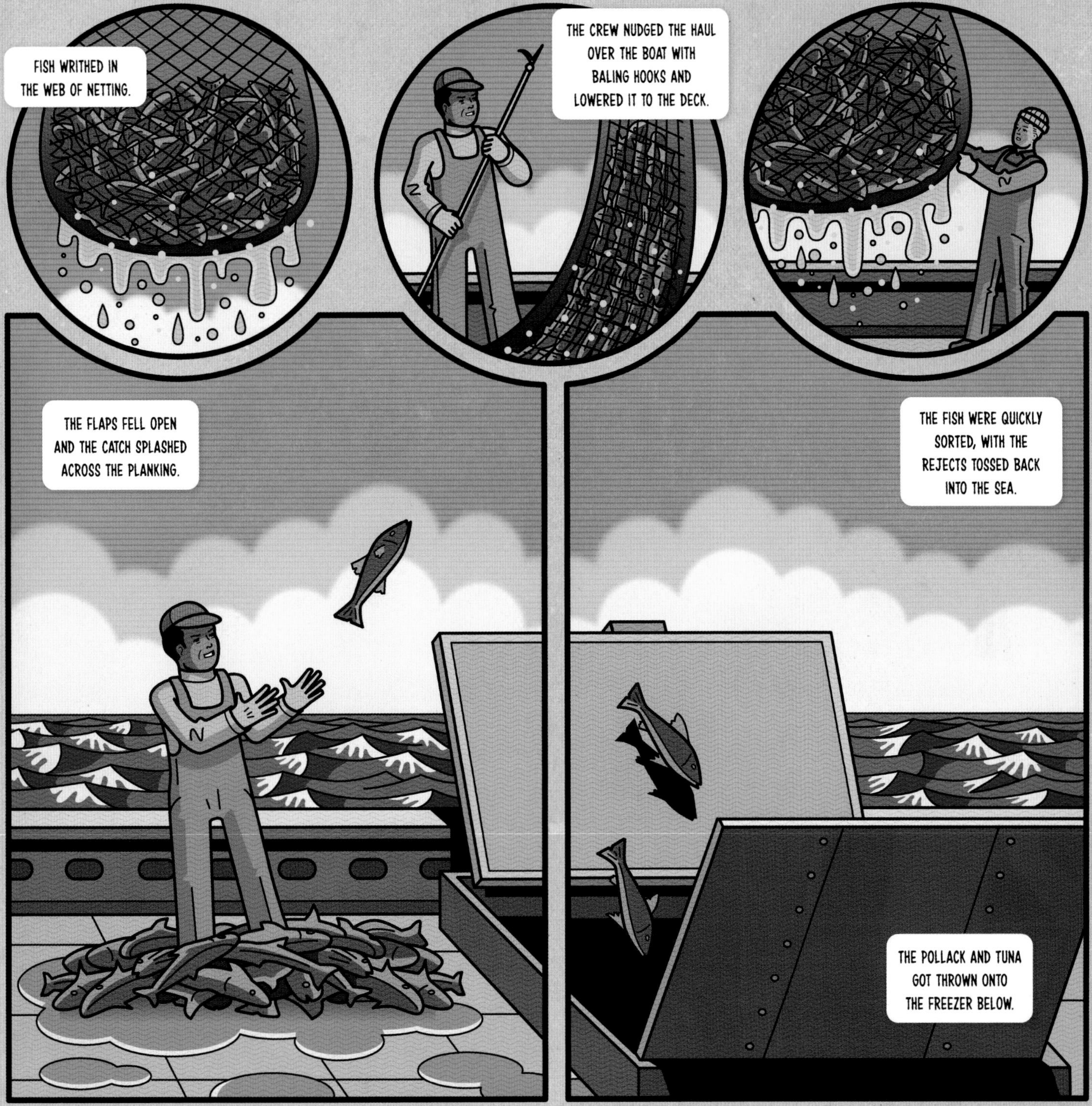
FISH WRITHED IN THE WEB OF NETTING.
THE CREW NUDGED THE HAUL OVER THE BOAT WITH BALING HOOKS AND LOWERED IT TO THE DECK.
THE FLAPS FELL OPEN AND THE CATCH SPLASHED ACROSS THE PLANKING.
THE FISH WERE QUICKLY SORTED, WITH THE REJECTS TOSSED BACK INTO THE SEA.
THE POLLACK AND TUNA GOT THROWN ONTO THE FREEZER BELOW.

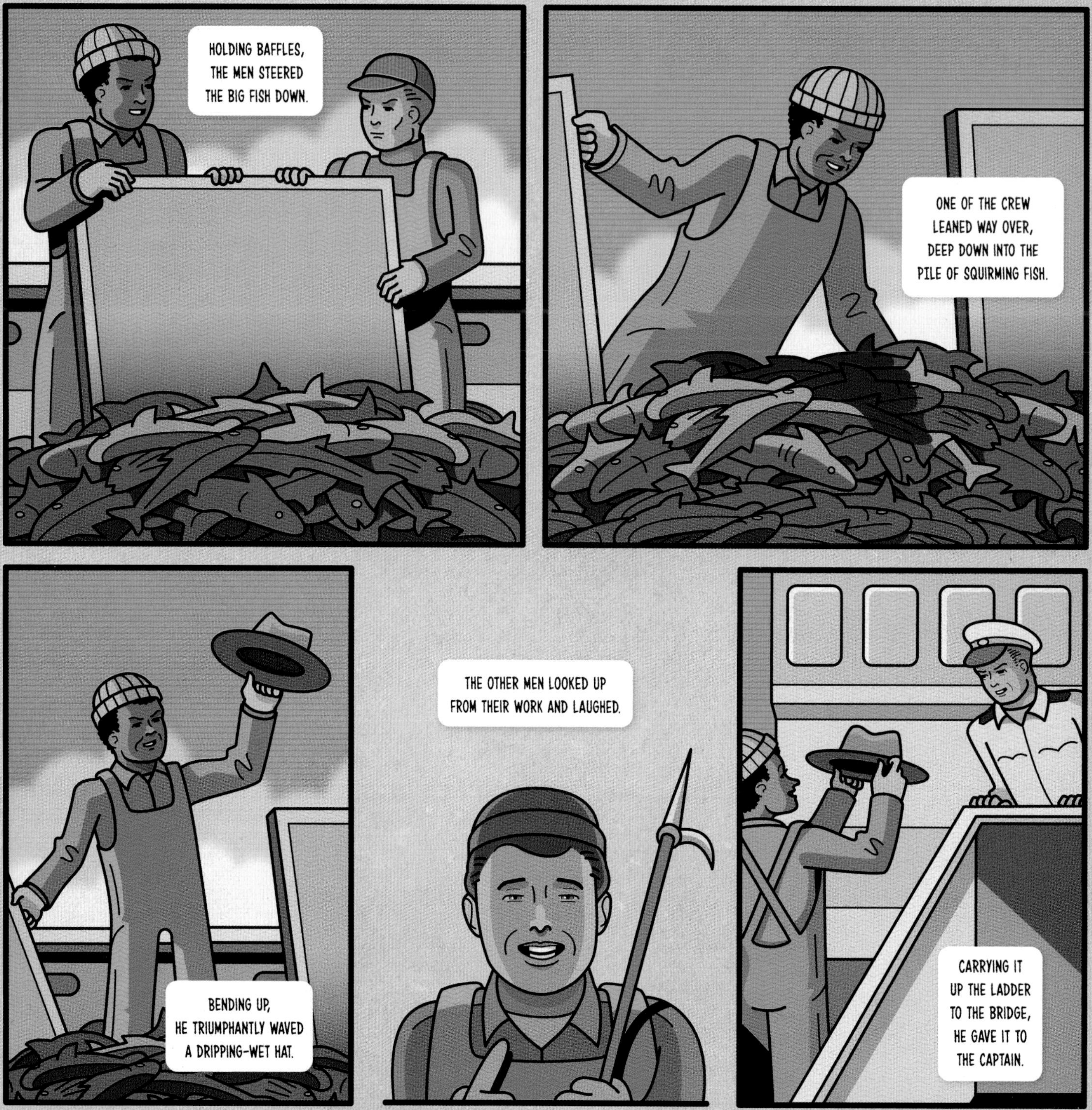
HOLDING BAFFLES, THE MEN STEERED THE BIG FISH DOWN.
ONE OF THE CREW LEANED WAY OVER, DEEP DOWN INTO THE PILE OF SQUIRMING FISH.
BENDING UP, HE TRIUMPHANTLY WAVED A DRIPPING-WET HAT.
THE OTHER MEN LOOKED UP FROM THEIR WORK AND LAUGHED.
CARRYING IT UP THE LADDER TO THE BRIDGE, HE GAVE IT TO THE CAPTAIN.

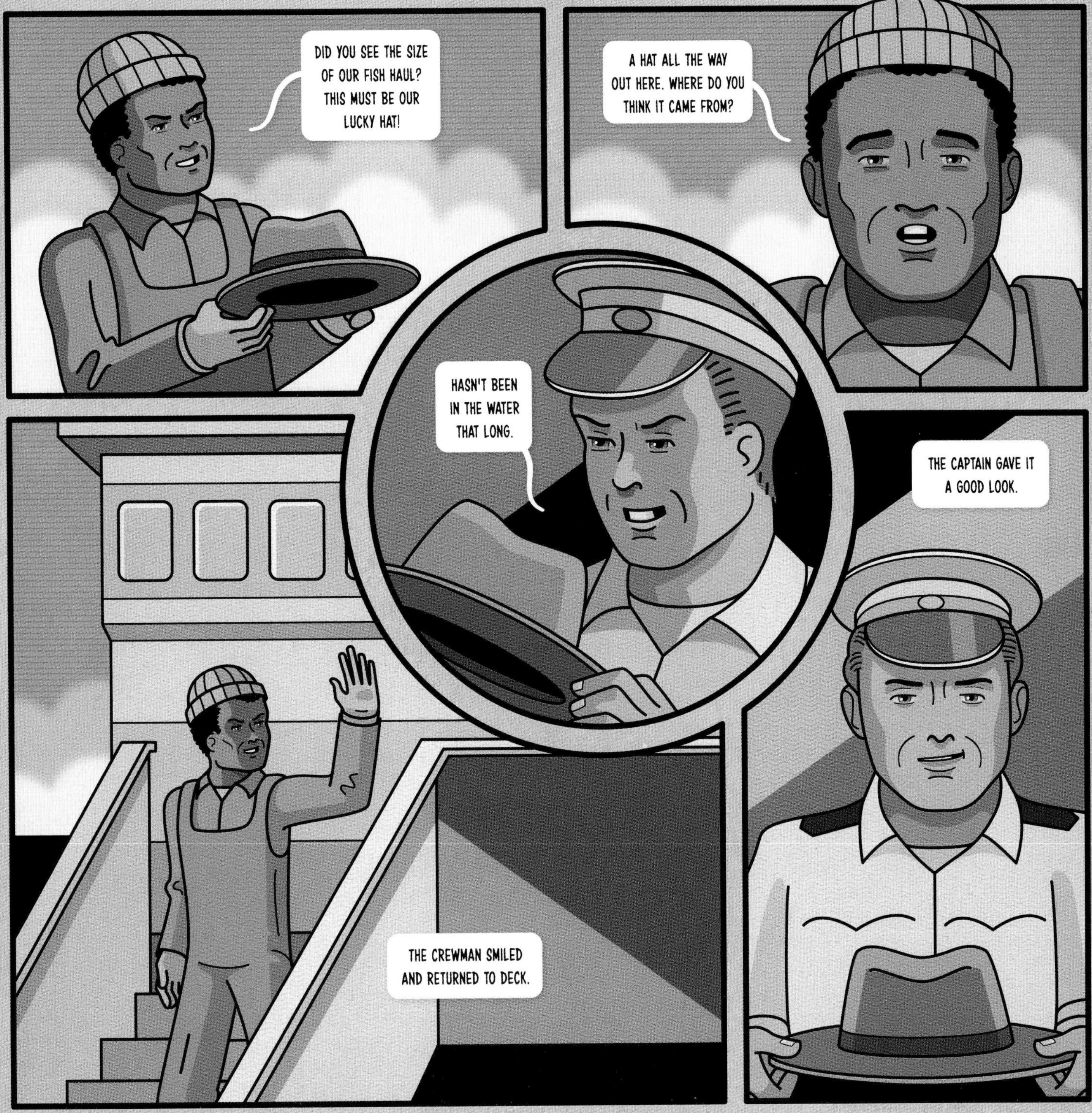
DID YOU SEE THE SIZE OF OUR FISH HAUL? THIS MUST BE OUR LUCKY HAT!
A HAT ALL THE WAY OUT HERE. WHERE DO YOU THINK IT CAME FROM?
HASN'T BEEN IN THE WATER THAT LONG.
THE CAPTAIN GAVE IT A GOOD LOOK.
THE CREWMAN SMILED AND RETURNED TO DECK.

EVENTUALLY HE TOOK OFF HIS OWN CAP AND TRIED IT ON.

IT FIT PERFECTLY.

AS HE TOOK IT OFF HE NOTICED A LABEL ON THE INSIDE.

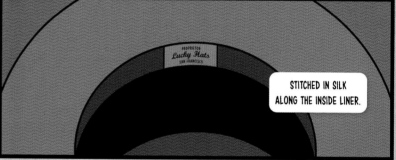

STITCHED IN SILK ALONG THE INSIDE LINER.

PROPRIETOR
Lucky Hats
SAN FRANCISCO

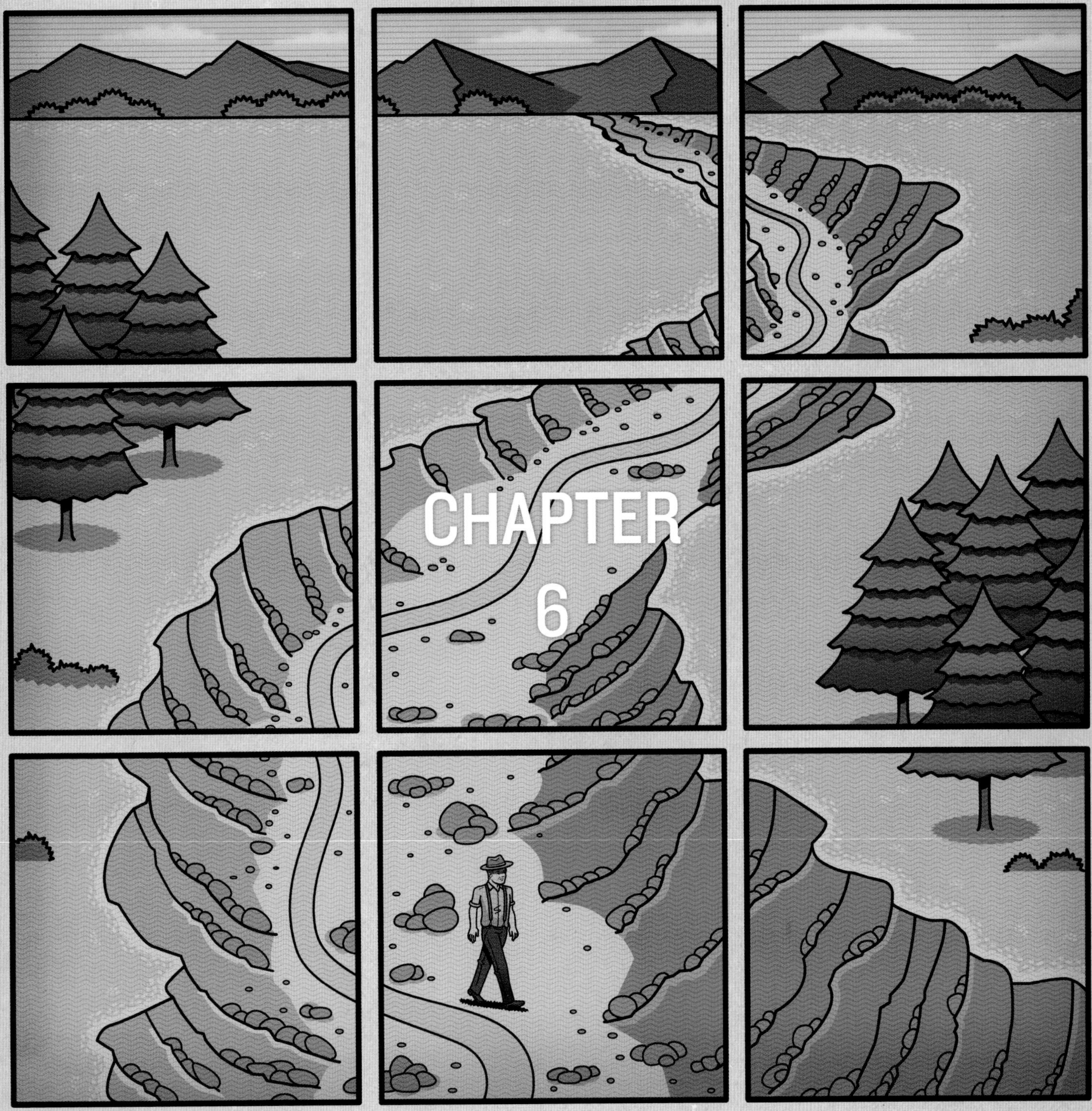
CHAPTER
6

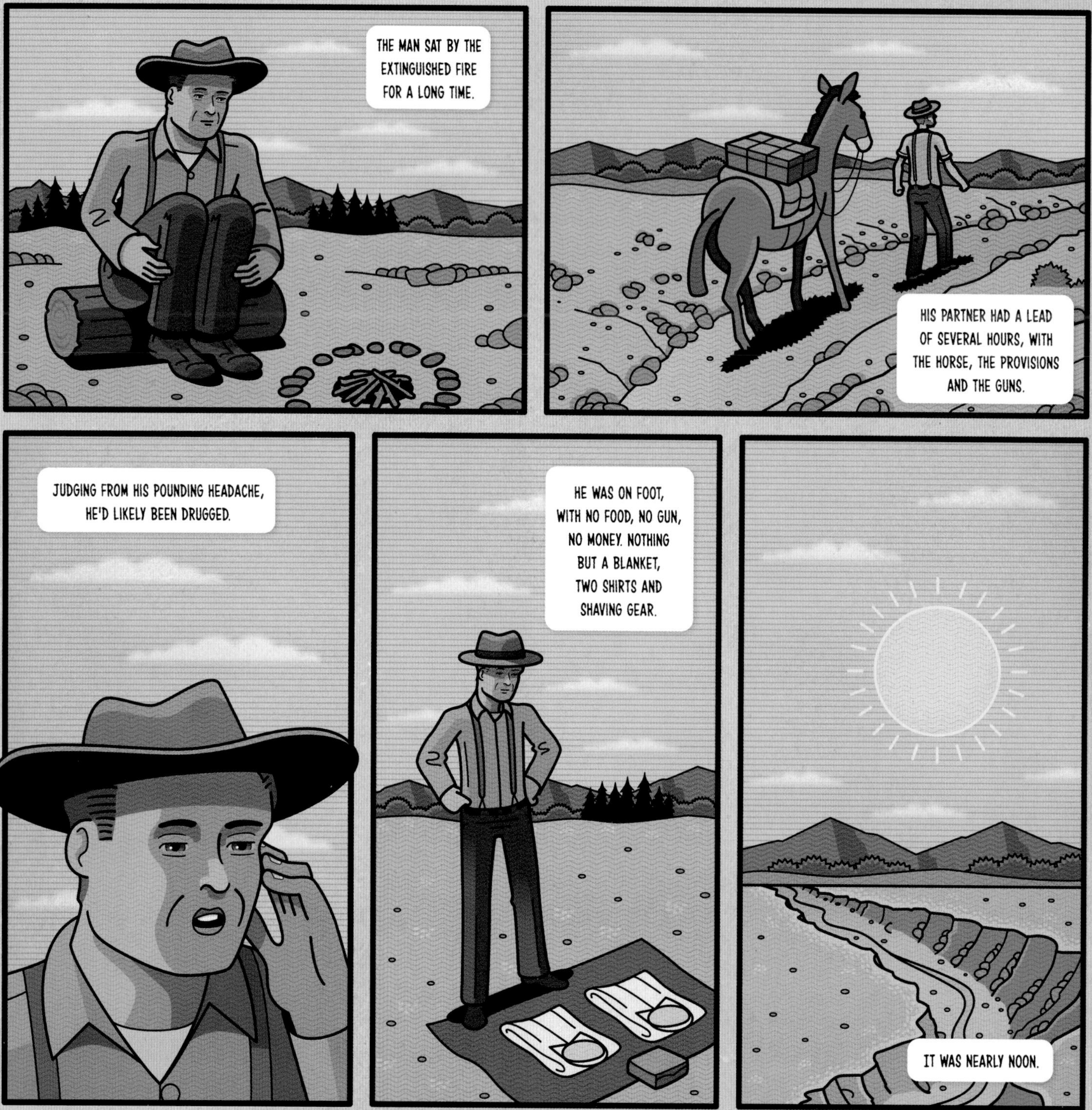
THE MAN SAT BY THE EXTINGUISHED FIRE FOR A LONG TIME.
HIS PARTNER HAD A LEAD OF SEVERAL HOURS, WITH THE HORSE, THE PROVISIONS AND THE GUNS.
JUDGING FROM HIS POUNDING HEADACHE, HE'D LIKELY BEEN DRUGGED.
HE WAS ON FOOT, WITH NO FOOD, NO GUN, NO MONEY. NOTHING BUT A BLANKET, TWO SHIRTS AND SHAVING GEAR.
IT WAS NEARLY NOON.

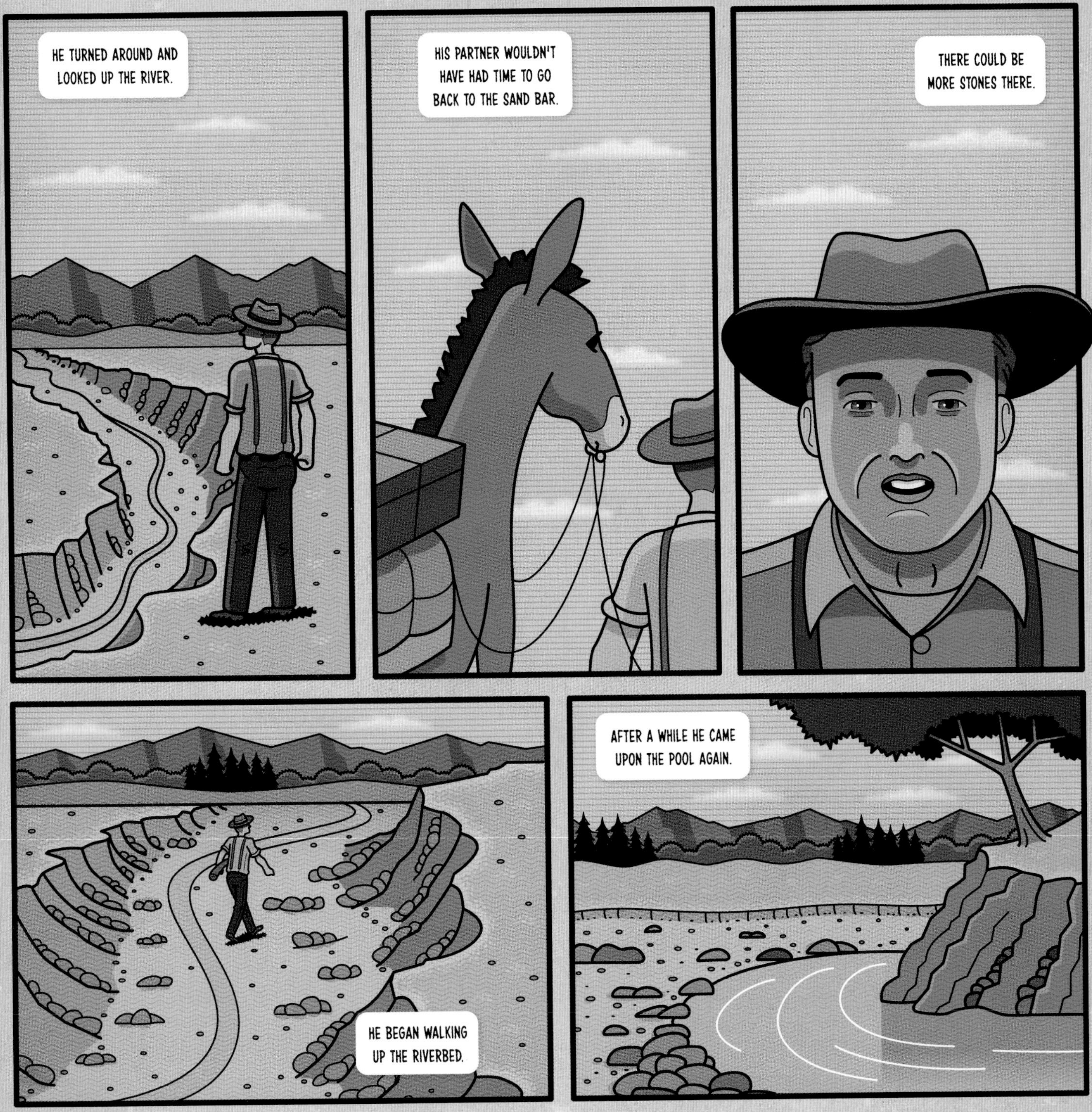
HE TURNED AROUND AND LOOKED UP THE RIVER.
HIS PARTNER WOULDN'T HAVE HAD TIME TO GO BACK TO THE SAND BAR.
THERE COULD BE MORE STONES THERE.
HE BEGAN WALKING UP THE RIVERBED.
AFTER A WHILE HE CAME UPON THE POOL AGAIN.

THE SANDBAR SHIMMERED OFF TO THE SIDE...

CATCHING THE AFTERNOON LIGHT.

HE WADED SLOWLY ACROSS THE WATER, TRYING NOT TO STIR THE SILT.

WHEN HE GOT TO THE MIDDLE HE BENT OVER AND PUT HIS HANDS INTO THE WATER.

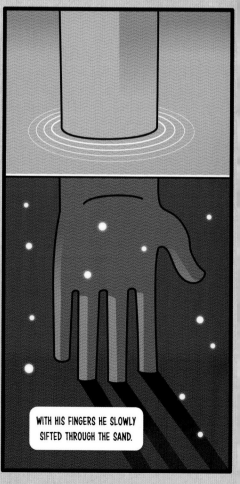

WITH HIS FINGERS HE SLOWLY SIFTED THROUGH THE SAND.

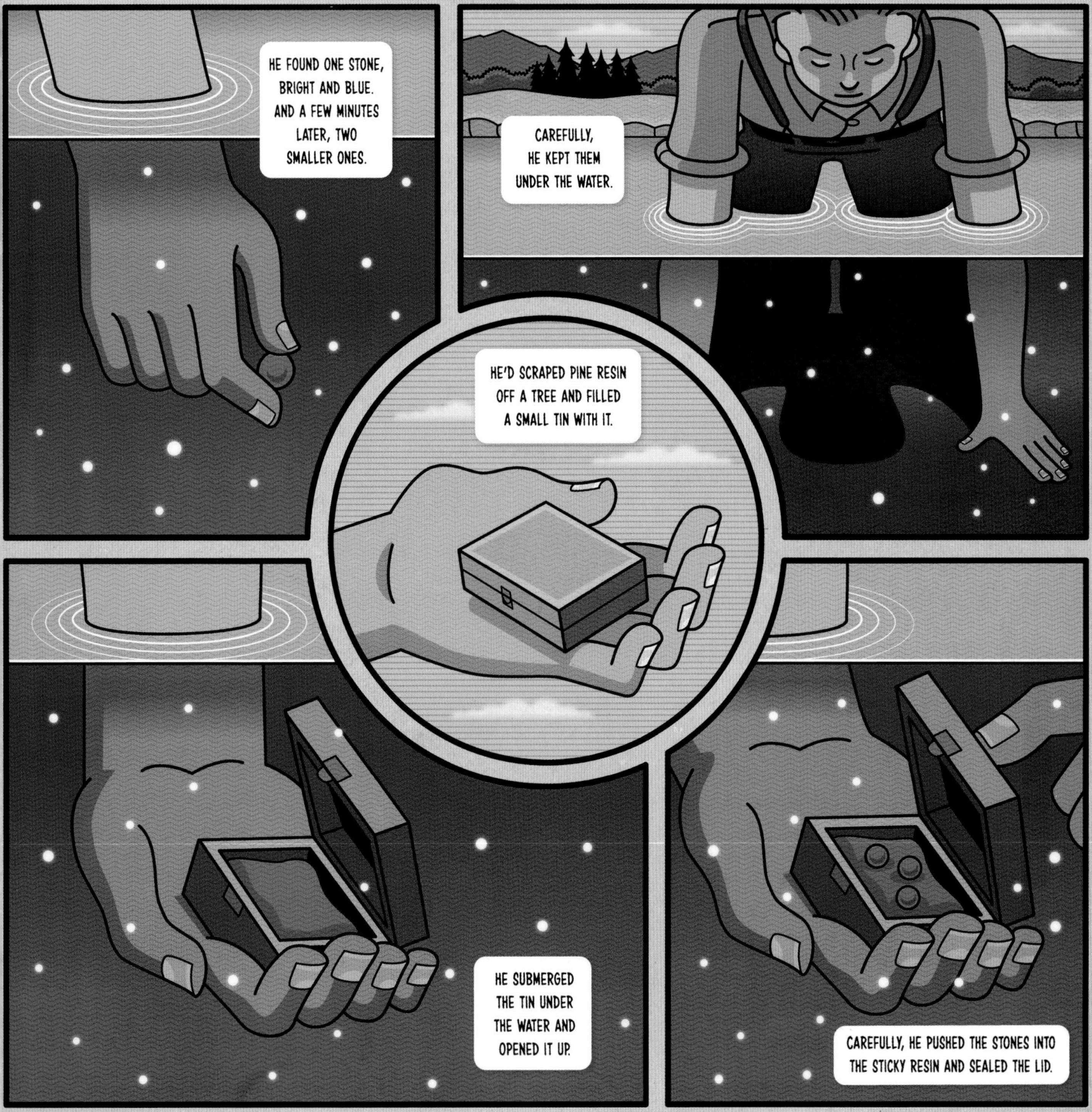
HE FOUND ONE STONE, BRIGHT AND BLUE. AND A FEW MINUTES LATER, TWO SMALLER ONES.
CAREFULLY, HE KEPT THEM UNDER THE WATER.
HE'D SCRAPED PINE RESIN OFF A TREE AND FILLED A SMALL TIN WITH IT.
HE SUBMERGED THE TIN UNDER THE WATER AND OPENED IT UP.
CAREFULLY, HE PUSHED THE STONES INTO THE STICKY RESIN AND SEALED THE LID.

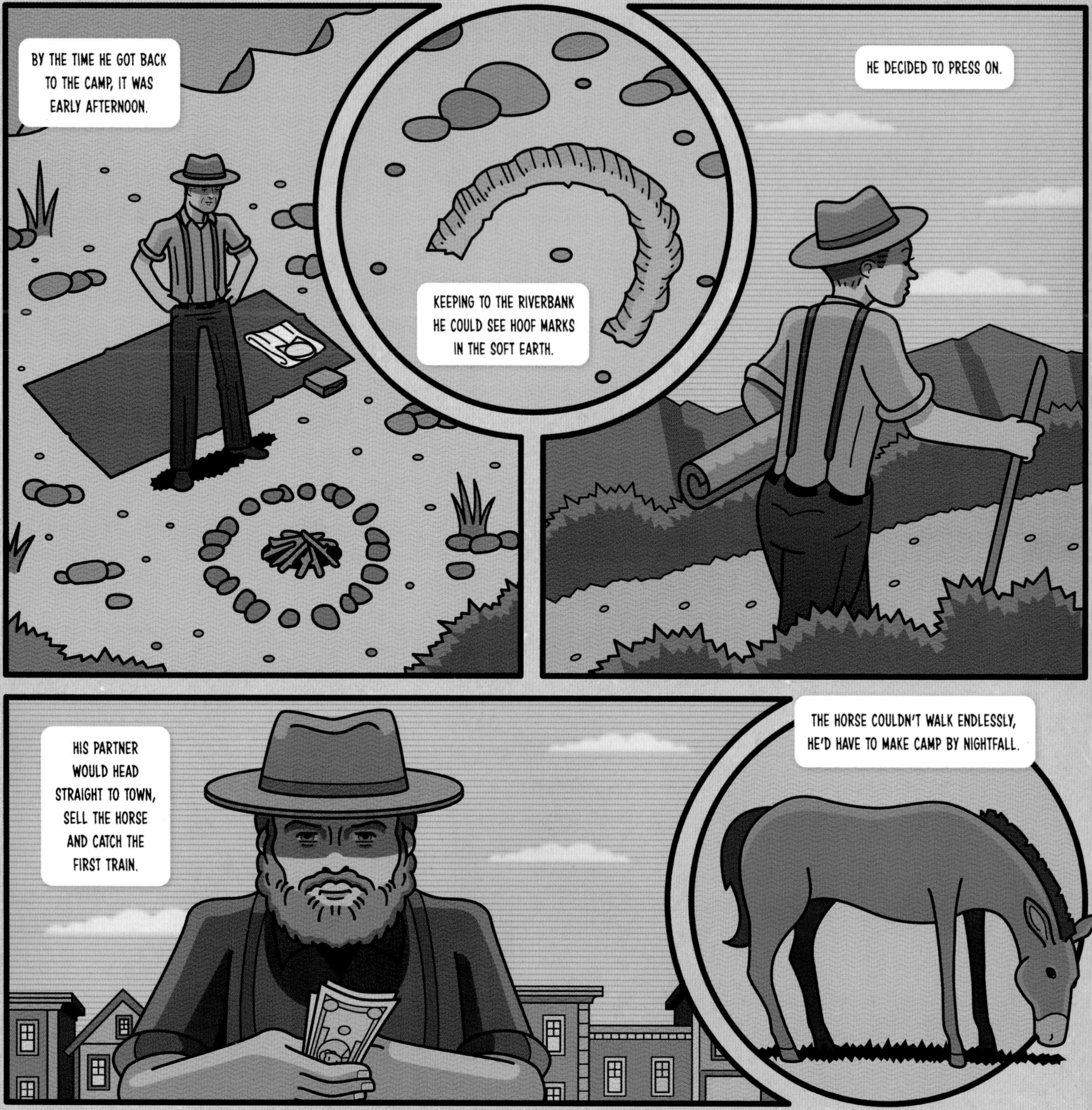
BY THE TIME HE GOT BACK TO THE CAMP, IT WAS EARLY AFTERNOON.
KEEPING TO THE RIVERBANK HE COULD SEE HOOF MARKS IN THE SOFT EARTH.
HE DECIDED TO PRESS ON.
HIS PARTNER WOULD HEAD STRAIGHT TO TOWN, SELL THE HORSE AND CATCH THE FIRST TRAIN.
THE HORSE COULDN'T WALK ENDLESSLY, HE'D HAVE TO MAKE CAMP BY NIGHTFALL.

BY WALKING STRAIGHT THROUGH THE NIGHT, THE MAN MIGHT CATCH THEM.

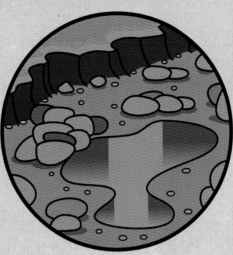

THERE WAS PLENTY OF WATER IN THE RIVER POOLS.

EVEN A FEW CRAYFISH.

BY EARLY EVENING HE CUT WEST THROUGH THE LOW MOUNTAIN PASS.

THIS WAS THE WAY THEY'D COME IN.

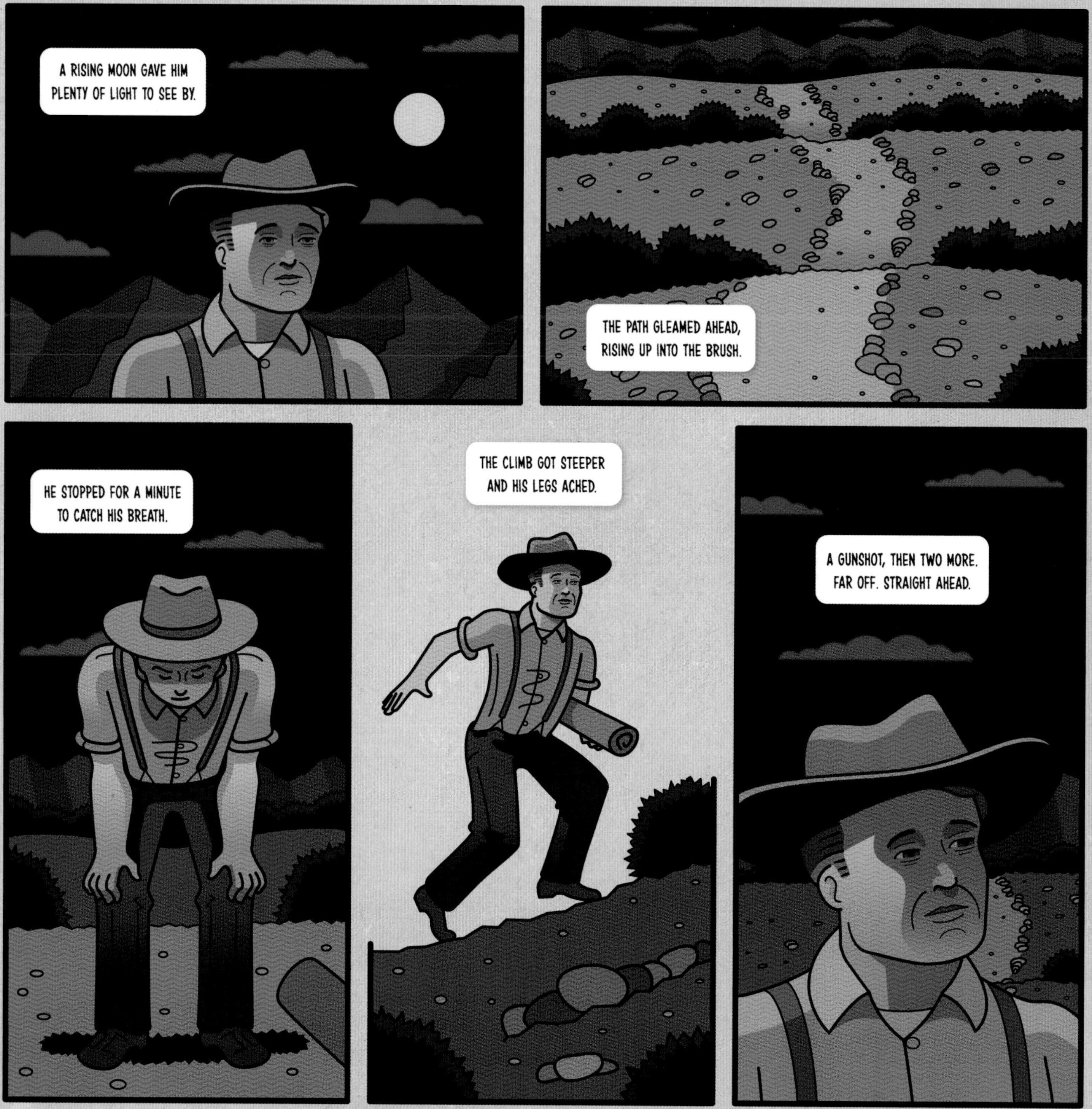
A RISING MOON GAVE HIM PLENTY OF LIGHT TO SEE BY.
THE PATH GLEAMED AHEAD, RISING UP INTO THE BRUSH.
HE STOPPED FOR A MINUTE TO CATCH HIS BREATH.
THE CLIMB GOT STEEPER AND HIS LEGS ACHED.
A GUNSHOT, THEN TWO MORE. FAR OFF. STRAIGHT AHEAD.

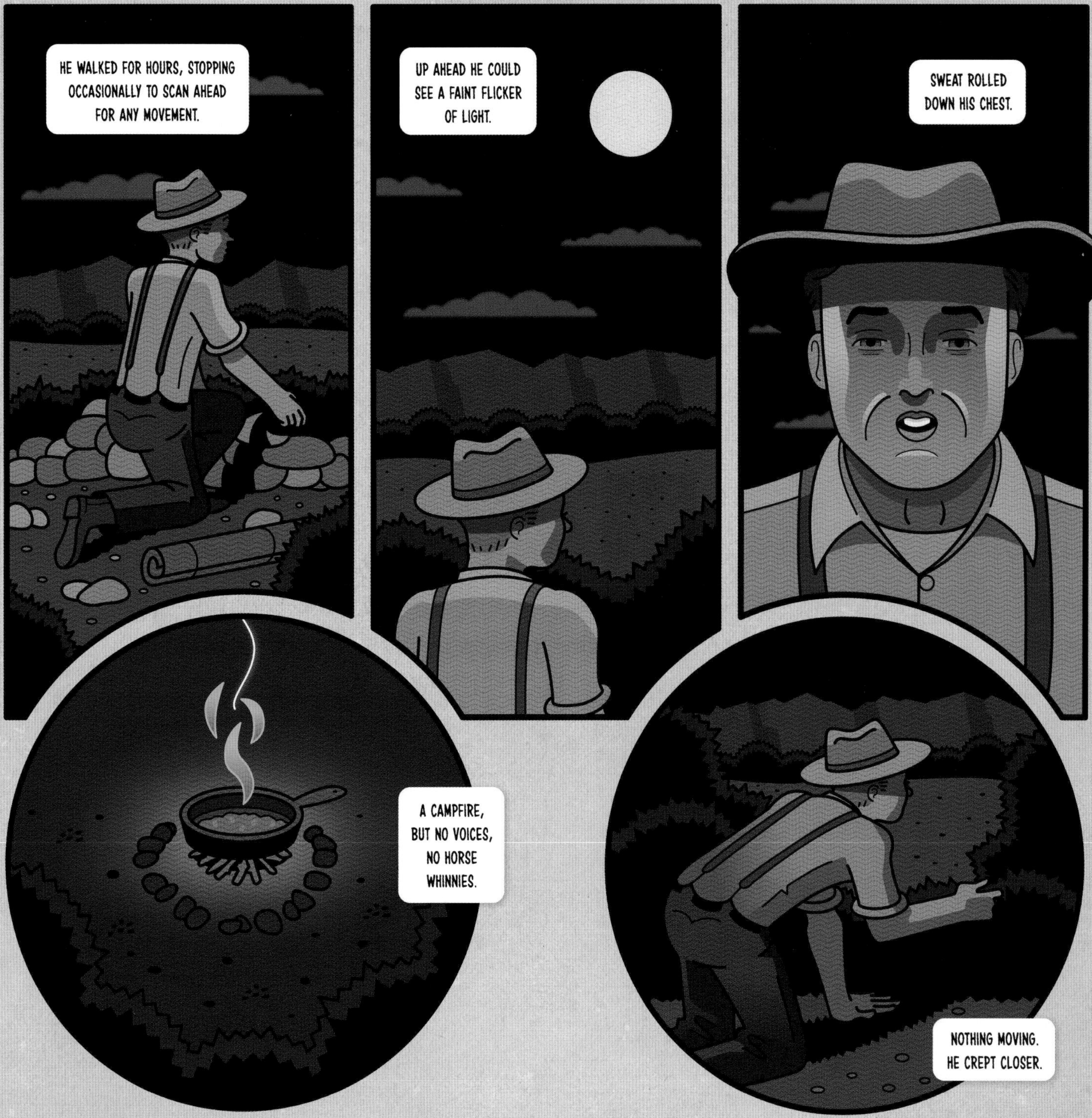
HE WALKED FOR HOURS, STOPPING OCCASIONALLY TO SCAN AHEAD FOR ANY MOVEMENT.
UP AHEAD HE COULD SEE A FAINT FLICKER OF LIGHT.
SWEAT ROLLED DOWN HIS CHEST.
A CAMPFIRE, BUT NO VOICES, NO HORSE WHINNIES.
NOTHING MOVING. HE CREPT CLOSER.

HE WAITED IN THE BRUSH FOR A LONG TIME. HE WAS UNARMED.

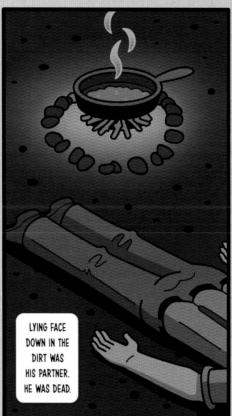

LYING FACE DOWN IN THE DIRT WAS HIS PARTNER. HE WAS DEAD.

THE HORSE AND GEAR WERE GONE. A SKILLET OF BEANS SMOLDERED ON THE FIRE.

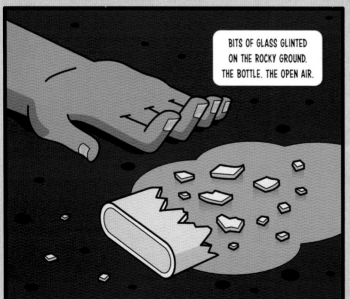

BITS OF GLASS GLINTED ON THE ROCKY GROUND. THE BOTTLE. THE OPEN AIR.

NO STONES.

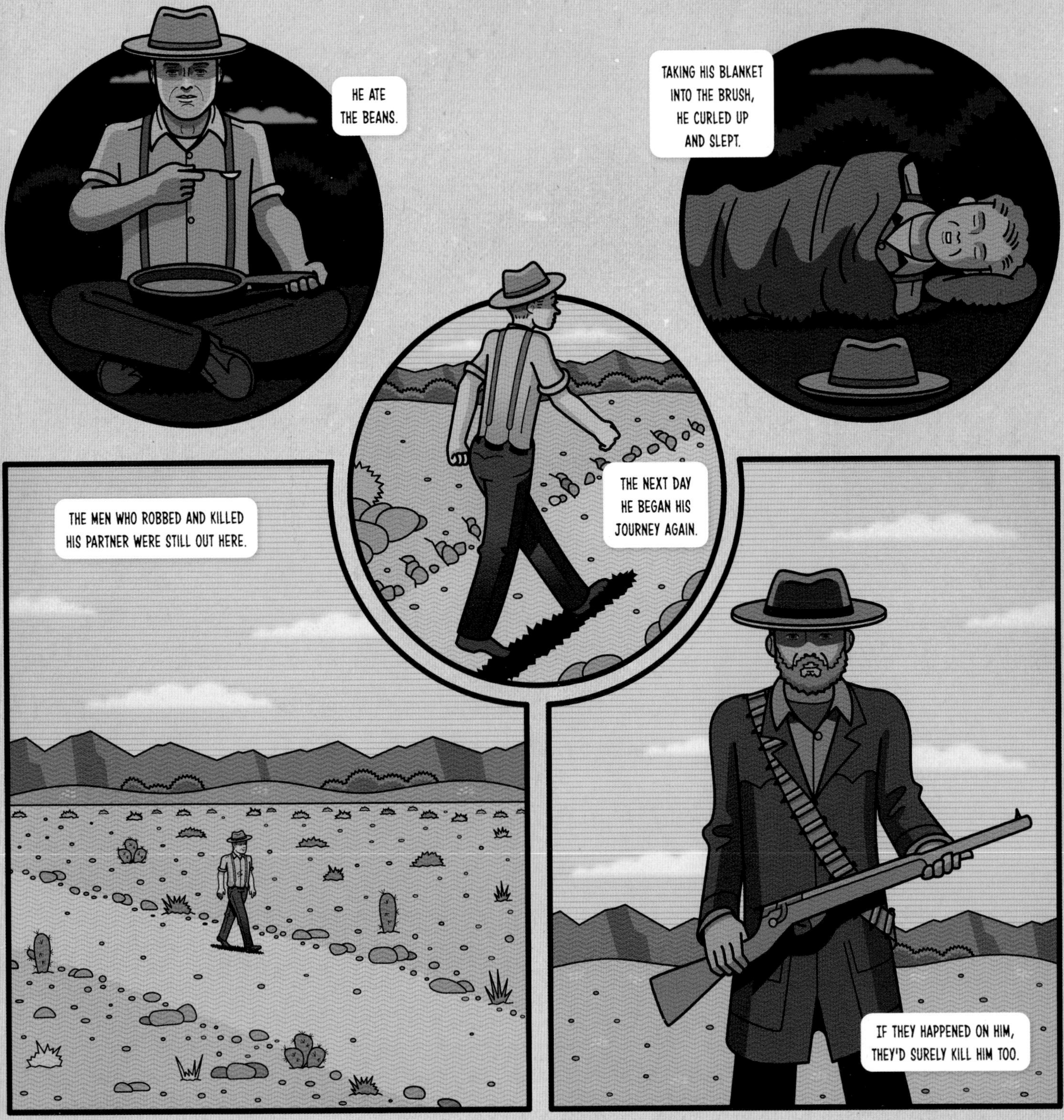
HE ATE
THE BEANS.
TAKING HIS BLANKET
INTO THE BRUSH,
HE CURLED UP
AND SLEPT.
THE NEXT DAY
HE BEGAN HIS
JOURNEY AGAIN.
THE MEN WHO ROBBED AND KILLED
HIS PARTNER WERE STILL OUT HERE.
IF THEY HAPPENED ON HIM,
THEY'D SURELY KILL HIM TOO.

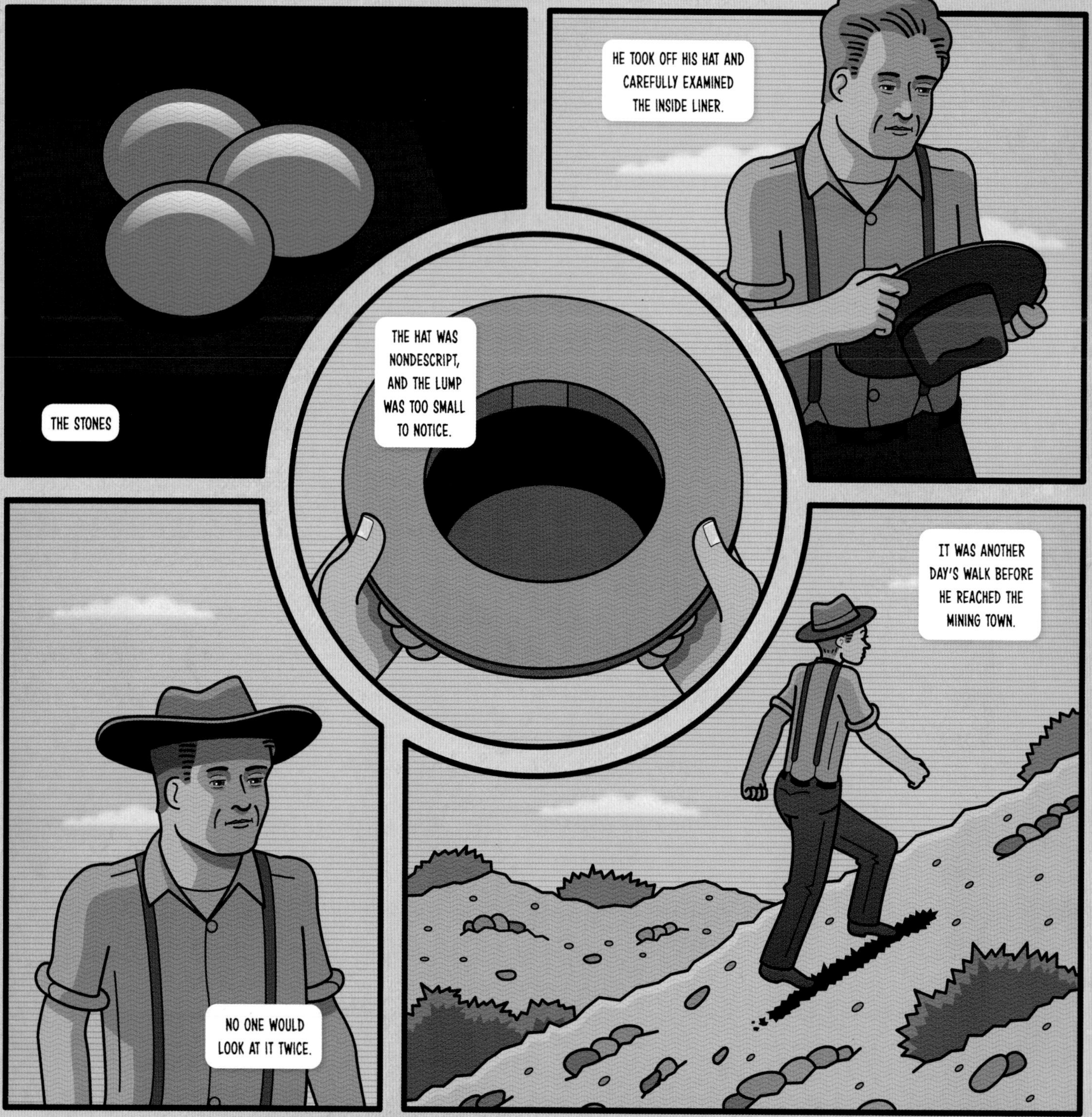
THE STONES
HE TOOK OFF HIS HAT AND CAREFULLY EXAMINED THE INSIDE LINER.
THE HAT WAS NONDESCRIPT, AND THE LUMP WAS TOO SMALL TO NOTICE.
NO ONE WOULD LOOK AT IT TWICE.
IT WAS ANOTHER DAY'S WALK BEFORE HE REACHED THE MINING TOWN.

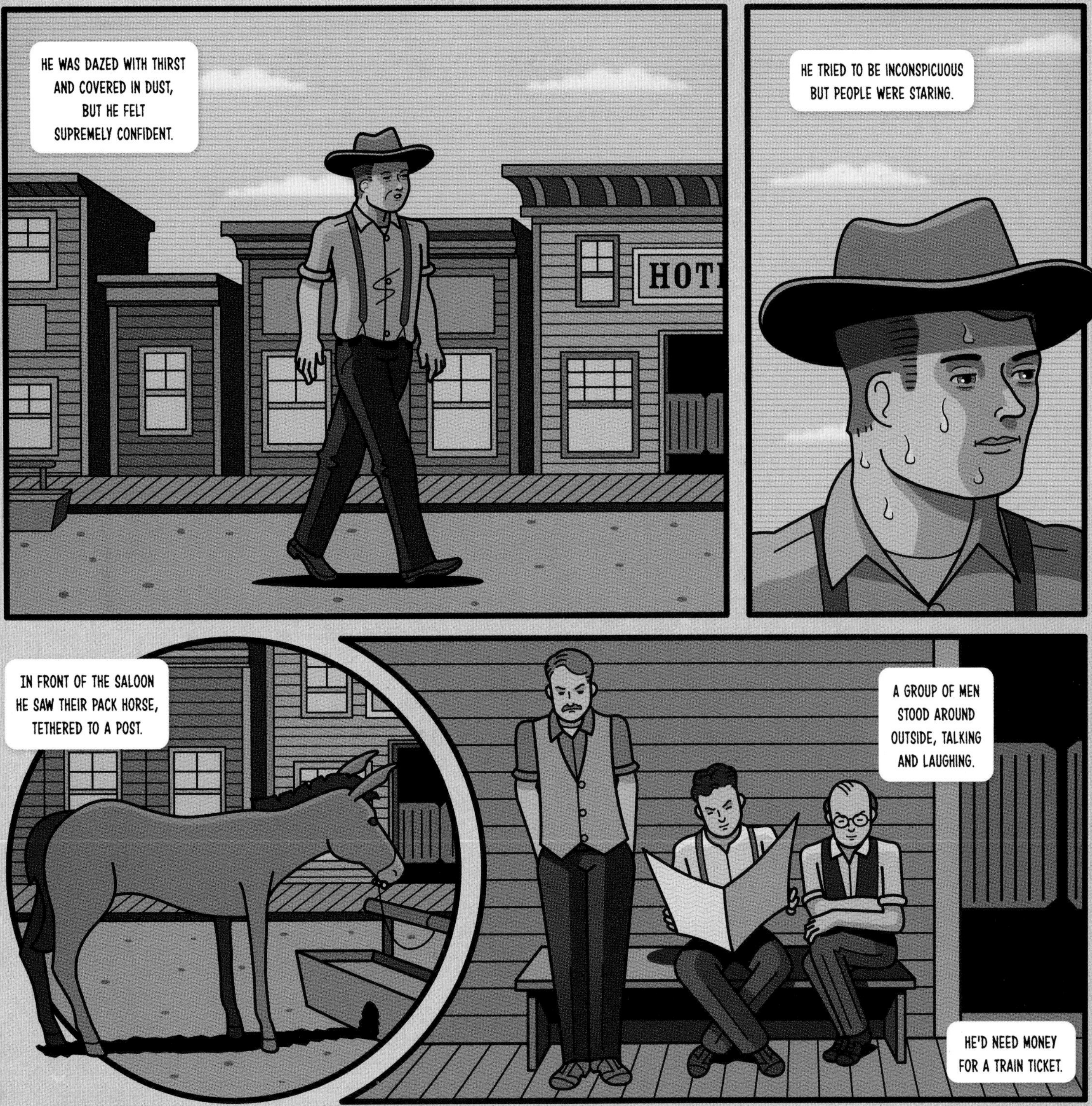
HE WAS DAZED WITH THIRST AND COVERED IN DUST, BUT HE FELT SUPREMELY CONFIDENT.
HOTE
HE TRIED TO BE INCONSPICUOUS BUT PEOPLE WERE STARING.
IN FRONT OF THE SALOON HE SAW THEIR PACK HORSE, TETHERED TO A POST.
A GROUP OF MEN STOOD AROUND OUTSIDE, TALKING AND LAUGHING.
HE'D NEED MONEY FOR A TRAIN TICKET.

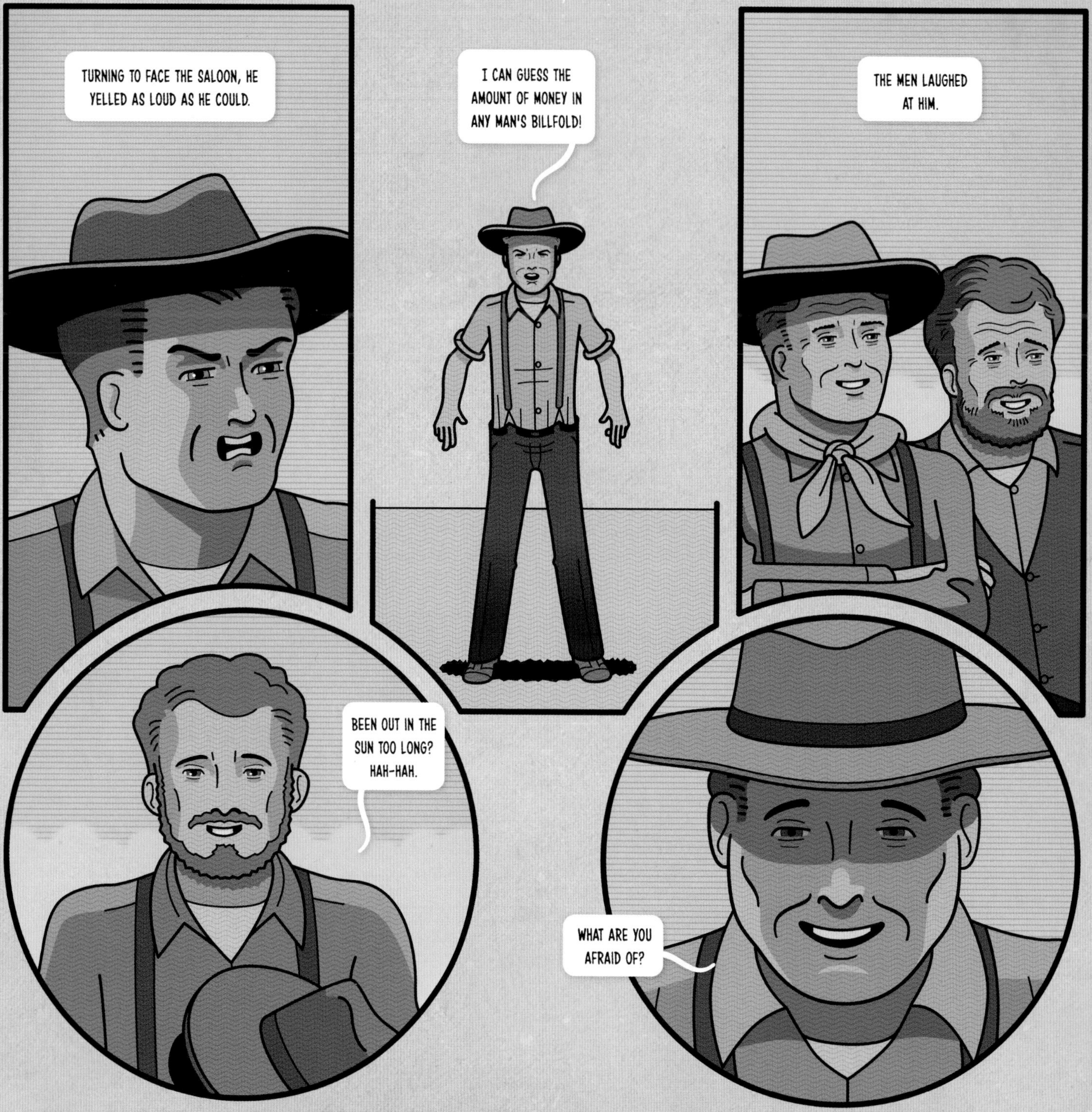
TURNING TO FACE THE SALOON, HE YELLED AS LOUD AS HE COULD.
I CAN GUESS THE AMOUNT OF MONEY IN ANY MAN'S BILLFOLD!
THE MEN LAUGHED AT HIM.
BEEN OUT IN THE SUN TOO LONG? HAH-HAH.
WHAT ARE YOU AFRAID OF?

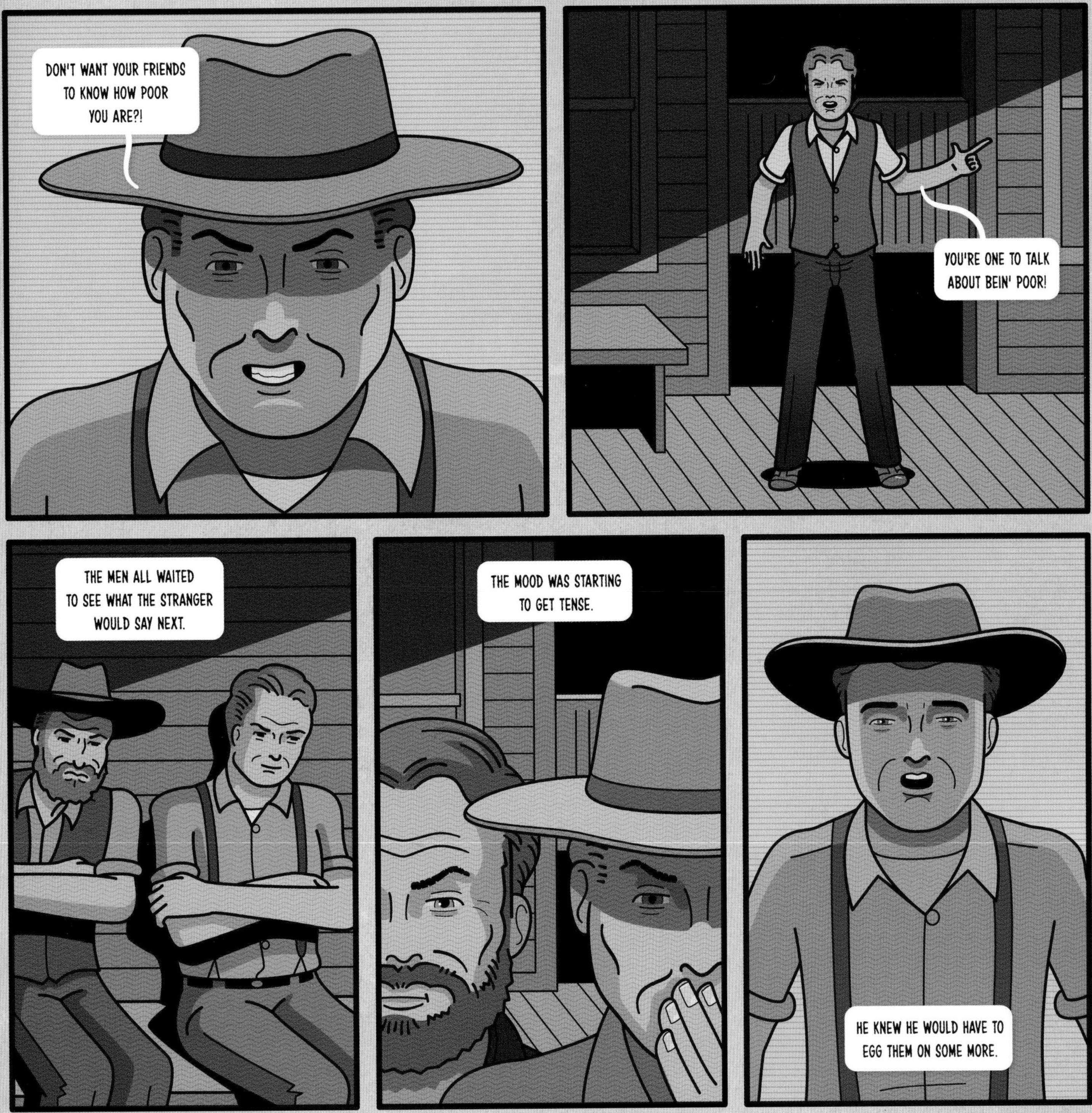
DON'T WANT YOUR FRIENDS TO KNOW HOW POOR YOU ARE?!
YOU'RE ONE TO TALK ABOUT BEIN' POOR!
THE MEN ALL WAITED TO SEE WHAT THE STRANGER WOULD SAY NEXT.
THE MOOD WAS STARTING TO GET TENSE.
HE KNEW HE WOULD HAVE TO EGG THEM ON SOME MORE.

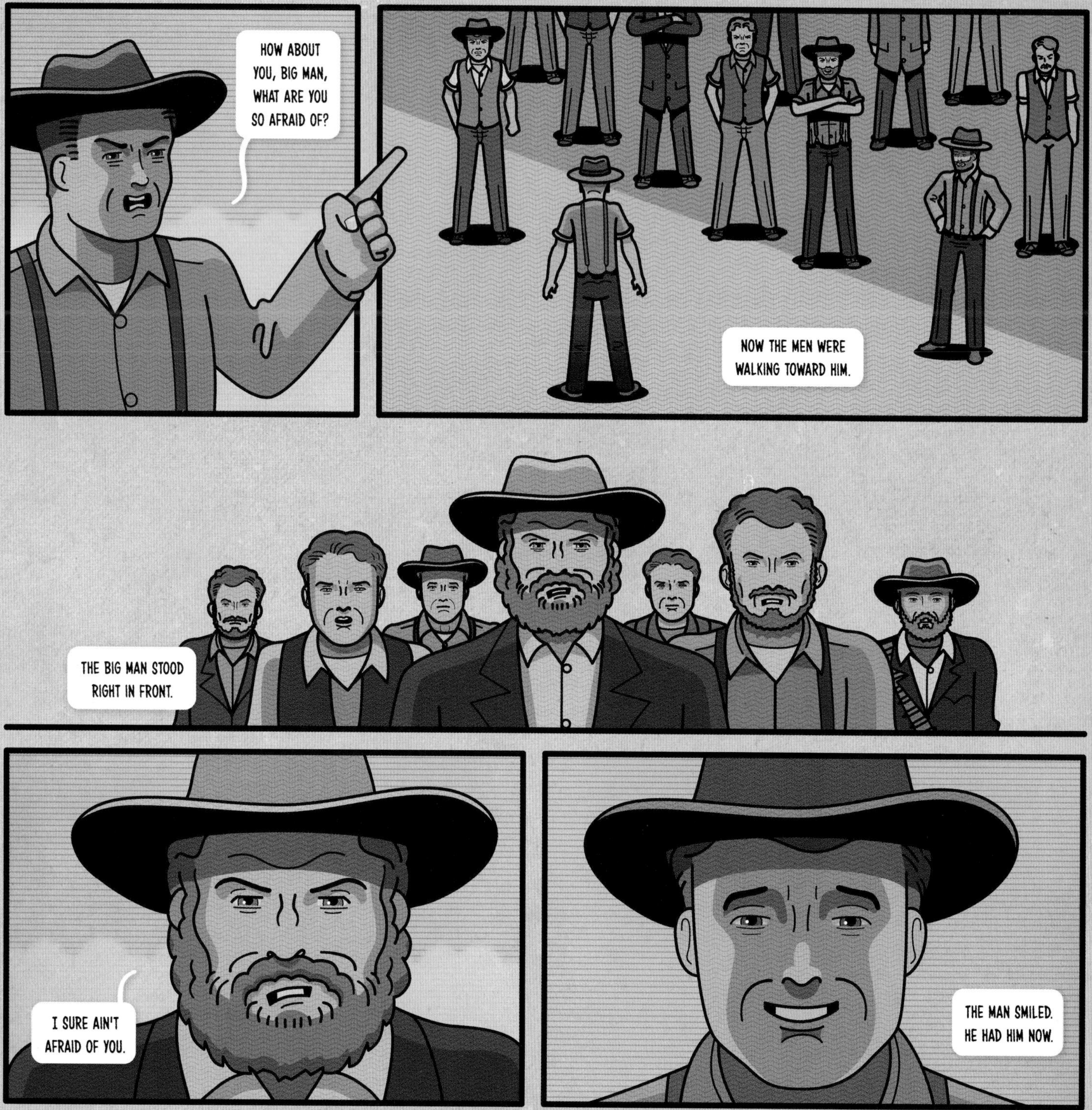
HOW ABOUT YOU, BIG MAN, WHAT ARE YOU SO AFRAID OF?
NOW THE MEN WERE WALKING TOWARD HIM.
THE BIG MAN STOOD RIGHT IN FRONT.
I SURE AIN'T AFRAID OF YOU.
THE MAN SMILED. HE HAD HIM NOW.

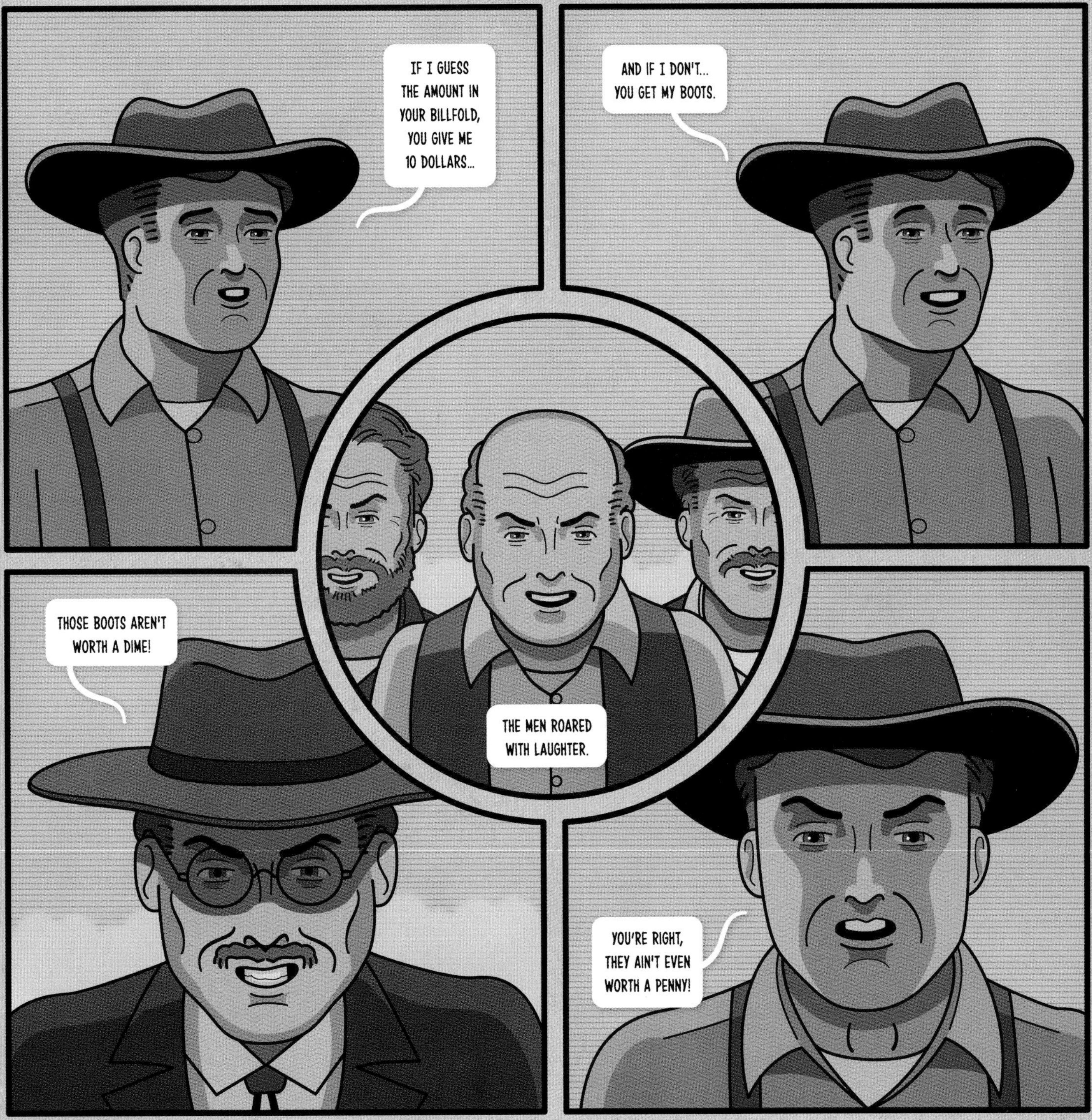
IF I GUESS THE AMOUNT IN YOUR BILLFOLD, YOU GIVE ME 10 DOLLARS...
AND IF I DON'T... YOU GET MY BOOTS.
THOSE BOOTS AREN'T WORTH A DIME!
THE MEN ROARED WITH LAUGHTER.
YOU'RE RIGHT, THEY AIN'T EVEN WORTH A PENNY!

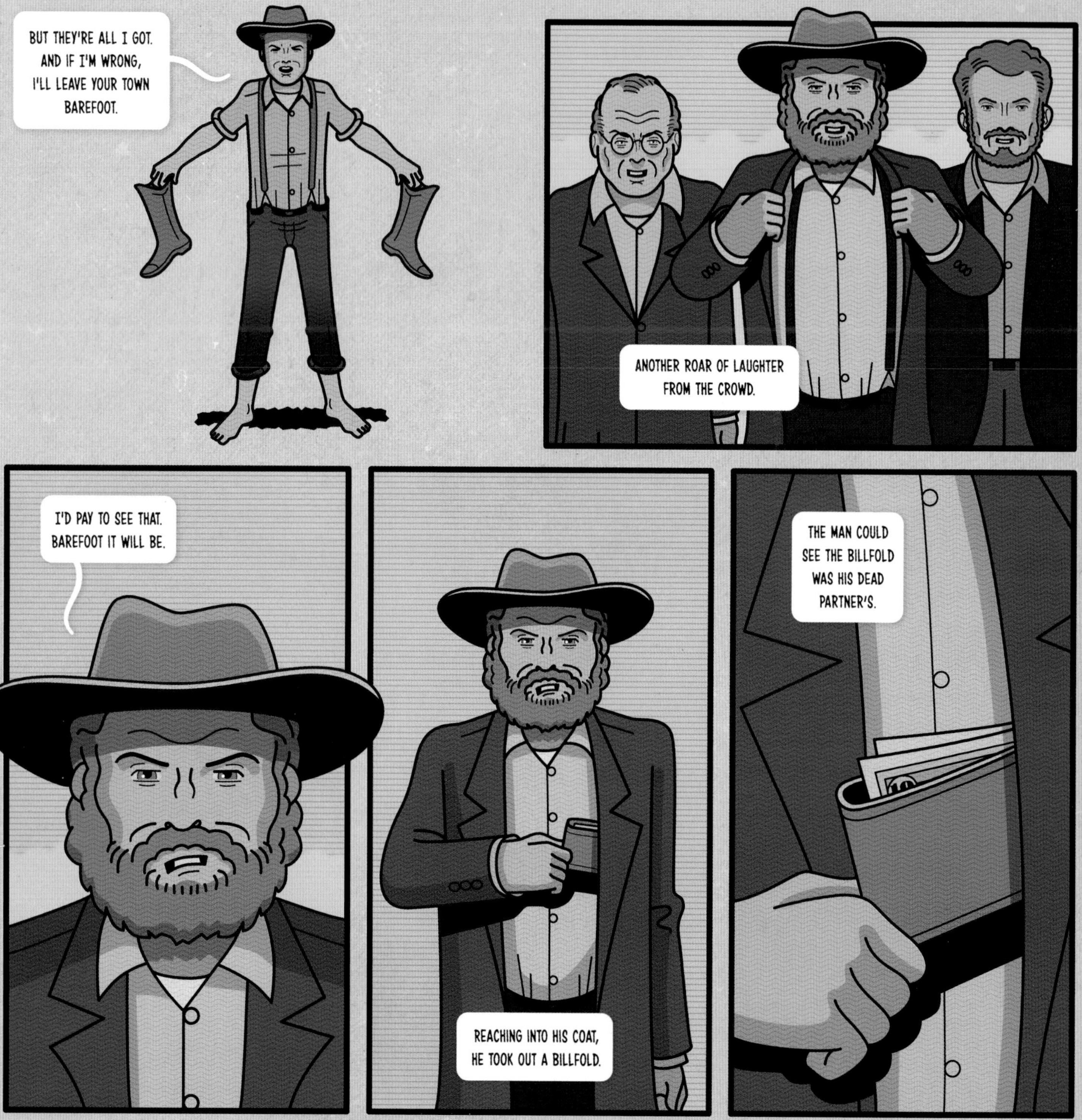
BUT THEY'RE ALL I GOT. AND IF I'M WRONG, I'LL LEAVE YOUR TOWN BAREFOOT.
ANOTHER ROAR OF LAUGHTER FROM THE CROWD.
I'D PAY TO SEE THAT. BAREFOOT IT WILL BE.
REACHING INTO HIS COAT, HE TOOK OUT A BILLFOLD.
THE MAN COULD SEE THE BILLFOLD WAS HIS DEAD PARTNER'S.

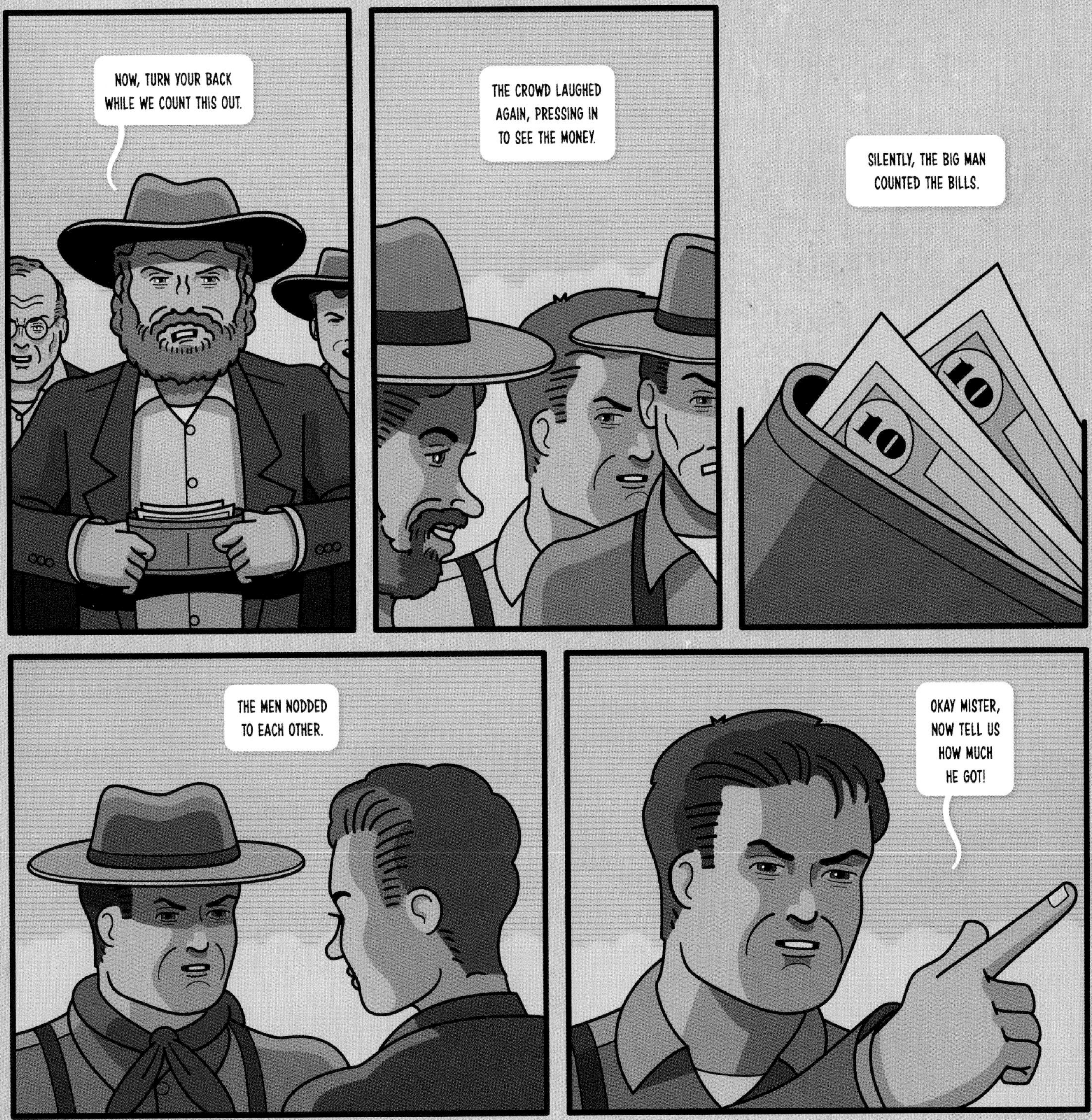
NOW, TURN YOUR BACK WHILE WE COUNT THIS OUT.
THE CROWD LAUGHED AGAIN, PRESSING IN TO SEE THE MONEY.
SILENTLY, THE BIG MAN COUNTED THE BILLS.
10
10
THE MEN NODDED TO EACH OTHER.
OKAY MISTER, NOW TELL US HOW MUCH HE GOT!

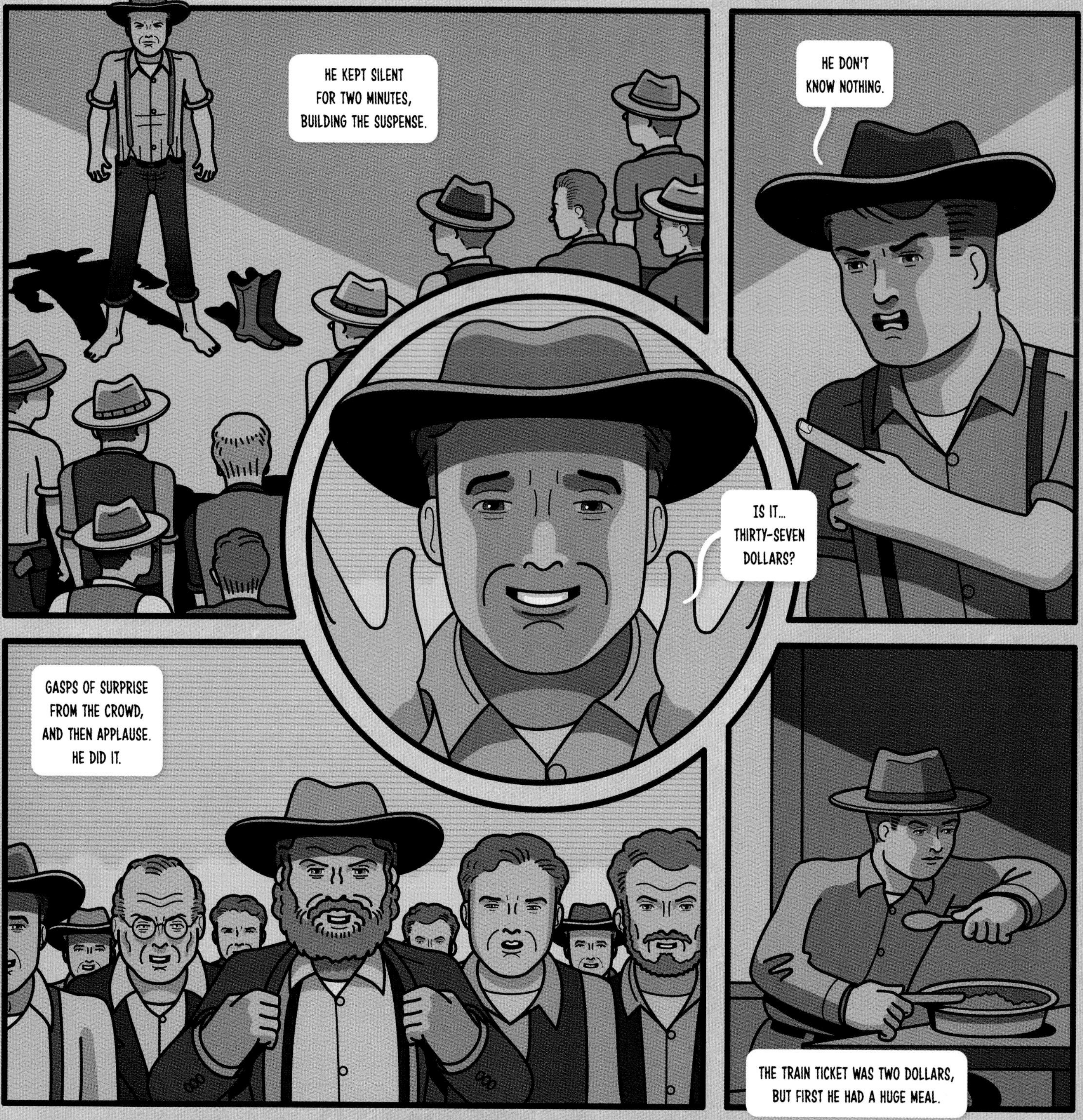
HE KEPT SILENT
FOR TWO MINUTES,
BUILDING THE SUSPENSE.
HE DON'T
KNOW NOTHING.
IS IT...
THIRTY-SEVEN
DOLLARS?
GASPS OF SURPRISE
FROM THE CROWD,
AND THEN APPLAUSE.
HE DID IT.
THE TRAIN TICKET WAS TWO DOLLARS,
BUT FIRST HE HAD A HUGE MEAL.

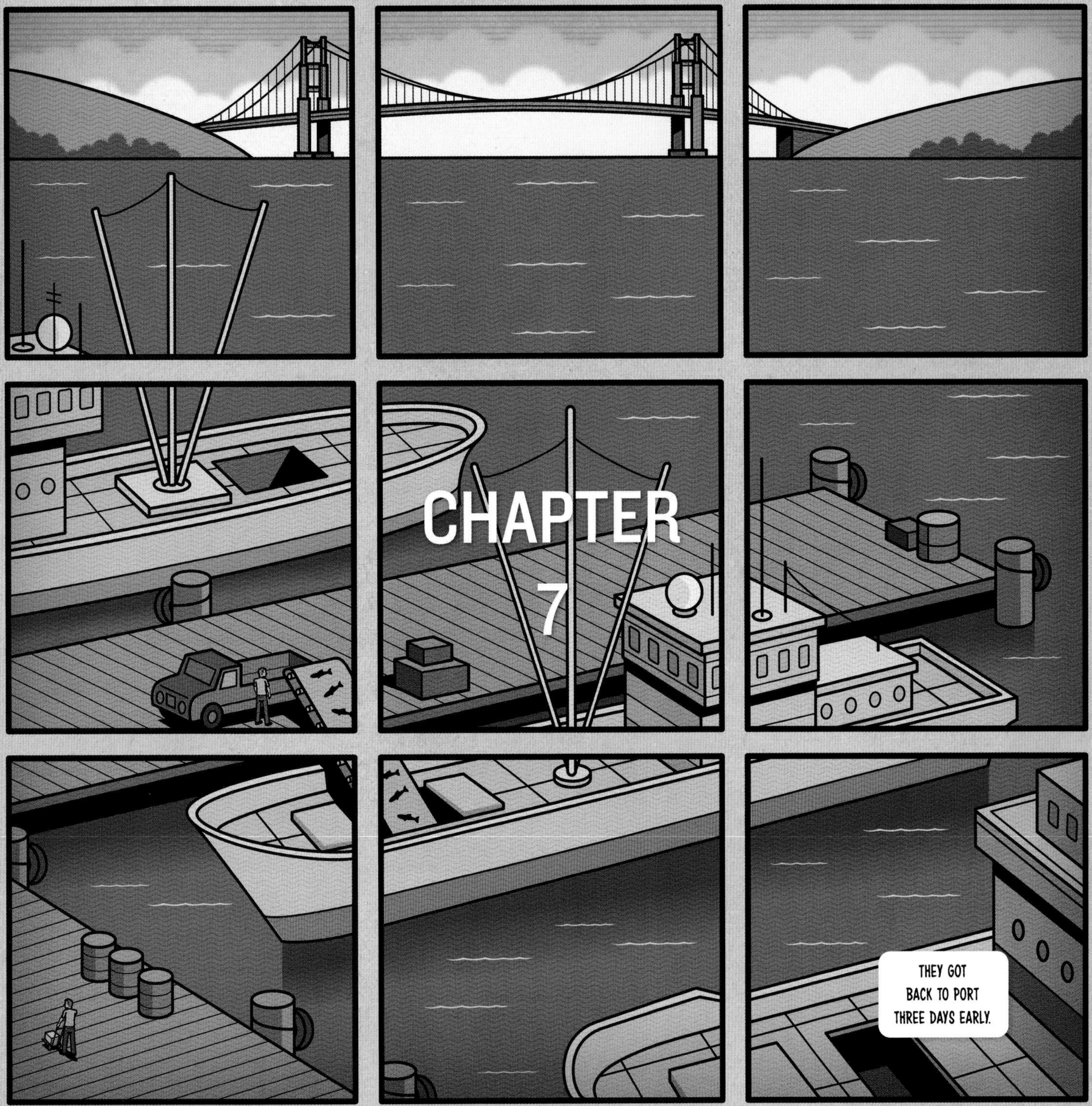
CHAPTER
7
THEY GOT BACK TO PORT THREE DAYS EARLY.

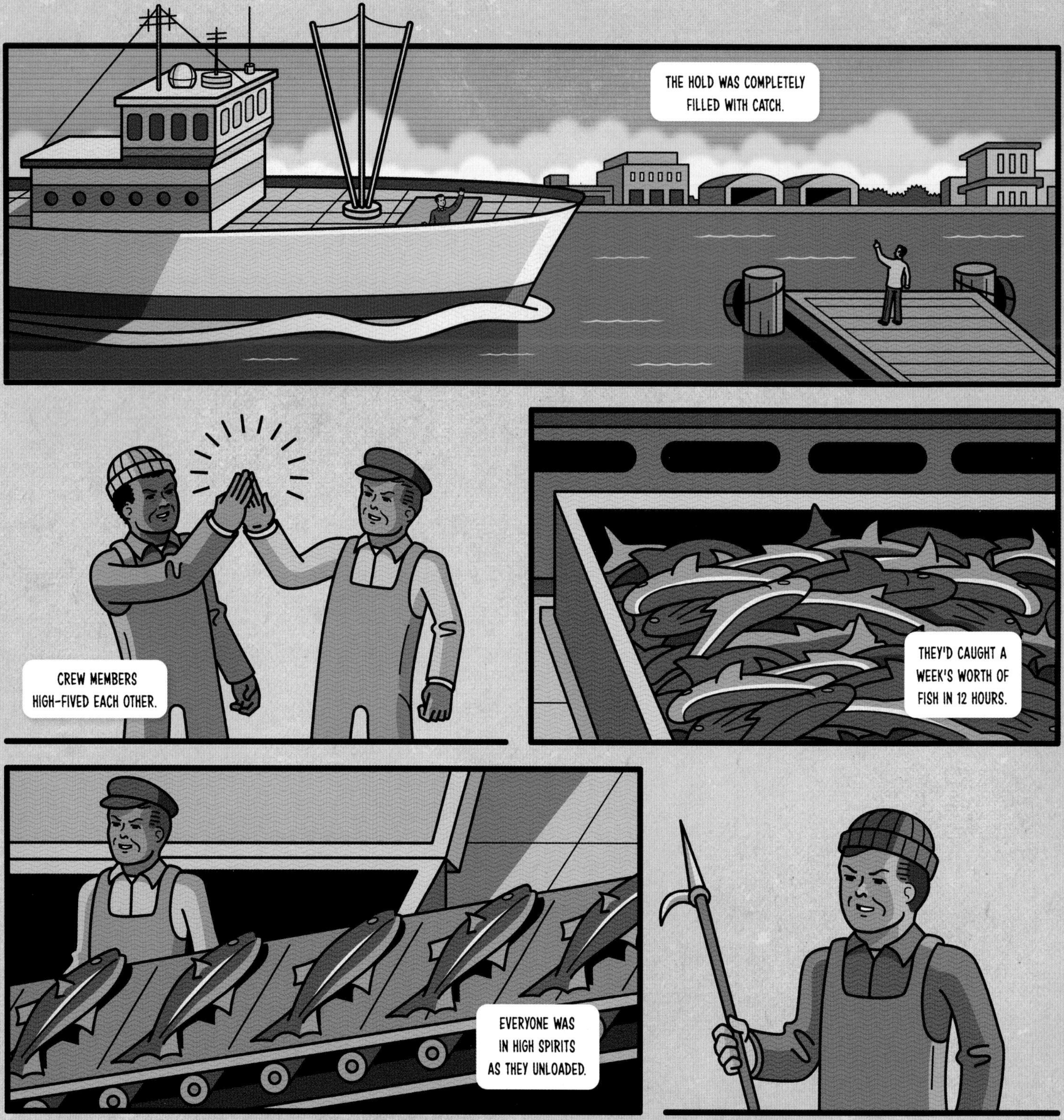
THE HOLD WAS COMPLETELY FILLED WITH CATCH.
CREW MEMBERS HIGH-FIVED EACH OTHER.
THEY'D CAUGHT A WEEK'S WORTH OF FISH IN 12 HOURS.
EVERYONE WAS IN HIGH SPIRITS AS THEY UNLOADED.

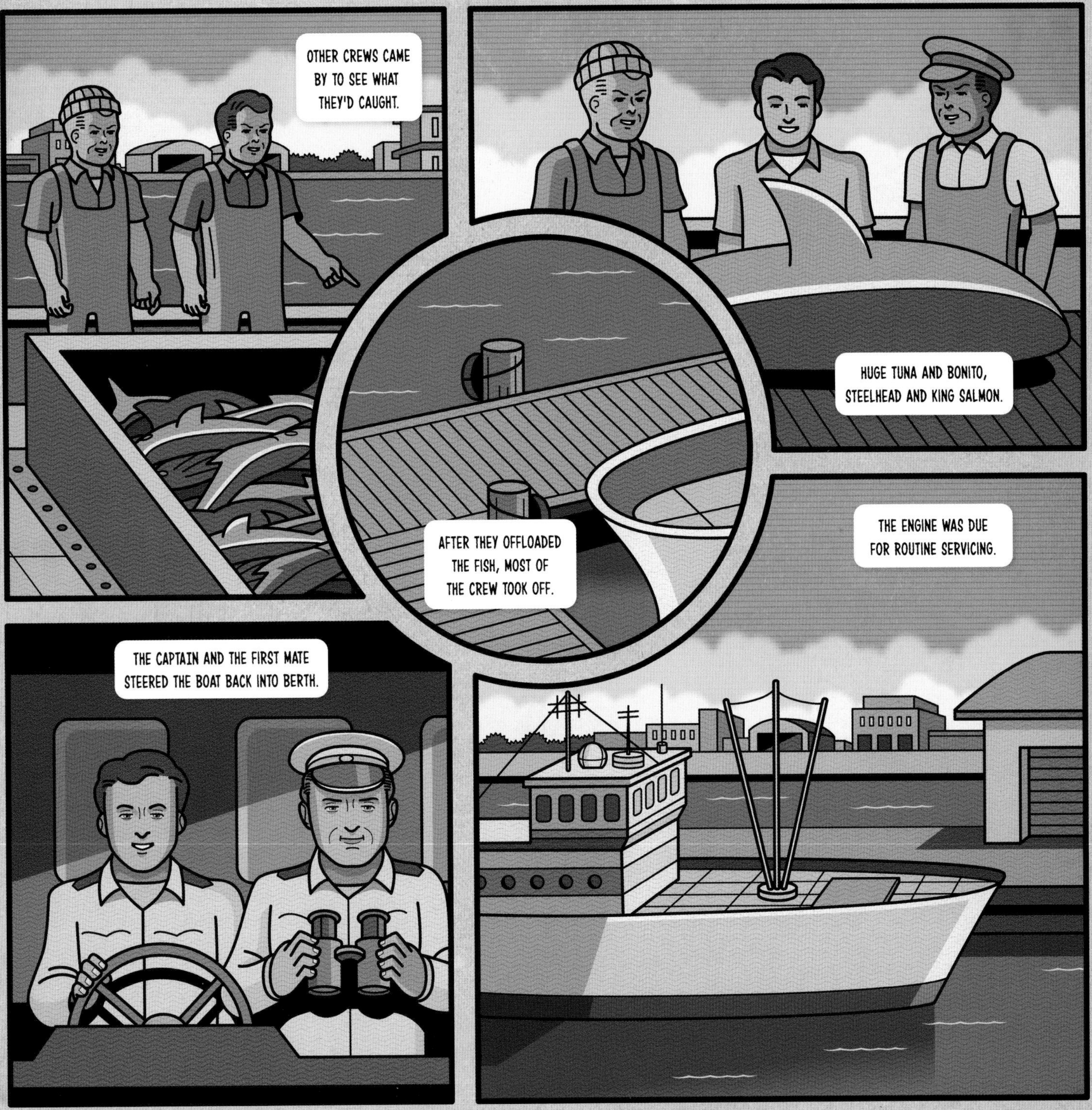
OTHER CREWS CAME BY TO SEE WHAT THEY'D CAUGHT.
HUGE TUNA AND BONITO, STEELHEAD AND KING SALMON.
AFTER THEY OFFLOADED THE FISH, MOST OF THE CREW TOOK OFF.
THE CAPTAIN AND THE FIRST MATE STEERED THE BOAT BACK INTO BERTH.
THE ENGINE WAS DUE FOR ROUTINE SERVICING.

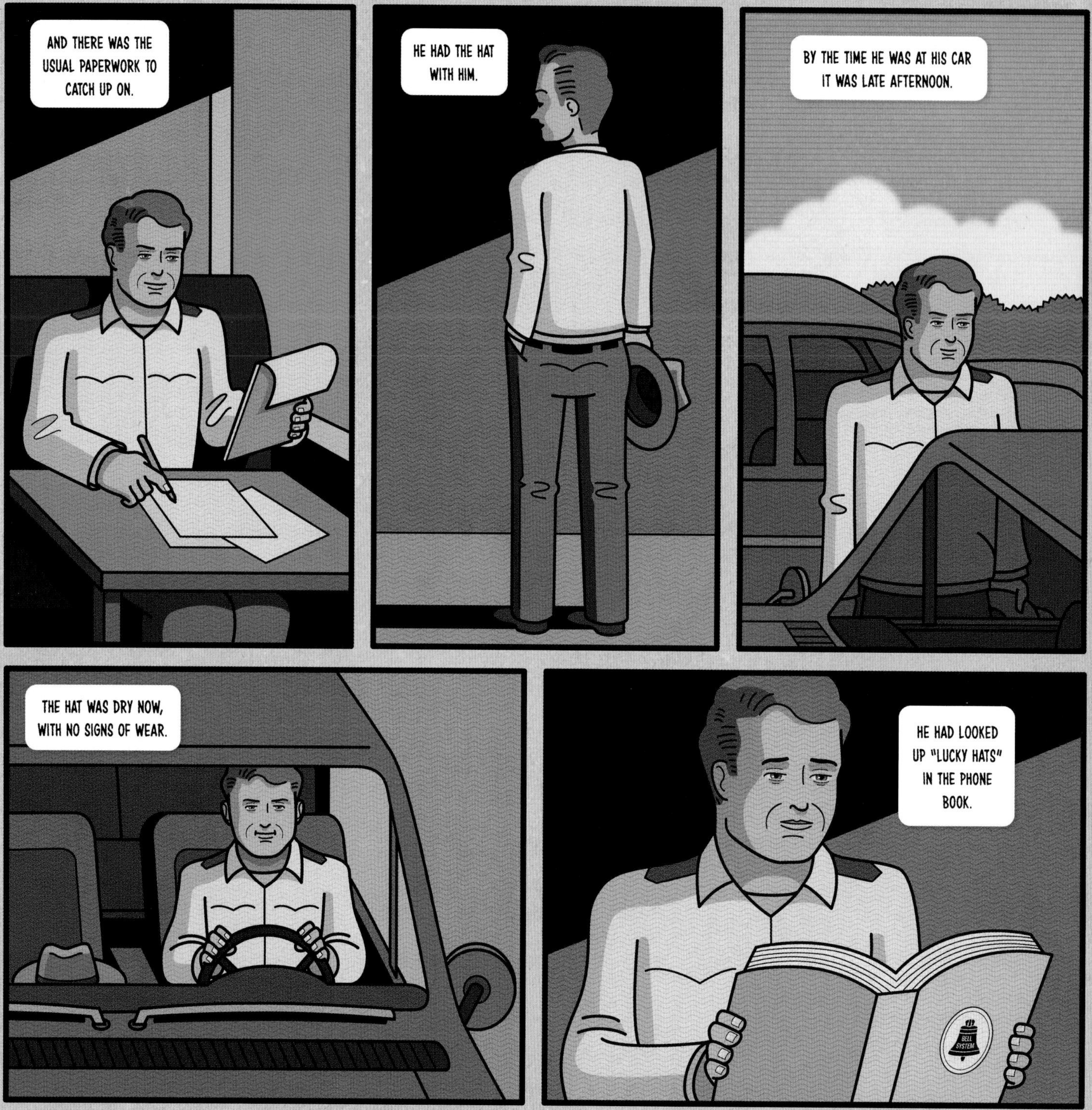
AND THERE WAS THE USUAL PAPERWORK TO CATCH UP ON.
HE HAD THE HAT WITH HIM.
BY THE TIME HE WAS AT HIS CAR IT WAS LATE AFTERNOON.
THE HAT WAS DRY NOW, WITH NO SIGNS OF WEAR.
HE HAD LOOKED UP "LUCKY HATS" IN THE PHONE BOOK.
BELL SYSTEM

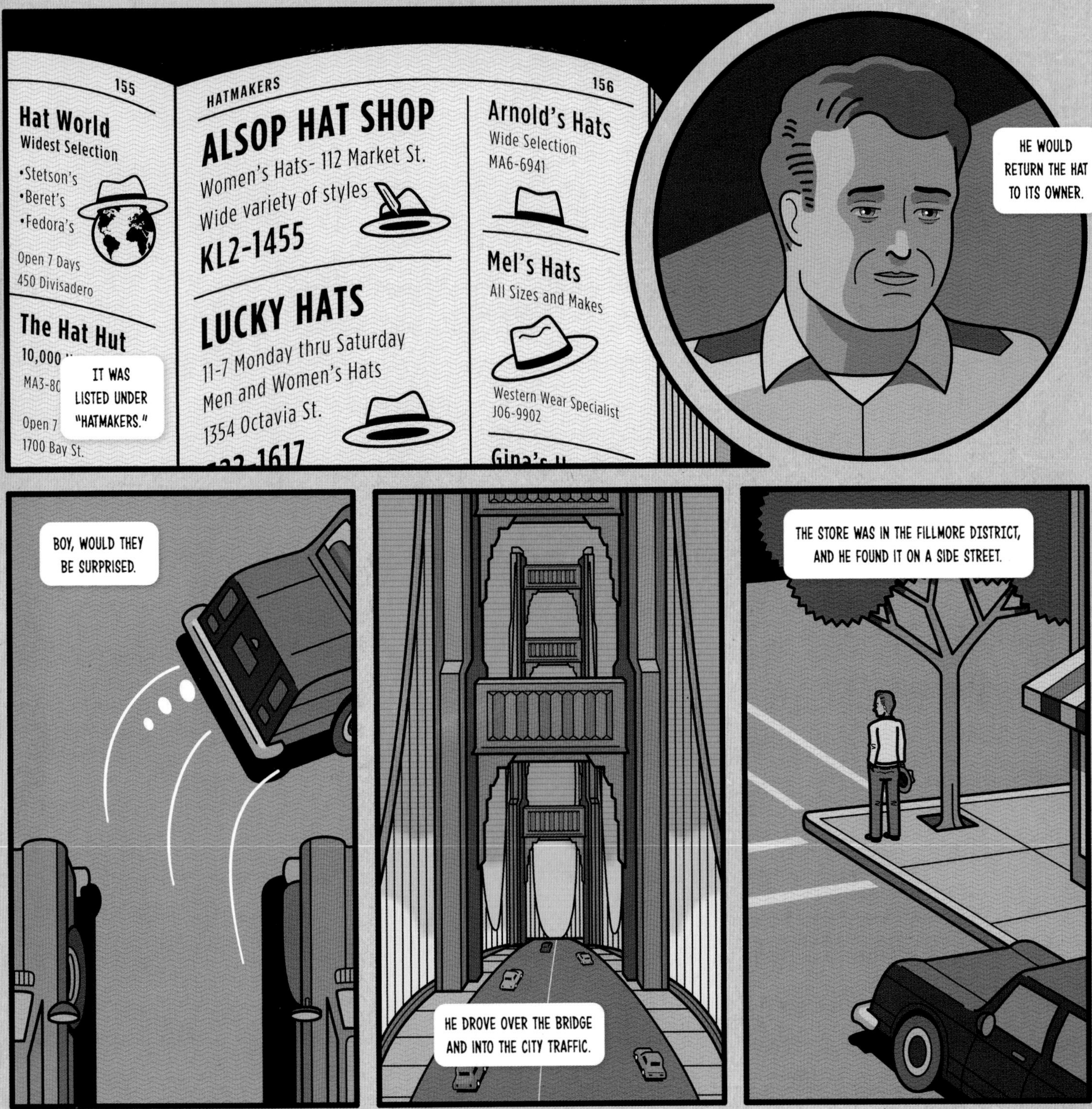
155
Hat World
Widest Selection
•Stetson's
•Beret's
•Fedora's
Open 7 Days
450 Divisadero
The Hat Hut
1700 Bay St.
HATMAKERS
156
ALSOP HAT SHOP
Women's Hats- 112 Market St.
Wide variety of styles
KL2-1455
LUCKY HATS
11-7 Monday thru Saturday
Men and Women's Hats
1354 Octavia St.
Arnold's Hats
Wide Selection
MA6-6941
Mel's Hats
All Sizes and Makes
Western Wear Specialist
JO6-9902
IT WAS LISTED UNDER "HATMAKERS."
HE WOULD RETURN THE HAT TO ITS OWNER.
BOY, WOULD THEY BE SURPRISED.
HE DROVE OVER THE BRIDGE AND INTO THE CITY TRAFFIC.
THE STORE WAS IN THE FILLMORE DISTRICT, AND HE FOUND IT ON A SIDE STREET.

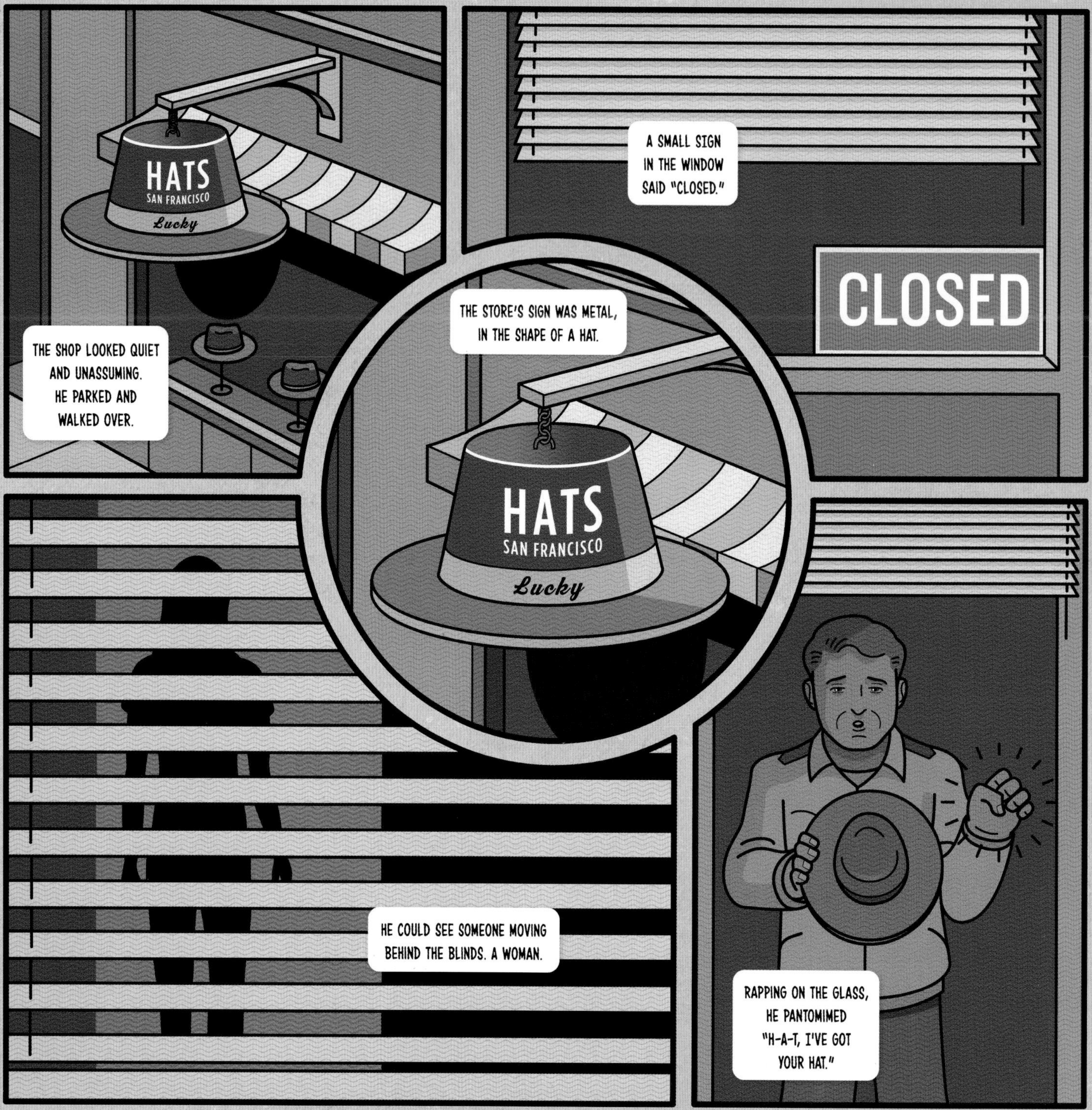
HATS
SAN FRANCISCO
Lucky
THE SHOP LOOKED QUIET AND UNASSUMING. HE PARKED AND WALKED OVER.
A SMALL SIGN IN THE WINDOW SAID "CLOSED."
CLOSED
THE STORE'S SIGN WAS METAL, IN THE SHAPE OF A HAT.
HATS
SAN FRANCISCO
Lucky
HE COULD SEE SOMEONE MOVING BEHIND THE BLINDS. A WOMAN.
RAPPING ON THE GLASS, HE PANTOMIMED "H-A-T, I'VE GOT YOUR HAT."

SHE HAD PUT ALL HIS PERSONAL THINGS IN A CARDBOARD BOX.

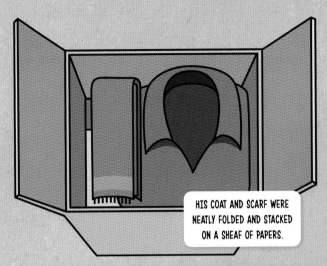

HIS COAT AND SCARF WERE NEATLY FOLDED AND STACKED ON A SHEAF OF PAPERS.

A SMALL FRAMED PHOTO OF THE TWO OF THEM SAT ON TOP.

IT WAS TAKEN ON THE DAY THEY WERE MARRIED.

BOTH OF THEM SMILING, EYES SQUINTING IN THE BRIGHT SUN.

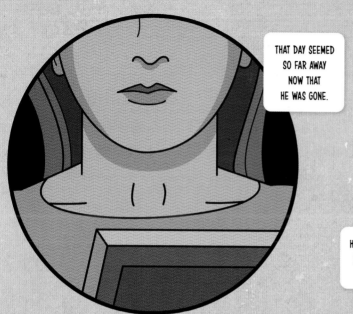

THAT DAY SEEMED SO FAR AWAY NOW THAT HE WAS GONE.

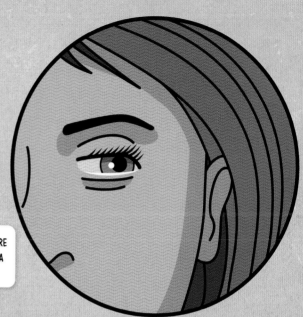

HER THOUGHTS WERE INTERRUPTED BY A TAPPING SOUND.

STARTLED, SHE LOOKED UP TO SEE A MAN AT THE DOOR.

HE WAS WAVING A HAT AND GESTURING TO HER.

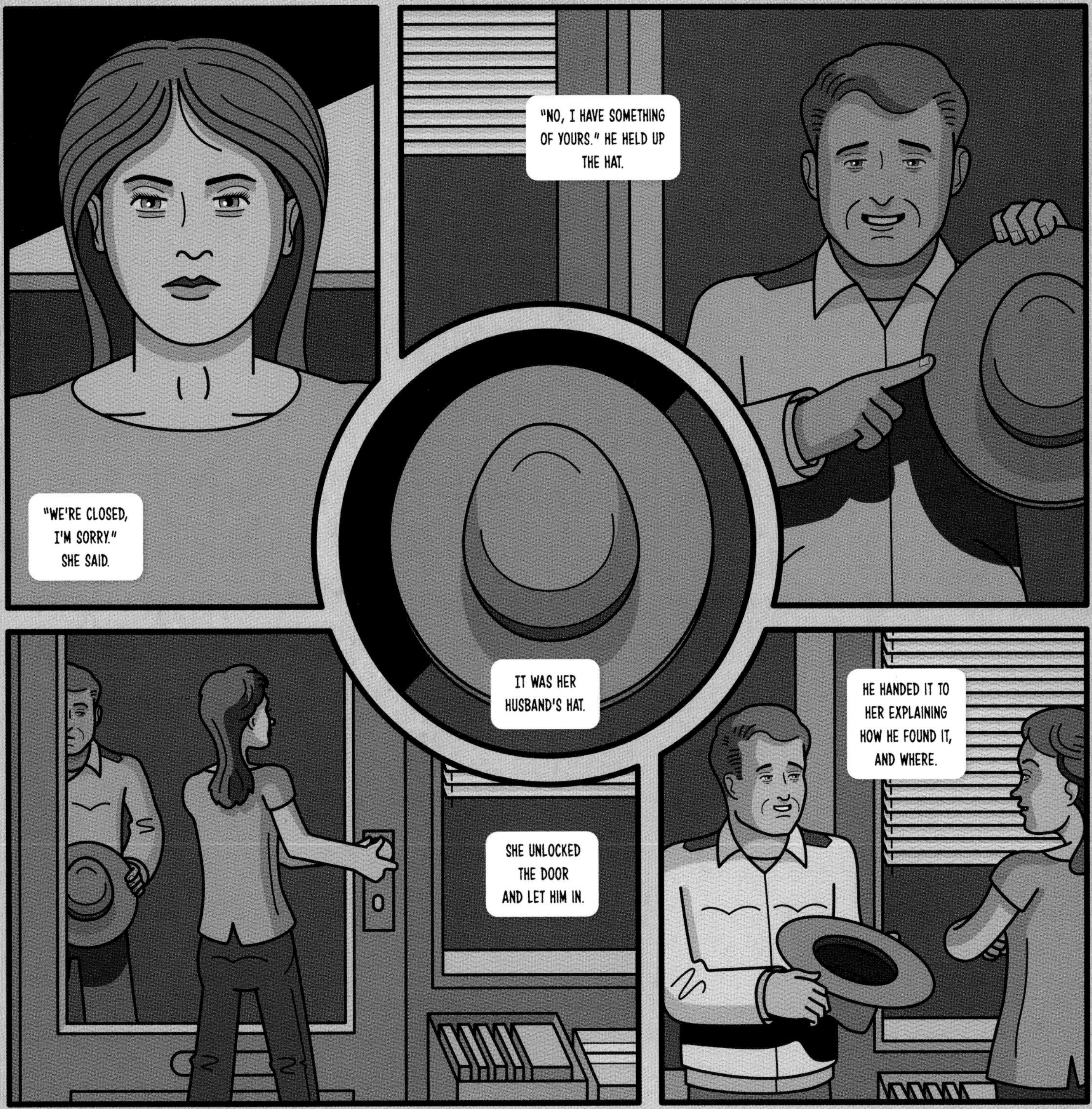
"WE'RE CLOSED, I'M SORRY." SHE SAID.
"NO, I HAVE SOMETHING OF YOURS." HE HELD UP THE HAT.
IT WAS HER HUSBAND'S HAT.
SHE UNLOCKED THE DOOR AND LET HIM IN.
HE HANDED IT TO HER EXPLAINING HOW HE FOUND IT, AND WHERE.

IT'S A VERY NICE HAT. I THOUGHT THE OWNER MIGHT APPRECIATE GETTING IT BACK.

HE STOOD QUIETLY, WATCHING HER EXAMINE THE HAT.

THIS WAS MY HUSBAND'S HAT.

HE DISAPPEARED A MONTH AGO.

NO ONE HAS FOUND HIM. NOT THE POLICE, NOT THE HOSPITALS, NOBODY.

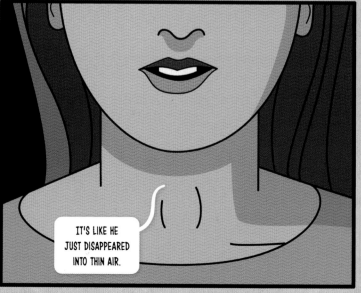

IT'S LIKE HE JUST DISAPPEARED INTO THIN AIR.

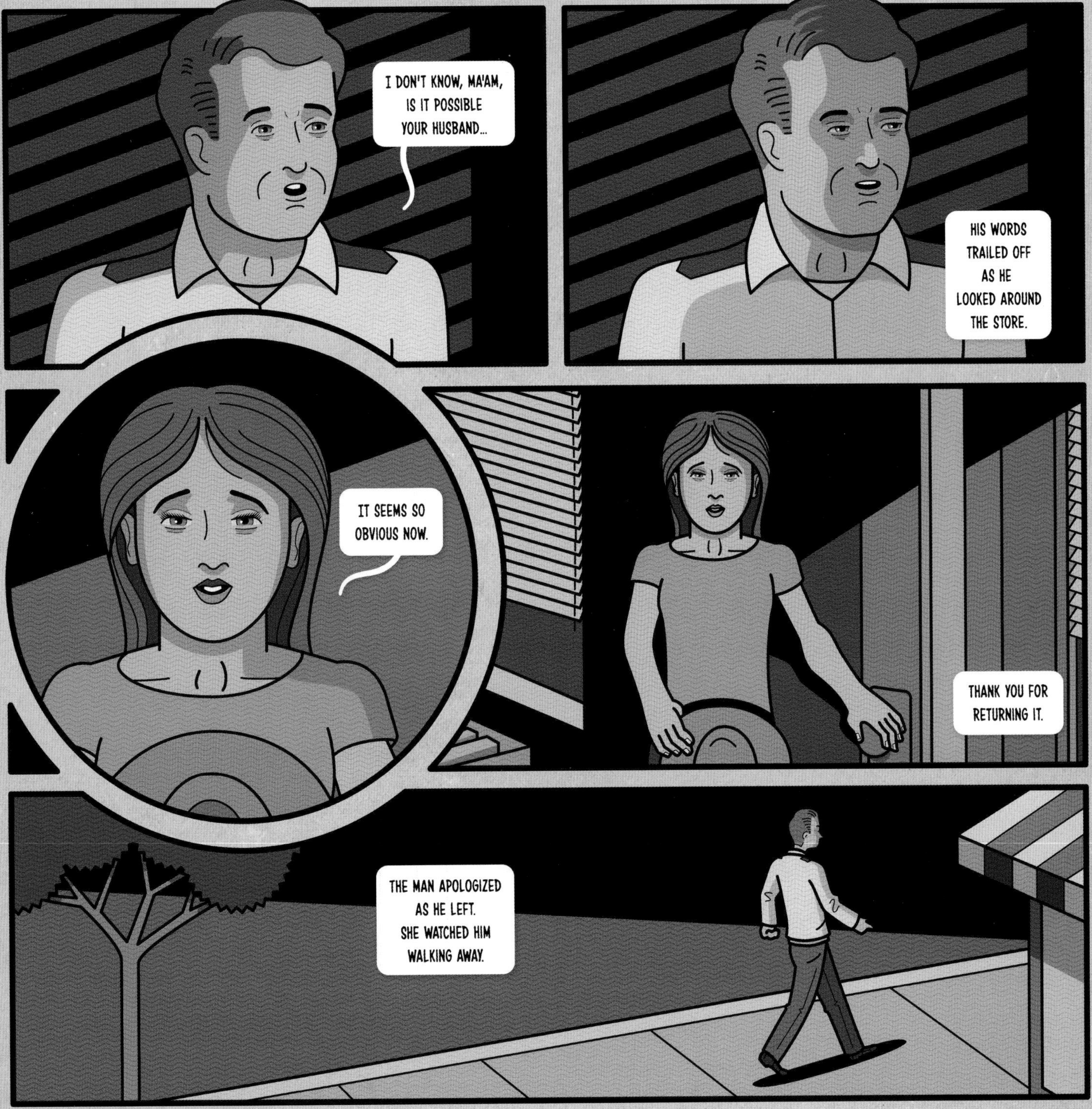
I DON'T KNOW, MA'AM, IS IT POSSIBLE YOUR HUSBAND...
HIS WORDS TRAILED OFF AS HE LOOKED AROUND THE STORE.
IT SEEMS SO OBVIOUS NOW.
THANK YOU FOR RETURNING IT.
THE MAN APOLOGIZED AS HE LEFT. SHE WATCHED HIM WALKING AWAY.

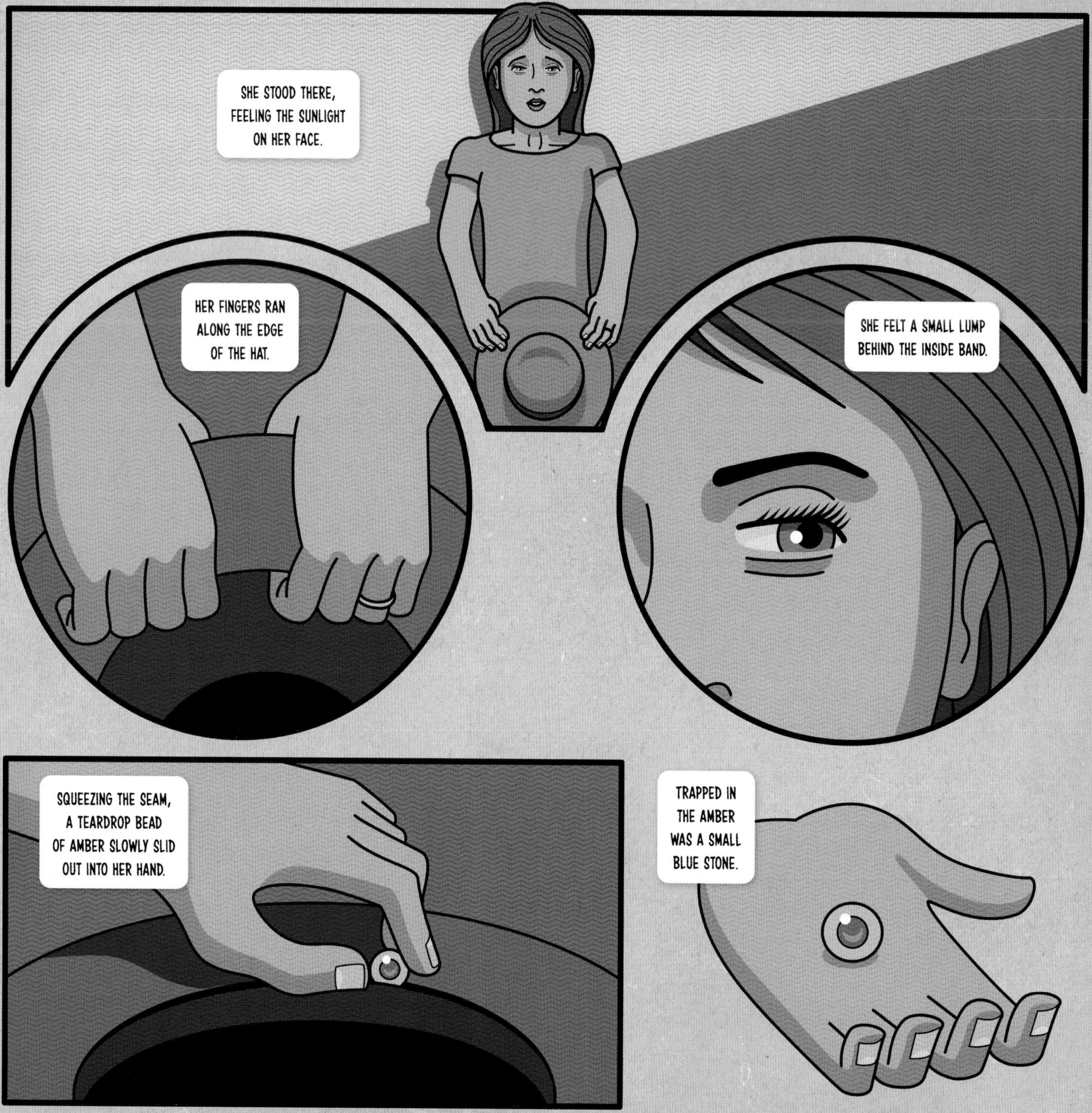
SHE STOOD THERE, FEELING THE SUNLIGHT ON HER FACE.
HER FINGERS RAN ALONG THE EDGE OF THE HAT.
SHE FELT A SMALL LUMP BEHIND THE INSIDE BAND.
SQUEEZING THE SEAM, A TEARDROP BEAD OF AMBER SLOWLY SLID OUT INTO HER HAND.
TRAPPED IN THE AMBER WAS A SMALL BLUE STONE.

CHAPTER

8

THEY HAD MET ON A RAINY AFTERNOON.

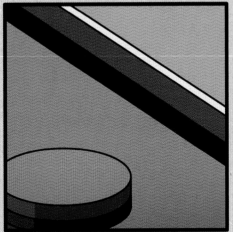

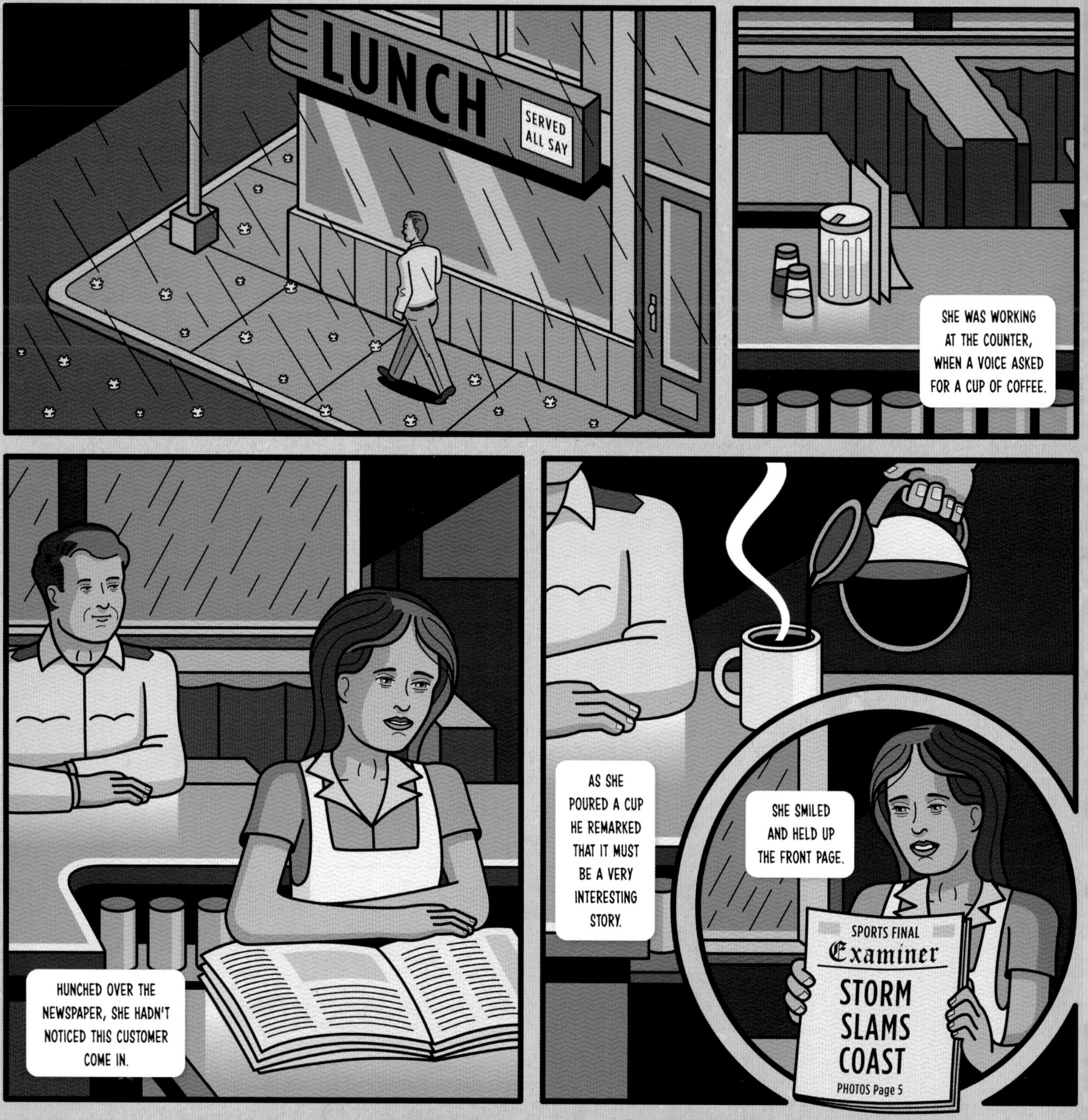
LUNCH
SERVED ALL SAY
SHE WAS WORKING AT THE COUNTER, WHEN A VOICE ASKED FOR A CUP OF COFFEE.
HUNCHED OVER THE NEWSPAPER, SHE HADN'T NOTICED THIS CUSTOMER COME IN.
AS SHE POURED A CUP HE REMARKED THAT IT MUST BE A VERY INTERESTING STORY.
SHE SMILED AND HELD UP THE FRONT PAGE.
SPORTS FINAL
Examiner
STORM SLAMS COAST
PHOTOS Page 5

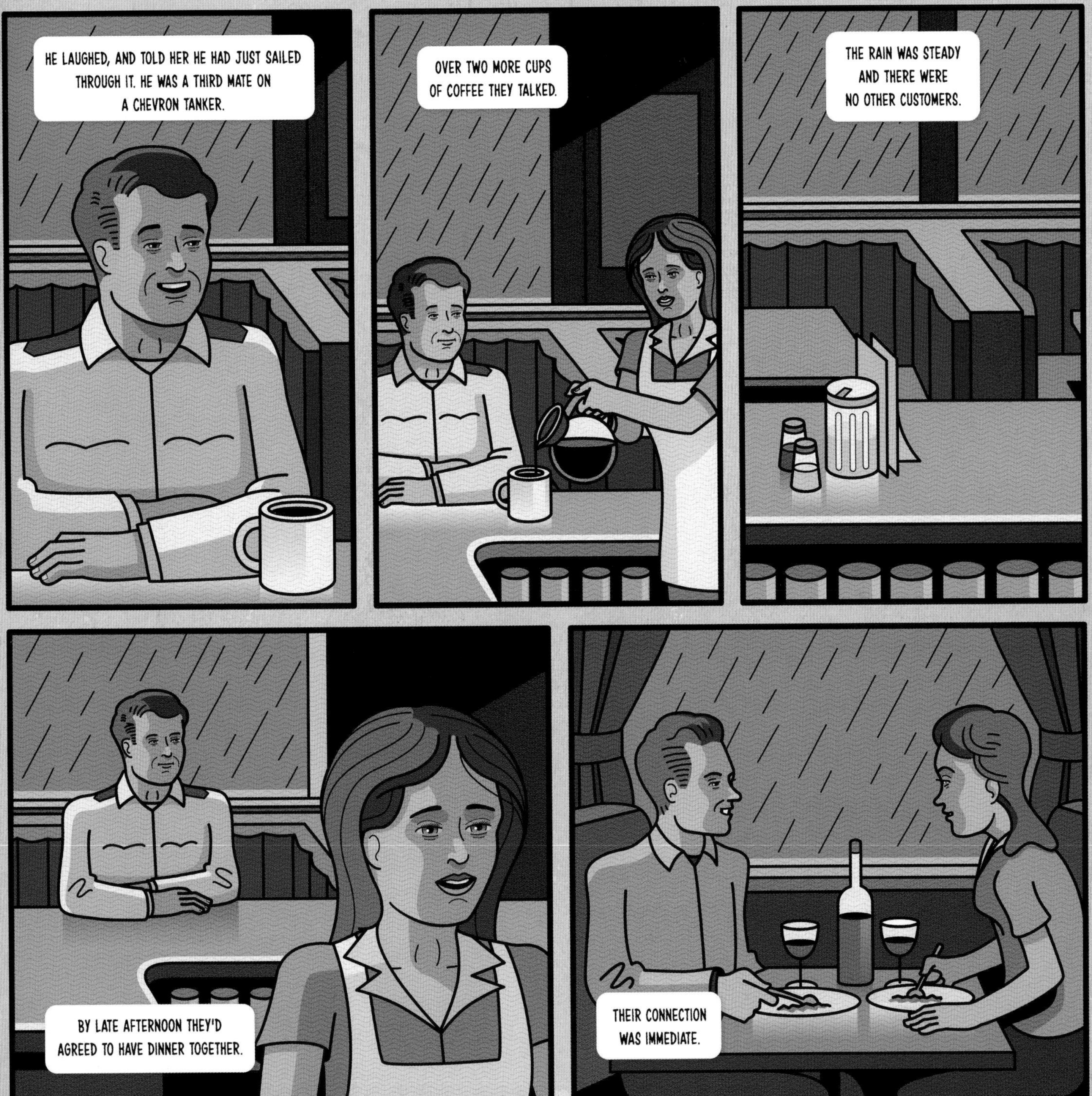
HE LAUGHED, AND TOLD HER HE HAD JUST SAILED THROUGH IT. HE WAS A THIRD MATE ON A CHEVRON TANKER.
OVER TWO MORE CUPS OF COFFEE THEY TALKED.
THE RAIN WAS STEADY AND THERE WERE NO OTHER CUSTOMERS.
BY LATE AFTERNOON THEY'D AGREED TO HAVE DINNER TOGETHER.
THEIR CONNECTION WAS IMMEDIATE.

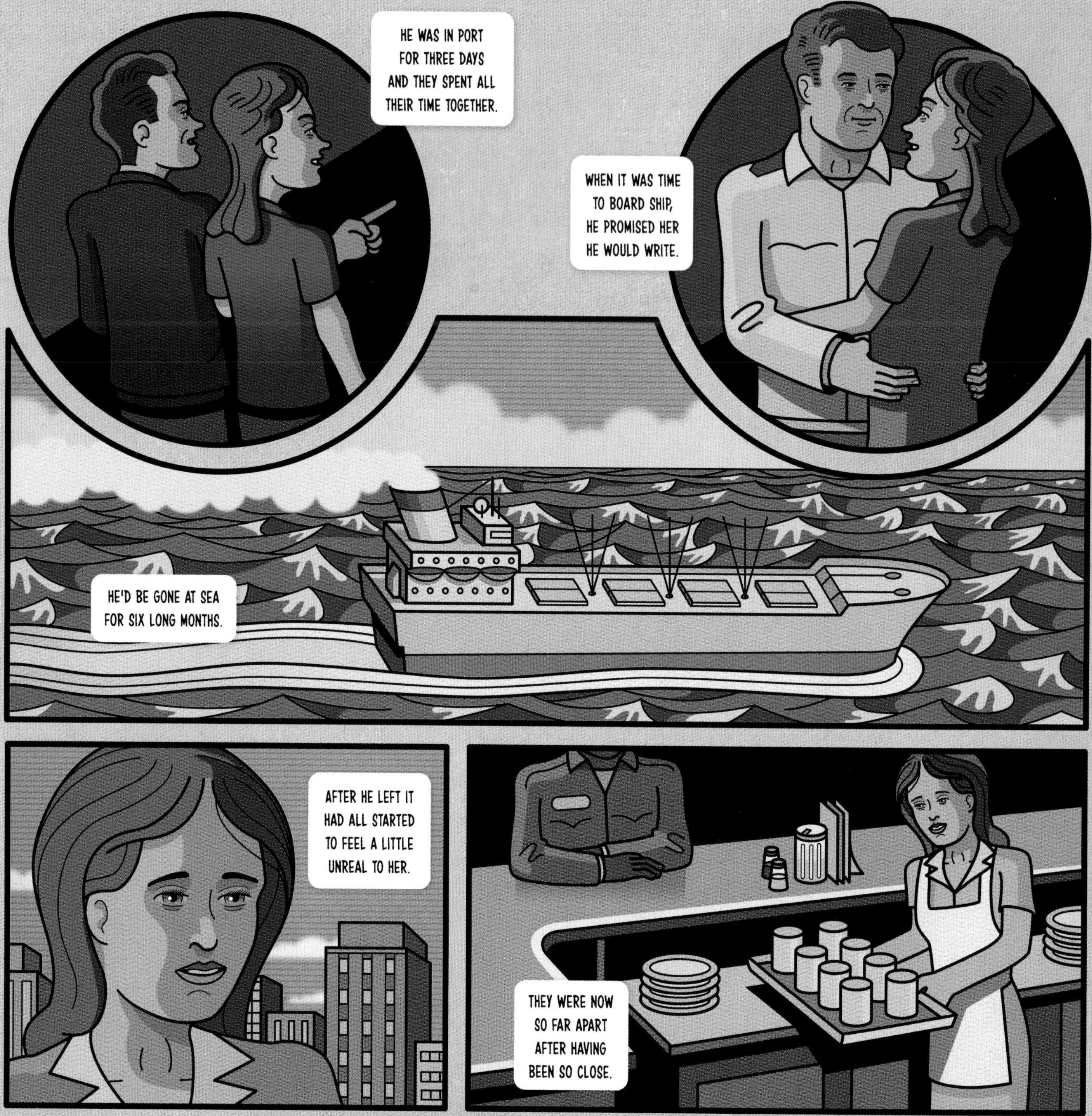
HE WAS IN PORT FOR THREE DAYS AND THEY SPENT ALL THEIR TIME TOGETHER.
WHEN IT WAS TIME TO BOARD SHIP, HE PROMISED HER HE WOULD WRITE.
HE'D BE GONE AT SEA FOR SIX LONG MONTHS.
AFTER HE LEFT IT HAD ALL STARTED TO FEEL A LITTLE UNREAL TO HER.
THEY WERE NOW SO FAR APART AFTER HAVING BEEN SO CLOSE.

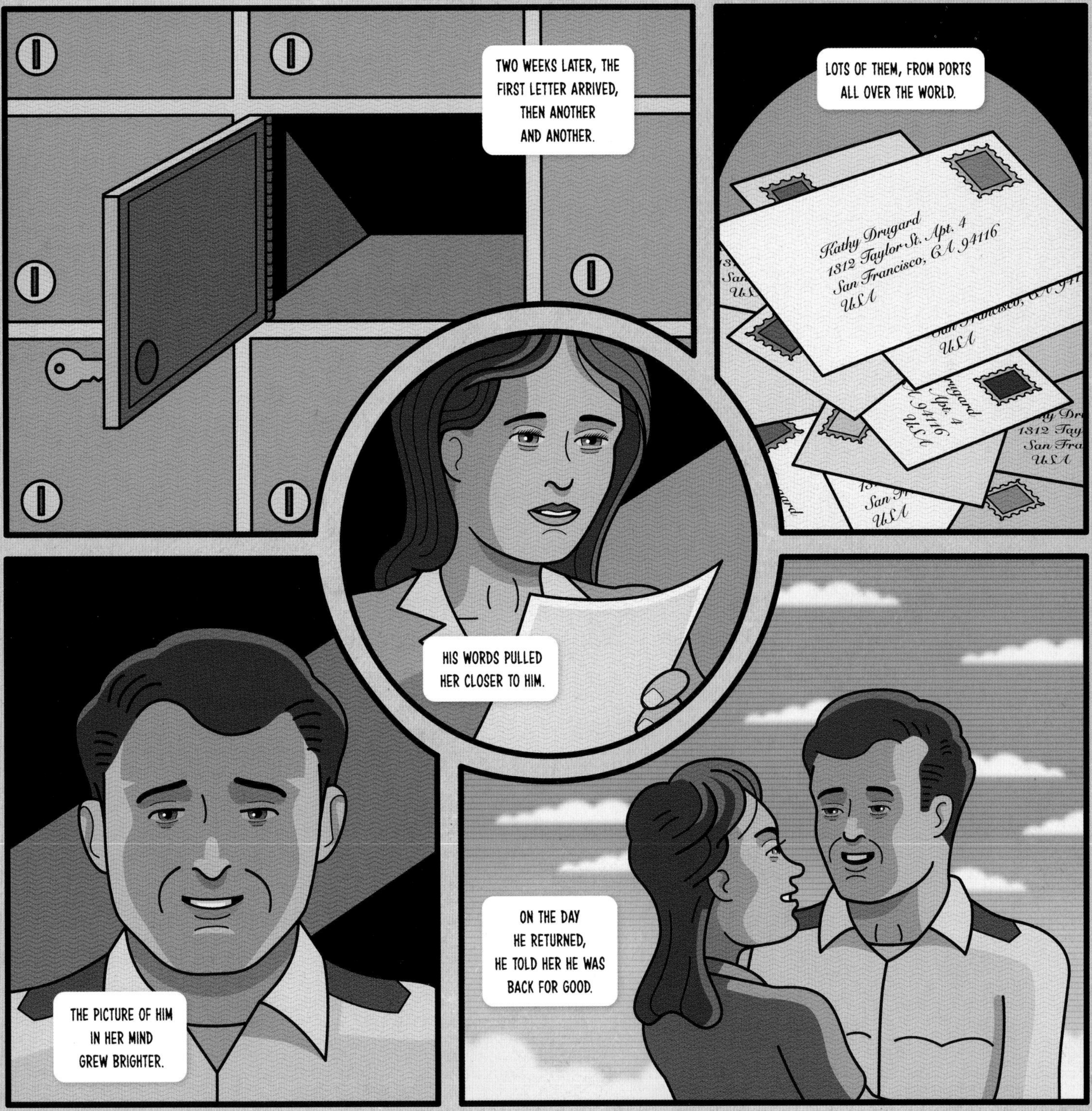
TWO WEEKS LATER, THE FIRST LETTER ARRIVED, THEN ANOTHER AND ANOTHER.
LOTS OF THEM, FROM PORTS ALL OVER THE WORLD.
Kathy Drugard
1312 Taylor St. Apt. 4
San Francisco, CA 94116
USA
HIS WORDS PULLED HER CLOSER TO HIM.
THE PICTURE OF HIM IN HER MIND GREW BRIGHTER.
ON THE DAY HE RETURNED, HE TOLD HER HE WAS BACK FOR GOOD.

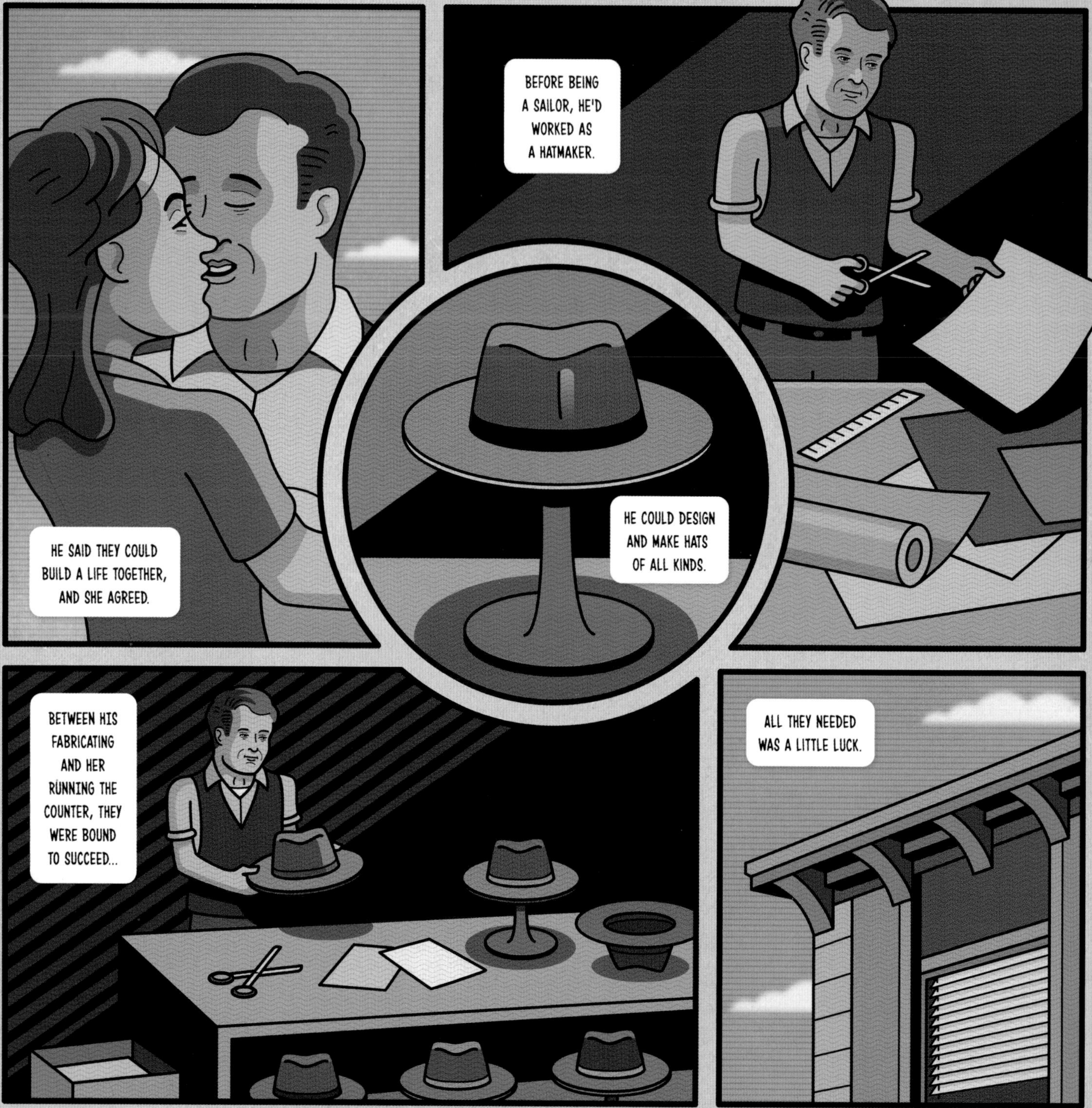
HE SAID THEY COULD BUILD A LIFE TOGETHER, AND SHE AGREED.
BEFORE BEING A SAILOR, HE'D WORKED AS A HATMAKER.
HE COULD DESIGN AND MAKE HATS OF ALL KINDS.
BETWEEN HIS FABRICATING AND HER RUNNING THE COUNTER, THEY WERE BOUND TO SUCCEED...
ALL THEY NEEDED WAS A LITTLE LUCK.

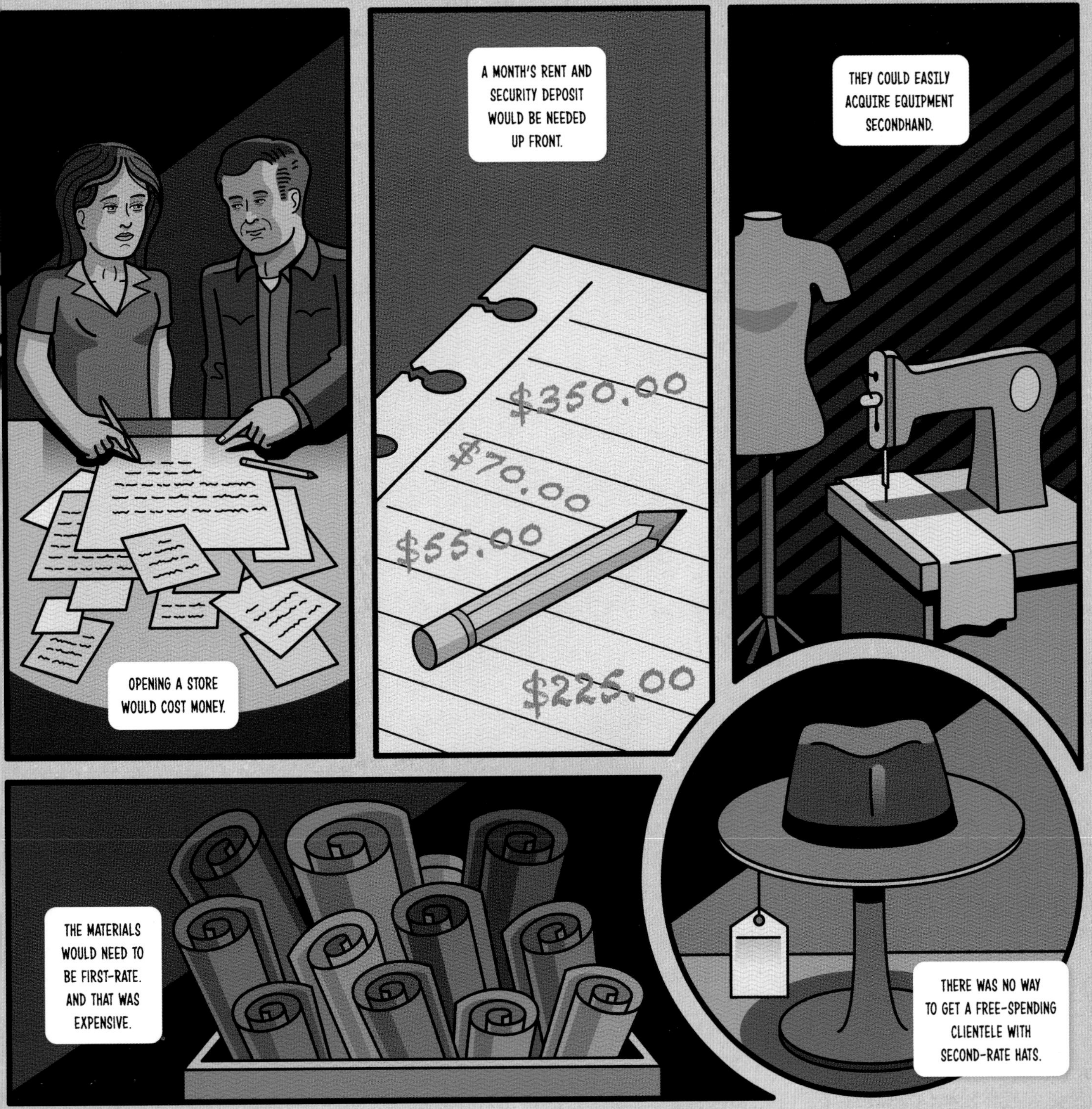
OPENING A STORE WOULD COST MONEY.
A MONTH'S RENT AND SECURITY DEPOSIT WOULD BE NEEDED UP FRONT.
$350.00
$70.00
$55.00
$225.00
THEY COULD EASILY ACQUIRE EQUIPMENT SECONDHAND.
THE MATERIALS WOULD NEED TO BE FIRST-RATE. AND THAT WAS EXPENSIVE.
THERE WAS NO WAY TO GET A FREE-SPENDING CLIENTELE WITH SECOND-RATE HATS.

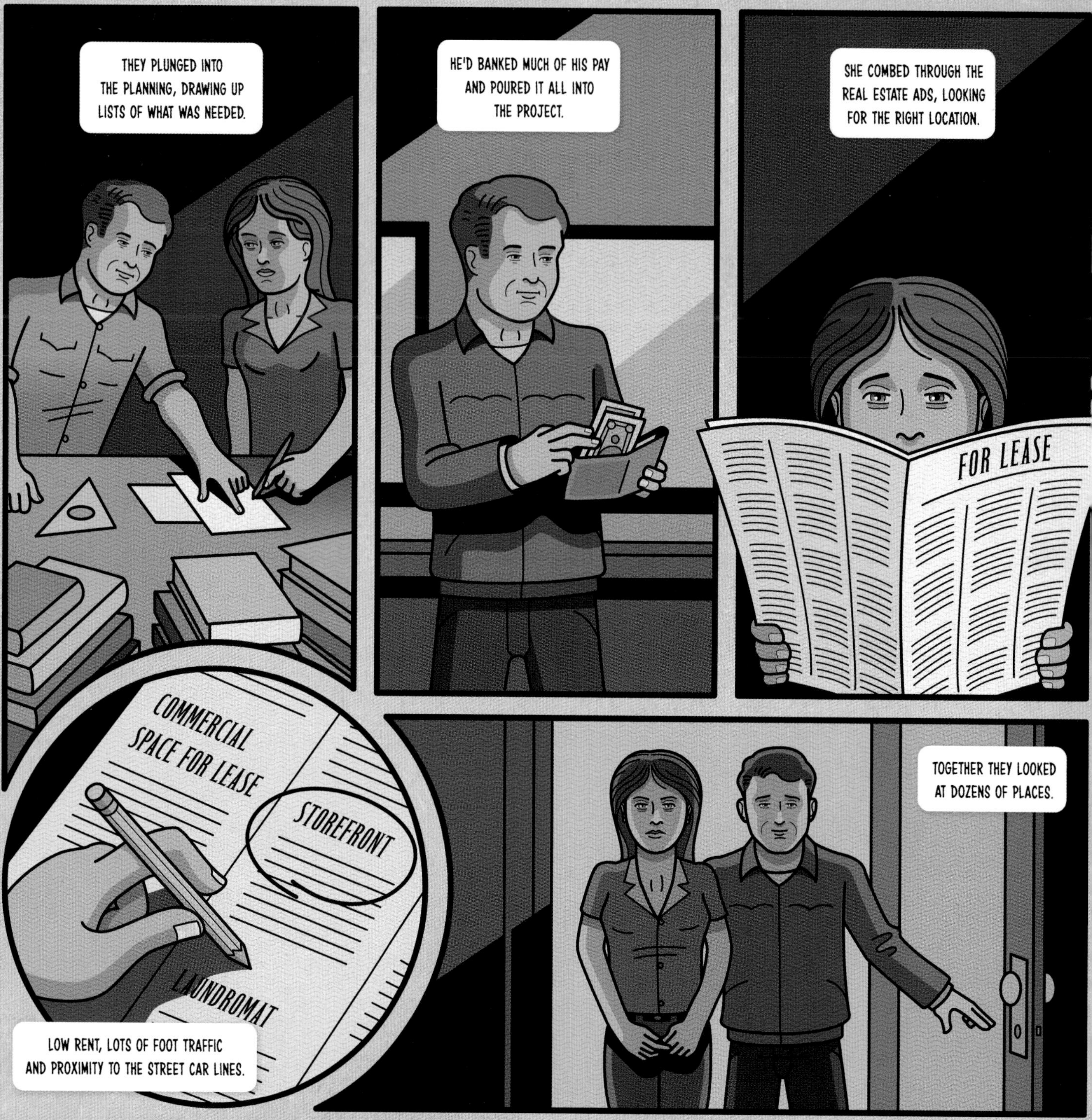
THEY PLUNGED INTO THE PLANNING, DRAWING UP LISTS OF WHAT WAS NEEDED.
HE'D BANKED MUCH OF HIS PAY AND POURED IT ALL INTO THE PROJECT.
SHE COMBED THROUGH THE REAL ESTATE ADS, LOOKING FOR THE RIGHT LOCATION.
FOR LEASE
COMMERCIAL SPACE FOR LEASE
STOREFRONT
LAUNDROMAT
LOW RENT, LOTS OF FOOT TRAFFIC AND PROXIMITY TO THE STREET CAR LINES.
TOGETHER THEY LOOKED AT DOZENS OF PLACES.

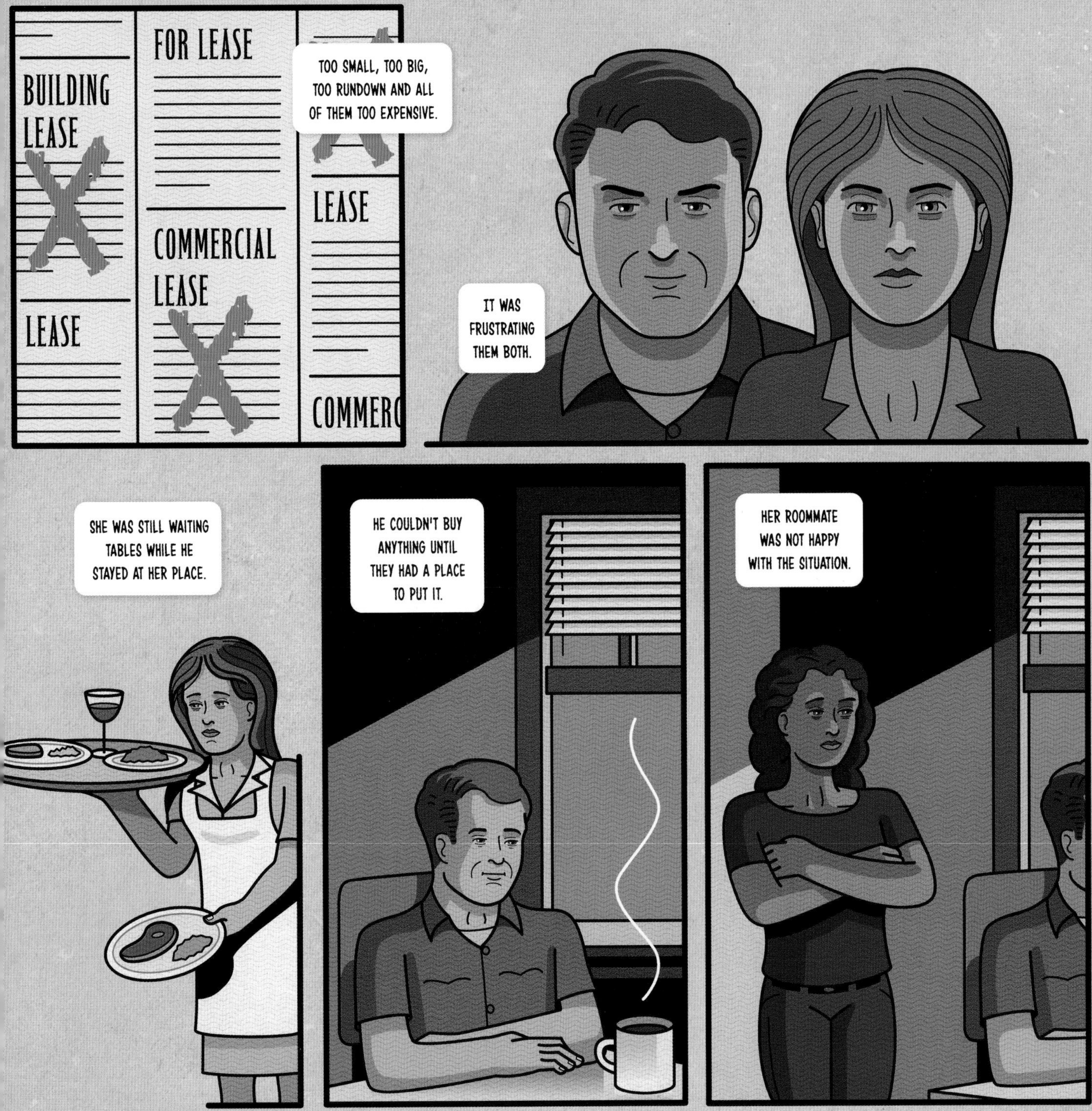
FOR LEASE
BUILDING LEASE
COMMERCIAL LEASE
LEASE
LEASE
COMMERC
TOO SMALL, TOO BIG, TOO RUNDOWN AND ALL OF THEM TOO EXPENSIVE.
IT WAS FRUSTRATING THEM BOTH.
SHE WAS STILL WAITING TABLES WHILE HE STAYED AT HER PLACE.
HE COULDN'T BUY ANYTHING UNTIL THEY HAD A PLACE TO PUT IT.
HER ROOMMATE WAS NOT HAPPY WITH THE SITUATION.

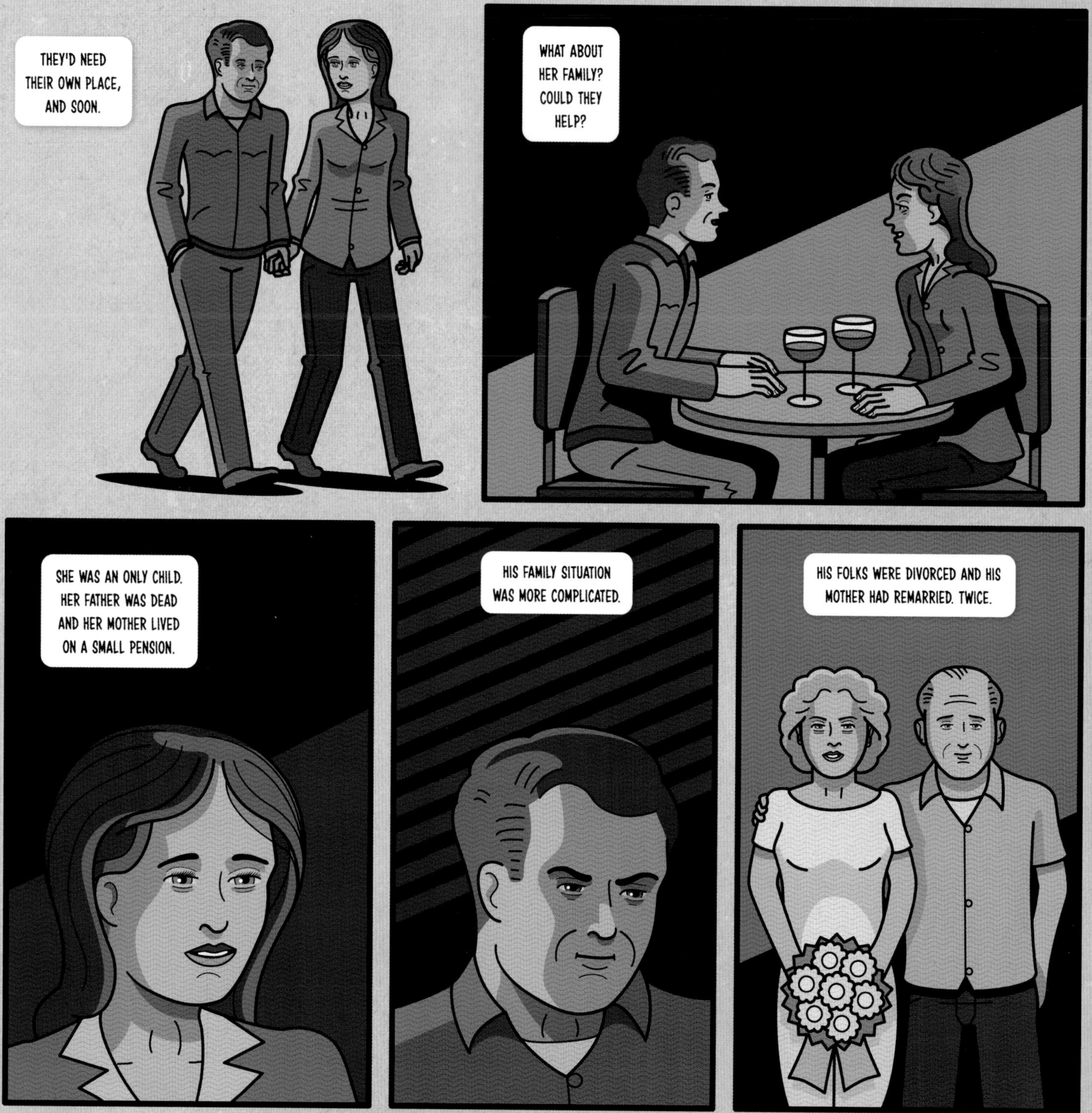
THEY'D NEED THEIR OWN PLACE, AND SOON.
WHAT ABOUT HER FAMILY? COULD THEY HELP?
SHE WAS AN ONLY CHILD. HER FATHER WAS DEAD AND HER MOTHER LIVED ON A SMALL PENSION.
HIS FAMILY SITUATION WAS MORE COMPLICATED.
HIS FOLKS WERE DIVORCED AND HIS MOTHER HAD REMARRIED. TWICE.

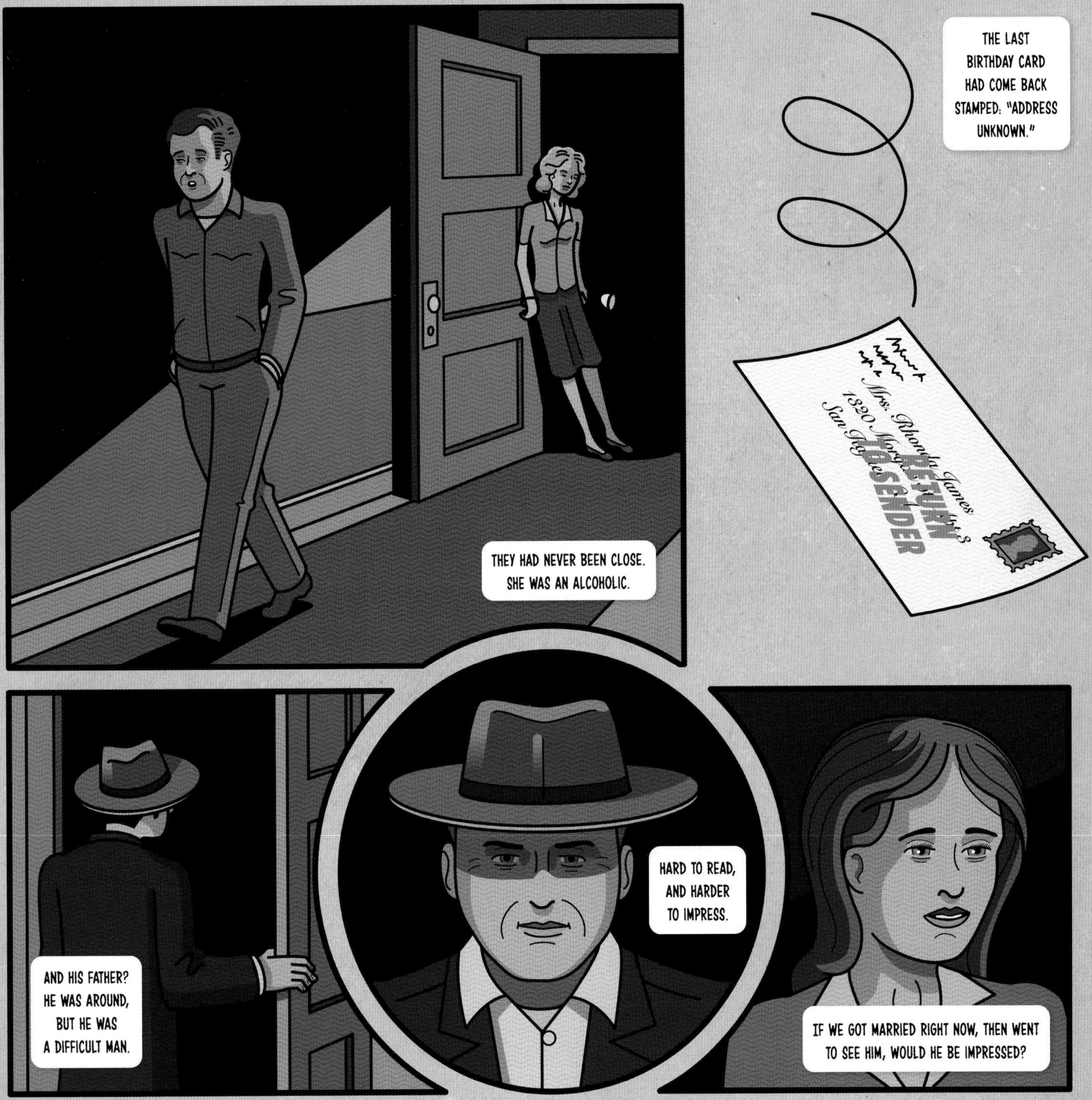
THEY HAD NEVER BEEN CLOSE. SHE WAS AN ALCOHOLIC.
THE LAST BIRTHDAY CARD HAD COME BACK STAMPED: "ADDRESS UNKNOWN."
Mrs. Rhonda James
RETURN TO SENDER
AND HIS FATHER? HE WAS AROUND, BUT HE WAS A DIFFICULT MAN.
HARD TO READ, AND HARDER TO IMPRESS.
IF WE GOT MARRIED RIGHT NOW, THEN WENT TO SEE HIM, WOULD HE BE IMPRESSED?

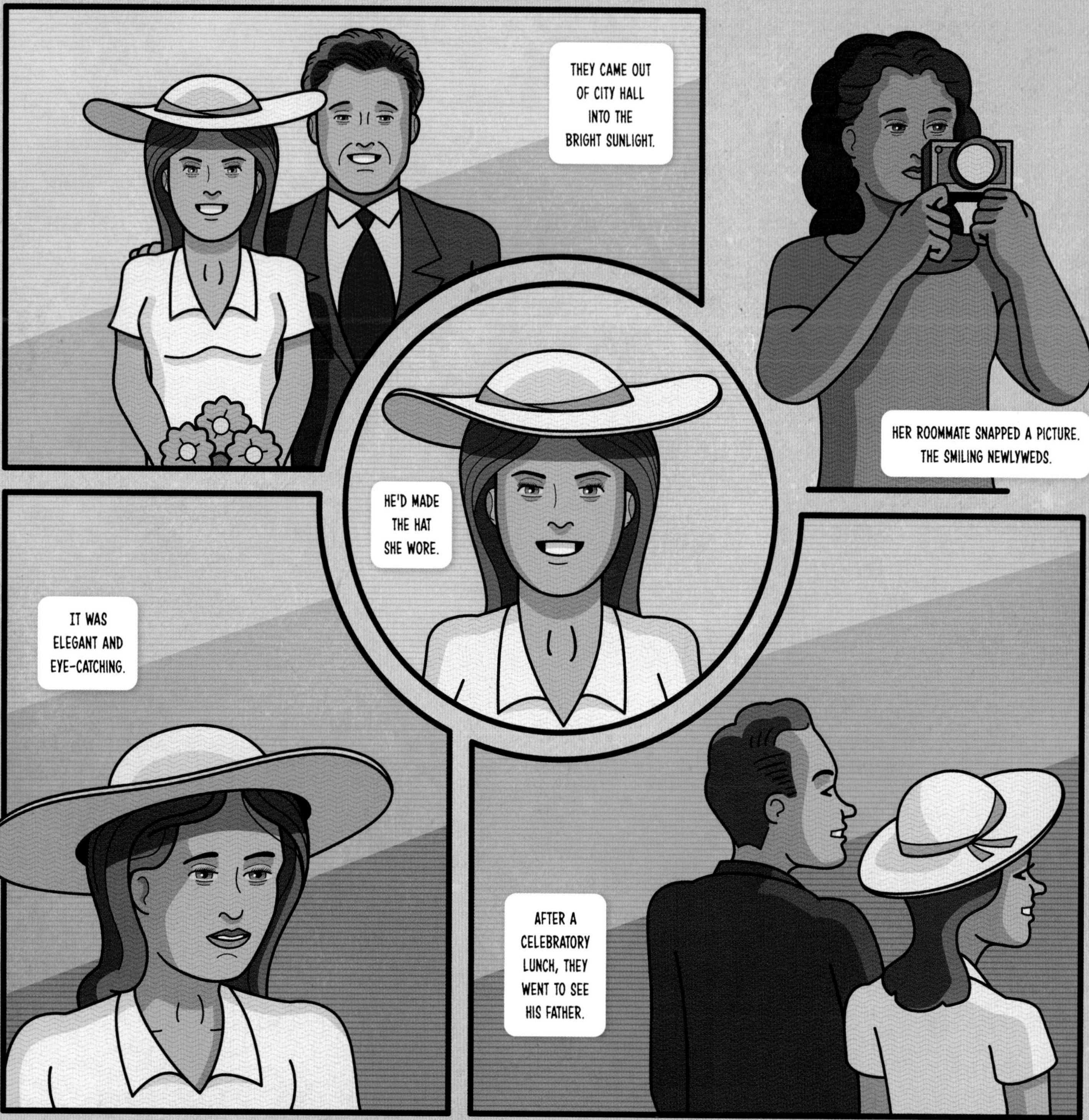
THEY CAME OUT OF CITY HALL INTO THE BRIGHT SUNLIGHT.
HER ROOMMATE SNAPPED A PICTURE. THE SMILING NEWLYWEDS.
HE'D MADE THE HAT SHE WORE.
IT WAS ELEGANT AND EYE-CATCHING.
AFTER A CELEBRATORY LUNCH, THEY WENT TO SEE HIS FATHER.

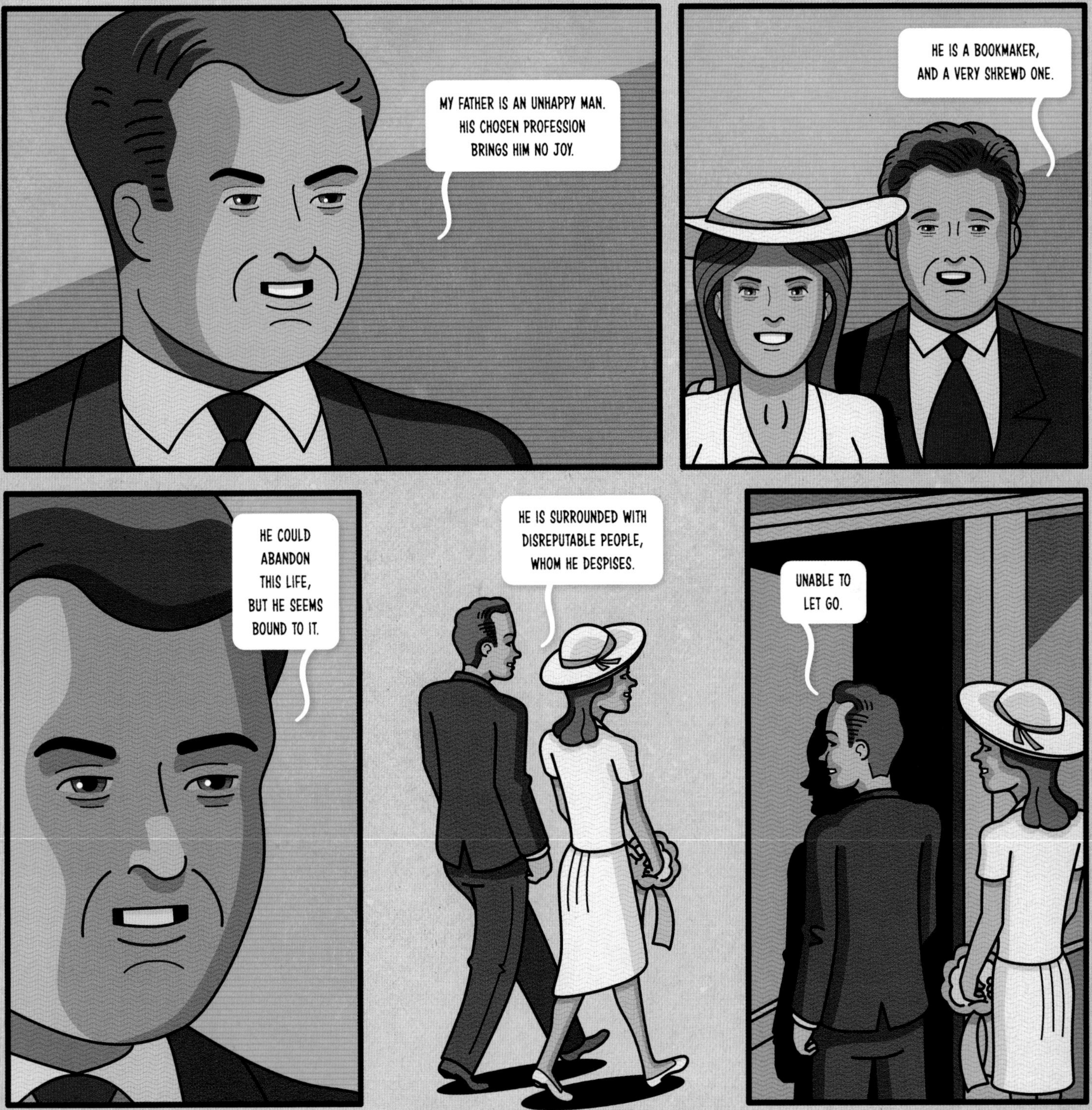
MY FATHER IS AN UNHAPPY MAN. HIS CHOSEN PROFESSION BRINGS HIM NO JOY.
HE IS A BOOKMAKER, AND A VERY SHREWD ONE.
HE COULD ABANDON THIS LIFE, BUT HE SEEMS BOUND TO IT.
HE IS SURROUNDED WITH DISREPUTABLE PEOPLE, WHOM HE DESPISES.
UNABLE TO LET GO.

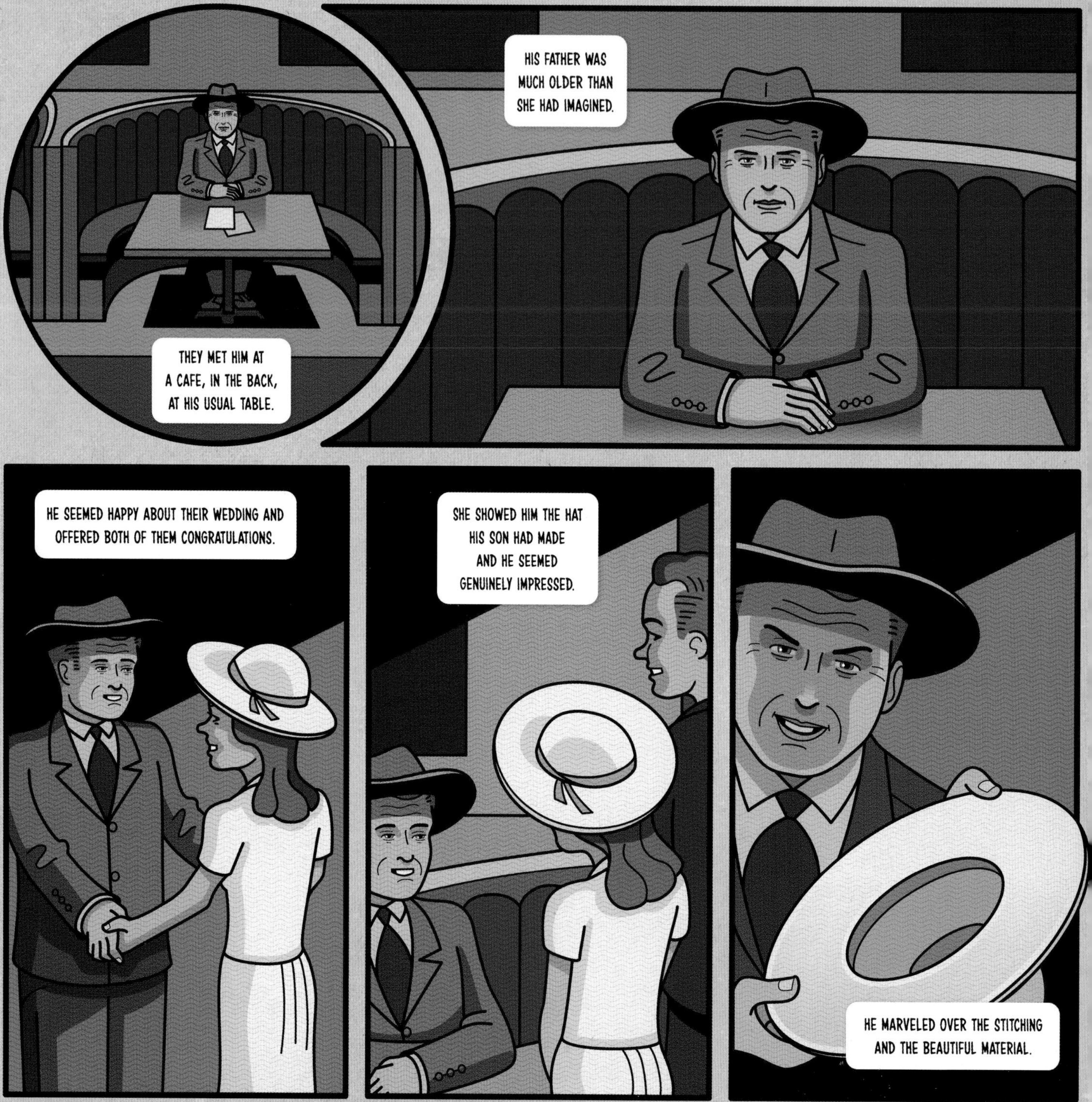
THEY MET HIM AT A CAFE, IN THE BACK, AT HIS USUAL TABLE.
HIS FATHER WAS MUCH OLDER THAN SHE HAD IMAGINED.
HE SEEMED HAPPY ABOUT THEIR WEDDING AND OFFERED BOTH OF THEM CONGRATULATIONS.
SHE SHOWED HIM THE HAT HIS SON HAD MADE AND HE SEEMED GENUINELY IMPRESSED.
HE MARVELED OVER THE STITCHING AND THE BEAUTIFUL MATERIAL.

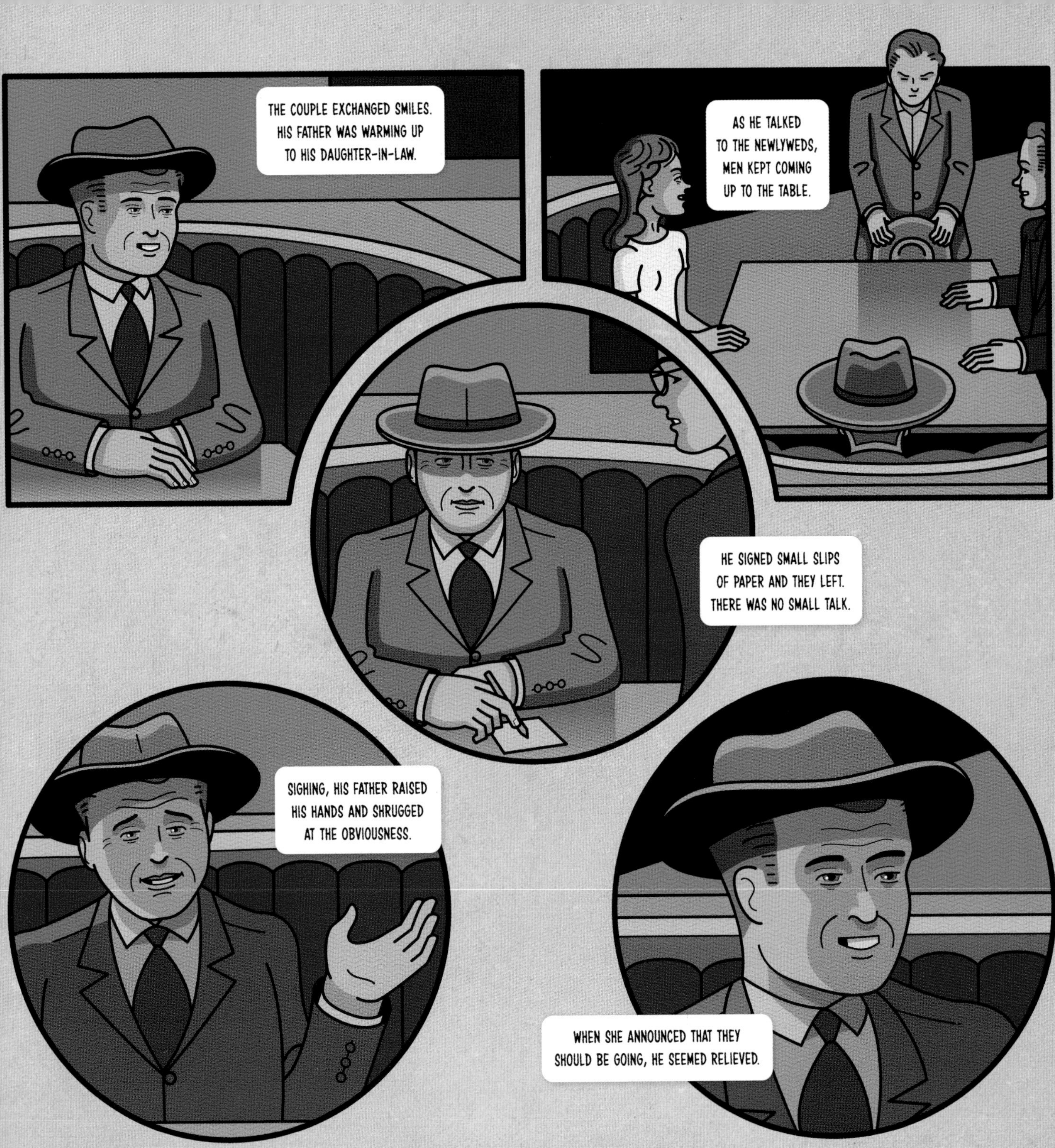
THE COUPLE EXCHANGED SMILES. HIS FATHER WAS WARMING UP TO HIS DAUGHTER-IN-LAW.
AS HE TALKED TO THE NEWLYWEDS, MEN KEPT COMING UP TO THE TABLE.
HE SIGNED SMALL SLIPS OF PAPER AND THEY LEFT. THERE WAS NO SMALL TALK.
SIGHING, HIS FATHER RAISED HIS HANDS AND SHRUGGED AT THE OBVIOUSNESS.
WHEN SHE ANNOUNCED THAT THEY SHOULD BE GOING, HE SEEMED RELIEVED.

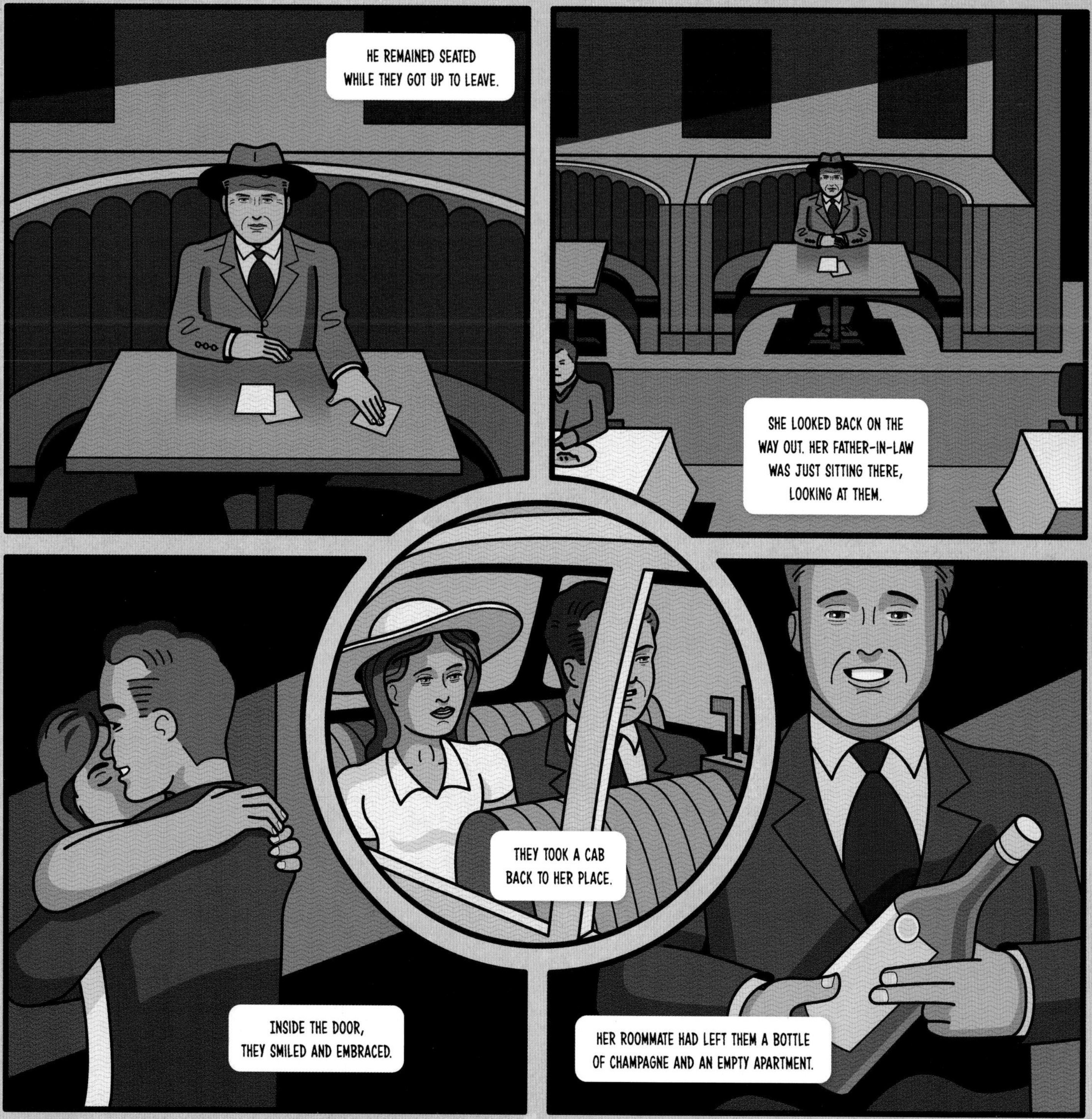
HE REMAINED SEATED WHILE THEY GOT UP TO LEAVE.
SHE LOOKED BACK ON THE WAY OUT. HER FATHER-IN-LAW WAS JUST SITTING THERE, LOOKING AT THEM.
THEY TOOK A CAB BACK TO HER PLACE.
INSIDE THE DOOR, THEY SMILED AND EMBRACED.
HER ROOMMATE HAD LEFT THEM A BOTTLE OF CHAMPAGNE AND AN EMPTY APARTMENT.

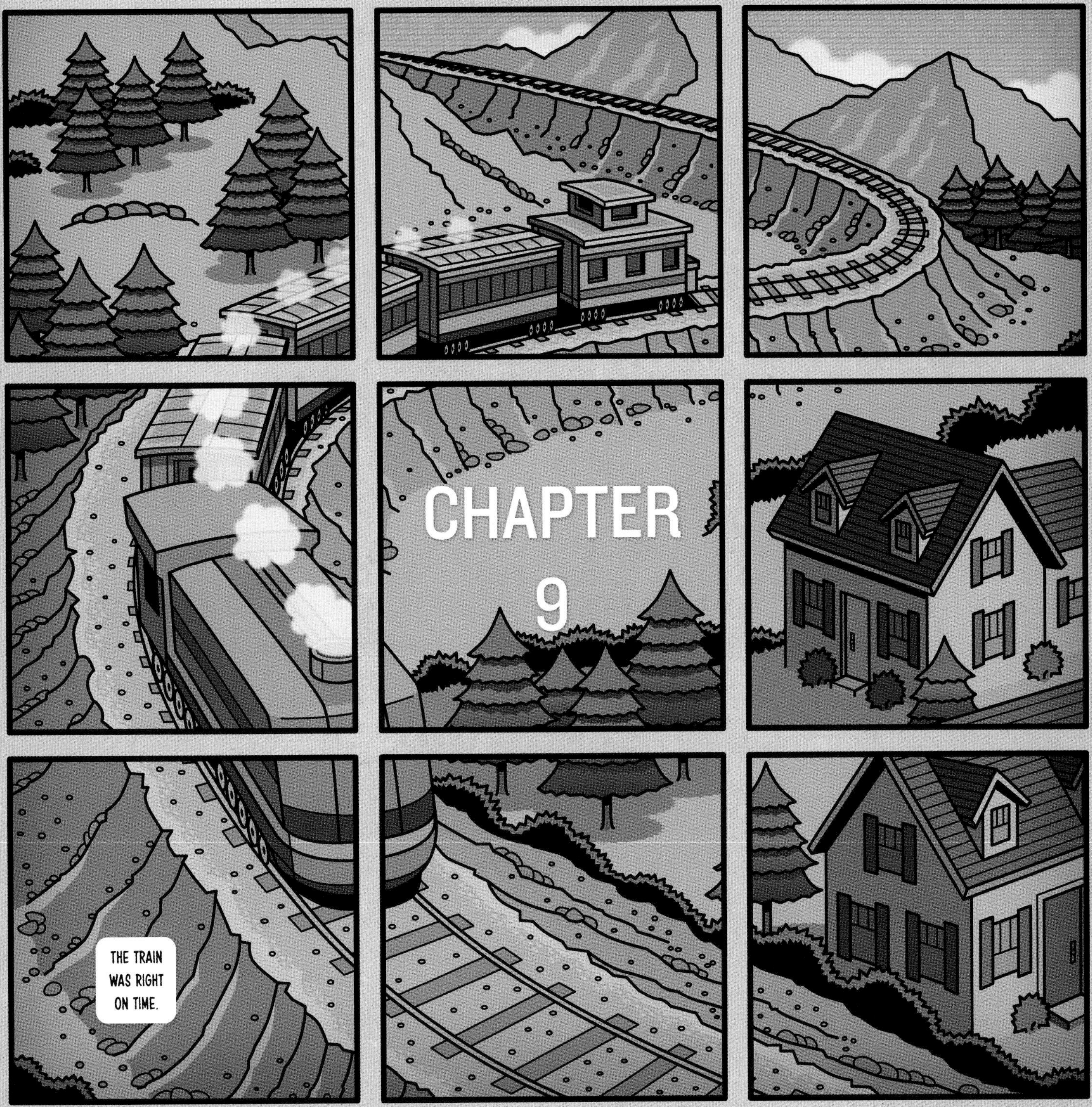
CHAPTER
9
THE TRAIN WAS RIGHT ON TIME.

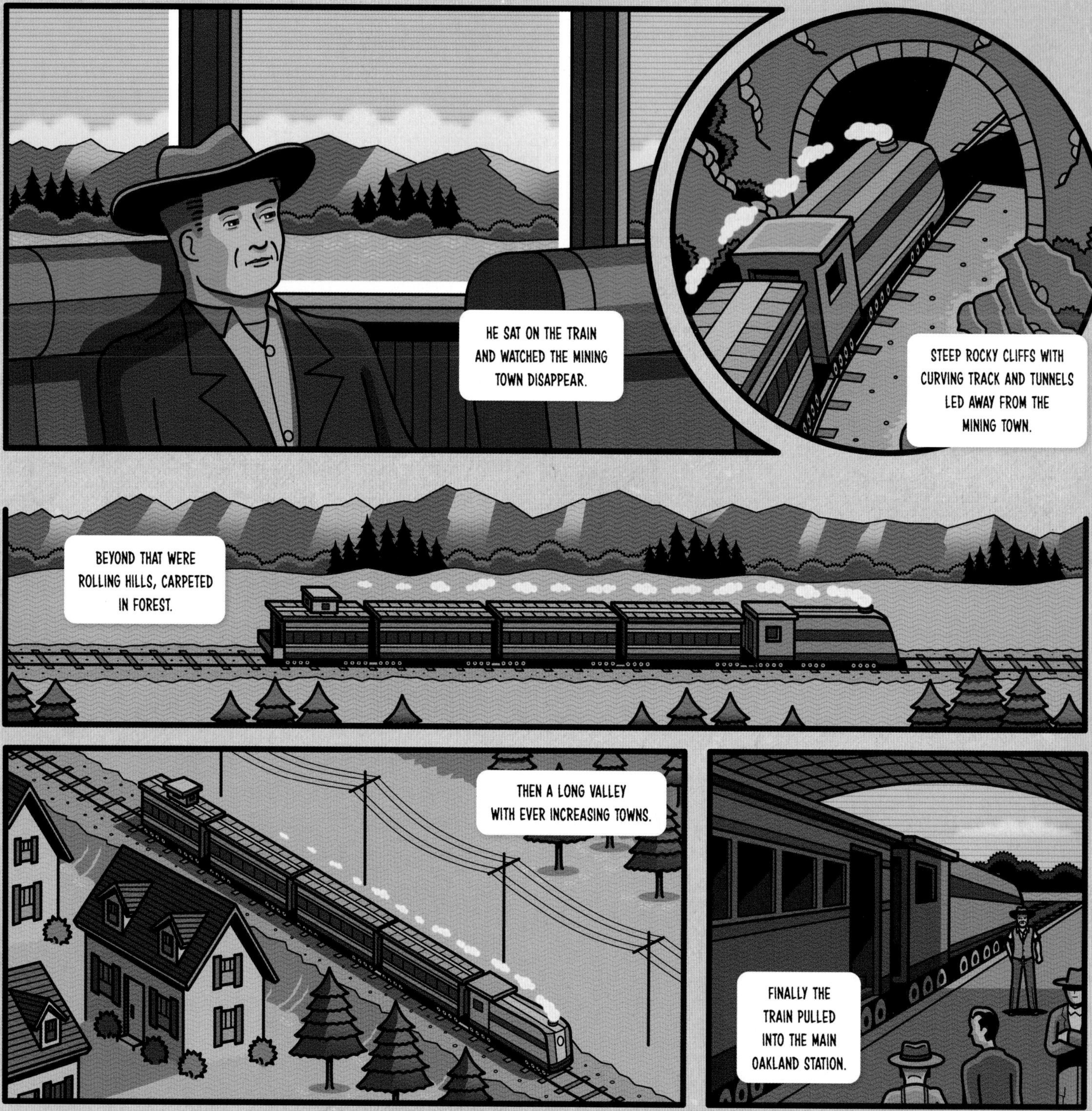
HE SAT ON THE TRAIN AND WATCHED THE MINING TOWN DISAPPEAR.
STEEP ROCKY CLIFFS WITH CURVING TRACK AND TUNNELS LED AWAY FROM THE MINING TOWN.
BEYOND THAT WERE ROLLING HILLS, CARPETED IN FOREST.
THEN A LONG VALLEY WITH EVER INCREASING TOWNS.
FINALLY THE TRAIN PULLED INTO THE MAIN OAKLAND STATION.

WITHOUT ANY LUGGAGE, HE SLIPPED UNNOTICED ONTO THE FERRY.

HE THOUGHT OF THE PARTNER WHO BETRAYED HIM, LYING DEAD IN THE DESERT.

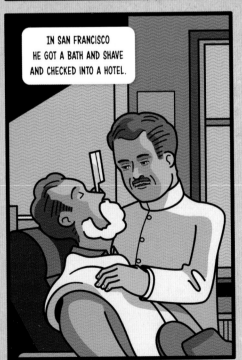

IN SAN FRANCISCO HE GOT A BATH AND SHAVE AND CHECKED INTO A HOTEL.

HE ALSO BOUGHT A NEW SET OF CLOTHES.

ALONE IN HIS ROOM HE TURNED OVER HIS OLD HAT.

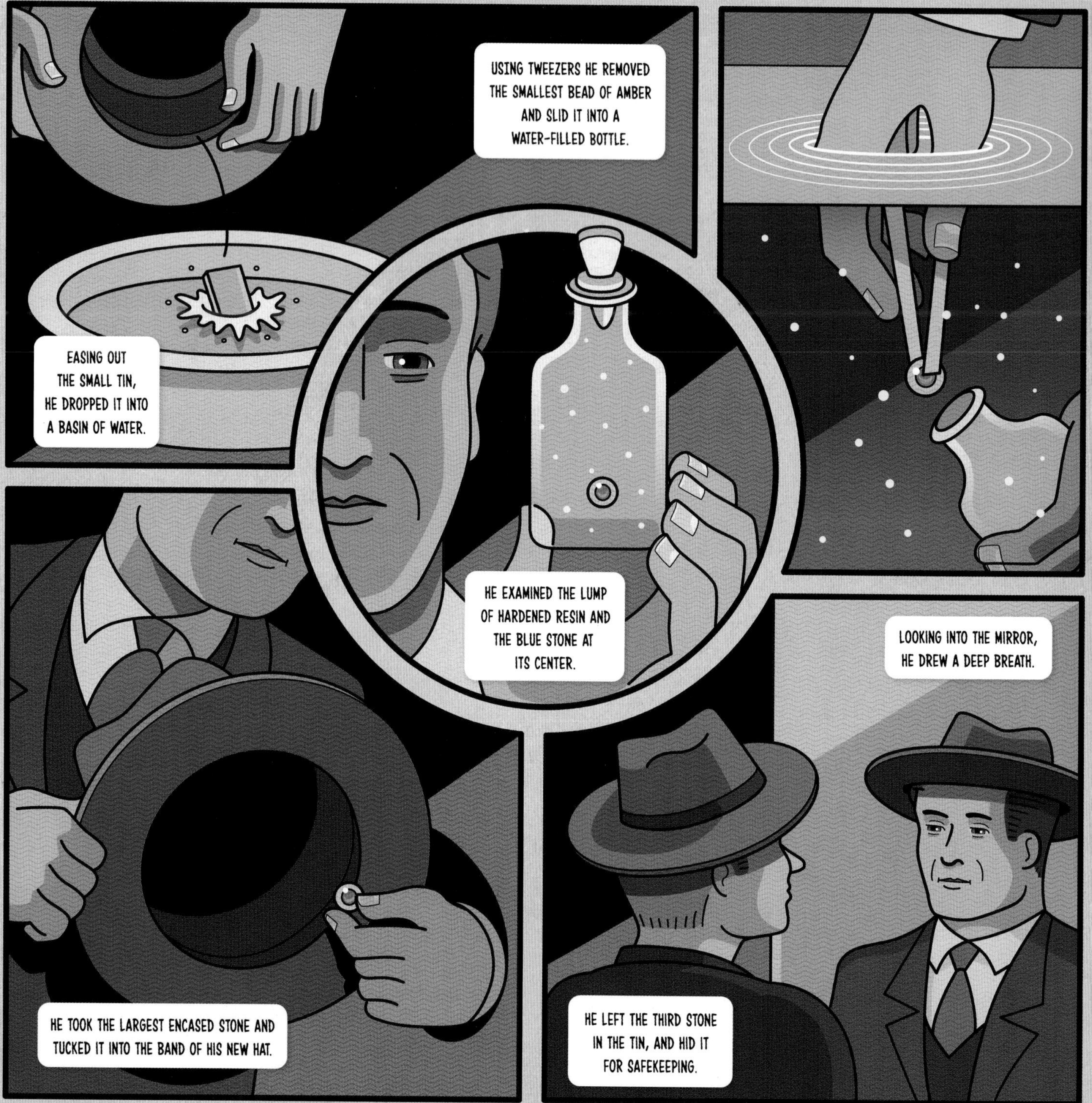
EASING OUT
THE SMALL TIN,
HE DROPPED IT INTO
A BASIN OF WATER.
USING TWEEZERS HE REMOVED
THE SMALLEST BEAD OF AMBER
AND SLID IT INTO A
WATER-FILLED BOTTLE.
HE EXAMINED THE LUMP
OF HARDENED RESIN AND
THE BLUE STONE AT
ITS CENTER.
HE TOOK THE LARGEST ENCASED STONE AND
TUCKED IT INTO THE BAND OF HIS NEW HAT.
HE LEFT THE THIRD STONE
IN THE TIN, AND HID IT
FOR SAFEKEEPING.
LOOKING INTO THE MIRROR,
HE DREW A DEEP BREATH.

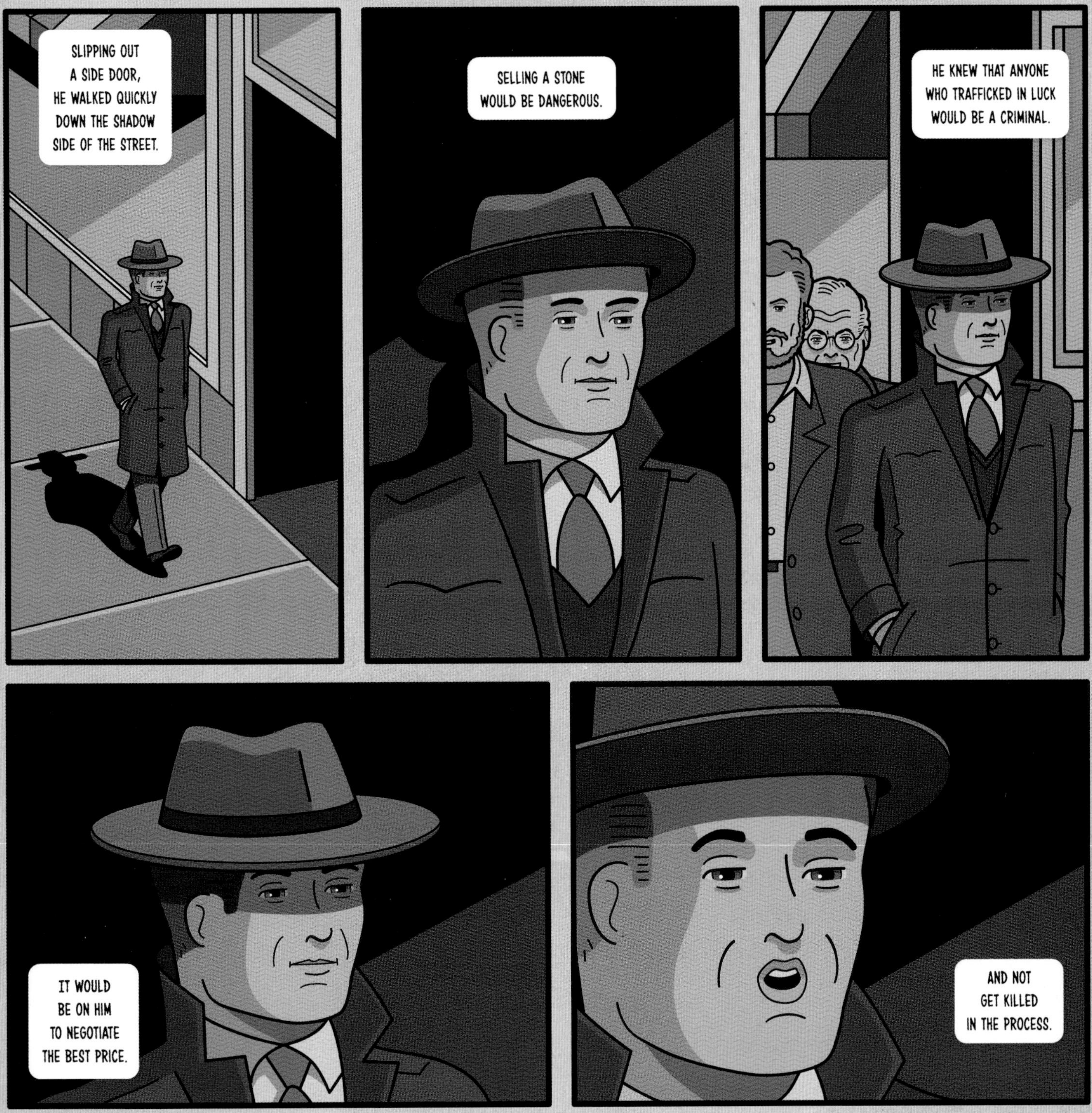
SLIPPING OUT A SIDE DOOR, HE WALKED QUICKLY DOWN THE SHADOW SIDE OF THE STREET.
SELLING A STONE WOULD BE DANGEROUS.
HE KNEW THAT ANYONE WHO TRAFFICKED IN LUCK WOULD BE A CRIMINAL.
IT WOULD BE ON HIM TO NEGOTIATE THE BEST PRICE.
AND NOT GET KILLED IN THE PROCESS.

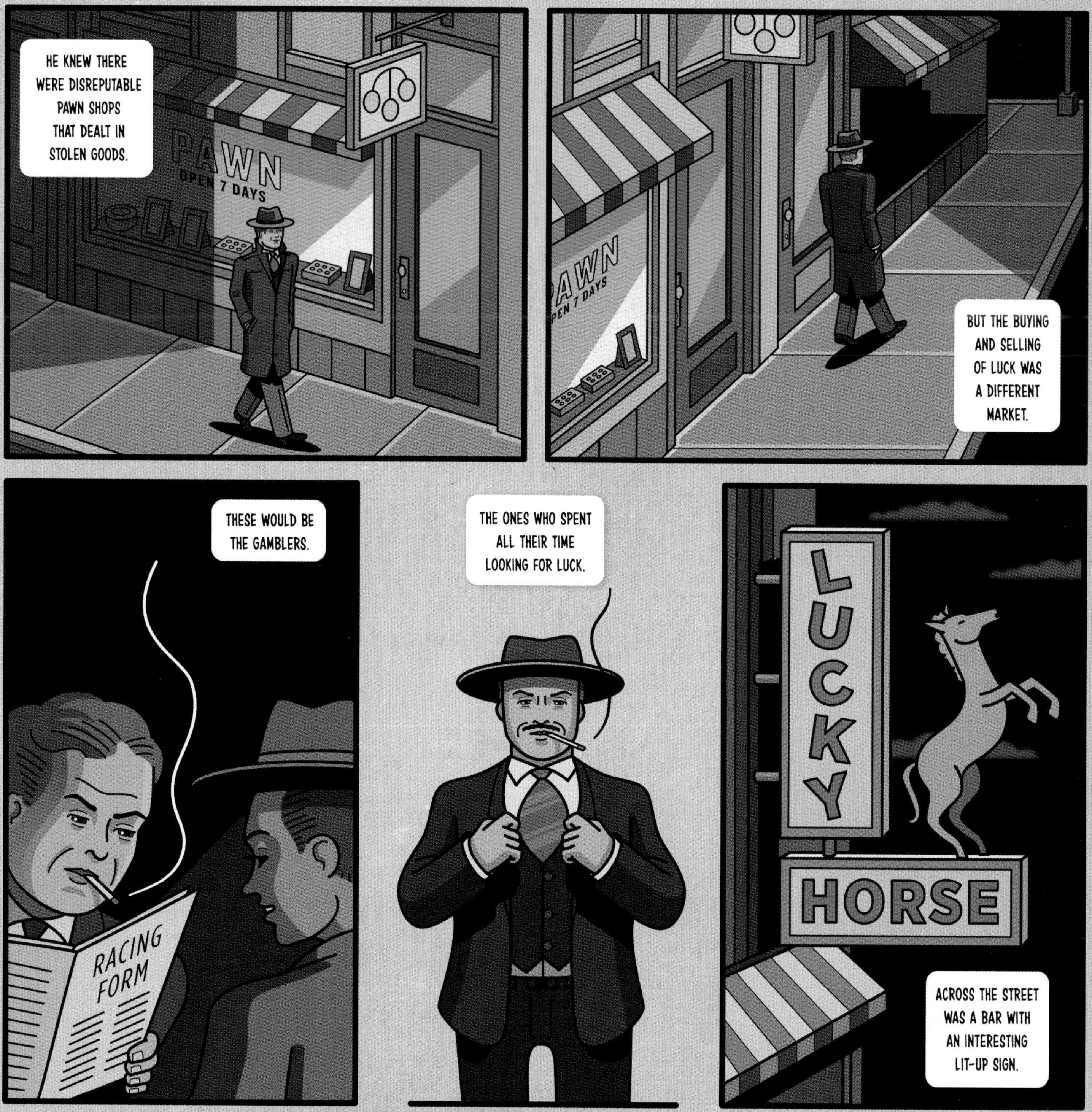
HE KNEW THERE WERE DISREPUTABLE PAWN SHOPS THAT DEALT IN STOLEN GOODS.
PAWN
OPEN 7 DAYS
BUT THE BUYING AND SELLING OF LUCK WAS A DIFFERENT MARKET.
THESE WOULD BE THE GAMBLERS.
RACING FORM
THE ONES WHO SPENT ALL THEIR TIME LOOKING FOR LUCK.
LUCKY
HORSE
ACROSS THE STREET WAS A BAR WITH AN INTERESTING LIT-UP SIGN.

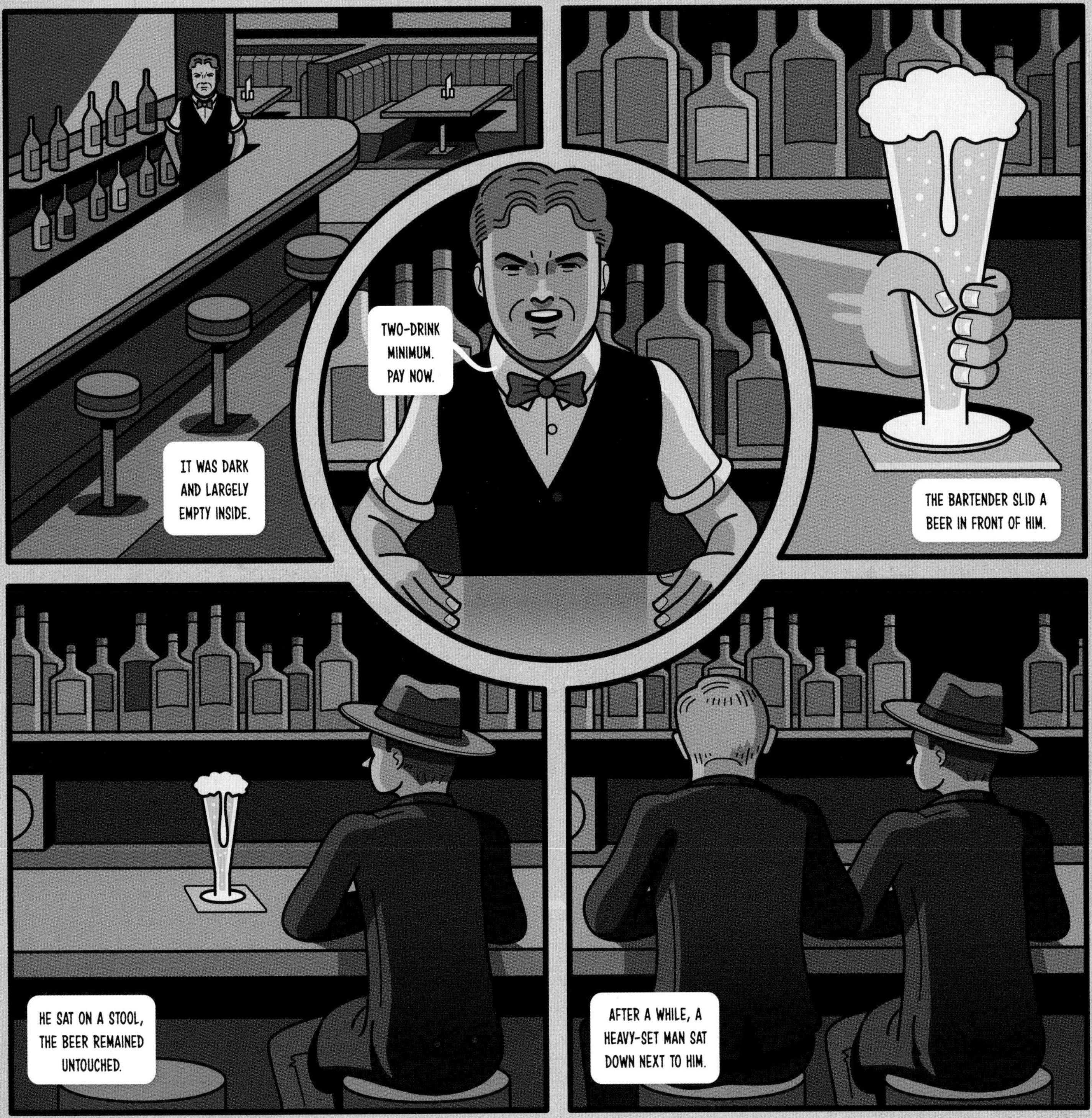
IT WAS DARK AND LARGELY EMPTY INSIDE.
TWO-DRINK MINIMUM. PAY NOW.
THE BARTENDER SLID A BEER IN FRONT OF HIM.
HE SAT ON A STOOL, THE BEER REMAINED UNTOUCHED.
AFTER A WHILE, A HEAVY-SET MAN SAT DOWN NEXT TO HIM.

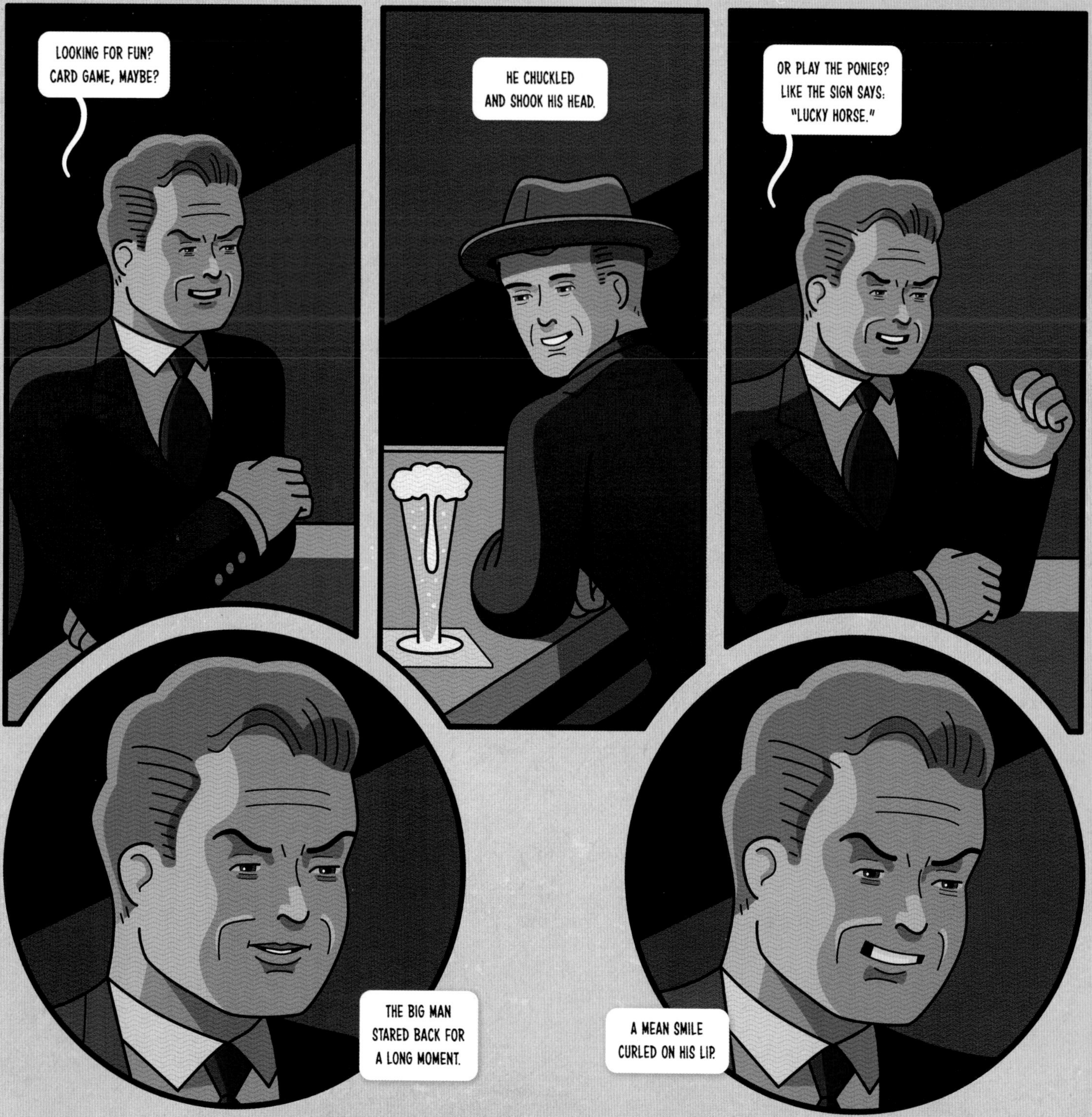
LOOKING FOR FUN?
CARD GAME, MAYBE?
HE CHUCKLED
AND SHOOK HIS HEAD.
OR PLAY THE PONIES?
LIKE THE SIGN SAYS:
"LUCKY HORSE."
THE BIG MAN
STARED BACK FOR
A LONG MOMENT.
A MEAN SMILE
CURLED ON HIS LIP.

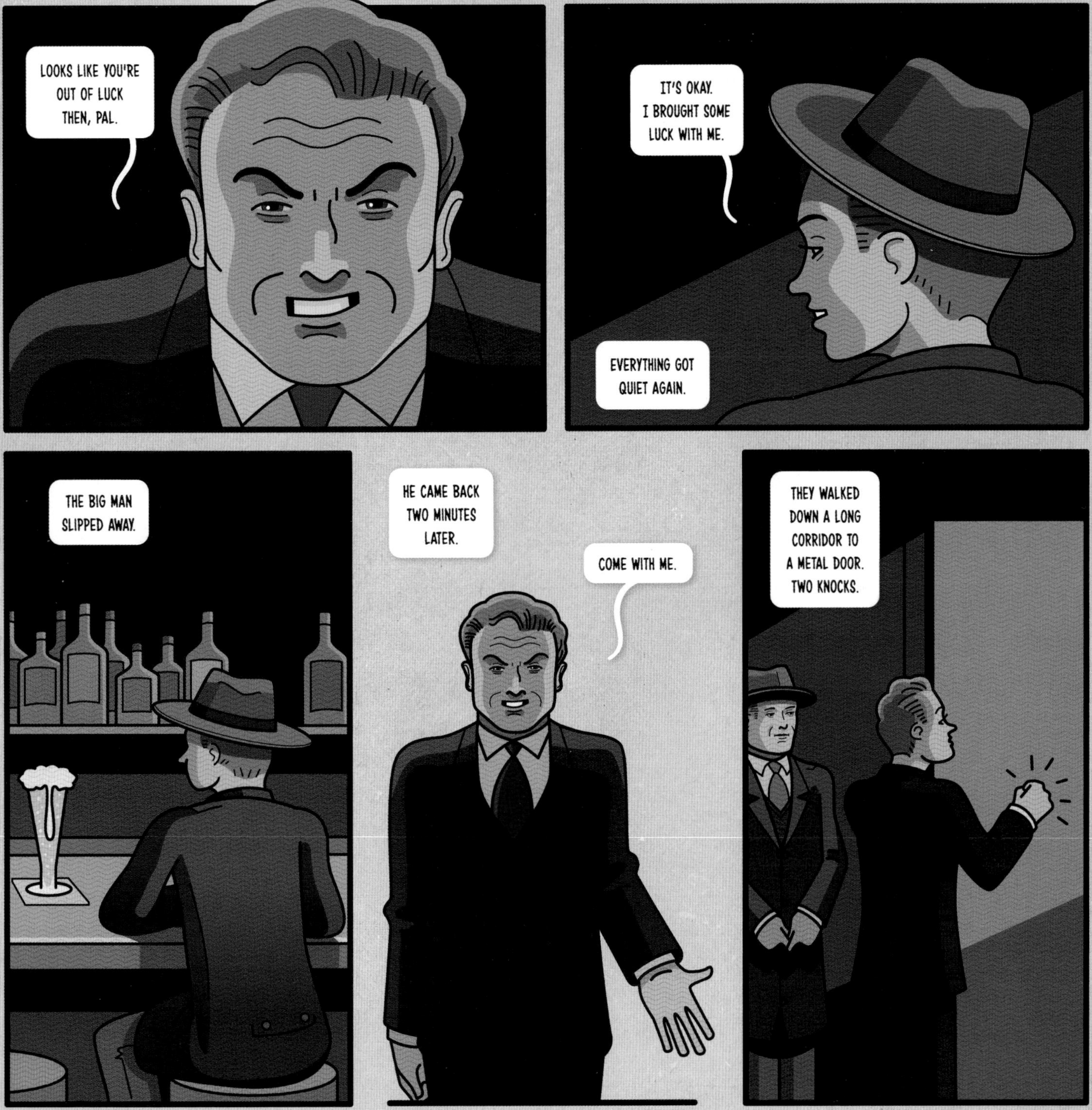
LOOKS LIKE YOU'RE OUT OF LUCK THEN, PAL.
IT'S OKAY. I BROUGHT SOME LUCK WITH ME.
EVERYTHING GOT QUIET AGAIN.
THE BIG MAN SLIPPED AWAY.
HE CAME BACK TWO MINUTES LATER.
COME WITH ME.
THEY WALKED DOWN A LONG CORRIDOR TO A METAL DOOR. TWO KNOCKS.

THE ROOM WAS SMALL WITH A SINGLE LIGHT.

A MAN SAT AT A FELT-COVERED TABLE. SILENT.

THERE WERE NO OTHER CHAIRS ON WHICH TO SIT, SO HE PUT THE GLASS VIAL ON TOP OF THE TABLE, AND TOOK A STEP BACK.

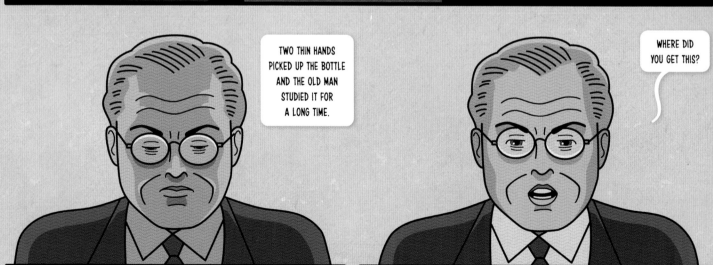

TWO THIN HANDS PICKED UP THE BOTTLE AND THE OLD MAN STUDIED IT FOR A LONG TIME.

WHERE DID YOU GET THIS?

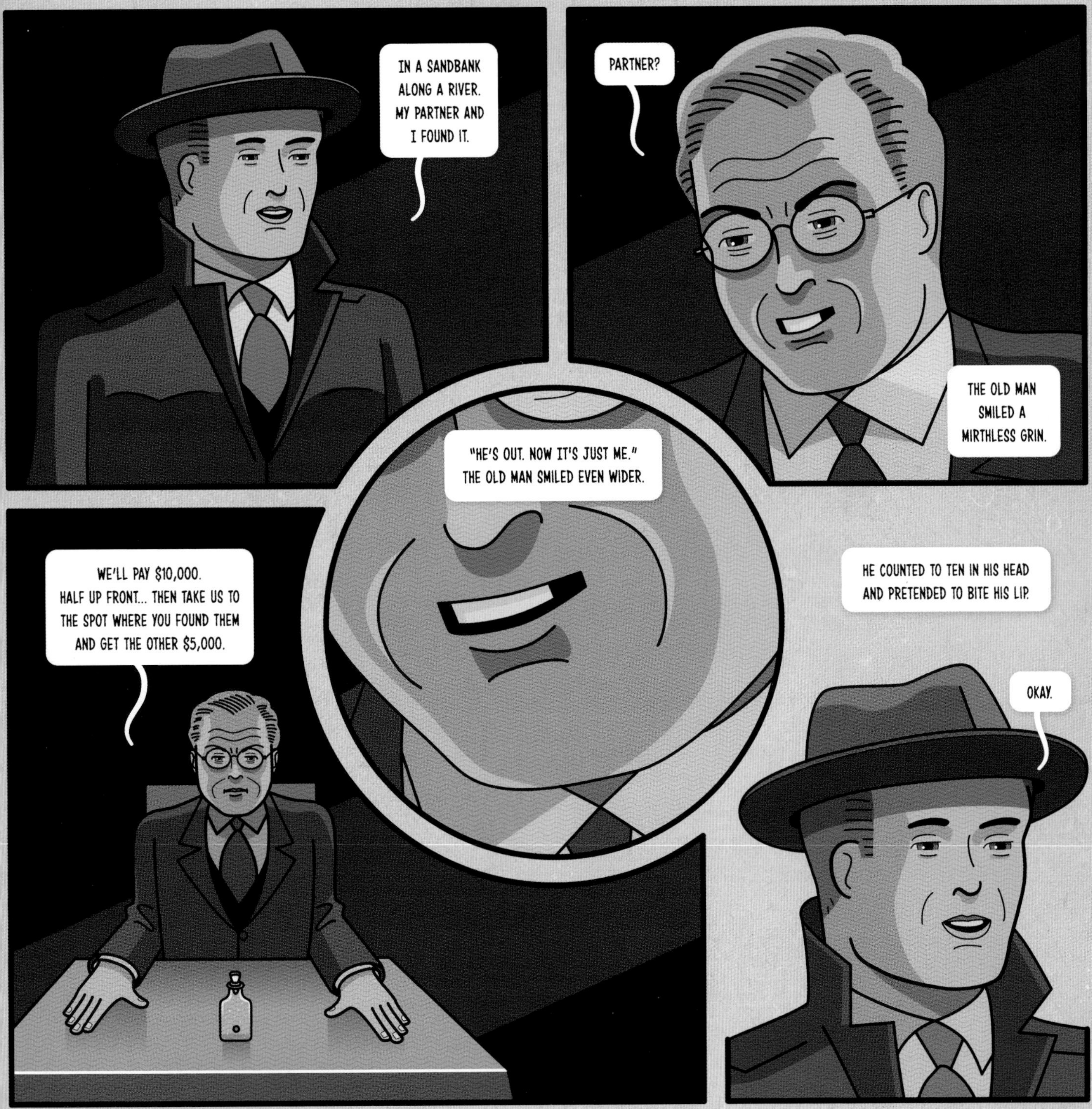
IN A SANDBANK ALONG A RIVER. MY PARTNER AND I FOUND IT.
PARTNER?
THE OLD MAN SMILED A MIRTHLESS GRIN.
"HE'S OUT. NOW IT'S JUST ME." THE OLD MAN SMILED EVEN WIDER.
WE'LL PAY $10,000. HALF UP FRONT... THEN TAKE US TO THE SPOT WHERE YOU FOUND THEM AND GET THE OTHER $5,000.
HE COUNTED TO TEN IN HIS HEAD AND PRETENDED TO BITE HIS LIP.
OKAY.

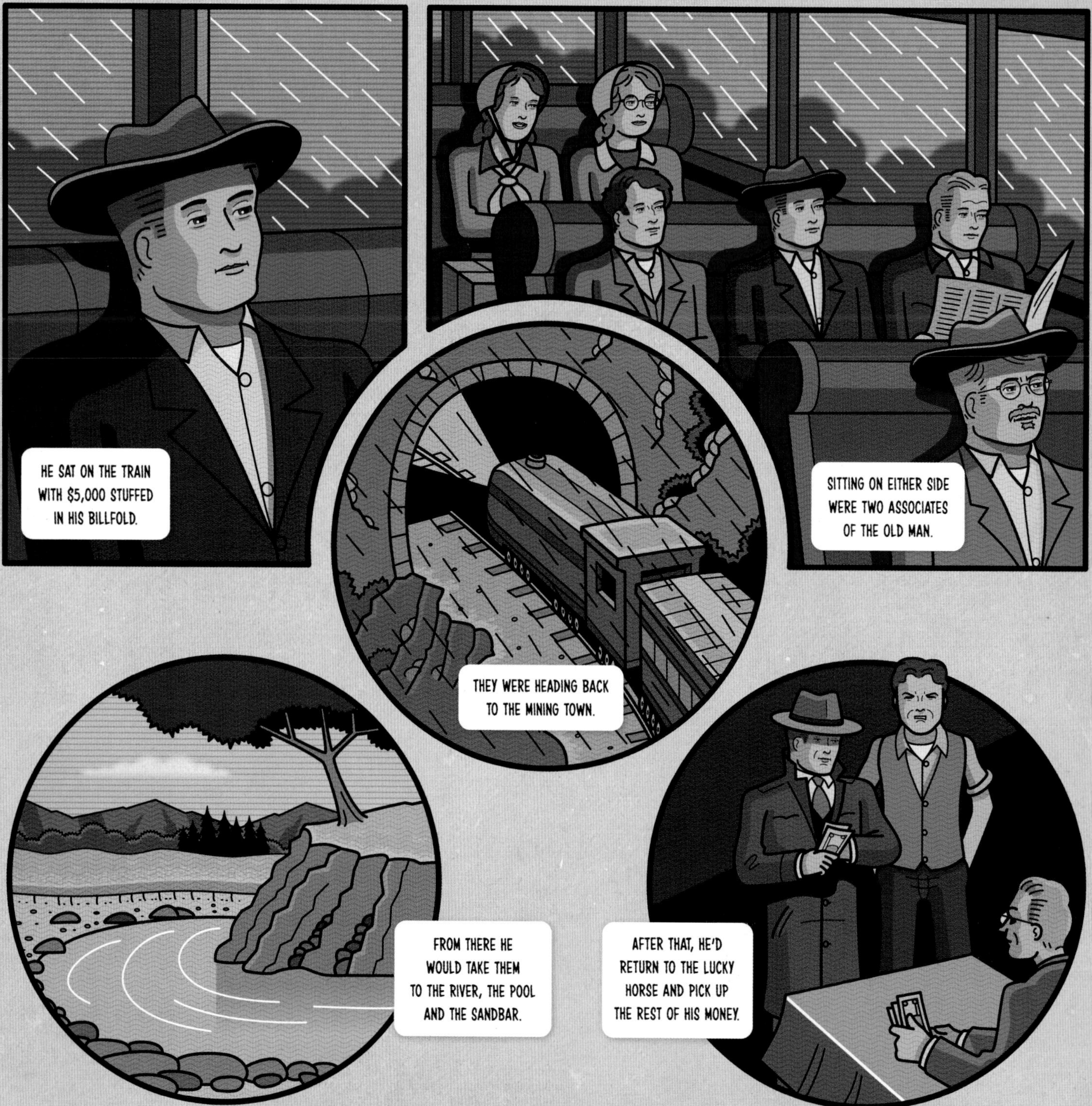
HE SAT ON THE TRAIN WITH $5,000 STUFFED IN HIS BILLFOLD.
SITTING ON EITHER SIDE WERE TWO ASSOCIATES OF THE OLD MAN.
THEY WERE HEADING BACK TO THE MINING TOWN.
FROM THERE HE WOULD TAKE THEM TO THE RIVER, THE POOL AND THE SANDBAR.
AFTER THAT, HE'D RETURN TO THE LUCKY HORSE AND PICK UP THE REST OF HIS MONEY.

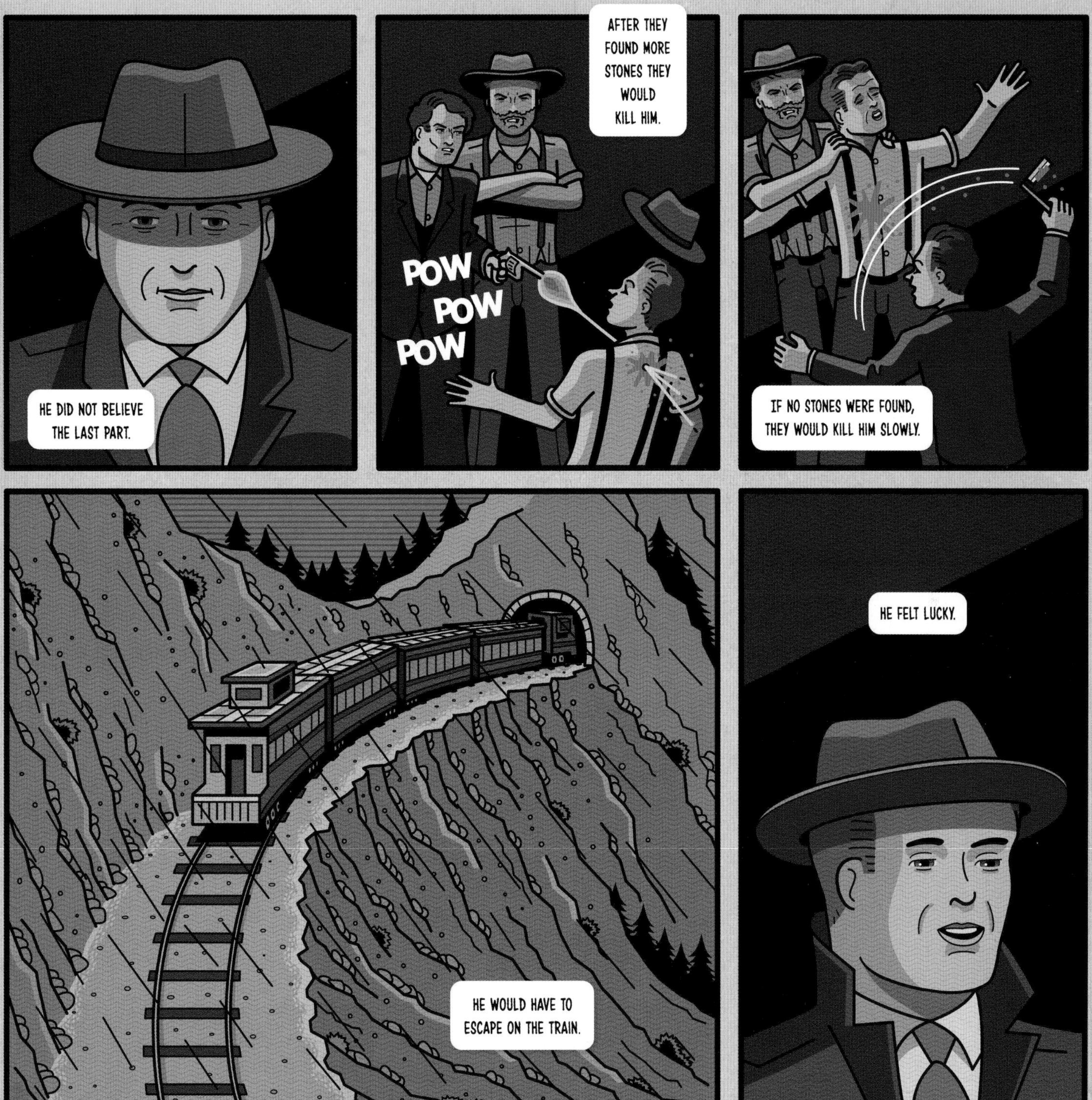
HE DID NOT BELIEVE THE LAST PART.
AFTER THEY FOUND MORE STONES THEY WOULD KILL HIM.
POW
POW
POW
IF NO STONES WERE FOUND, THEY WOULD KILL HIM SLOWLY.
HE WOULD HAVE TO ESCAPE ON THE TRAIN.
HE FELT LUCKY.

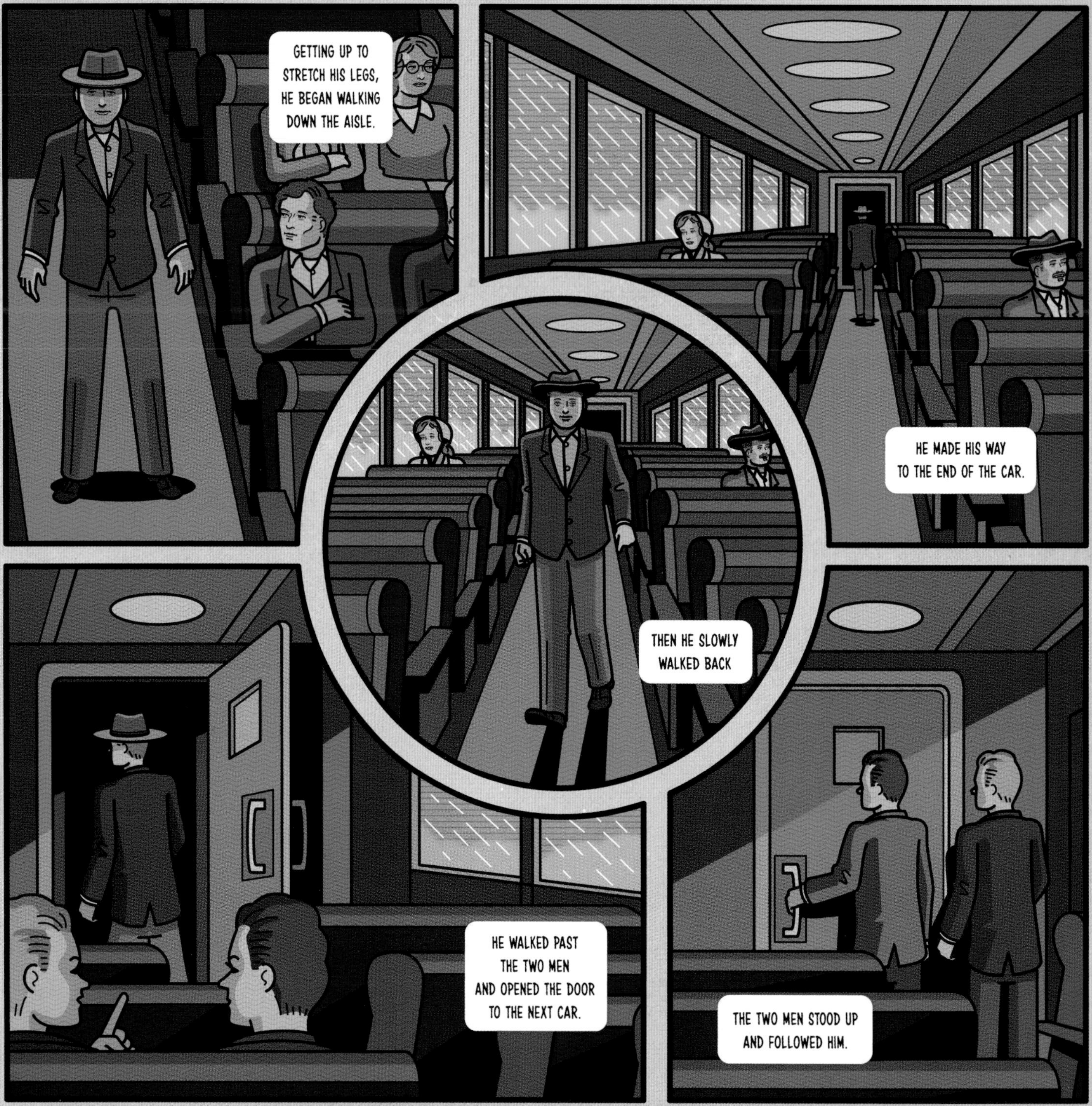
GETTING UP TO STRETCH HIS LEGS, HE BEGAN WALKING DOWN THE AISLE.
HE MADE HIS WAY TO THE END OF THE CAR.
THEN HE SLOWLY WALKED BACK
HE WALKED PAST THE TWO MEN AND OPENED THE DOOR TO THE NEXT CAR.
THE TWO MEN STOOD UP AND FOLLOWED HIM.

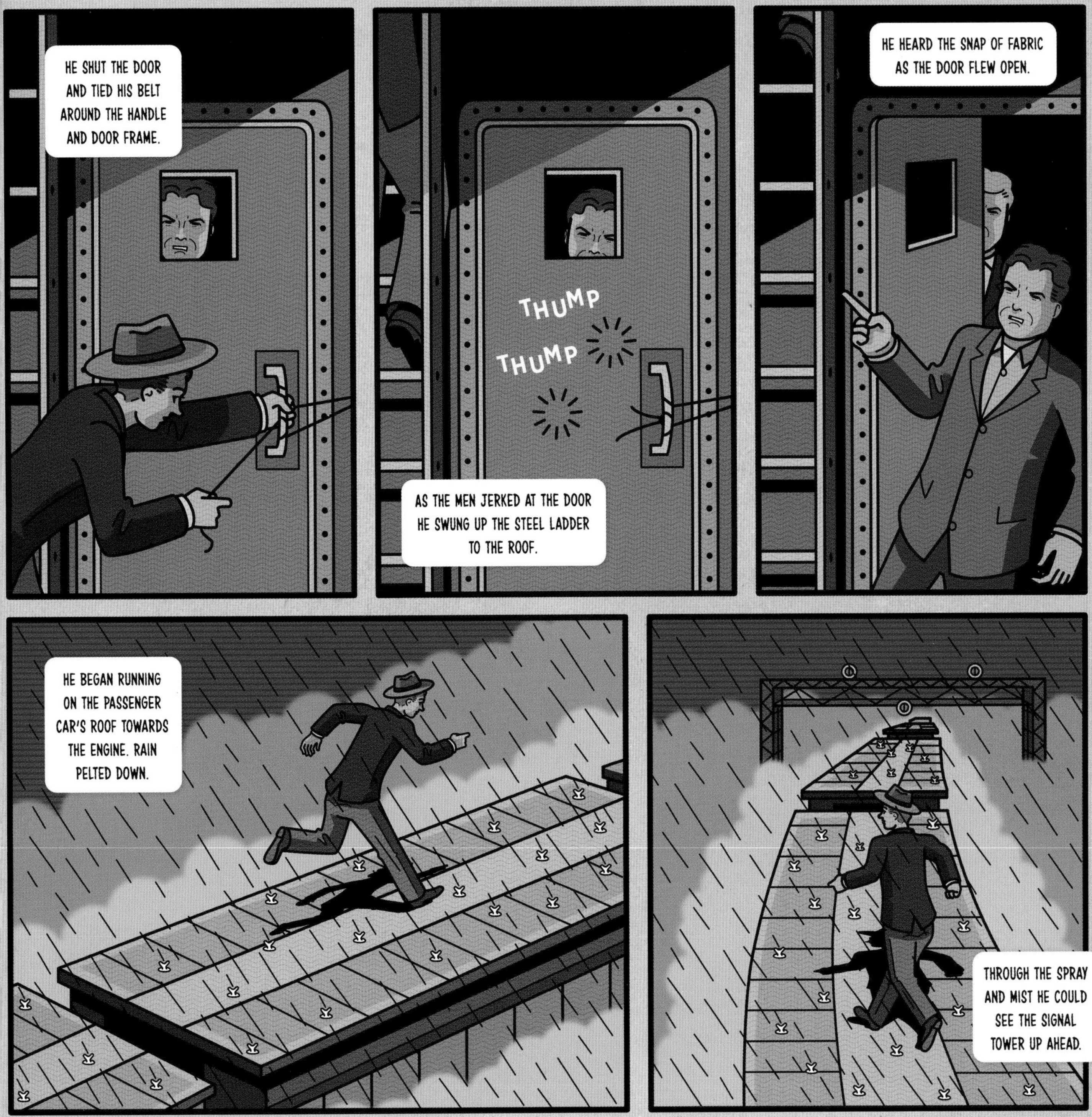
HE SHUT THE DOOR AND TIED HIS BELT AROUND THE HANDLE AND DOOR FRAME.
THUMP
THUMP
AS THE MEN JERKED AT THE DOOR HE SWUNG UP THE STEEL LADDER TO THE ROOF.
HE HEARD THE SNAP OF FABRIC AS THE DOOR FLEW OPEN.
HE BEGAN RUNNING ON THE PASSENGER CAR'S ROOF TOWARDS THE ENGINE. RAIN PELTED DOWN.
THROUGH THE SPRAY AND MIST HE COULD SEE THE SIGNAL TOWER UP AHEAD.

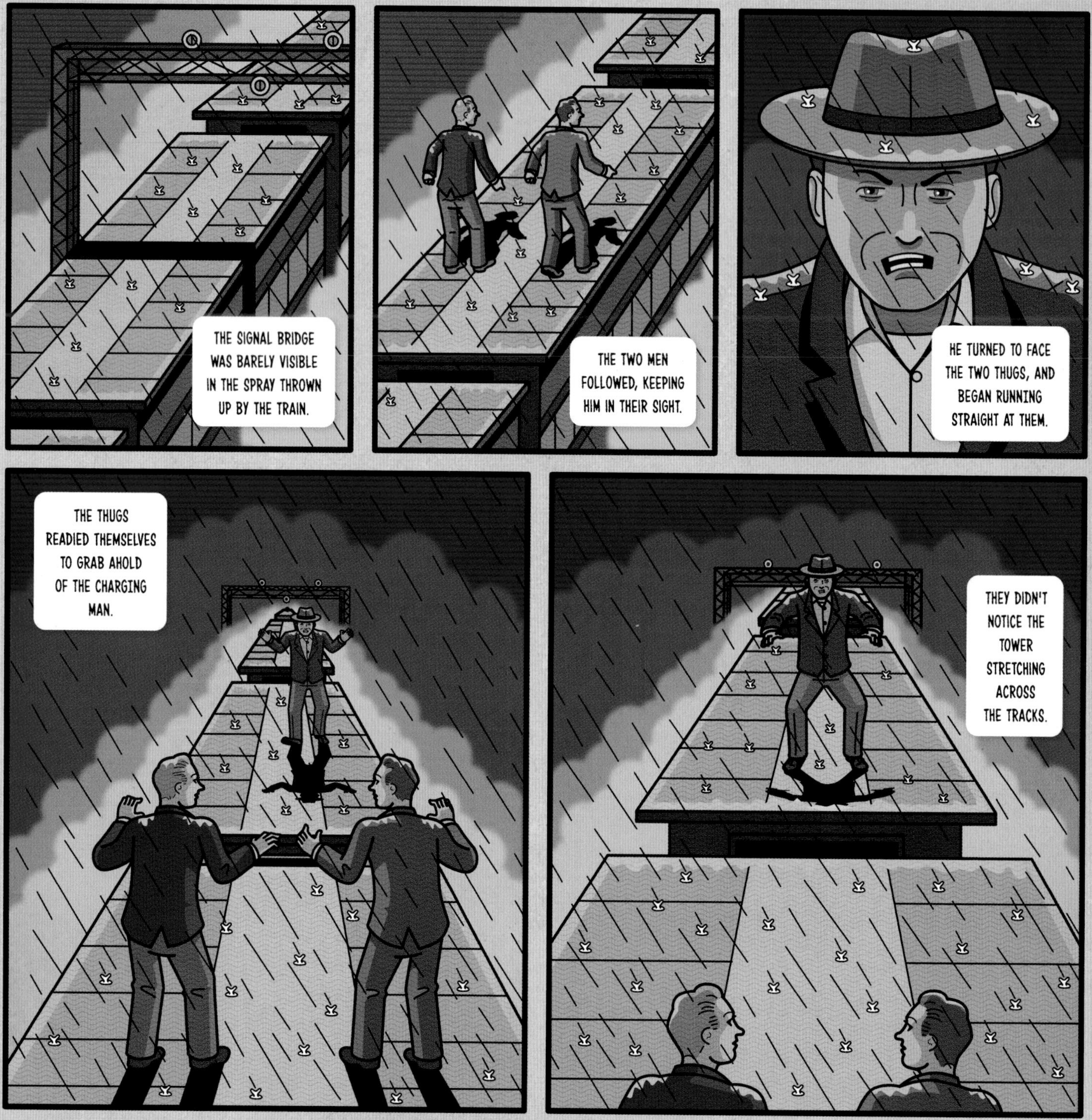
THE SIGNAL BRIDGE WAS BARELY VISIBLE IN THE SPRAY THROWN UP BY THE TRAIN.
THE TWO MEN FOLLOWED, KEEPING HIM IN THEIR SIGHT.
HE TURNED TO FACE THE TWO THUGS, AND BEGAN RUNNING STRAIGHT AT THEM.
THE THUGS READIED THEMSELVES TO GRAB AHOLD OF THE CHARGING MAN.
THEY DIDN'T NOTICE THE TOWER STRETCHING ACROSS THE TRACKS.

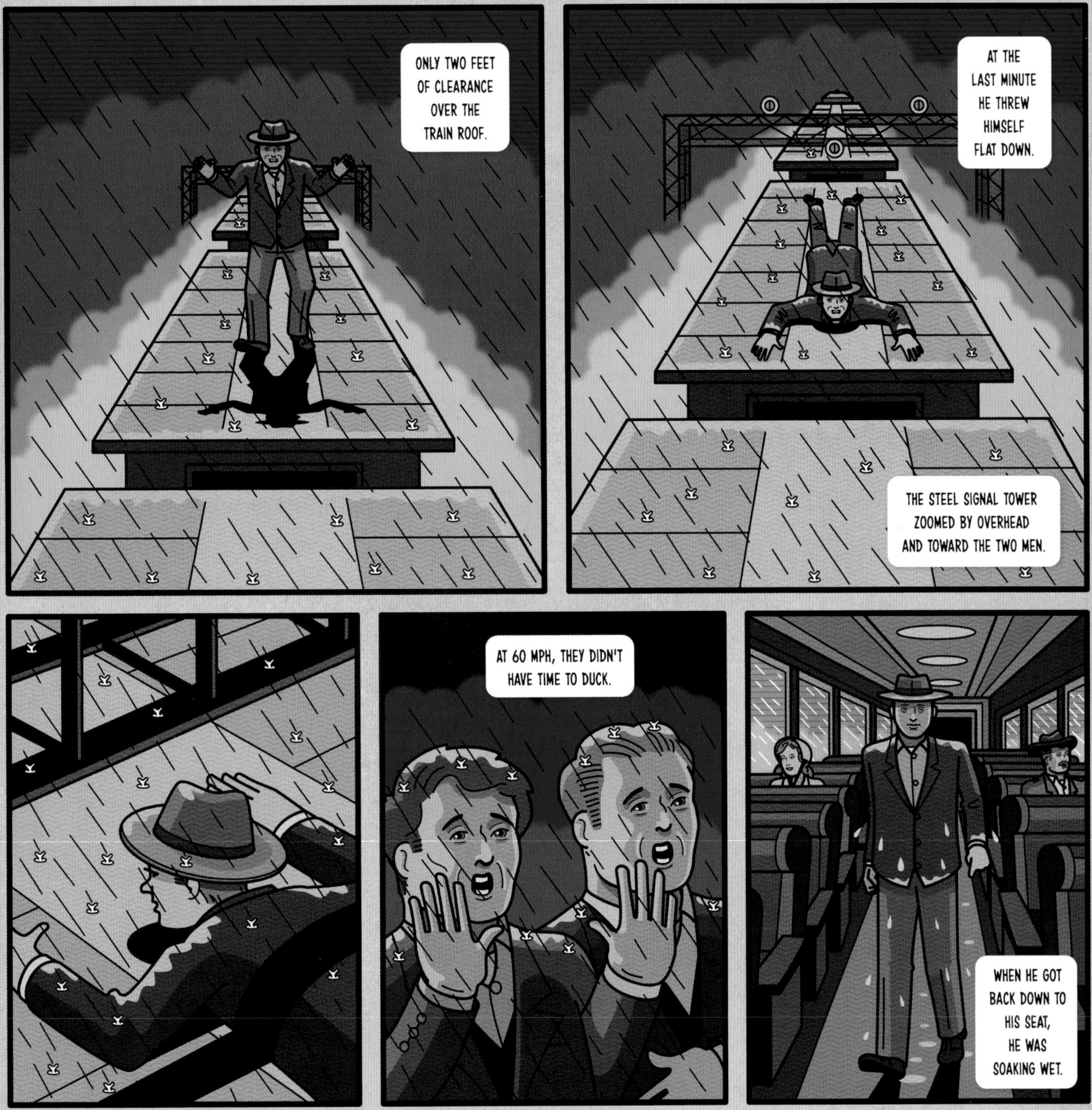
ONLY TWO FEET OF CLEARANCE OVER THE TRAIN ROOF.
AT THE LAST MINUTE HE THREW HIMSELF FLAT DOWN.
THE STEEL SIGNAL TOWER ZOOMED BY OVERHEAD AND TOWARD THE TWO MEN.
AT 60 MPH, THEY DIDN'T HAVE TIME TO DUCK.
WHEN HE GOT BACK DOWN TO HIS SEAT, HE WAS SOAKING WET.

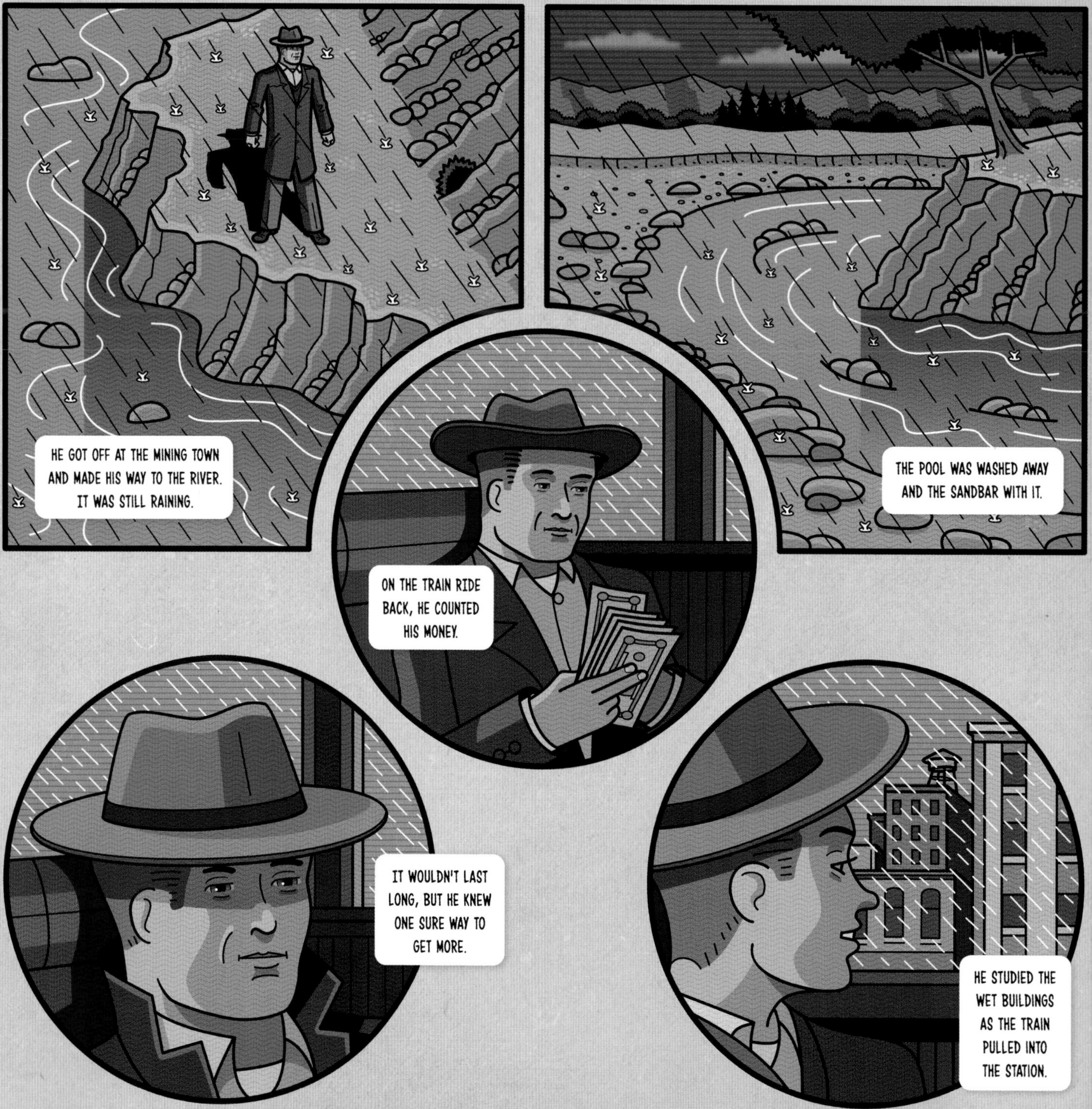
HE GOT OFF AT THE MINING TOWN AND MADE HIS WAY TO THE RIVER. IT WAS STILL RAINING.
THE POOL WAS WASHED AWAY AND THE SANDBAR WITH IT.
ON THE TRAIN RIDE BACK, HE COUNTED HIS MONEY.
IT WOULDN'T LAST LONG, BUT HE KNEW ONE SURE WAY TO GET MORE.
HE STUDIED THE WET BUILDINGS AS THE TRAIN PULLED INTO THE STATION.

CHAPTER 10

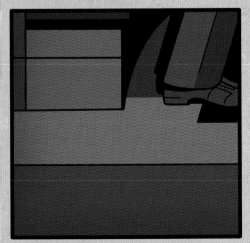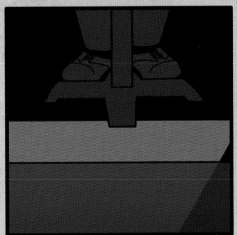

HE MADE HIS WAY TO THE BACK OF THE CAFE AND SAT DOWN AT THE BANQUETTE WITH HIS FATHER.

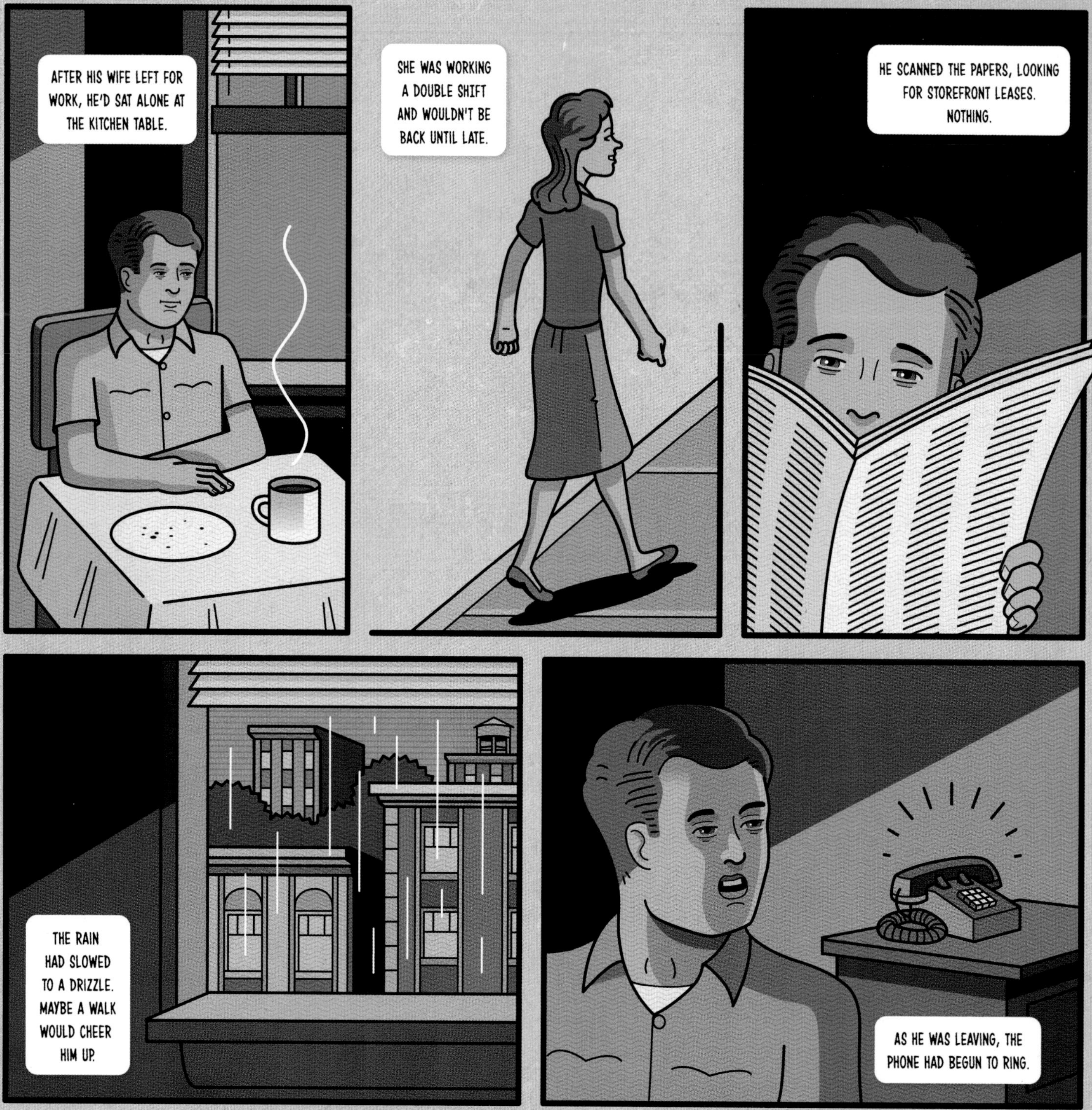
AFTER HIS WIFE LEFT FOR WORK, HE'D SAT ALONE AT THE KITCHEN TABLE.
SHE WAS WORKING A DOUBLE SHIFT AND WOULDN'T BE BACK UNTIL LATE.
HE SCANNED THE PAPERS, LOOKING FOR STOREFRONT LEASES. NOTHING.
THE RAIN HAD SLOWED TO A DRIZZLE. MAYBE A WALK WOULD CHEER HIM UP.
AS HE WAS LEAVING, THE PHONE HAD BEGUN TO RING.

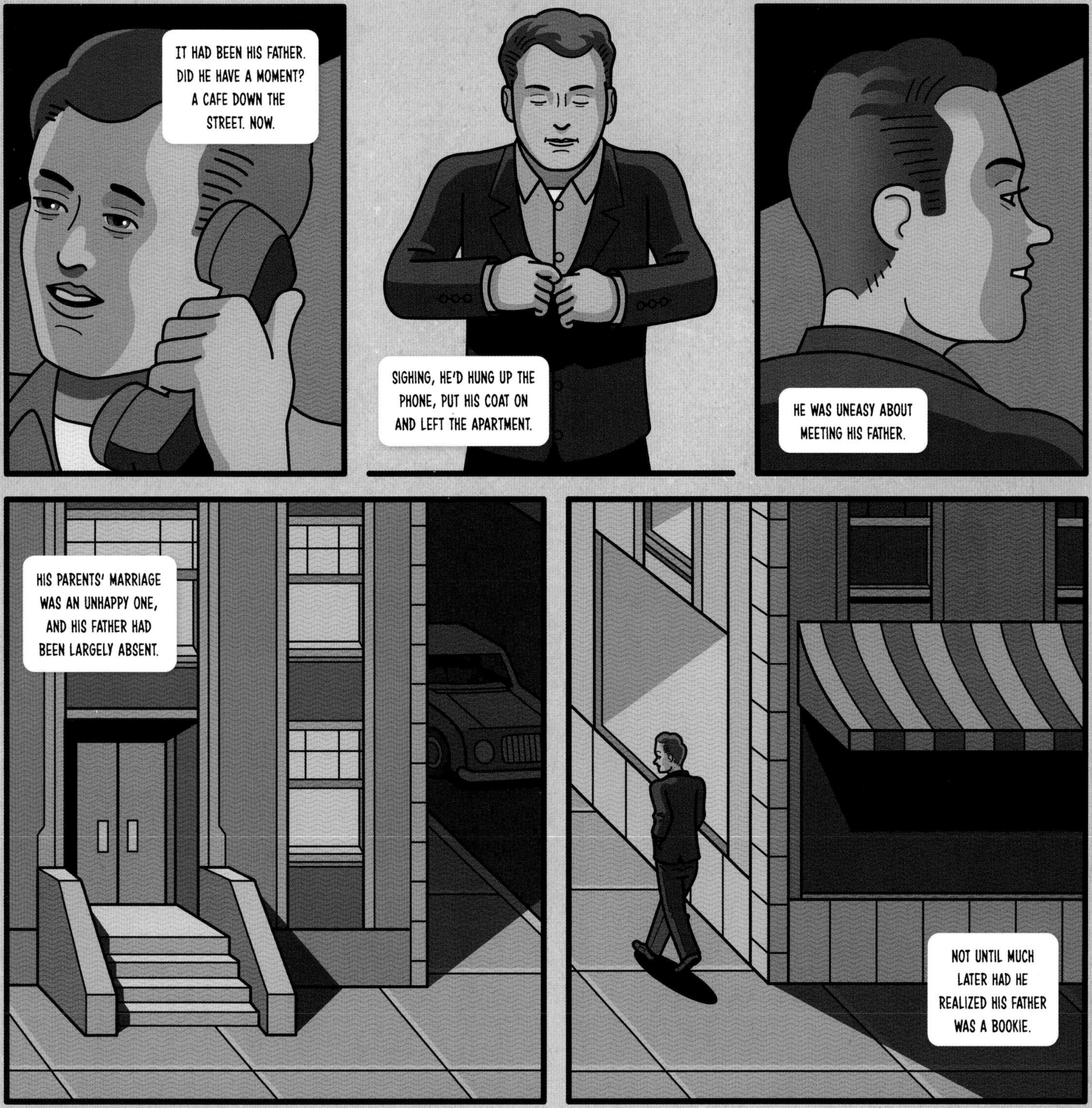
IT HAD BEEN HIS FATHER. DID HE HAVE A MOMENT? A CAFE DOWN THE STREET. NOW.
SIGHING, HE'D HUNG UP THE PHONE, PUT HIS COAT ON AND LEFT THE APARTMENT.
HE WAS UNEASY ABOUT MEETING HIS FATHER.
HIS PARENTS' MARRIAGE WAS AN UNHAPPY ONE, AND HIS FATHER HAD BEEN LARGELY ABSENT.
NOT UNTIL MUCH LATER HAD HE REALIZED HIS FATHER WAS A BOOKIE.

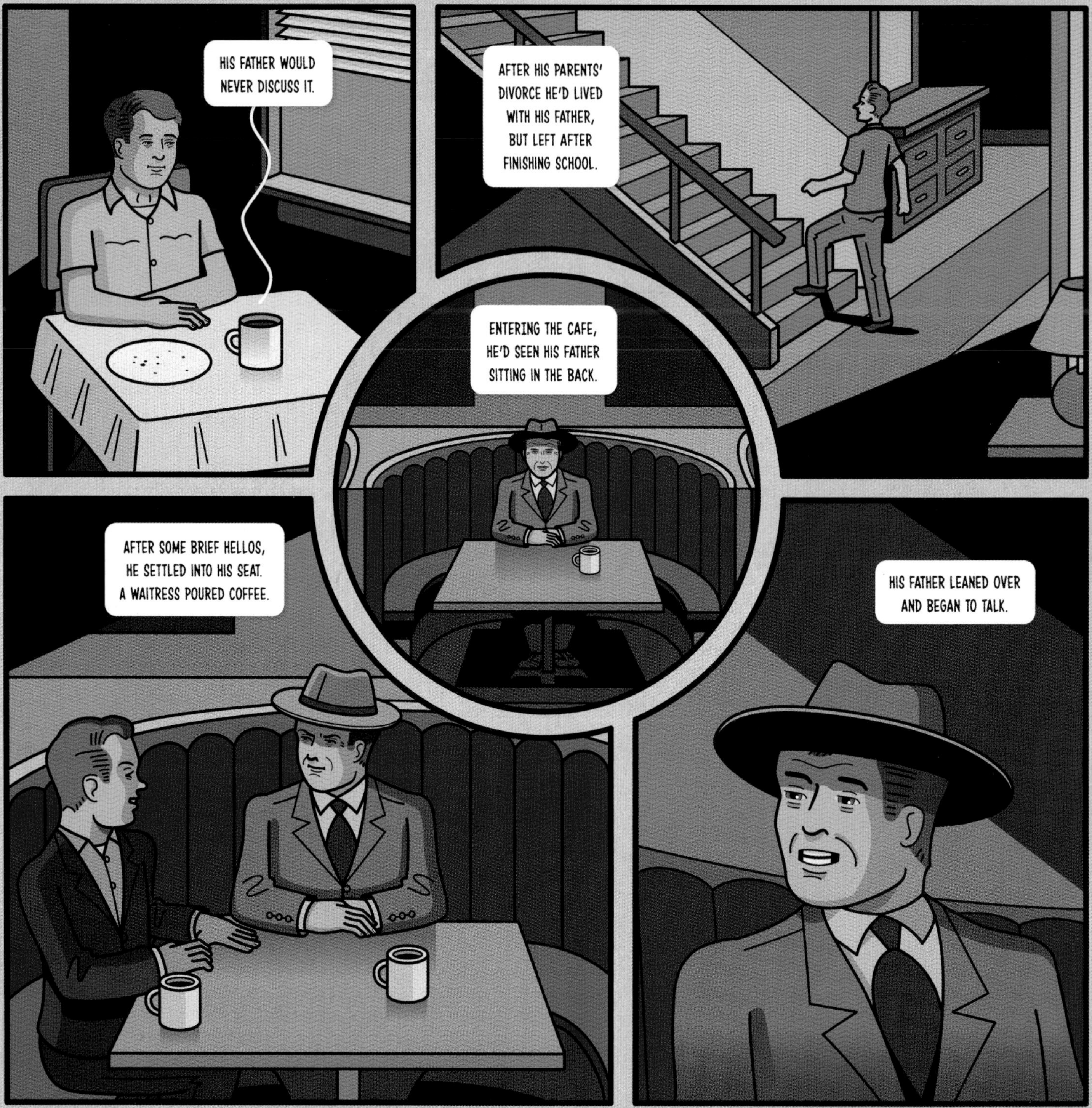
HIS FATHER WOULD NEVER DISCUSS IT.
AFTER HIS PARENTS' DIVORCE HE'D LIVED WITH HIS FATHER, BUT LEFT AFTER FINISHING SCHOOL.
ENTERING THE CAFE, HE'D SEEN HIS FATHER SITTING IN THE BACK.
AFTER SOME BRIEF HELLOS, HE SETTLED INTO HIS SEAT. A WAITRESS POURED COFFEE.
HIS FATHER LEANED OVER AND BEGAN TO TALK.

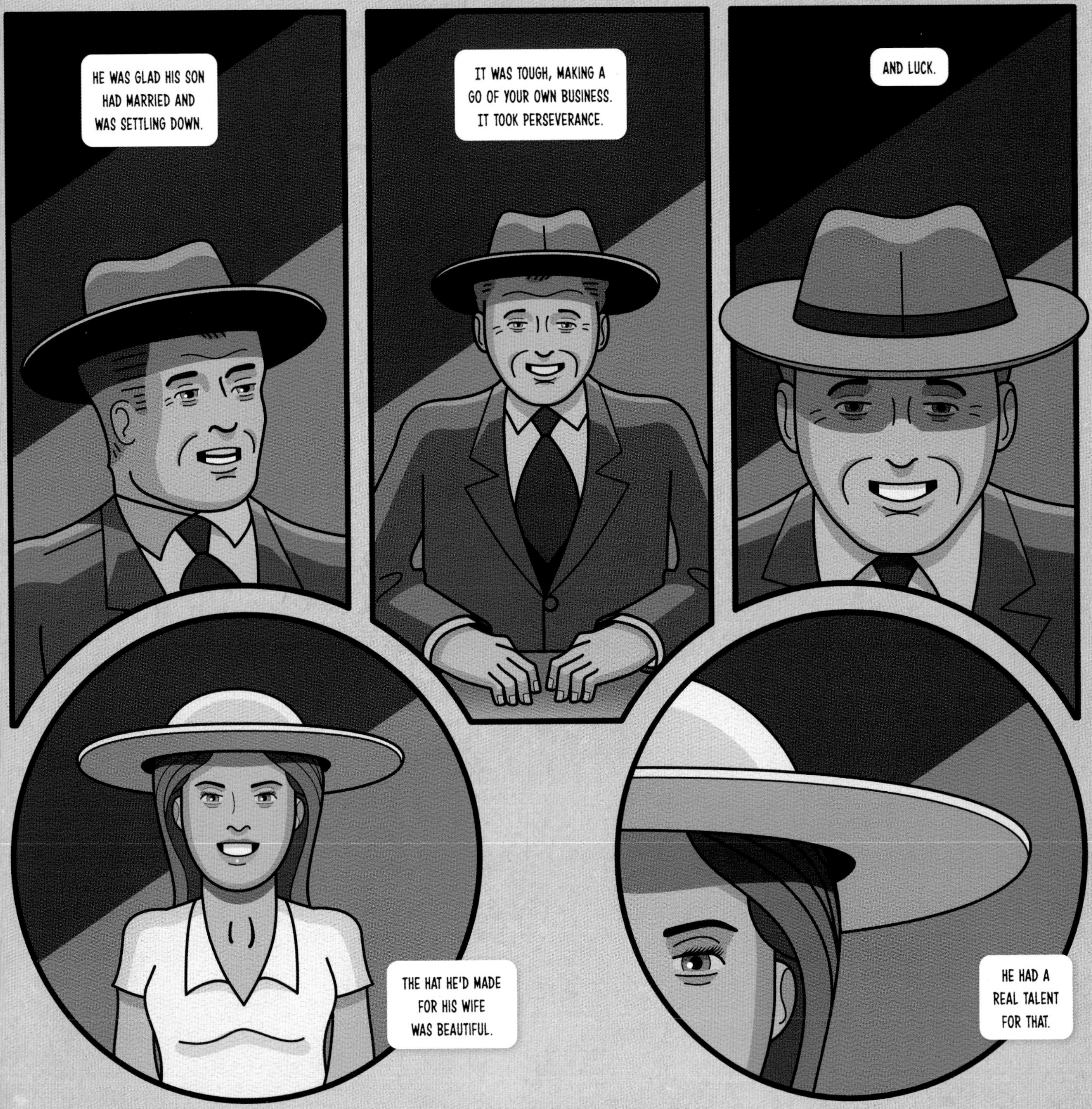
HE WAS GLAD HIS SON HAD MARRIED AND WAS SETTLING DOWN.
IT WAS TOUGH, MAKING A GO OF YOUR OWN BUSINESS. IT TOOK PERSEVERANCE.
AND LUCK.
THE HAT HE'D MADE FOR HIS WIFE WAS BEAUTIFUL.
HE HAD A REAL TALENT FOR THAT.

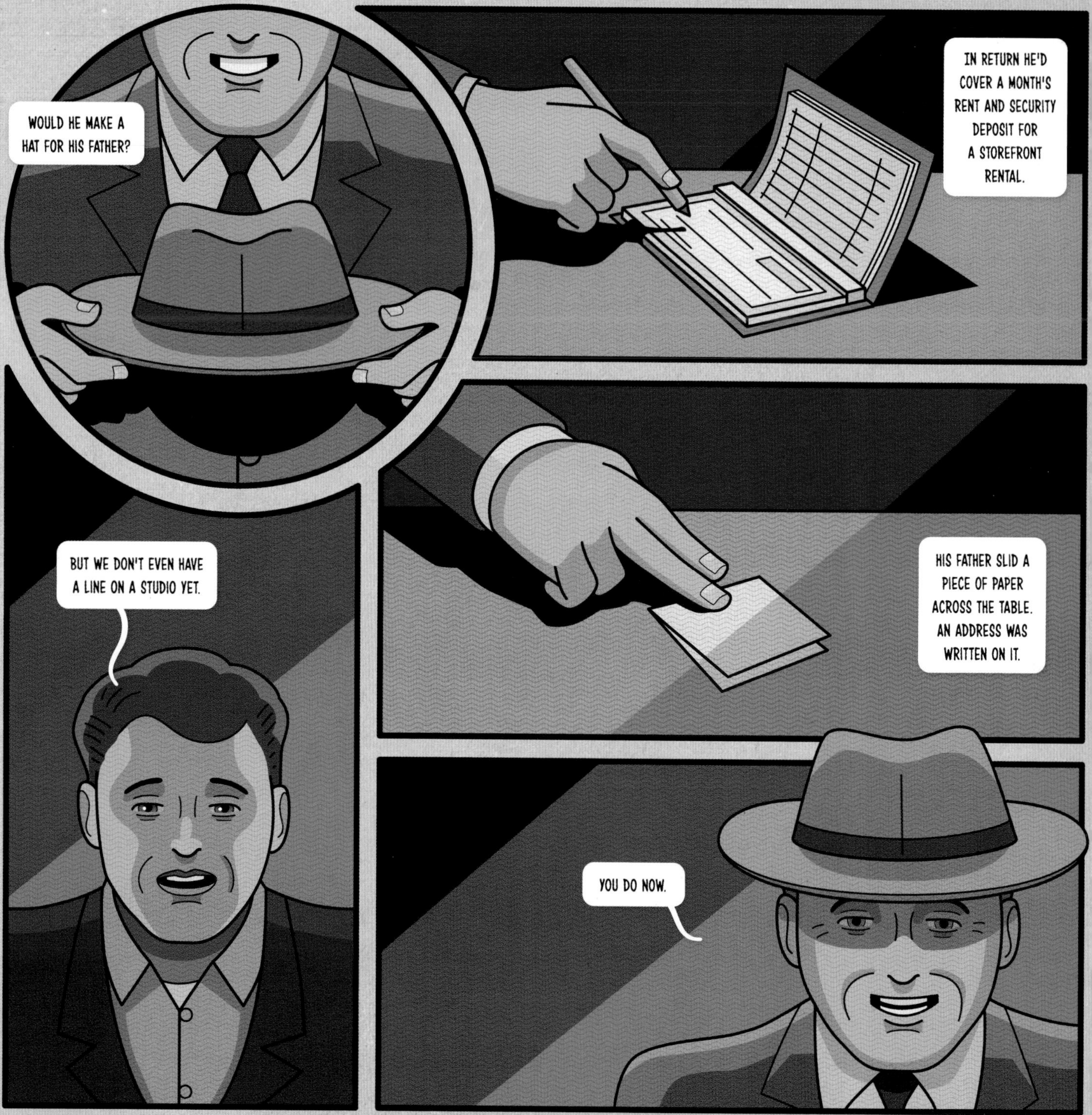
WOULD HE MAKE A HAT FOR HIS FATHER?
IN RETURN HE'D COVER A MONTH'S RENT AND SECURITY DEPOSIT FOR A STOREFRONT RENTAL.
BUT WE DON'T EVEN HAVE A LINE ON A STUDIO YET.
HIS FATHER SLID A PIECE OF PAPER ACROSS THE TABLE. AN ADDRESS WAS WRITTEN ON IT.
YOU DO NOW.

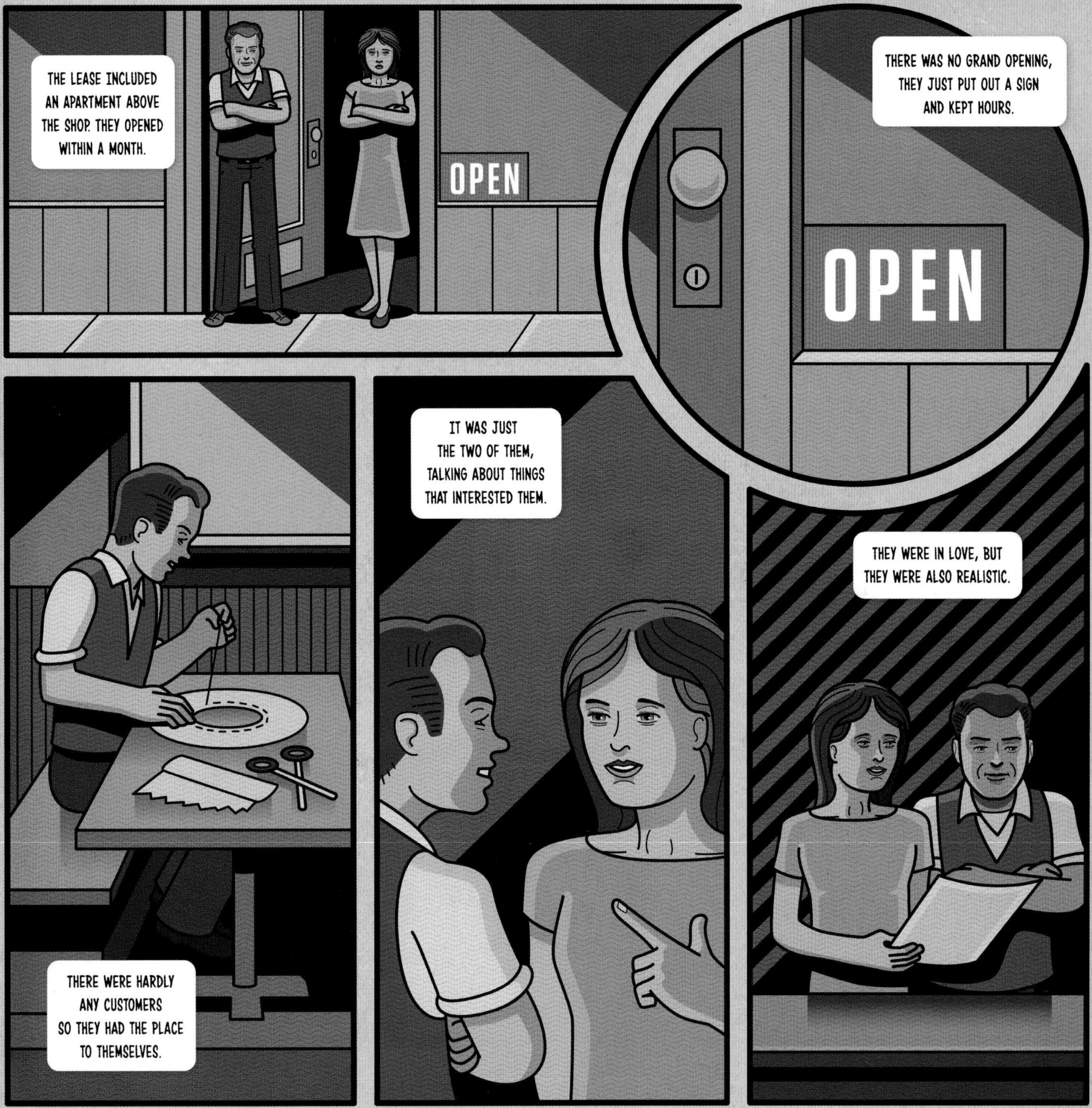
THE LEASE INCLUDED AN APARTMENT ABOVE THE SHOP. THEY OPENED WITHIN A MONTH.
OPEN
THERE WAS NO GRAND OPENING, THEY JUST PUT OUT A SIGN AND KEPT HOURS.
OPEN
THERE WERE HARDLY ANY CUSTOMERS SO THEY HAD THE PLACE TO THEMSELVES.
IT WAS JUST THE TWO OF THEM, TALKING ABOUT THINGS THAT INTERESTED THEM.
THEY WERE IN LOVE, BUT THEY WERE ALSO REALISTIC.

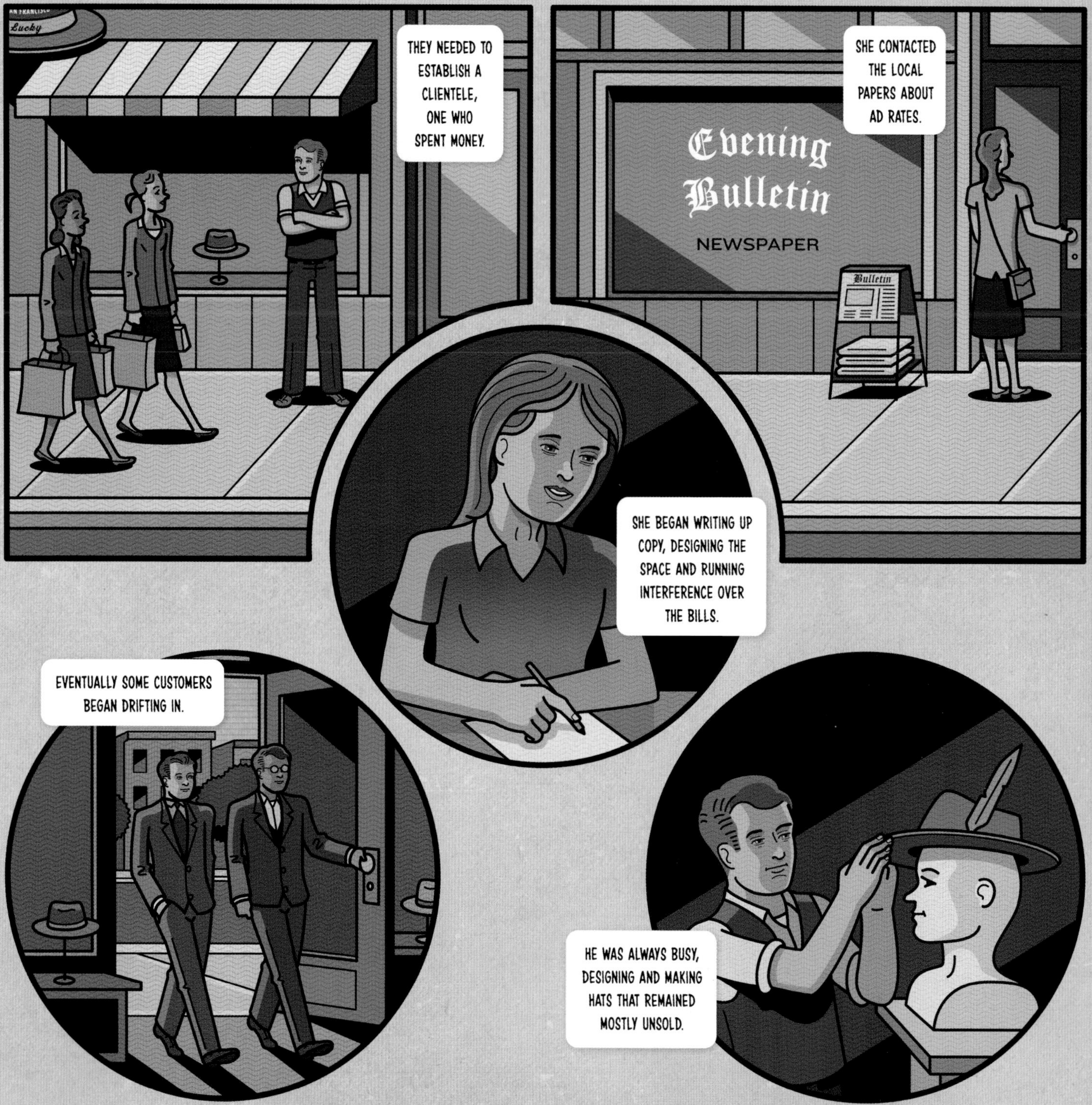
Lucky
THEY NEEDED TO ESTABLISH A CLIENTELE, ONE WHO SPENT MONEY.
Evening Bulletin
NEWSPAPER
Bulletin
SHE CONTACTED THE LOCAL PAPERS ABOUT AD RATES.
SHE BEGAN WRITING UP COPY, DESIGNING THE SPACE AND RUNNING INTERFERENCE OVER THE BILLS.
EVENTUALLY SOME CUSTOMERS BEGAN DRIFTING IN.
HE WAS ALWAYS BUSY, DESIGNING AND MAKING HATS THAT REMAINED MOSTLY UNSOLD.

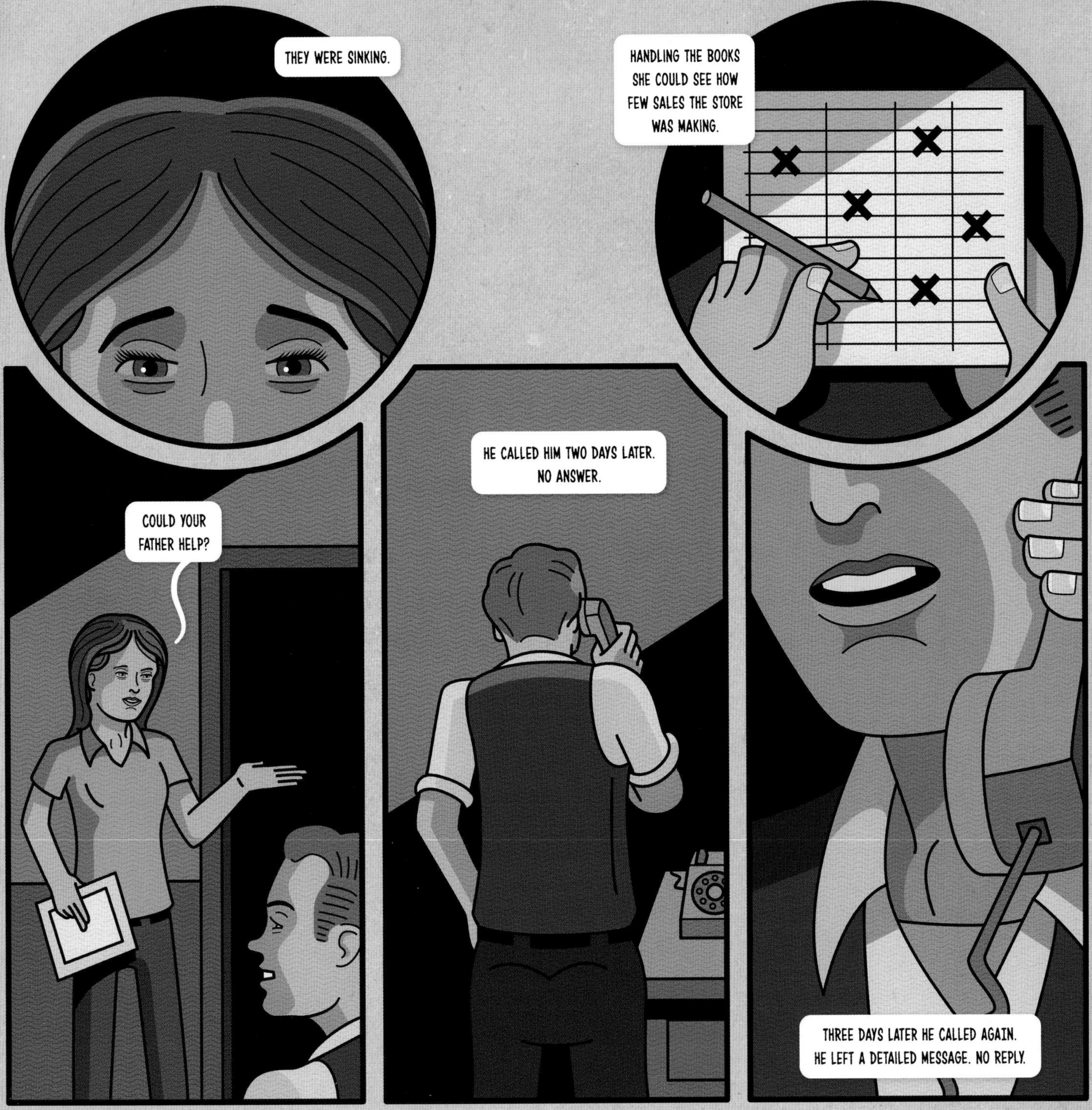
THEY WERE SINKING.
HANDLING THE BOOKS SHE COULD SEE HOW FEW SALES THE STORE WAS MAKING.
COULD YOUR FATHER HELP?
HE CALLED HIM TWO DAYS LATER. NO ANSWER.
THREE DAYS LATER HE CALLED AGAIN. HE LEFT A DETAILED MESSAGE. NO REPLY.

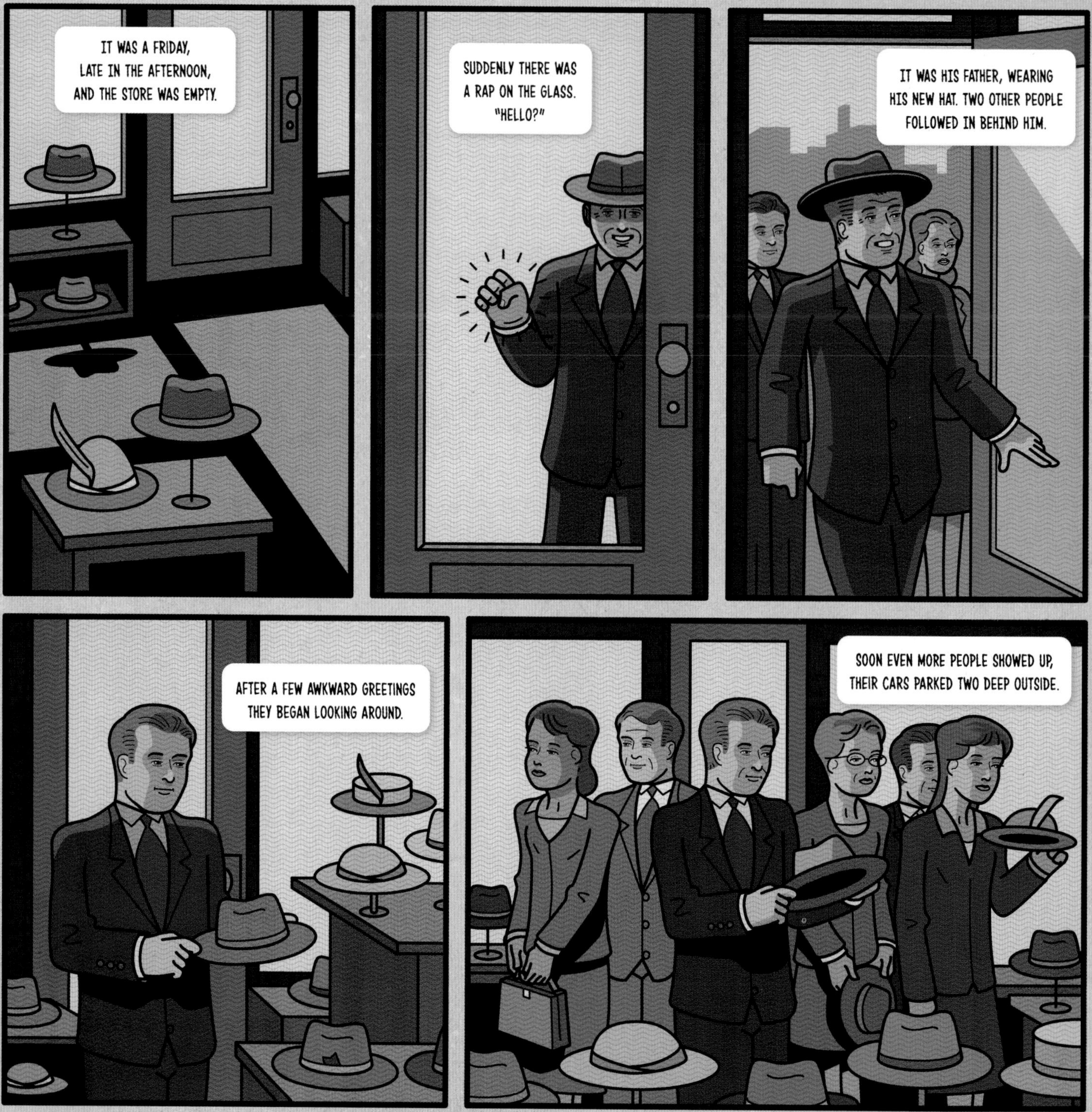
IT WAS A FRIDAY, LATE IN THE AFTERNOON, AND THE STORE WAS EMPTY.
SUDDENLY THERE WAS A RAP ON THE GLASS. "HELLO?"
IT WAS HIS FATHER, WEARING HIS NEW HAT. TWO OTHER PEOPLE FOLLOWED IN BEHIND HIM.
AFTER A FEW AWKWARD GREETINGS THEY BEGAN LOOKING AROUND.
SOON EVEN MORE PEOPLE SHOWED UP, THEIR CARS PARKED TWO DEEP OUTSIDE.

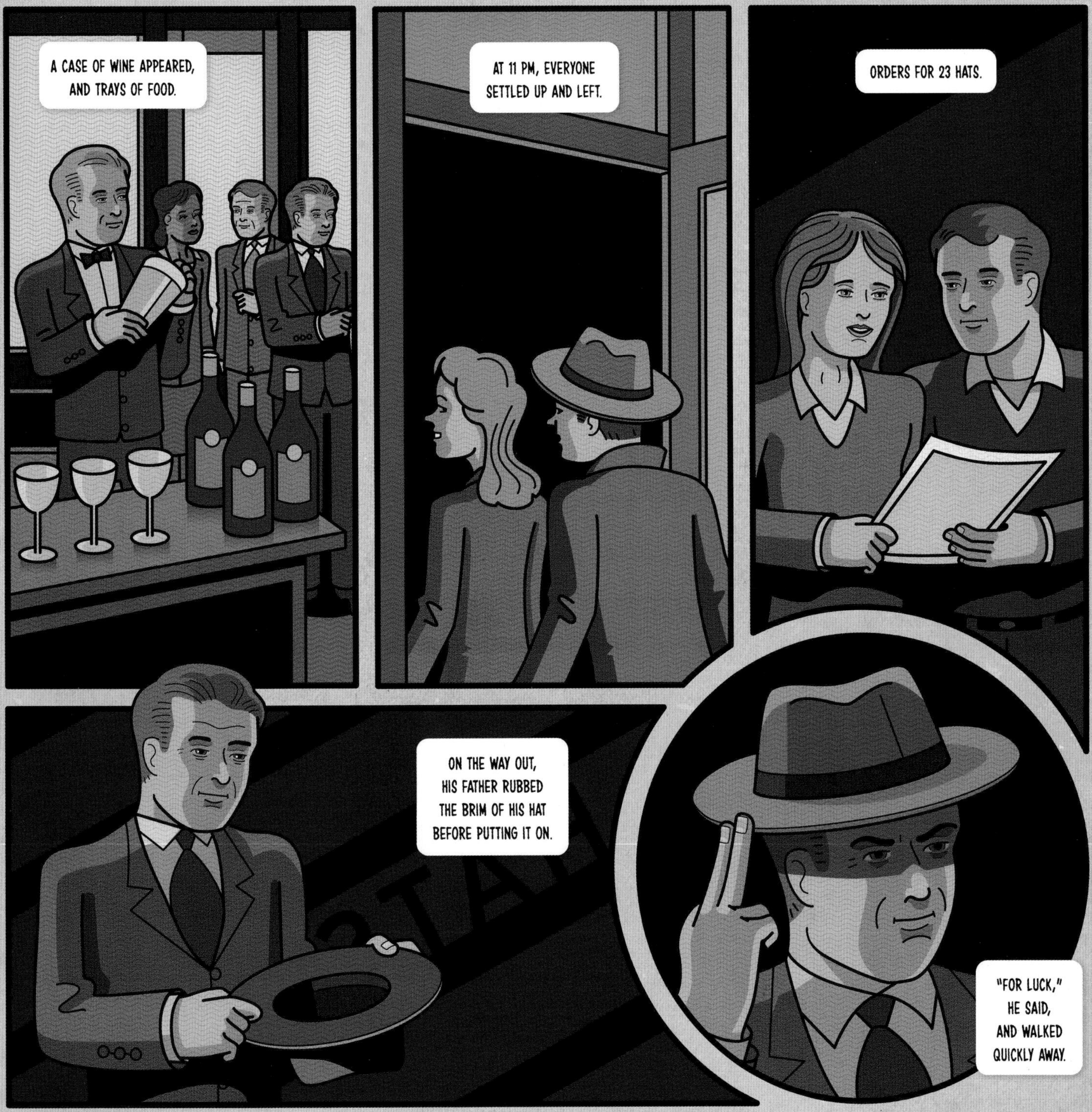
A CASE OF WINE APPEARED, AND TRAYS OF FOOD.
AT 11 PM, EVERYONE SETTLED UP AND LEFT.
ORDERS FOR 23 HATS.
ON THE WAY OUT, HIS FATHER RUBBED THE BRIM OF HIS HAT BEFORE PUTTING IT ON.
"FOR LUCK," HE SAID, AND WALKED QUICKLY AWAY.

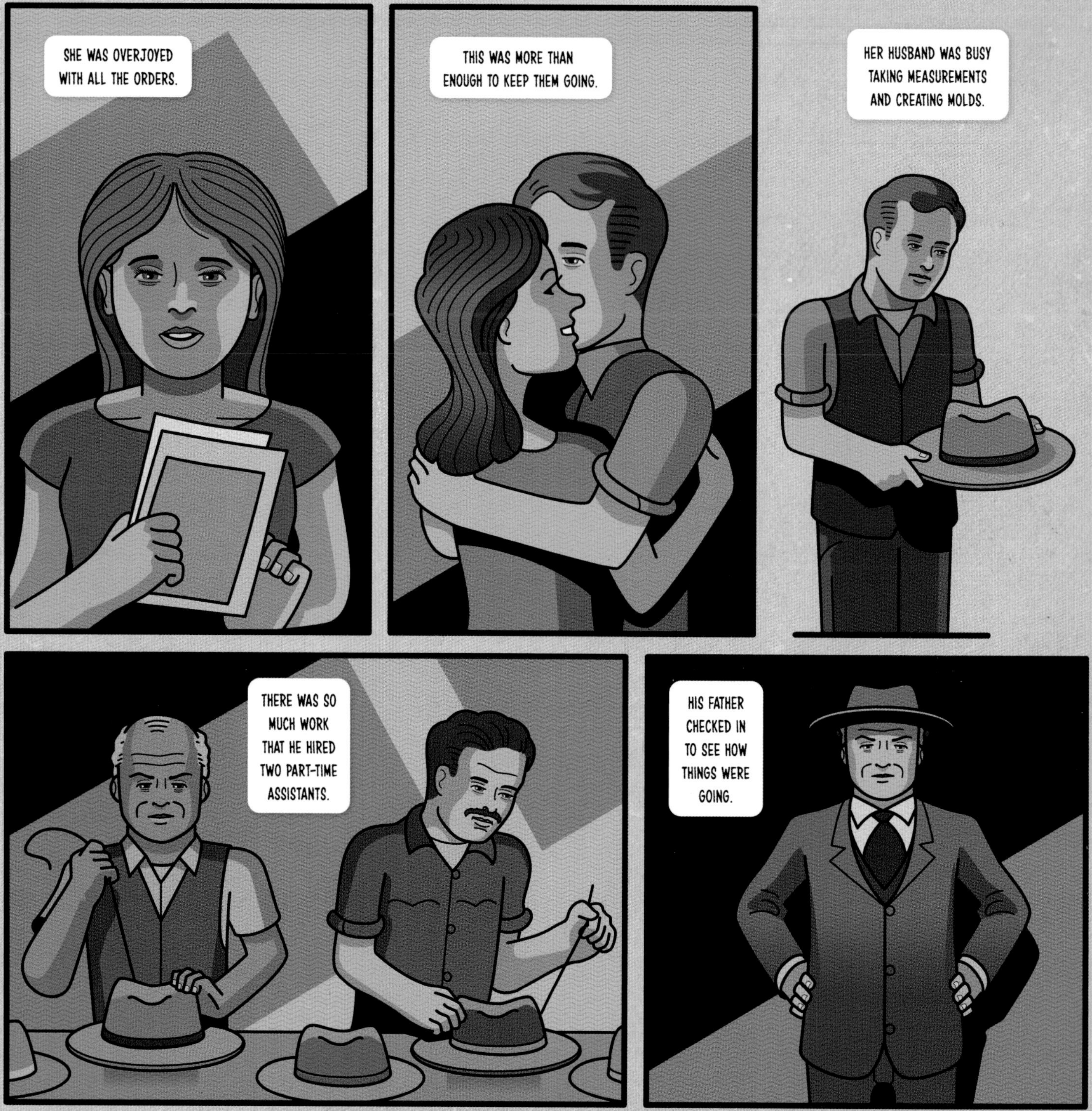
SHE WAS OVERJOYED WITH ALL THE ORDERS.
THIS WAS MORE THAN ENOUGH TO KEEP THEM GOING.
HER HUSBAND WAS BUSY TAKING MEASUREMENTS AND CREATING MOLDS.
THERE WAS SO MUCH WORK THAT HE HIRED TWO PART-TIME ASSISTANTS.
HIS FATHER CHECKED IN TO SEE HOW THINGS WERE GOING.

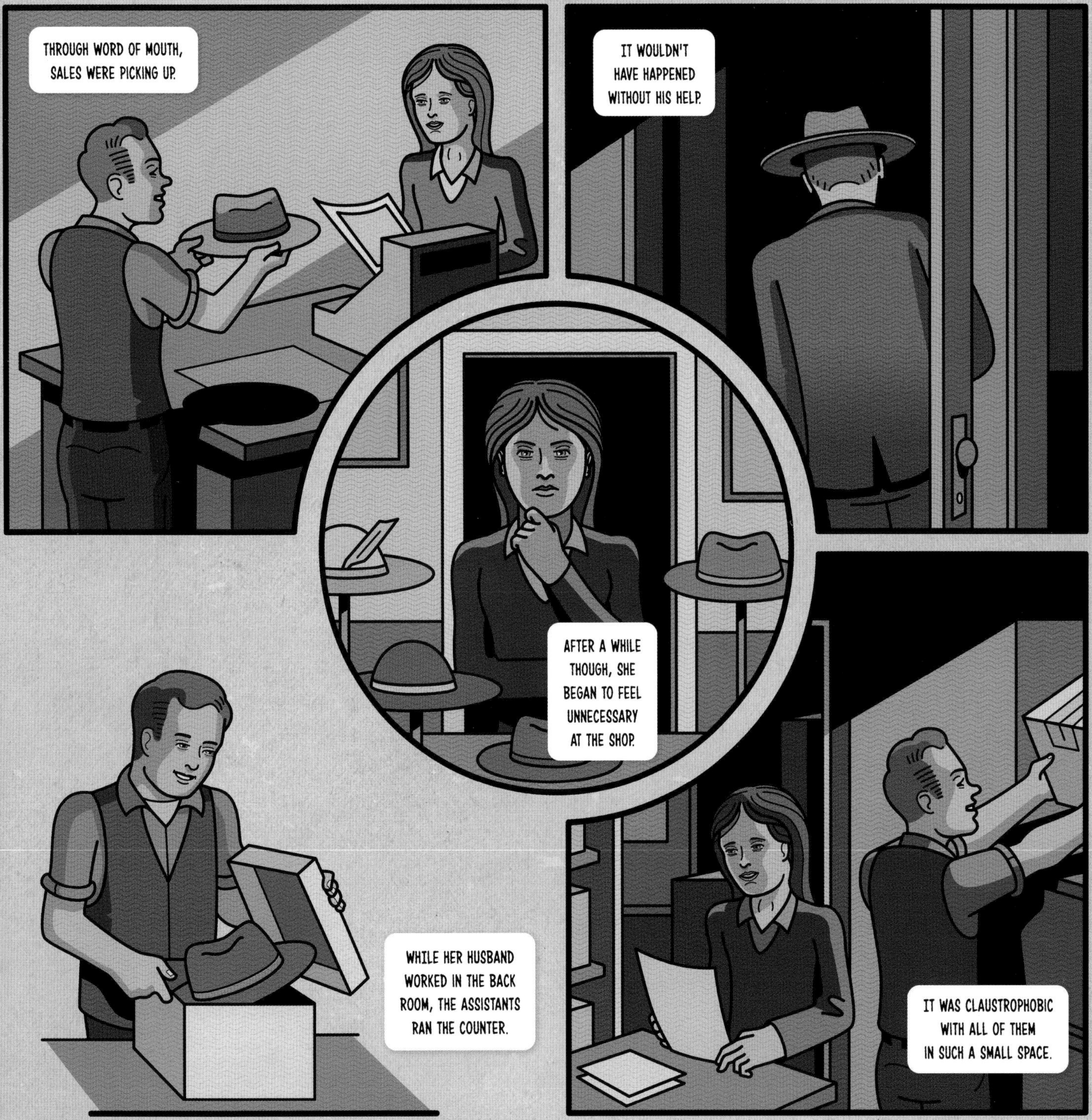
THROUGH WORD OF MOUTH, SALES WERE PICKING UP.
IT WOULDN'T HAVE HAPPENED WITHOUT HIS HELP.
AFTER A WHILE THOUGH, SHE BEGAN TO FEEL UNNECESSARY AT THE SHOP.
WHILE HER HUSBAND WORKED IN THE BACK ROOM, THE ASSISTANTS RAN THE COUNTER.
IT WAS CLAUSTROPHOBIC WITH ALL OF THEM IN SUCH A SMALL SPACE.

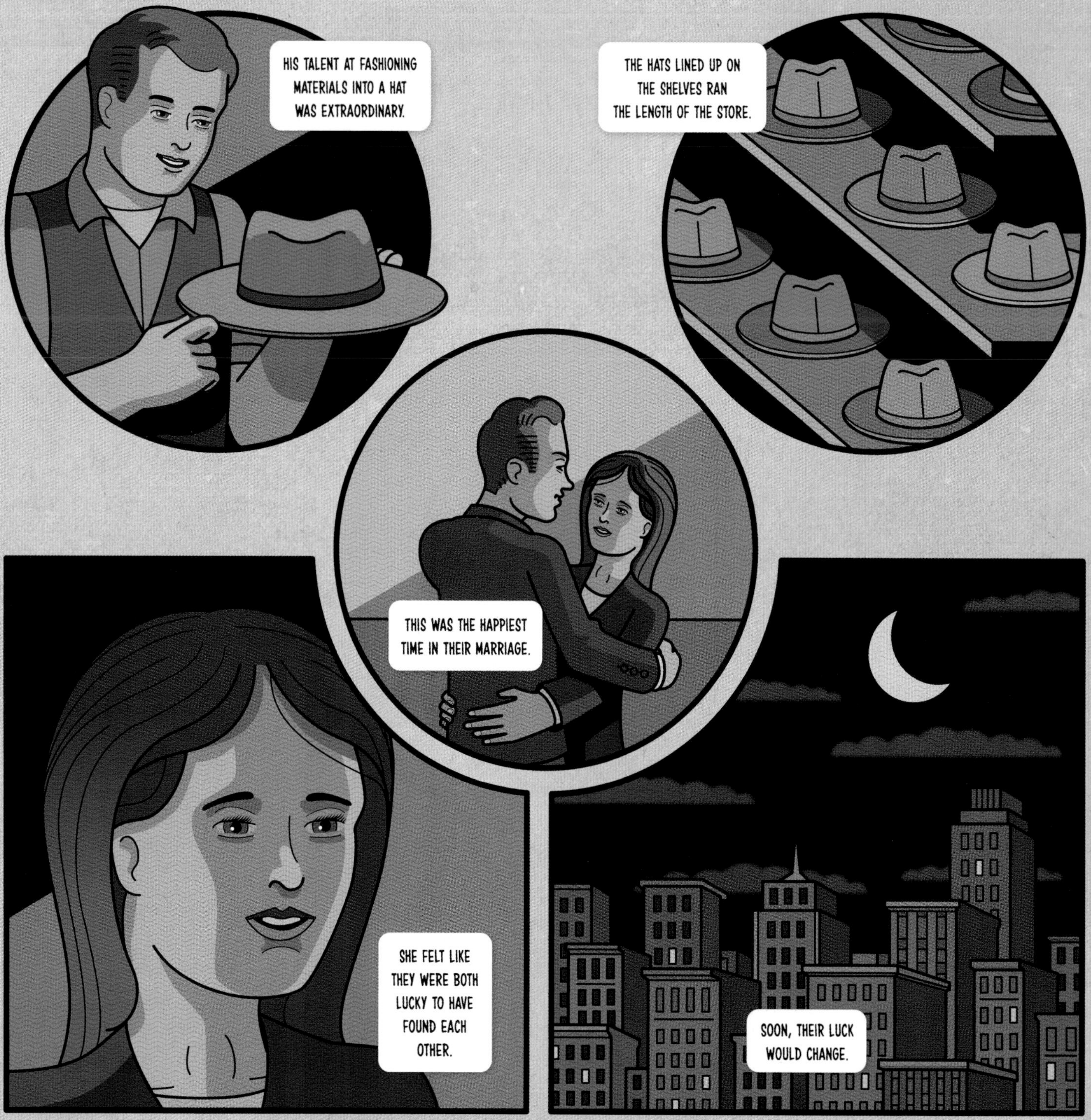
HIS TALENT AT FASHIONING MATERIALS INTO A HAT WAS EXTRAORDINARY.
THE HATS LINED UP ON THE SHELVES RAN THE LENGTH OF THE STORE.
THIS WAS THE HAPPIEST TIME IN THEIR MARRIAGE.
SHE FELT LIKE THEY WERE BOTH LUCKY TO HAVE FOUND EACH OTHER.
SOON, THEIR LUCK WOULD CHANGE.

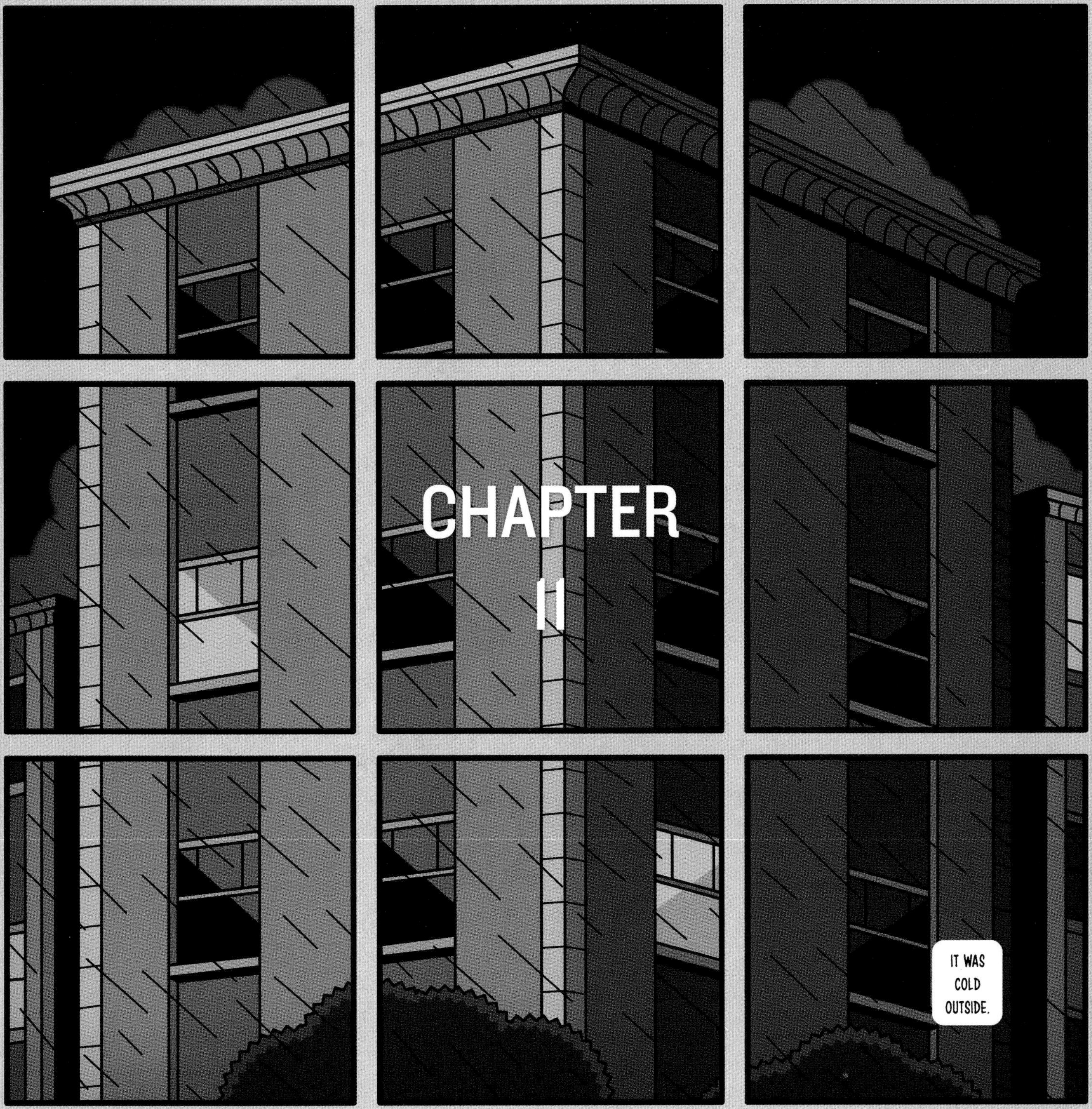
CHAPTER
11
IT WAS COLD OUTSIDE.

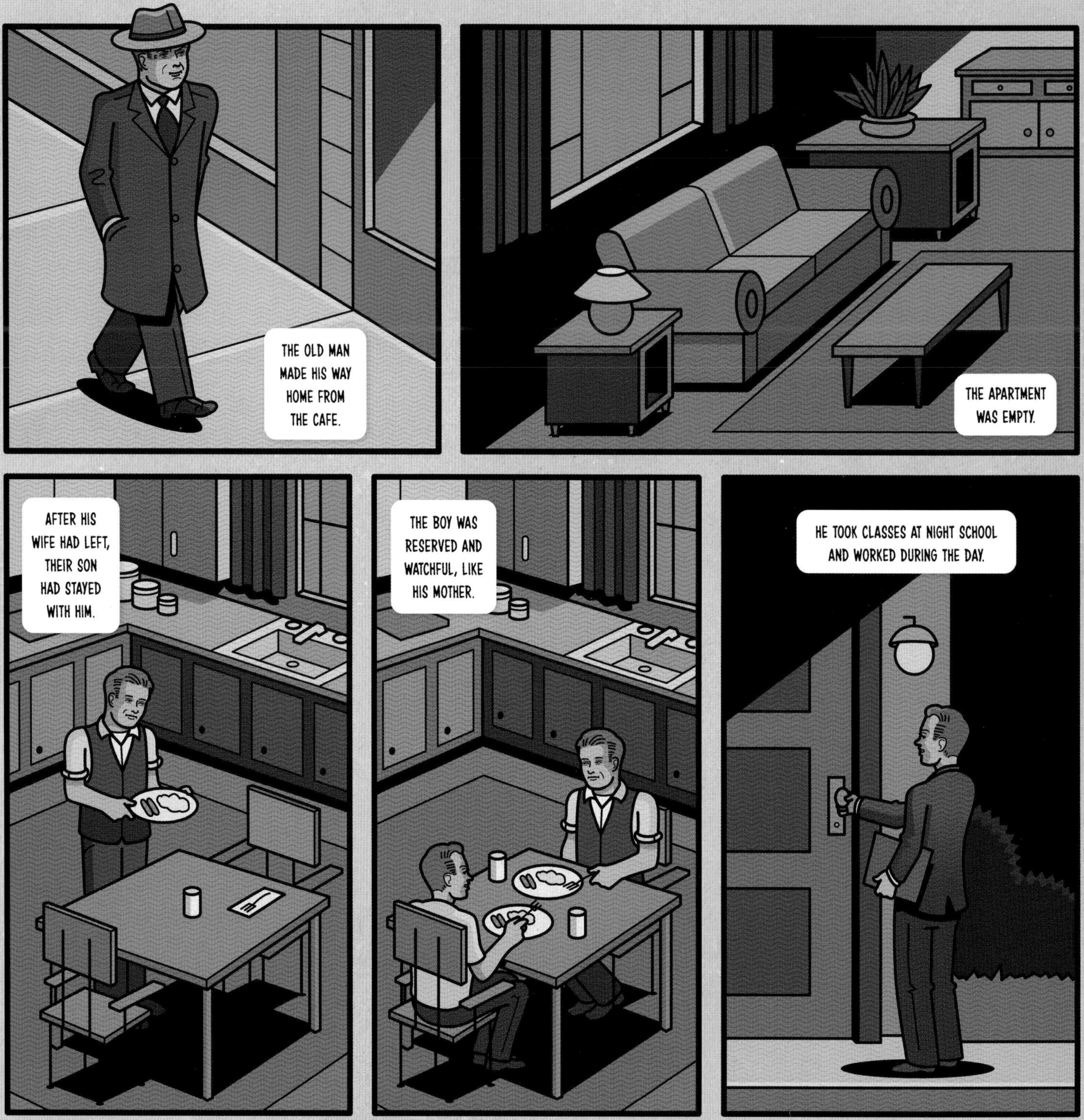
THE OLD MAN MADE HIS WAY HOME FROM THE CAFE.
THE APARTMENT WAS EMPTY.
AFTER HIS WIFE HAD LEFT, THEIR SON HAD STAYED WITH HIM.
THE BOY WAS RESERVED AND WATCHFUL, LIKE HIS MOTHER.
HE TOOK CLASSES AT NIGHT SCHOOL AND WORKED DURING THE DAY.

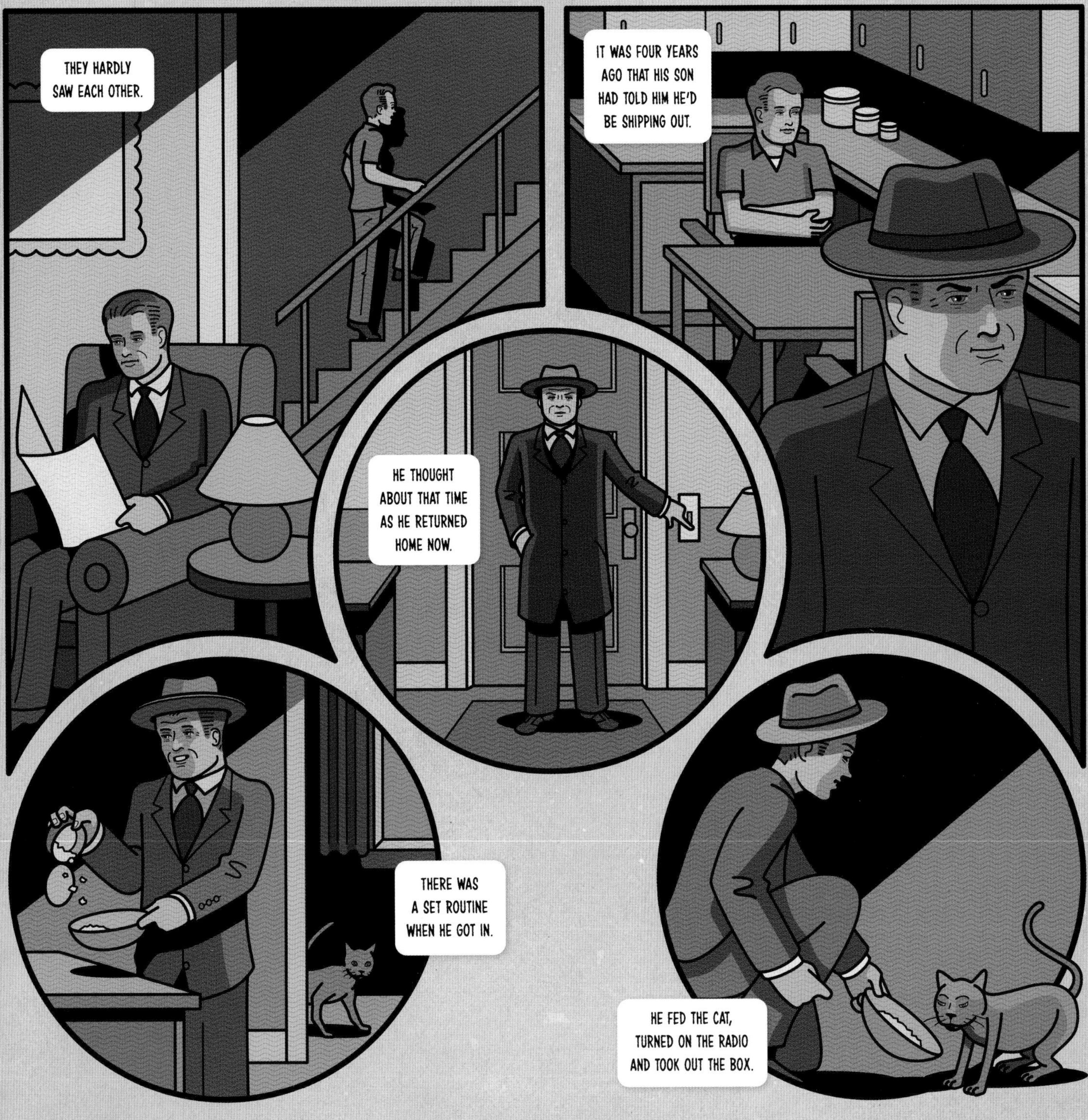
THEY HARDLY SAW EACH OTHER.
IT WAS FOUR YEARS AGO THAT HIS SON HAD TOLD HIM HE'D BE SHIPPING OUT.
HE THOUGHT ABOUT THAT TIME AS HE RETURNED HOME NOW.
THERE WAS A SET ROUTINE WHEN HE GOT IN.
HE FED THE CAT, TURNED ON THE RADIO AND TOOK OUT THE BOX.

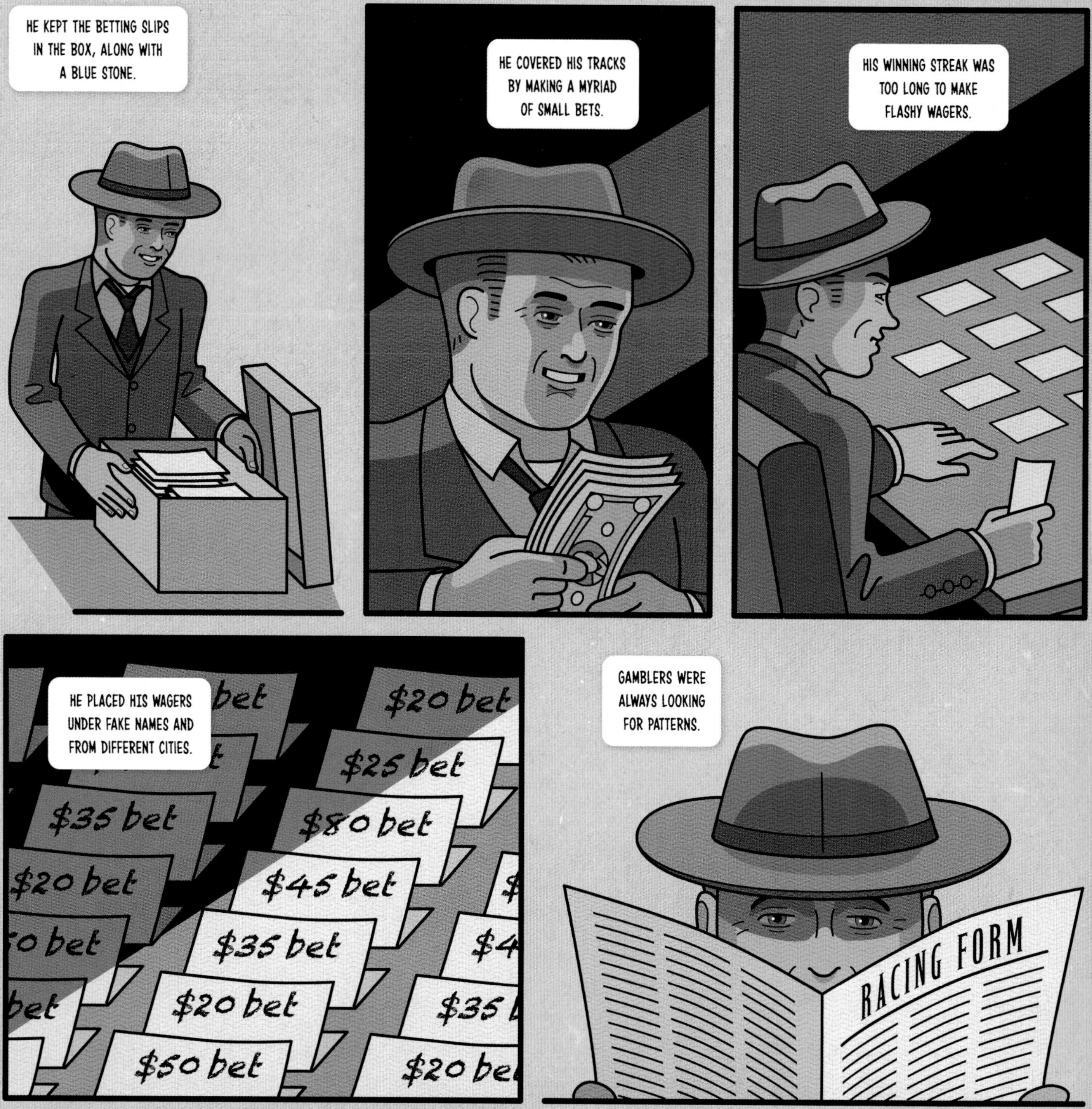
HE KEPT THE BETTING SLIPS IN THE BOX, ALONG WITH A BLUE STONE.
HE COVERED HIS TRACKS BY MAKING A MYRIAD OF SMALL BETS.
HIS WINNING STREAK WAS TOO LONG TO MAKE FLASHY WAGERS.
HE PLACED HIS WAGERS UNDER FAKE NAMES AND FROM DIFFERENT CITIES.
$20 bet
$25 bet
$35 bet
$80 bet
$20 bet
$45 bet
$35 bet
$20 bet
$50 bet
GAMBLERS WERE ALWAYS LOOKING FOR PATTERNS.
RACING FORM

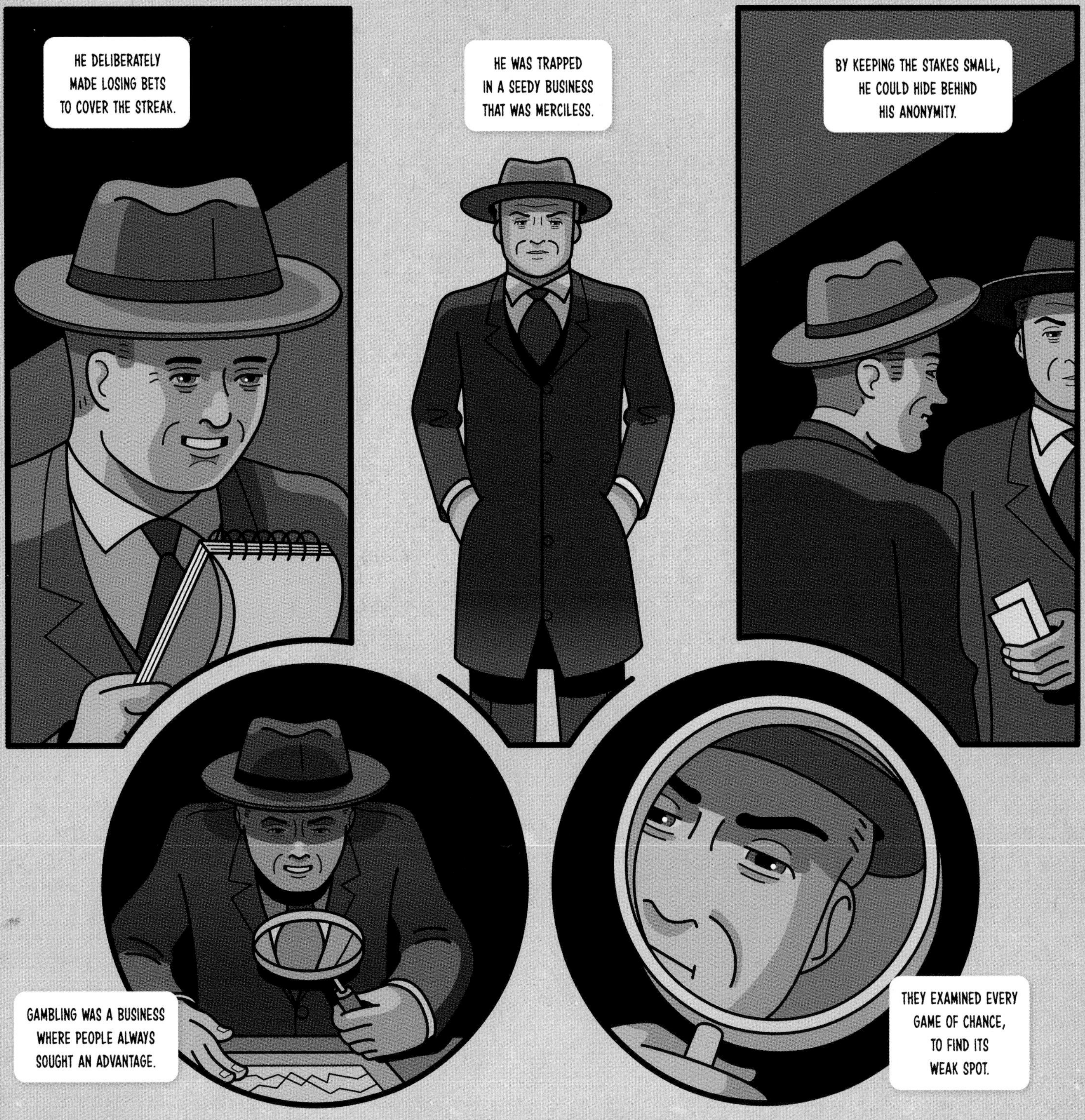
HE DELIBERATELY MADE LOSING BETS TO COVER THE STREAK.
HE WAS TRAPPED IN A SEEDY BUSINESS THAT WAS MERCILESS.
BY KEEPING THE STAKES SMALL, HE COULD HIDE BEHIND HIS ANONYMITY.
GAMBLING WAS A BUSINESS WHERE PEOPLE ALWAYS SOUGHT AN ADVANTAGE.
THEY EXAMINED EVERY GAME OF CHANCE, TO FIND ITS WEAK SPOT.

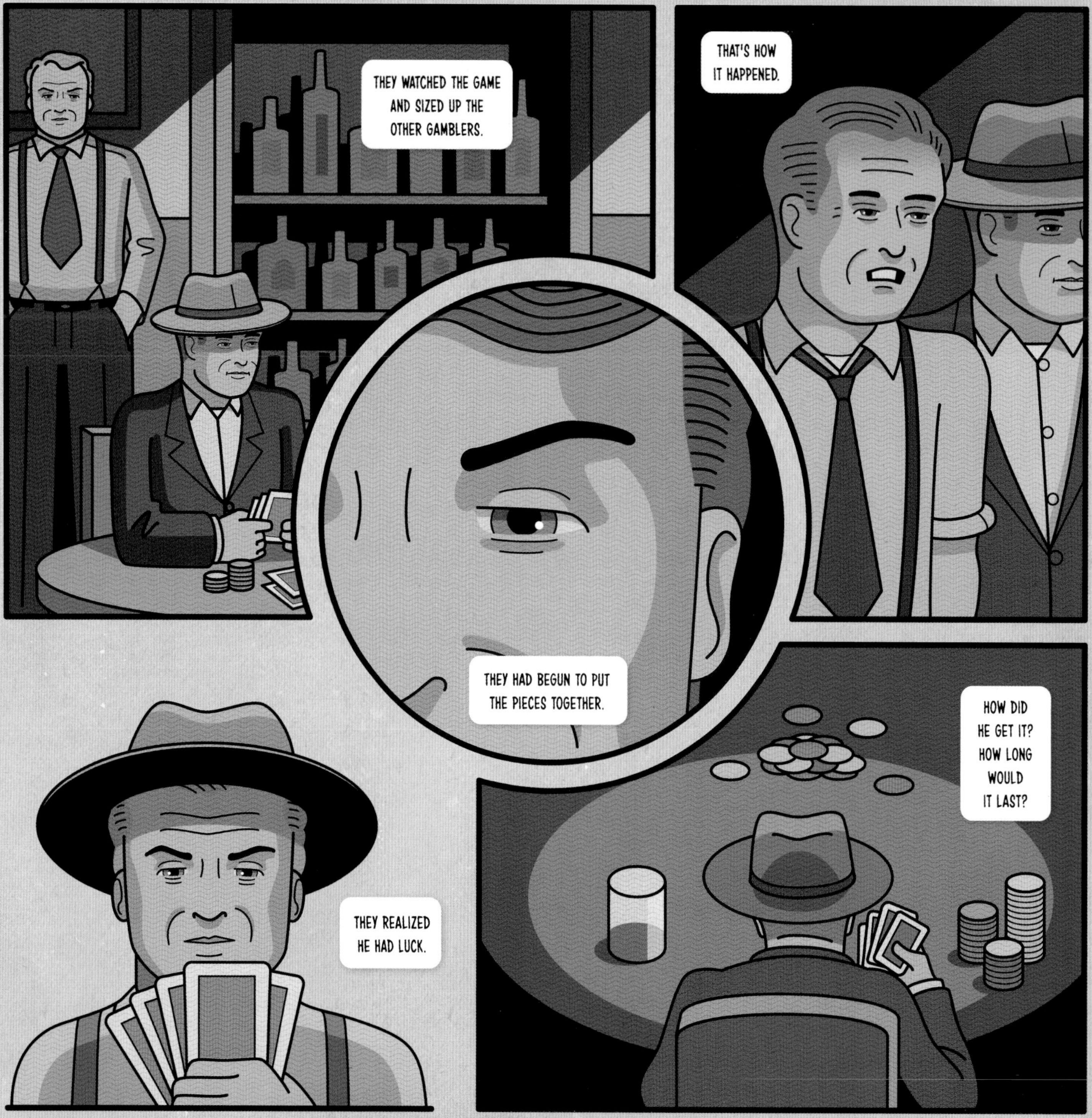
THEY WATCHED THE GAME AND SIZED UP THE OTHER GAMBLERS.
THAT'S HOW IT HAPPENED.
THEY HAD BEGUN TO PUT THE PIECES TOGETHER.
THEY REALIZED HE HAD LUCK.
HOW DID HE GET IT? HOW LONG WOULD IT LAST?

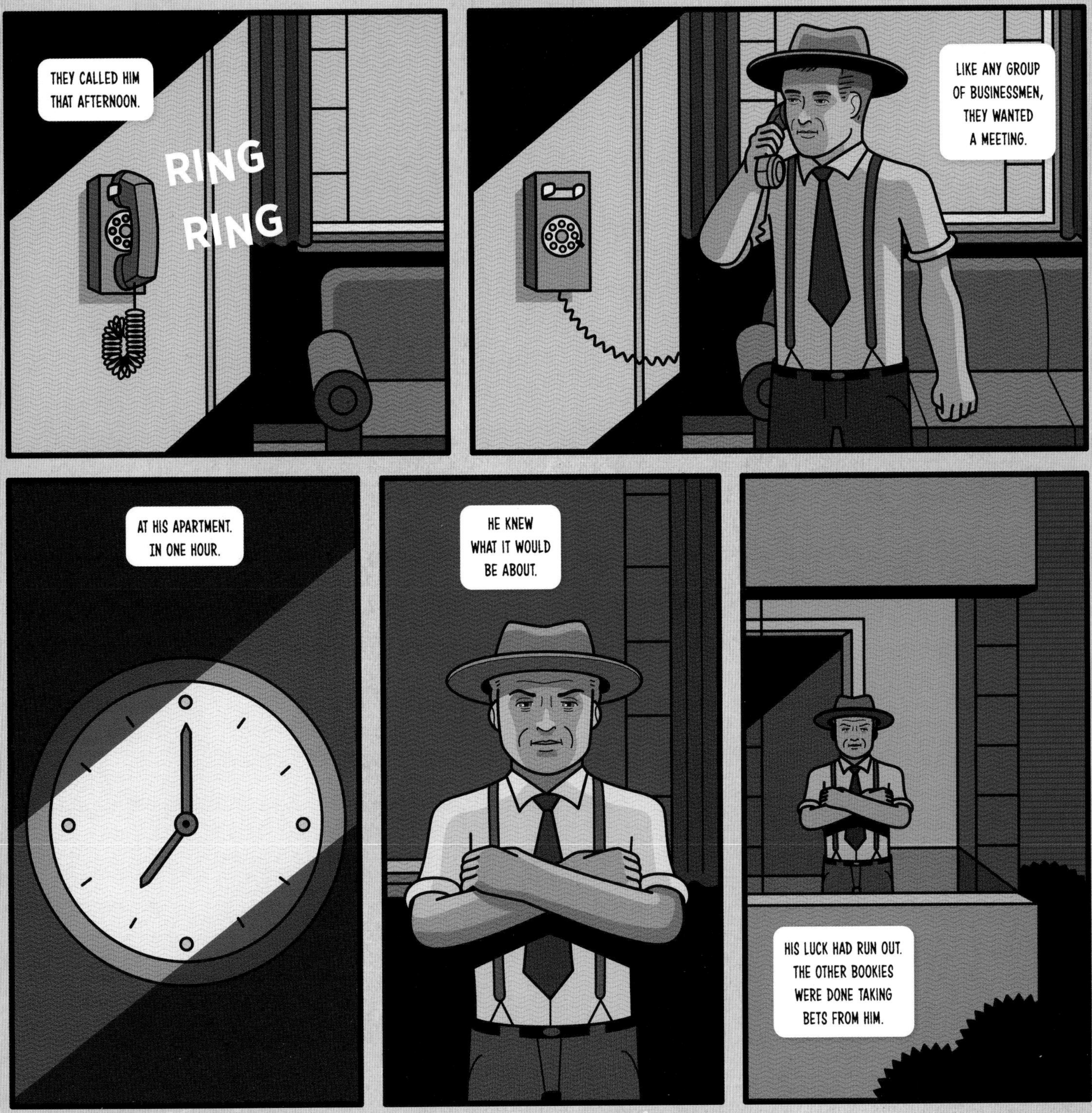
THEY CALLED HIM THAT AFTERNOON.
RING RING
LIKE ANY GROUP OF BUSINESSMEN, THEY WANTED A MEETING.
AT HIS APARTMENT. IN ONE HOUR.
HE KNEW WHAT IT WOULD BE ABOUT.
HIS LUCK HAD RUN OUT. THE OTHER BOOKIES WERE DONE TAKING BETS FROM HIM.

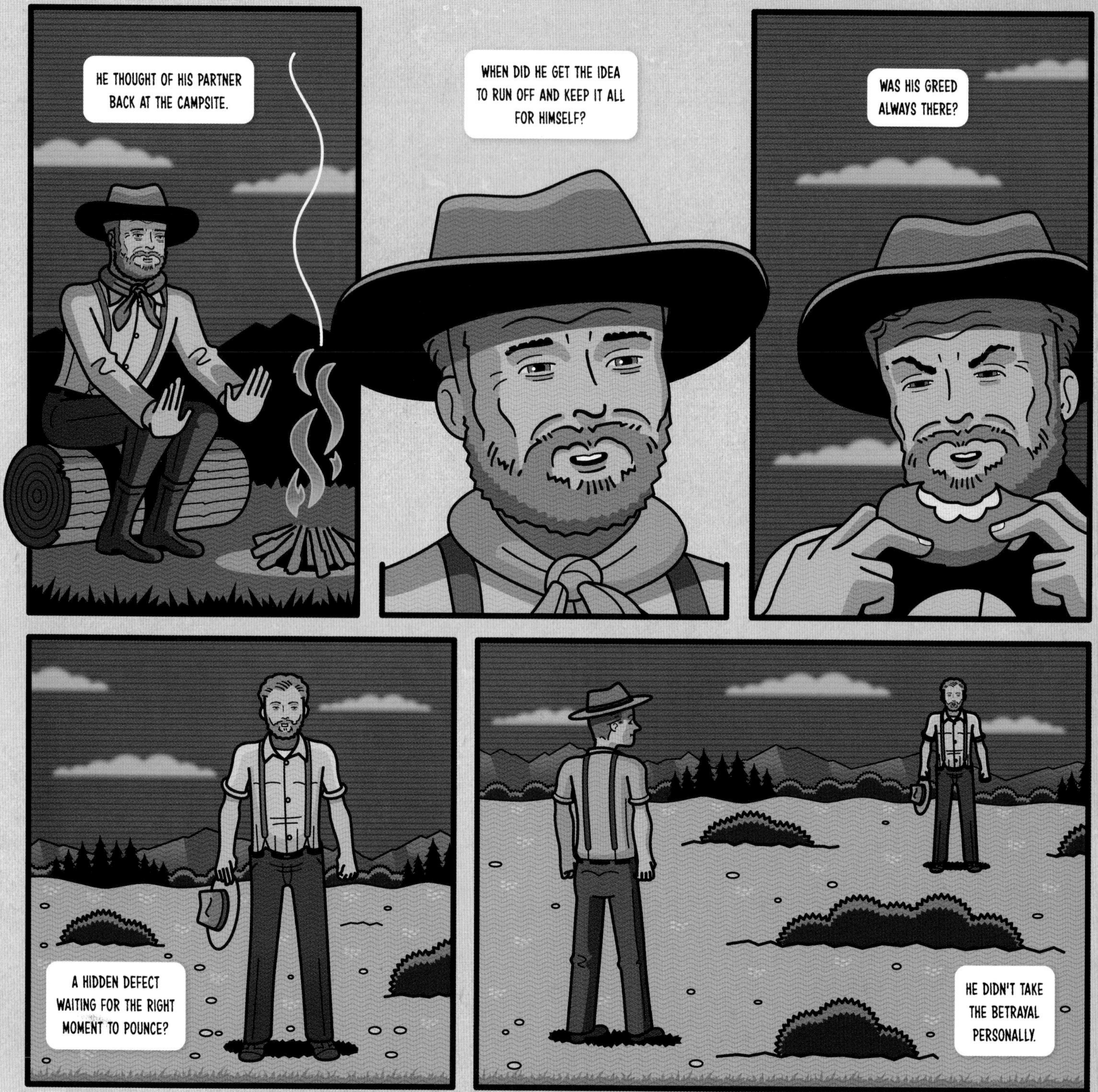
HE THOUGHT OF HIS PARTNER BACK AT THE CAMPSITE.
WHEN DID HE GET THE IDEA TO RUN OFF AND KEEP IT ALL FOR HIMSELF?
WAS HIS GREED ALWAYS THERE?
A HIDDEN DEFECT WAITING FOR THE RIGHT MOMENT TO POUNCE?
HE DIDN'T TAKE THE BETRAYAL PERSONALLY.

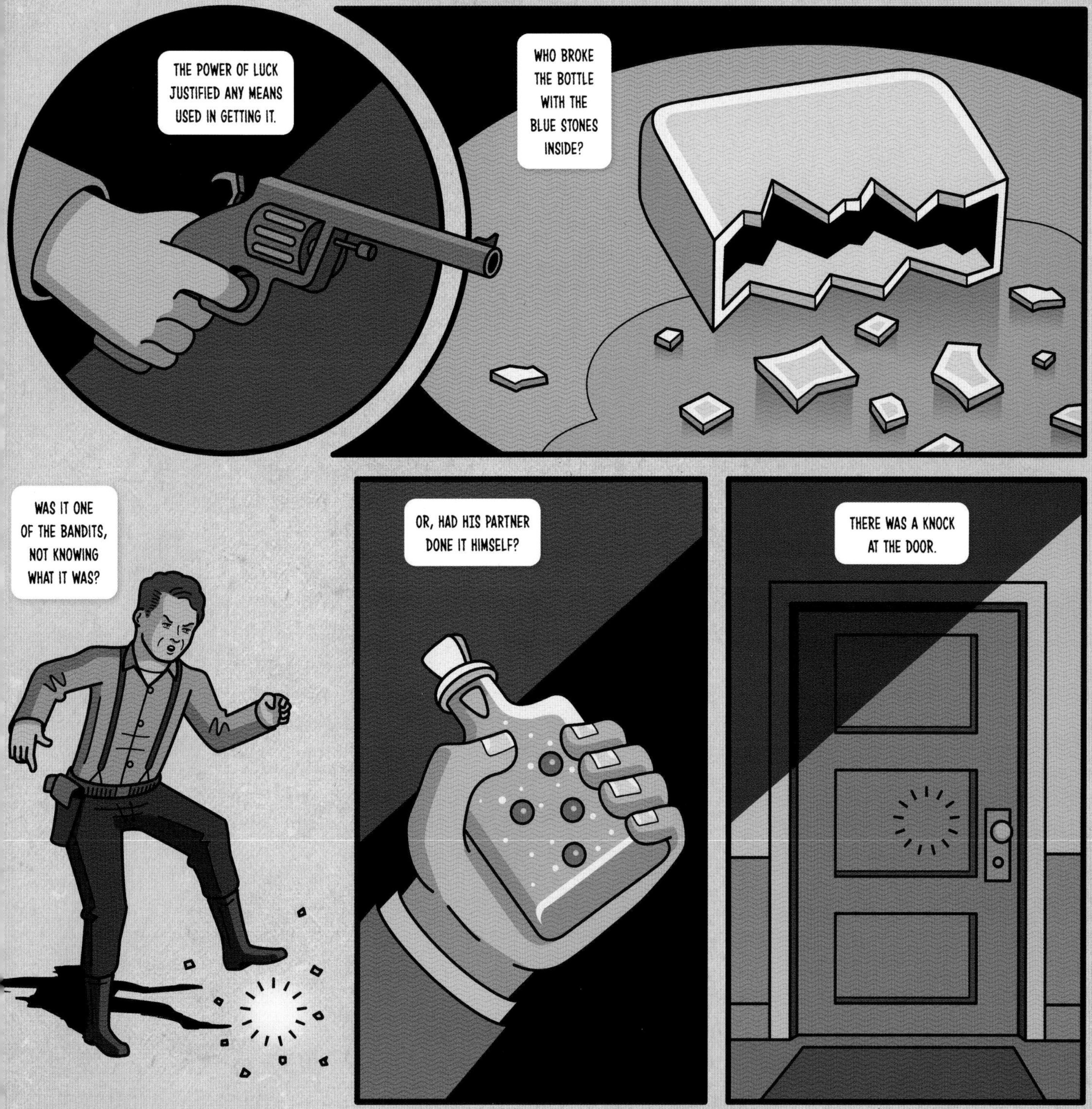
THE POWER OF LUCK JUSTIFIED ANY MEANS USED IN GETTING IT.
WHO BROKE THE BOTTLE WITH THE BLUE STONES INSIDE?
WAS IT ONE OF THE BANDITS, NOT KNOWING WHAT IT WAS?
OR, HAD HIS PARTNER DONE IT HIMSELF?
THERE WAS A KNOCK AT THE DOOR.

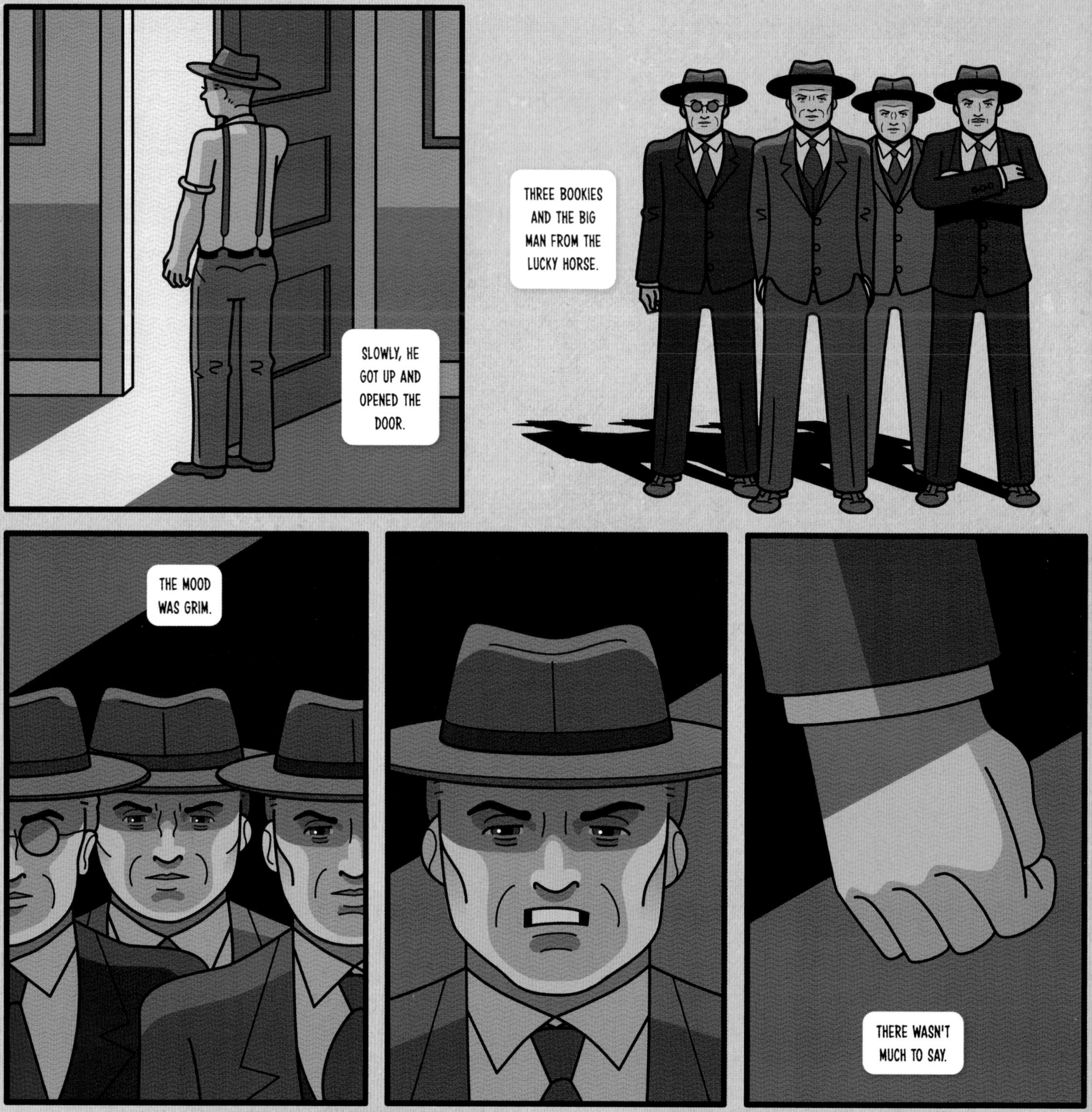
SLOWLY, HE GOT UP AND OPENED THE DOOR.
THREE BOOKIES AND THE BIG MAN FROM THE LUCKY HORSE.
THE MOOD WAS GRIM.
THERE WASN'T MUCH TO SAY.

HE'D USED LUCK FOR YEARS, AND NOW THEY KNEW.

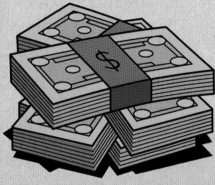

THE MEN TOOK ALL HIS MONEY AND THE SEALED STONE IN THE TIN BOX.

NOT ONE OF THEM LOOKED HAPPY ABOUT IT.

THE BIG MAN STUDIED THE STONE CLOSELY THROUGH A MAGNIFYING GLASS.

SETTING IT DOWN, HE GRINNED.

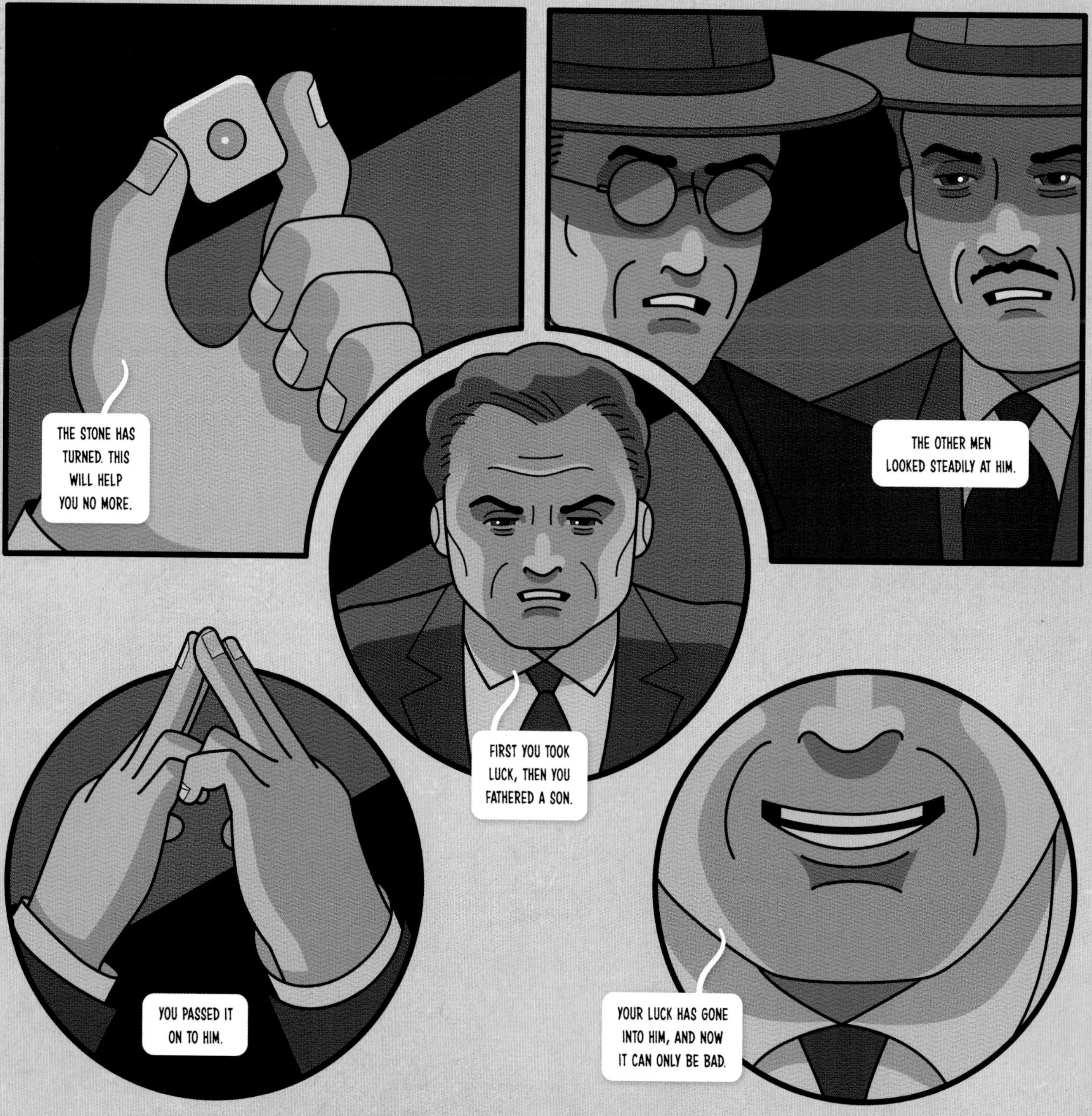
THE STONE HAS TURNED. THIS WILL HELP YOU NO MORE.
THE OTHER MEN LOOKED STEADILY AT HIM.
FIRST YOU TOOK LUCK, THEN YOU FATHERED A SON.
YOU PASSED IT ON TO HIM.
YOUR LUCK HAS GONE INTO HIM, AND NOW IT CAN ONLY BE BAD.

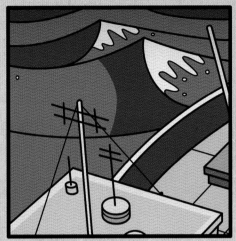
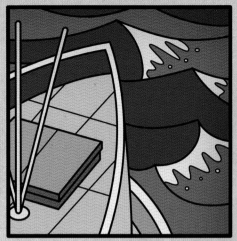
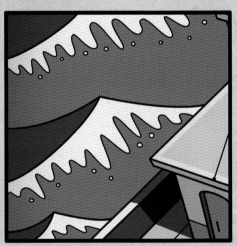

CHAPTER

12

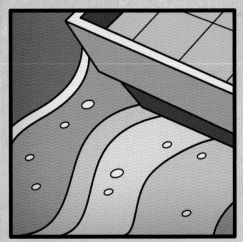
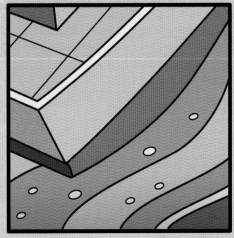
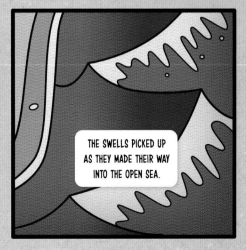

THE SWELLS PICKED UP
AS THEY MADE THEIR WAY
INTO THE OPEN SEA.

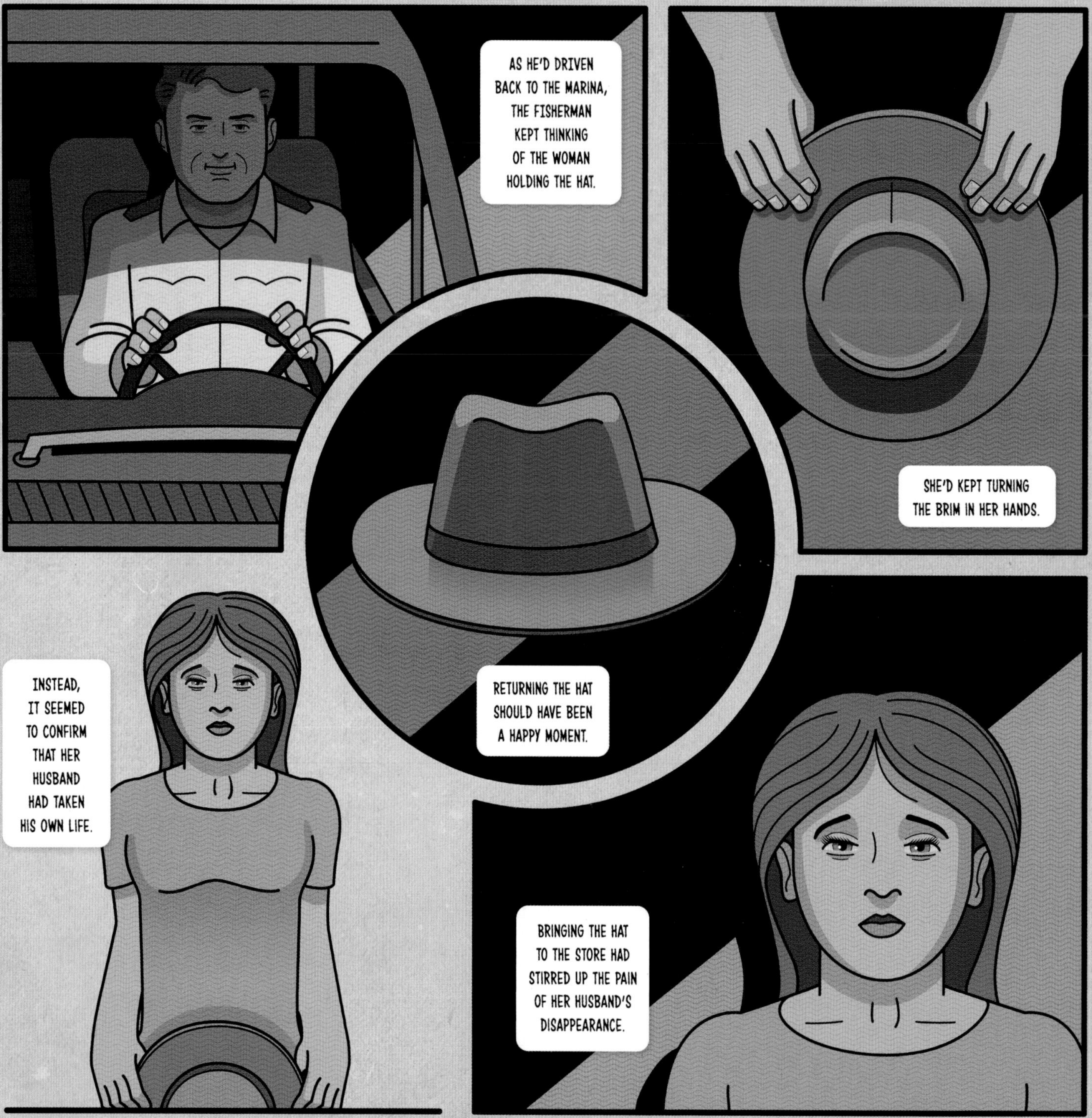
AS HE'D DRIVEN BACK TO THE MARINA, THE FISHERMAN KEPT THINKING OF THE WOMAN HOLDING THE HAT.
SHE'D KEPT TURNING THE BRIM IN HER HANDS.
RETURNING THE HAT SHOULD HAVE BEEN A HAPPY MOMENT.
INSTEAD, IT SEEMED TO CONFIRM THAT HER HUSBAND HAD TAKEN HIS OWN LIFE.
BRINGING THE HAT TO THE STORE HAD STIRRED UP THE PAIN OF HER HUSBAND'S DISAPPEARANCE.

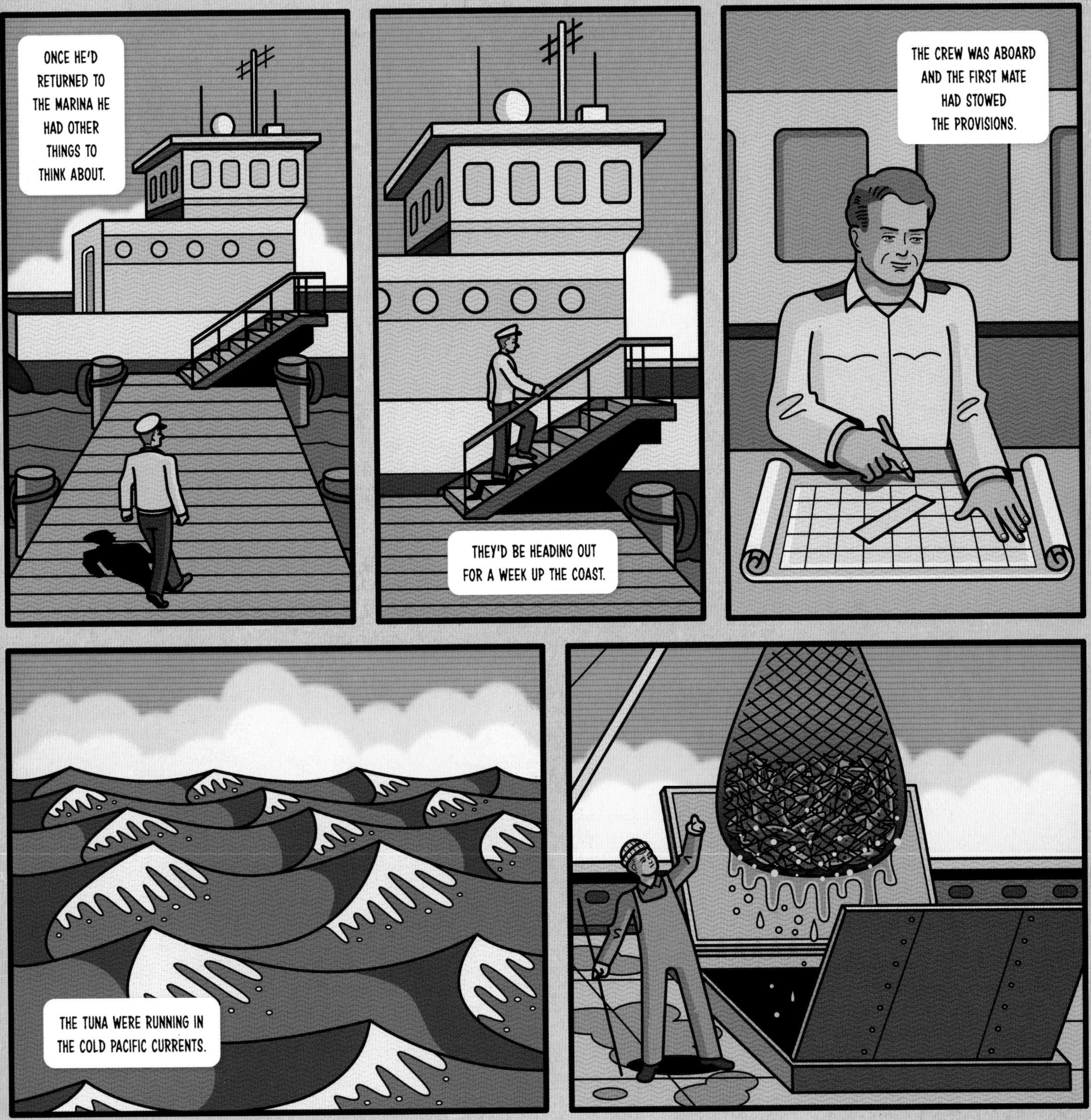
ONCE HE'D RETURNED TO THE MARINA HE HAD OTHER THINGS TO THINK ABOUT.
THEY'D BE HEADING OUT FOR A WEEK UP THE COAST.
THE CREW WAS ABOARD AND THE FIRST MATE HAD STOWED THE PROVISIONS.
THE TUNA WERE RUNNING IN THE COLD PACIFIC CURRENTS.

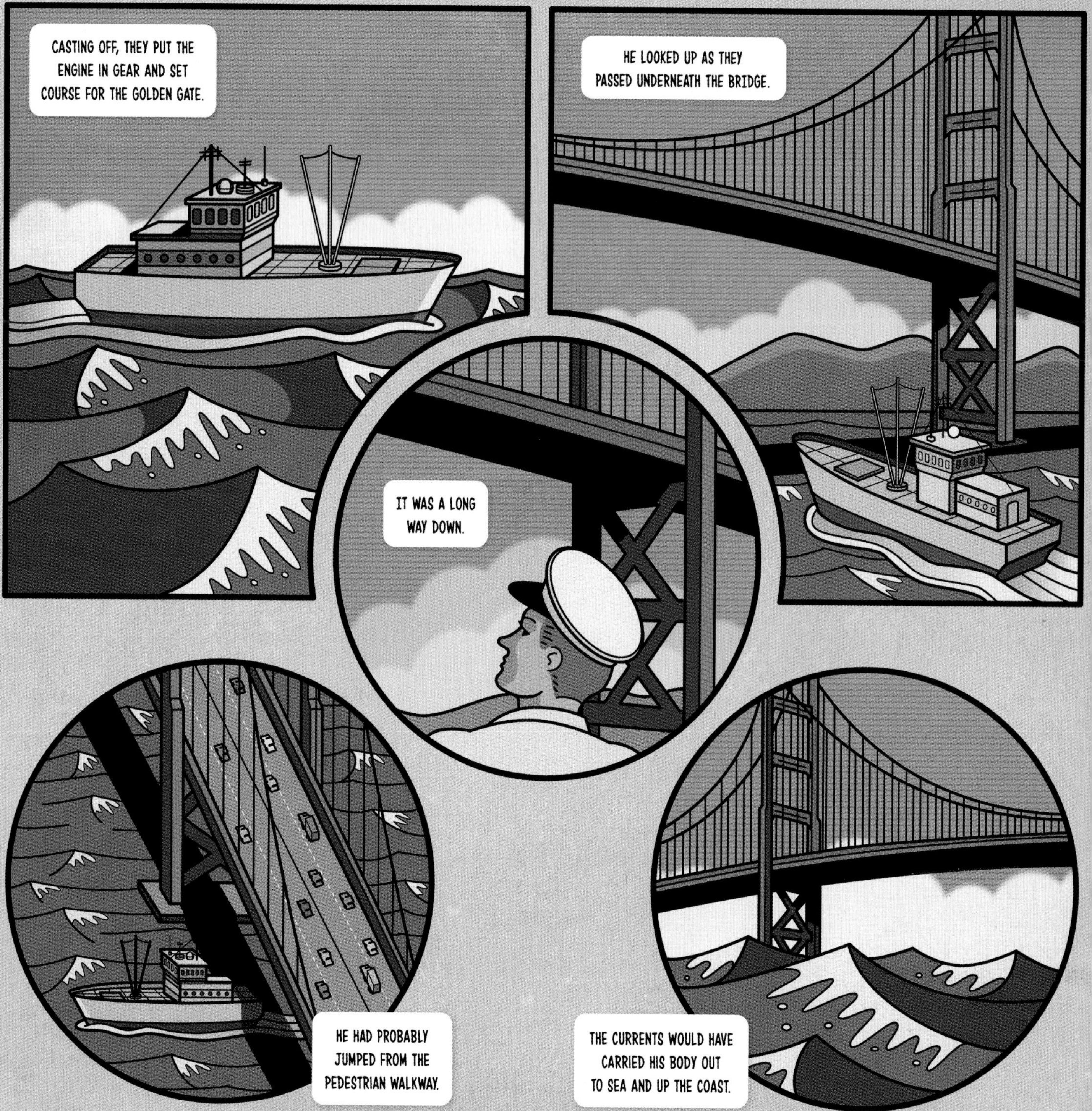
CASTING OFF, THEY PUT THE ENGINE IN GEAR AND SET COURSE FOR THE GOLDEN GATE.
HE LOOKED UP AS THEY PASSED UNDERNEATH THE BRIDGE.
IT WAS A LONG WAY DOWN.
HE HAD PROBABLY JUMPED FROM THE PEDESTRIAN WALKWAY.
THE CURRENTS WOULD HAVE CARRIED HIS BODY OUT TO SEA AND UP THE COAST.

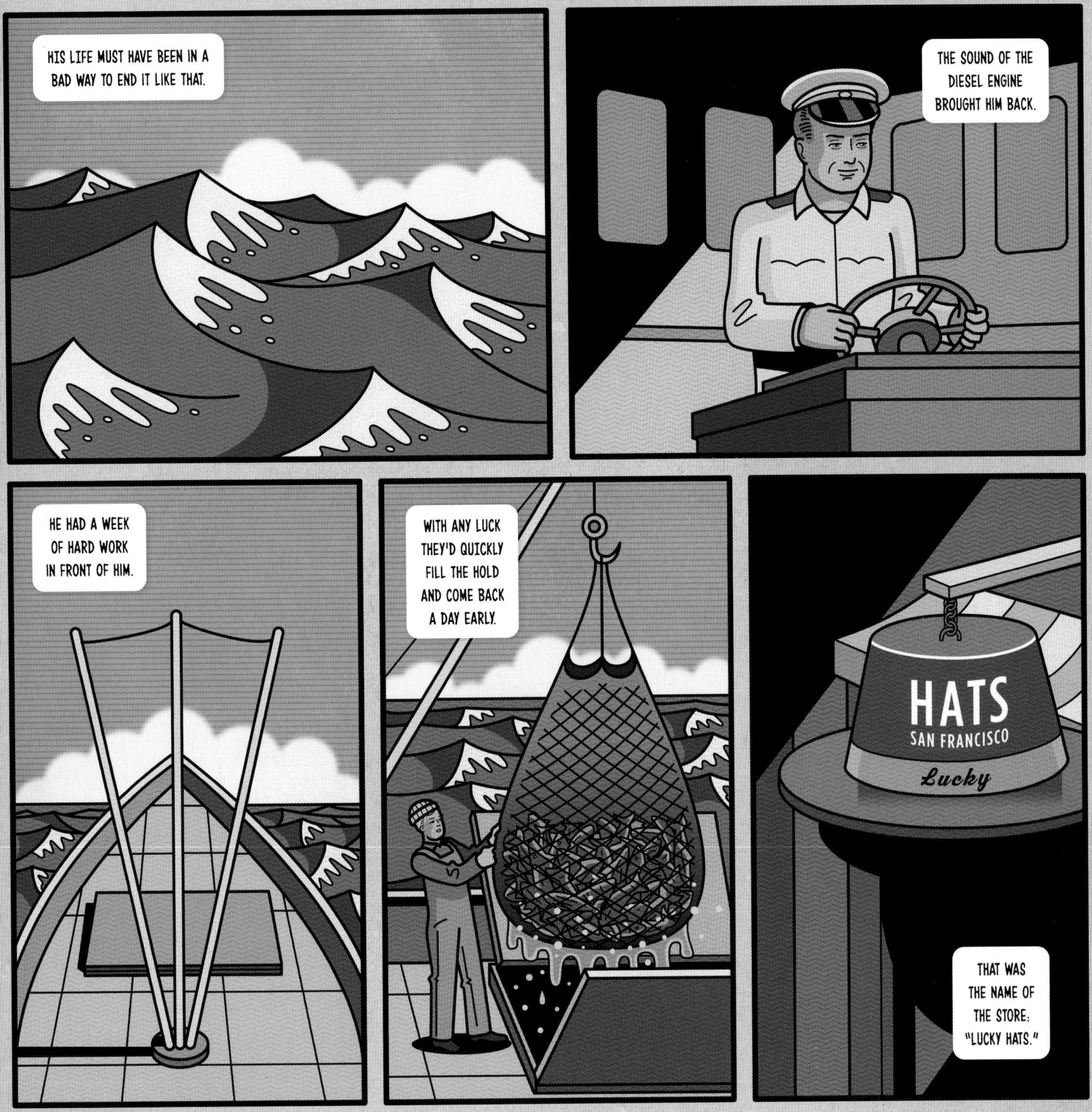
HIS LIFE MUST HAVE BEEN IN A BAD WAY TO END IT LIKE THAT.
THE SOUND OF THE DIESEL ENGINE BROUGHT HIM BACK.
HE HAD A WEEK OF HARD WORK IN FRONT OF HIM.
WITH ANY LUCK THEY'D QUICKLY FILL THE HOLD AND COME BACK A DAY EARLY.
HATS
SAN FRANCISCO
Lucky
THAT WAS THE NAME OF THE STORE: "LUCKY HATS."

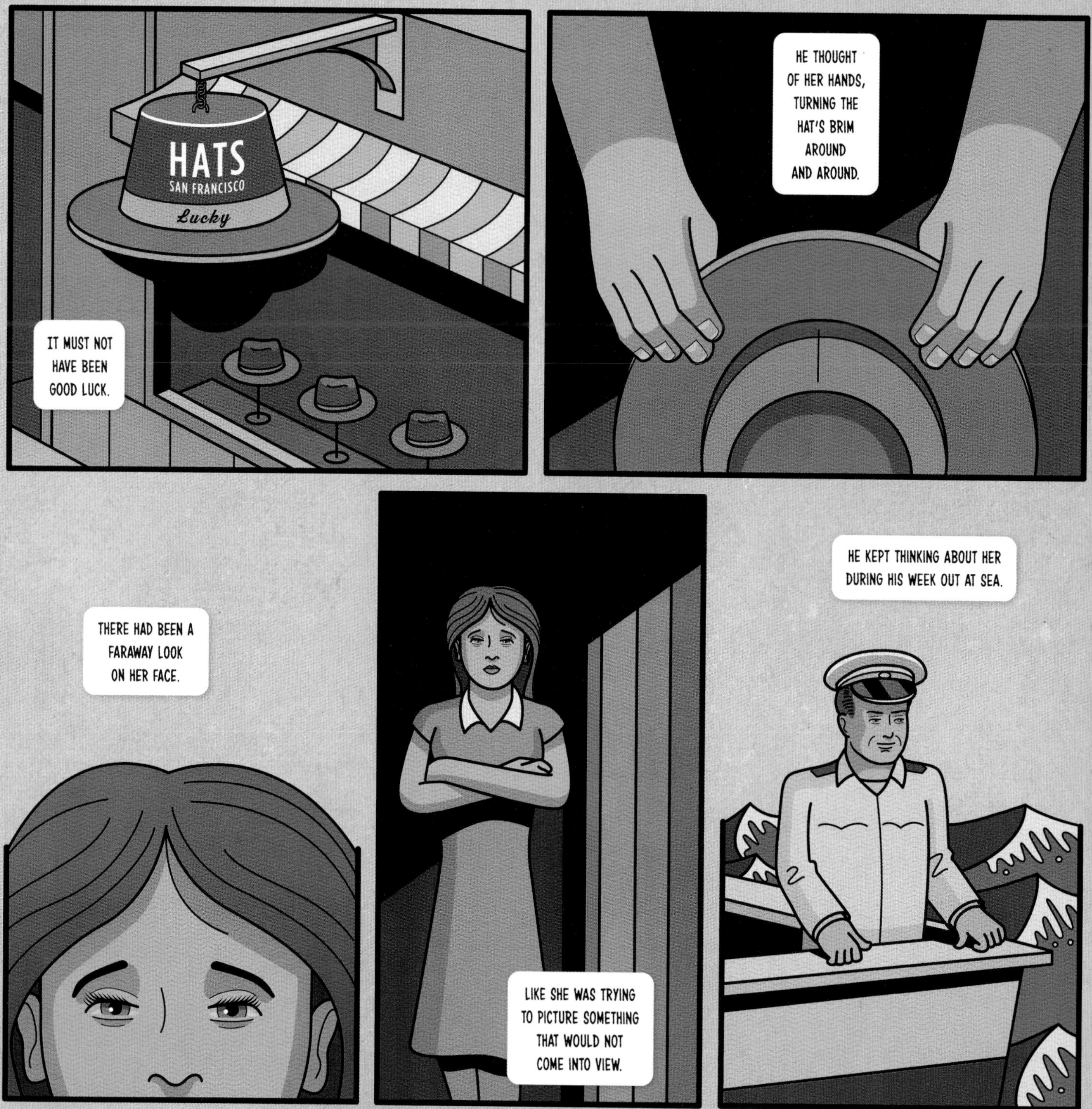
HATS
SAN FRANCISCO
Lucky
IT MUST NOT HAVE BEEN GOOD LUCK.
HE THOUGHT OF HER HANDS, TURNING THE HAT'S BRIM AROUND AND AROUND.
THERE HAD BEEN A FARAWAY LOOK ON HER FACE.
LIKE SHE WAS TRYING TO PICTURE SOMETHING THAT WOULD NOT COME INTO VIEW.
HE KEPT THINKING ABOUT HER DURING HIS WEEK OUT AT SEA.

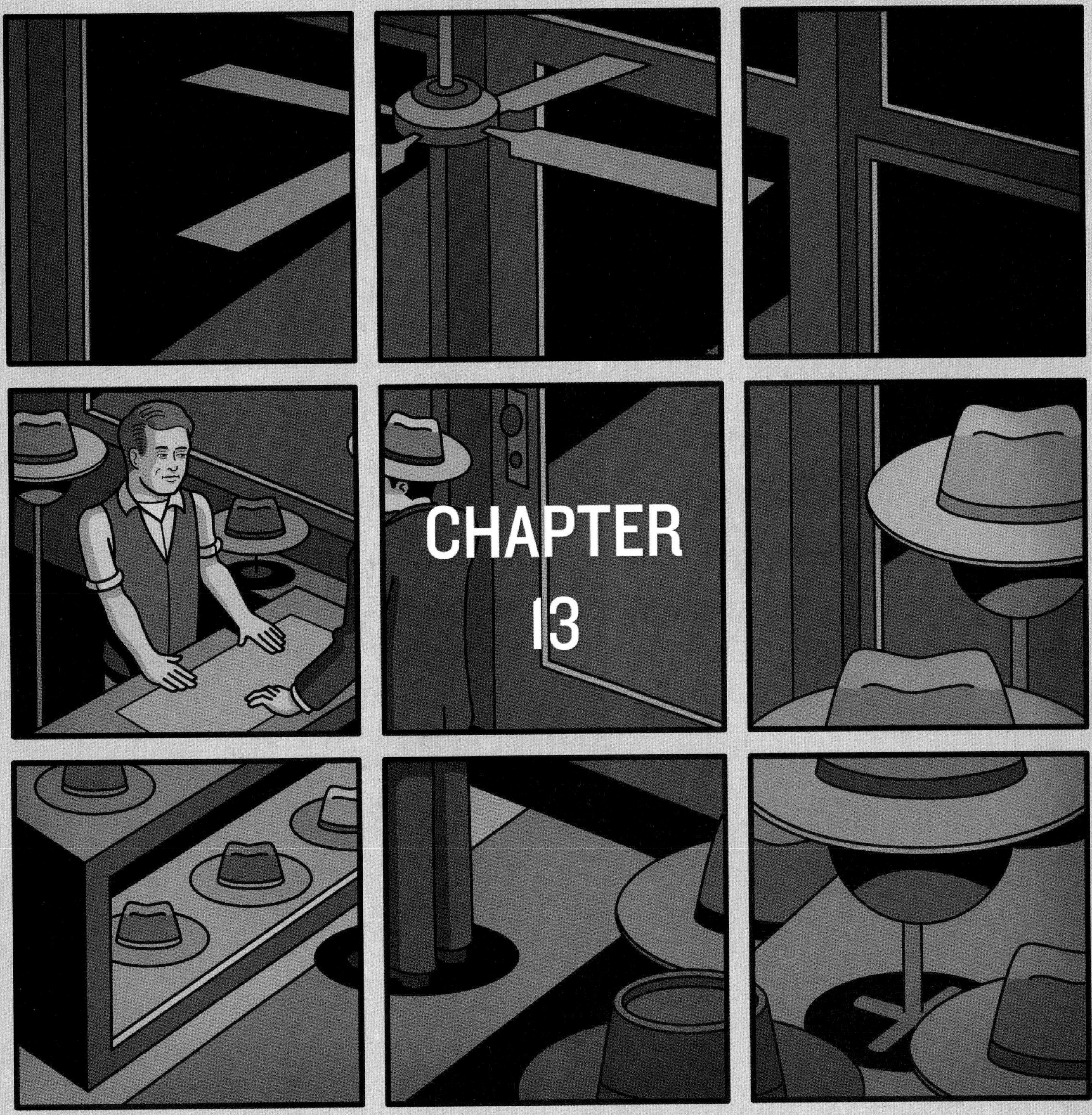
CHAPTER
13

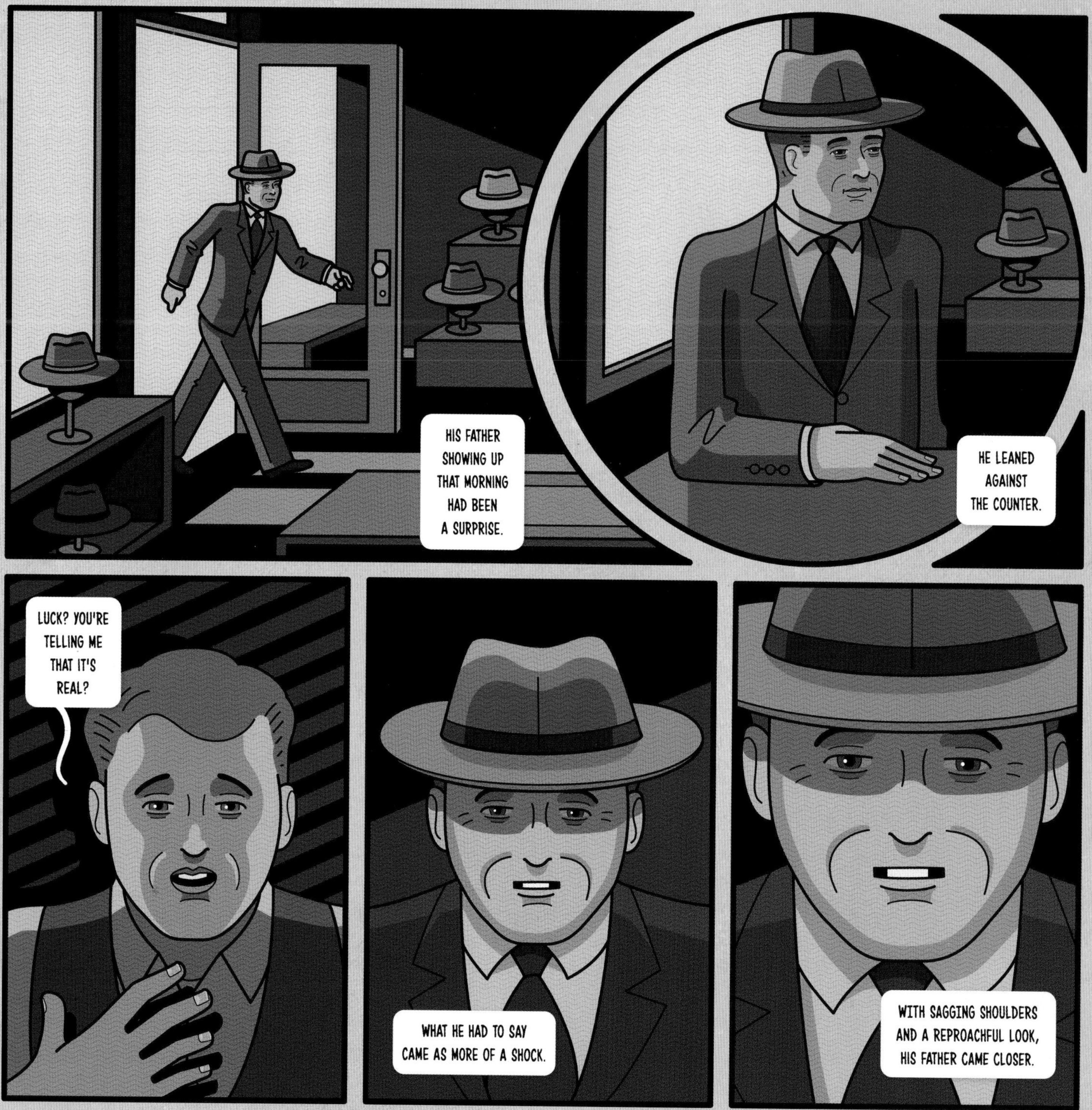
HIS FATHER SHOWING UP THAT MORNING HAD BEEN A SURPRISE.
HE LEANED AGAINST THE COUNTER.
LUCK? YOU'RE TELLING ME THAT IT'S REAL?
WHAT HE HAD TO SAY CAME AS MORE OF A SHOCK.
WITH SAGGING SHOULDERS AND A REPROACHFUL LOOK, HIS FATHER CAME CLOSER.

IT'S WORSE THAN REAL. IT WAS HERE AND NOW IT'S GONE.

HE TOOK OFF THE HAT HIS SON HAD GIVEN HIM.

TURNING IT UPSIDE DOWN, HE CAREFULLY RAN HIS FINGERS ALONG THE BAND.

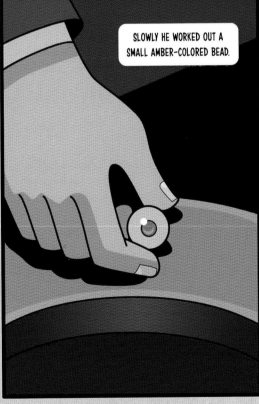

SLOWLY HE WORKED OUT A SMALL AMBER-COLORED BEAD.

SUSPENDED IN THE MIDDLE WAS A BRIGHT BLUE STONE.

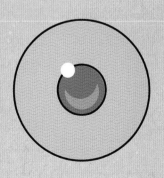

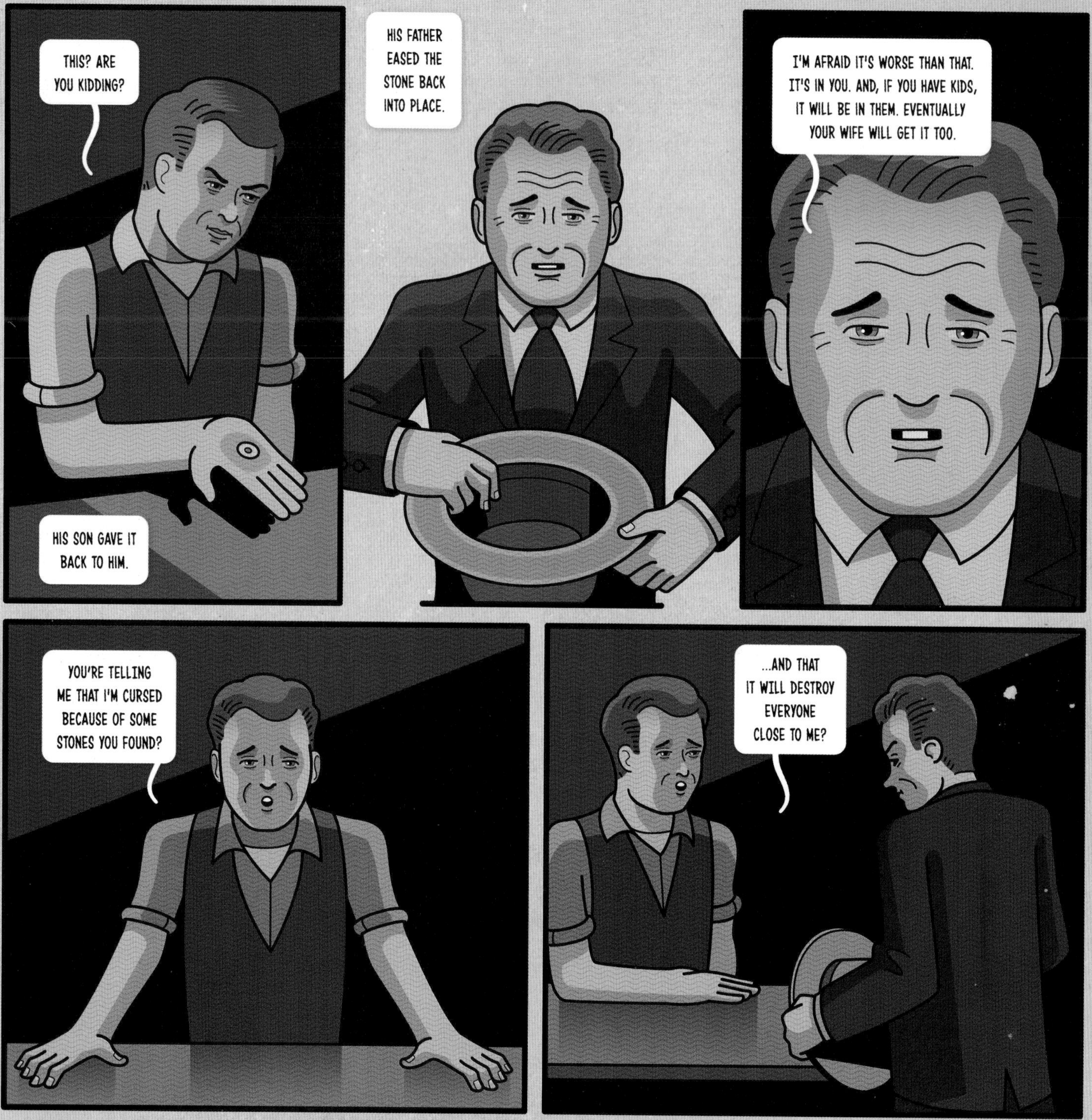
THIS? ARE YOU KIDDING?
HIS SON GAVE IT BACK TO HIM.
HIS FATHER EASED THE STONE BACK INTO PLACE.
I'M AFRAID IT'S WORSE THAN THAT. IT'S IN YOU. AND, IF YOU HAVE KIDS, IT WILL BE IN THEM. EVENTUALLY YOUR WIFE WILL GET IT TOO.
YOU'RE TELLING ME THAT I'M CURSED BECAUSE OF SOME STONES YOU FOUND?
...AND THAT IT WILL DESTROY EVERYONE CLOSE TO ME?

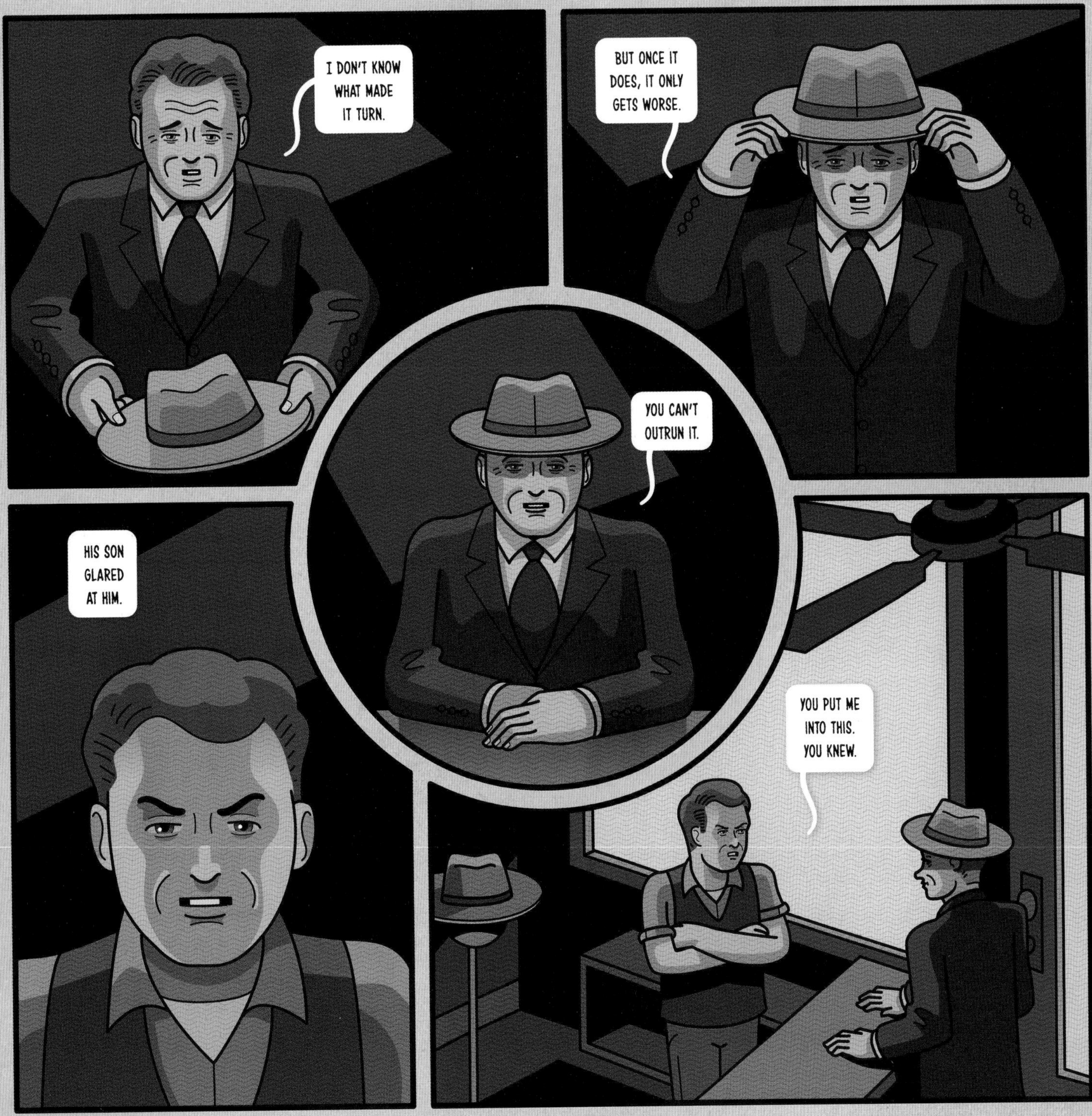
I DON'T KNOW WHAT MADE IT TURN.
BUT ONCE IT DOES, IT ONLY GETS WORSE.
YOU CAN'T OUTRUN IT.
HIS SON GLARED AT HIM.
YOU PUT ME INTO THIS. YOU KNEW.

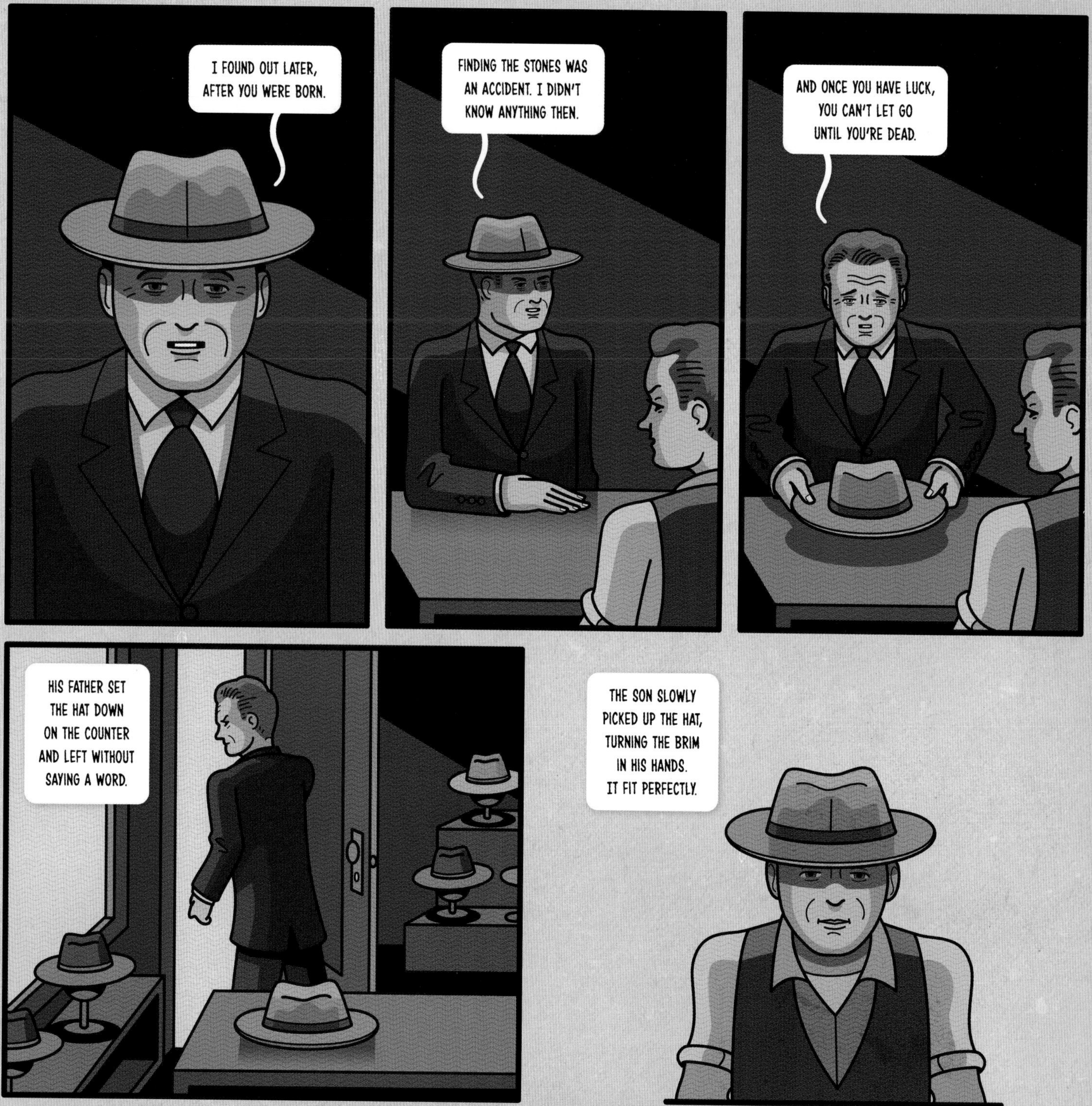
I FOUND OUT LATER, AFTER YOU WERE BORN.
FINDING THE STONES WAS AN ACCIDENT. I DIDN'T KNOW ANYTHING THEN.
AND ONCE YOU HAVE LUCK, YOU CAN'T LET GO UNTIL YOU'RE DEAD.
HIS FATHER SET THE HAT DOWN ON THE COUNTER AND LEFT WITHOUT SAYING A WORD.
THE SON SLOWLY PICKED UP THE HAT, TURNING THE BRIM IN HIS HANDS. IT FIT PERFECTLY.

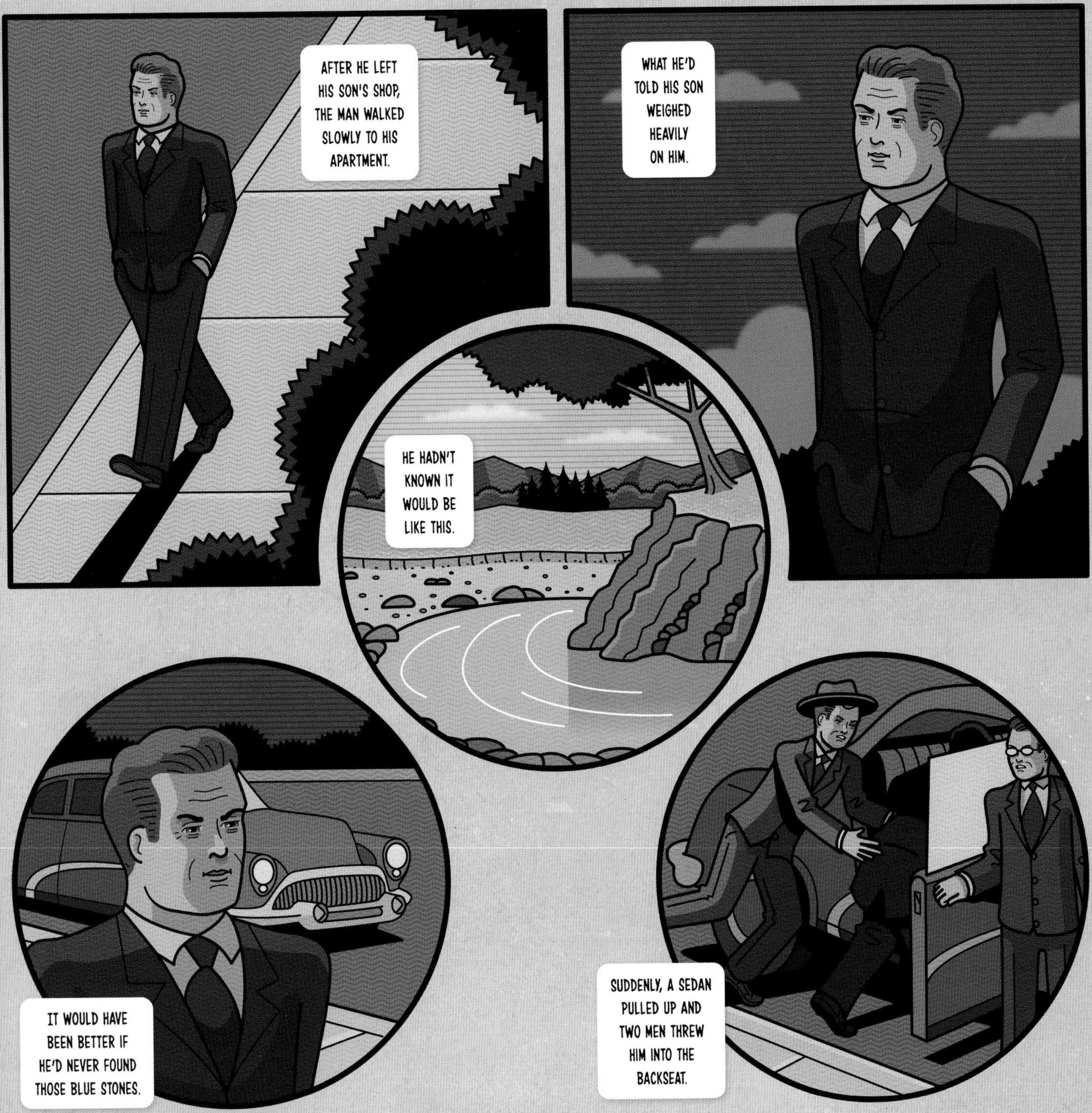
AFTER HE LEFT HIS SON'S SHOP, THE MAN WALKED SLOWLY TO HIS APARTMENT.
WHAT HE'D TOLD HIS SON WEIGHED HEAVILY ON HIM.
HE HADN'T KNOWN IT WOULD BE LIKE THIS.
IT WOULD HAVE BEEN BETTER IF HE'D NEVER FOUND THOSE BLUE STONES.
SUDDENLY, A SEDAN PULLED UP AND TWO MEN THREW HIM INTO THE BACKSEAT.

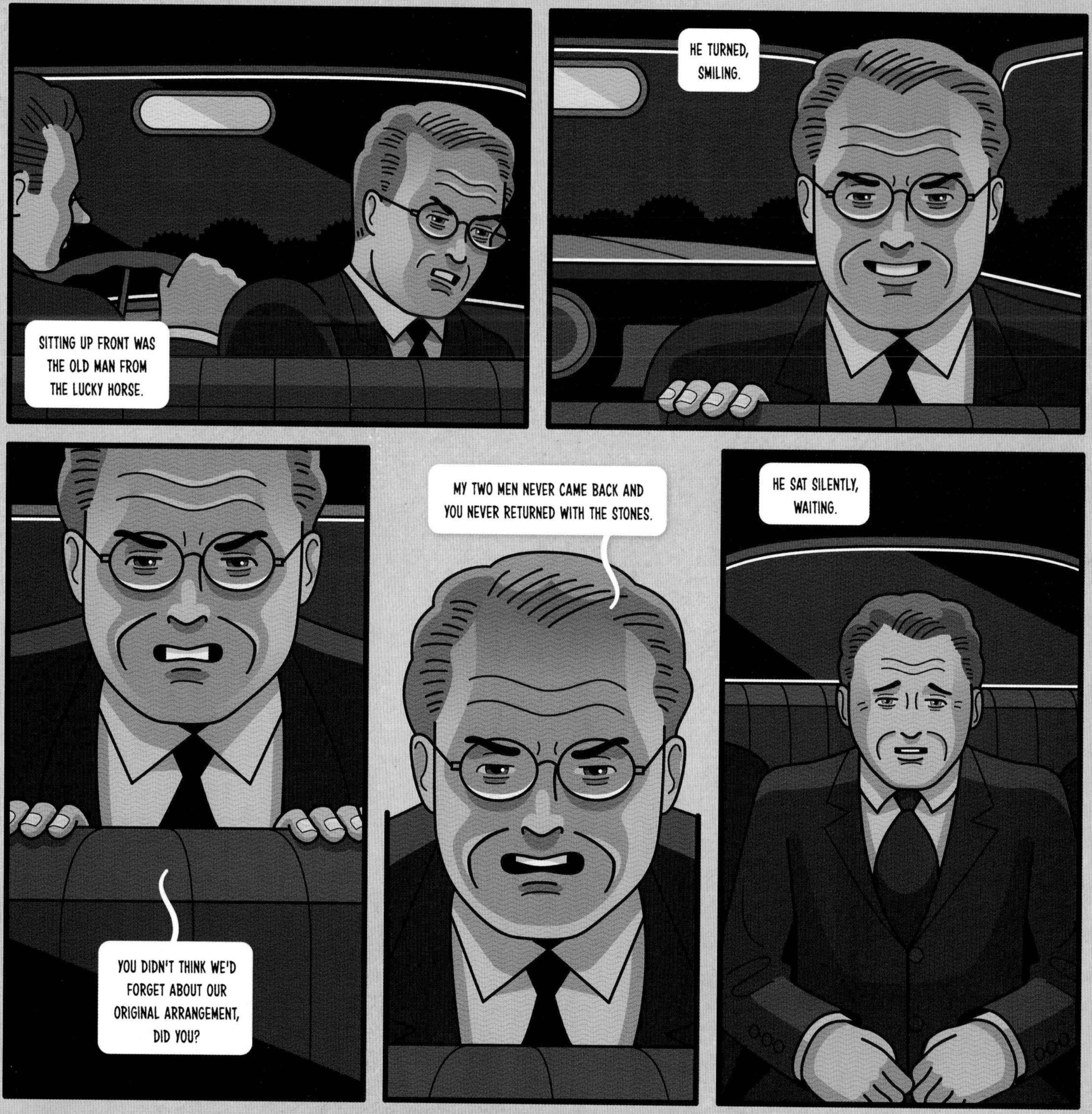
SITTING UP FRONT WAS THE OLD MAN FROM THE LUCKY HORSE.
HE TURNED, SMILING.
YOU DIDN'T THINK WE'D FORGET ABOUT OUR ORIGINAL ARRANGEMENT, DID YOU?
MY TWO MEN NEVER CAME BACK AND YOU NEVER RETURNED WITH THE STONES.
HE SAT SILENTLY, WAITING.

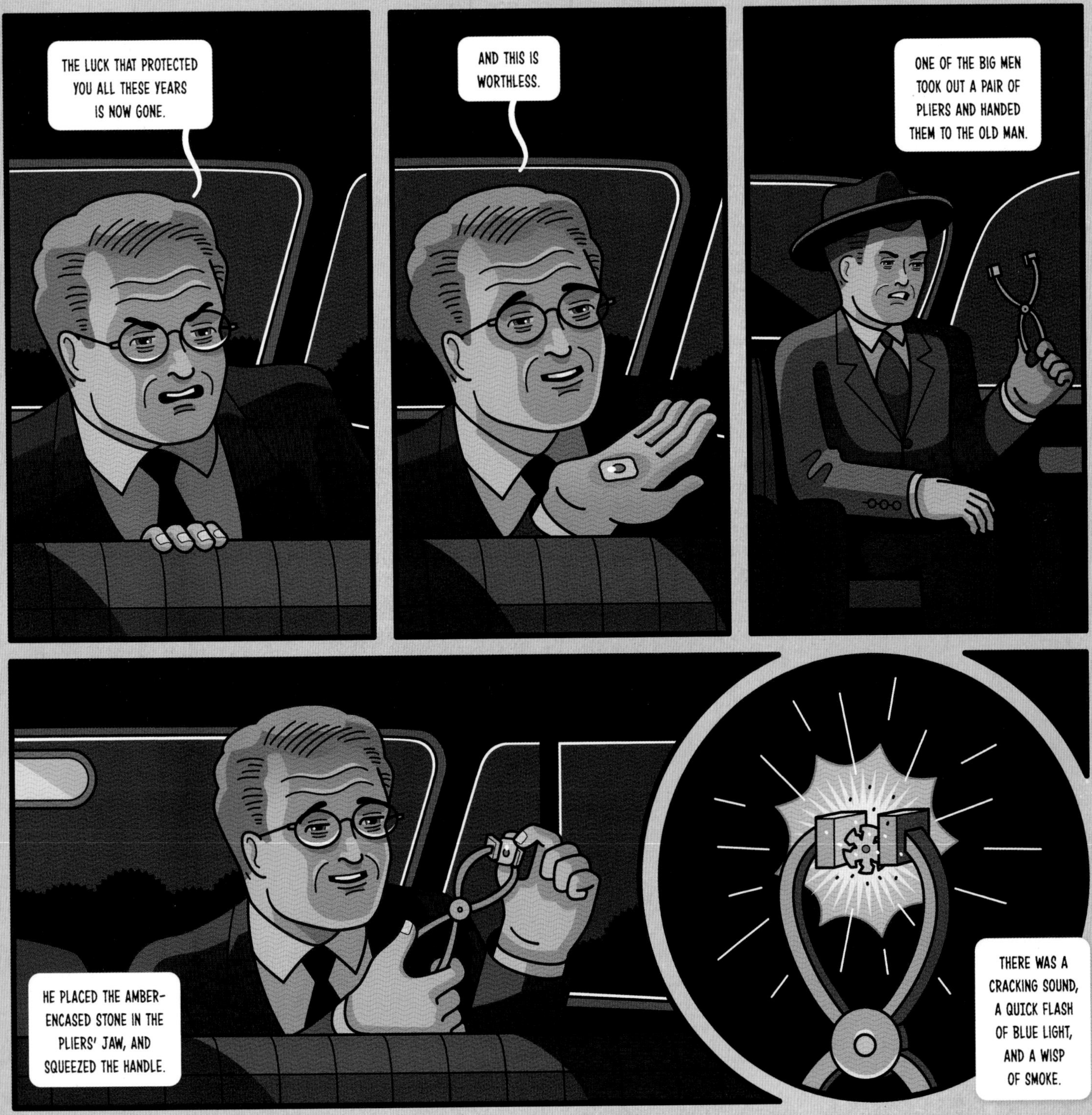
THE LUCK THAT PROTECTED YOU ALL THESE YEARS IS NOW GONE.
AND THIS IS WORTHLESS.
ONE OF THE BIG MEN TOOK OUT A PAIR OF PLIERS AND HANDED THEM TO THE OLD MAN.
HE PLACED THE AMBER-ENCASED STONE IN THE PLIERS' JAW, AND SQUEEZED THE HANDLE.
THERE WAS A CRACKING SOUND, A QUICK FLASH OF BLUE LIGHT, AND A WISP OF SMOKE.

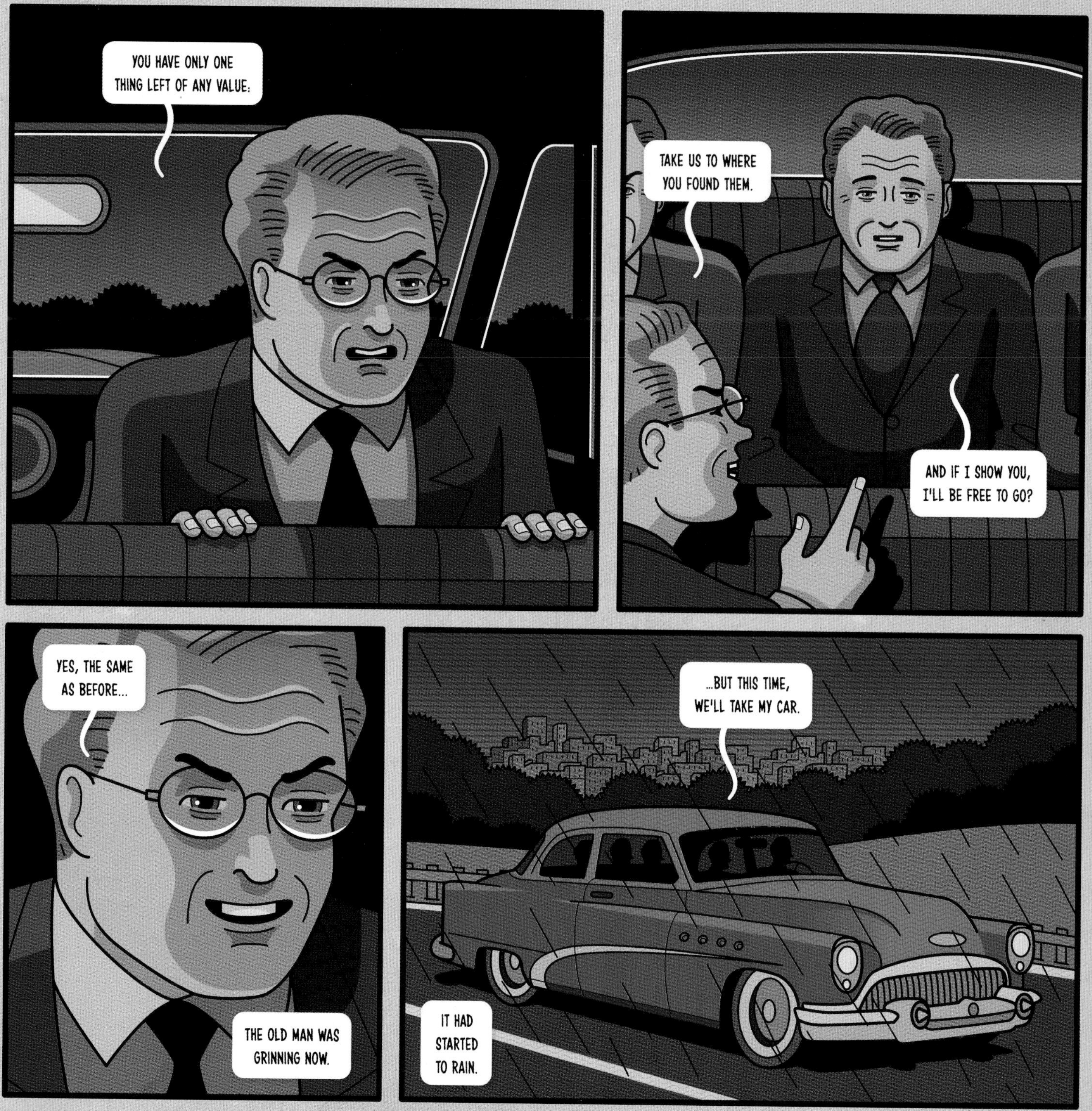
YOU HAVE ONLY ONE THING LEFT OF ANY VALUE:
TAKE US TO WHERE YOU FOUND THEM.
AND IF I SHOW YOU, I'LL BE FREE TO GO?
YES, THE SAME AS BEFORE...
THE OLD MAN WAS GRINNING NOW.
...BUT THIS TIME, WE'LL TAKE MY CAR.
IT HAD STARTED TO RAIN.

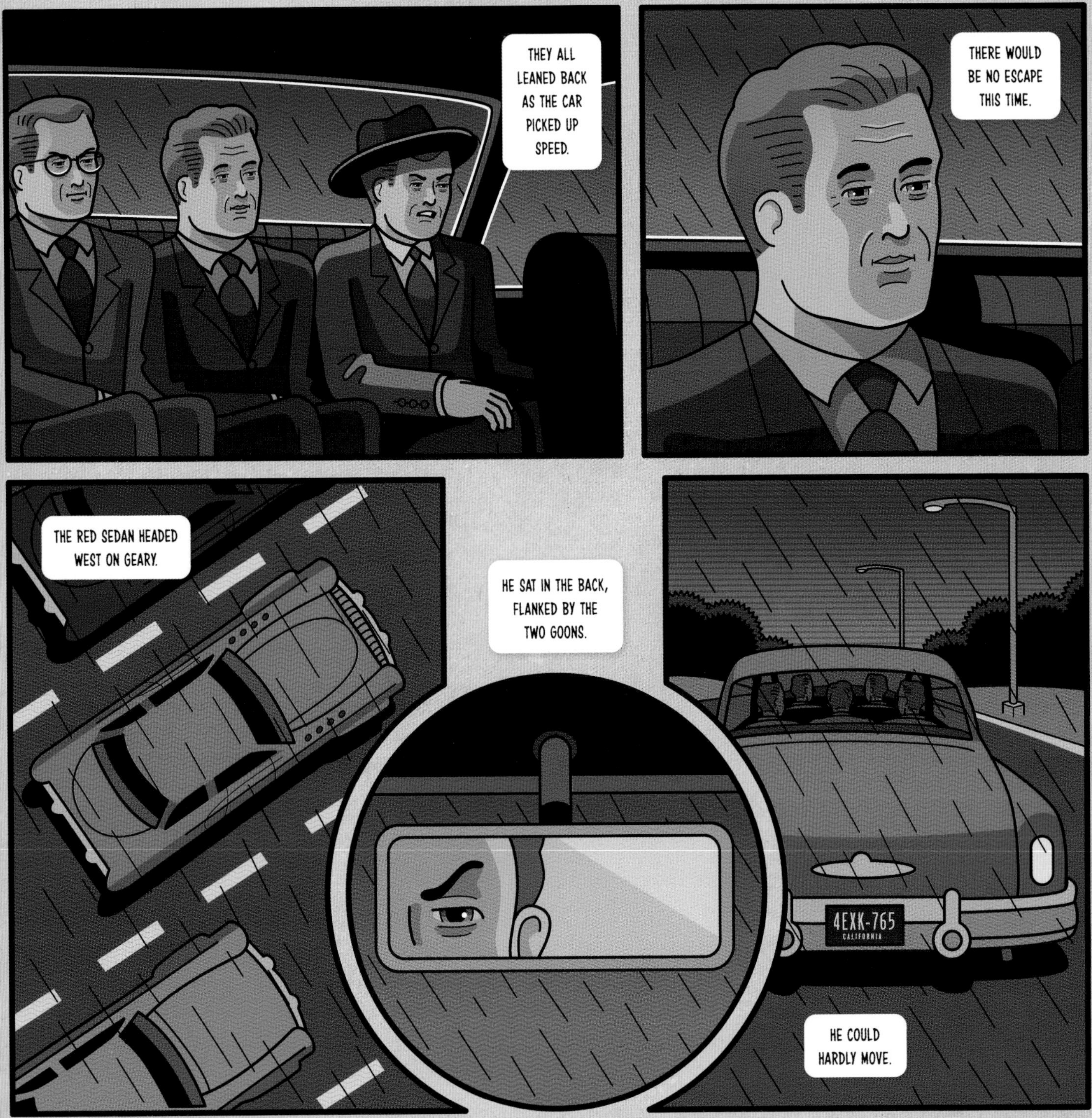
THEY ALL LEANED BACK AS THE CAR PICKED UP SPEED.
THERE WOULD BE NO ESCAPE THIS TIME.
THE RED SEDAN HEADED WEST ON GEARY.
HE SAT IN THE BACK, FLANKED BY THE TWO GOONS.
4EXK-765
CALIFORNIA
HE COULD HARDLY MOVE.

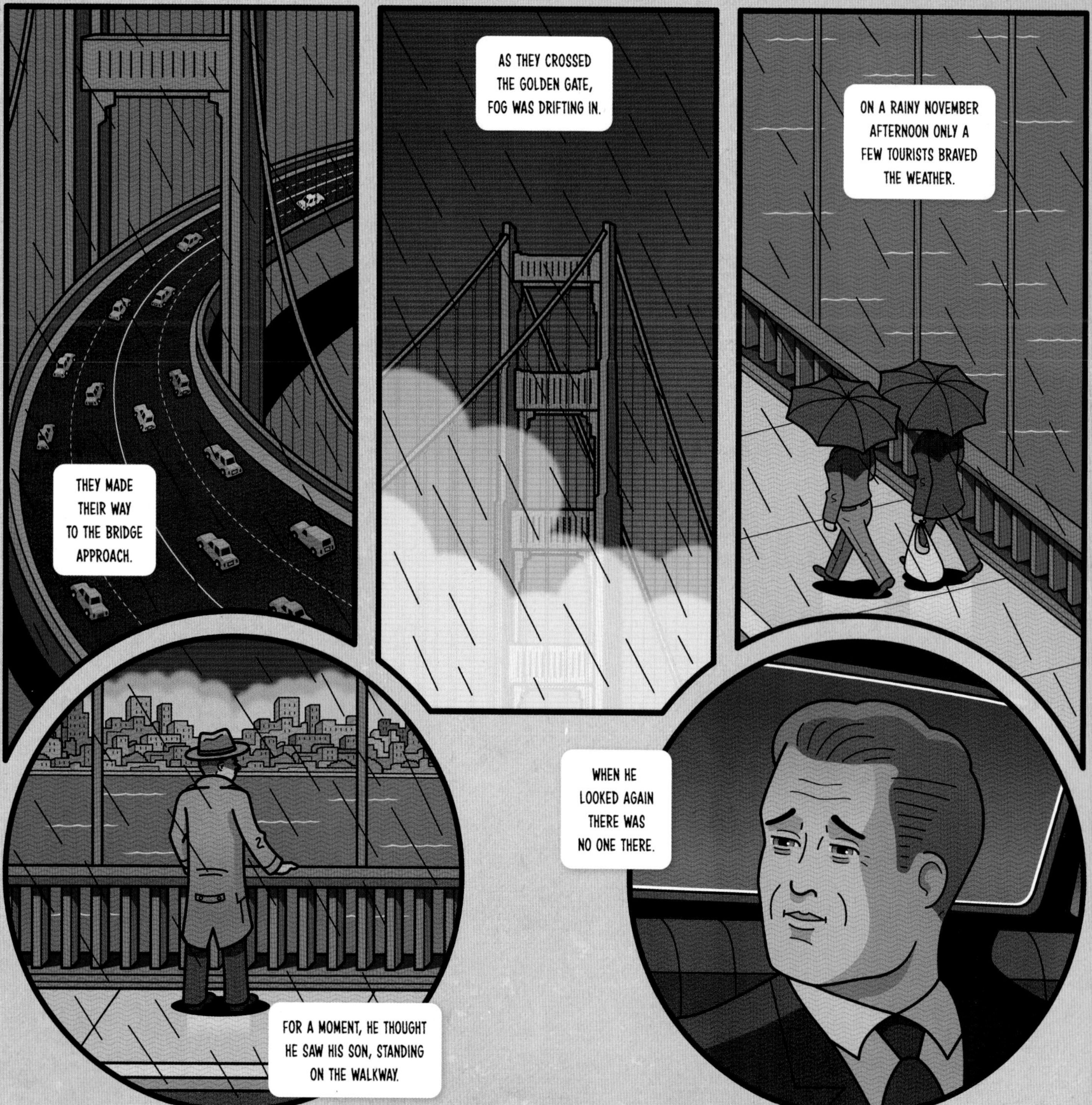
THEY MADE THEIR WAY TO THE BRIDGE APPROACH.
AS THEY CROSSED THE GOLDEN GATE, FOG WAS DRIFTING IN.
ON A RAINY NOVEMBER AFTERNOON ONLY A FEW TOURISTS BRAVED THE WEATHER.
FOR A MOMENT, HE THOUGHT HE SAW HIS SON, STANDING ON THE WALKWAY.
WHEN HE LOOKED AGAIN THERE WAS NO ONE THERE.

CHAPTER
14

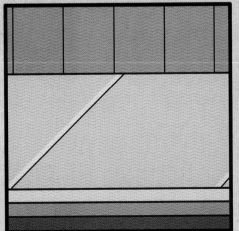

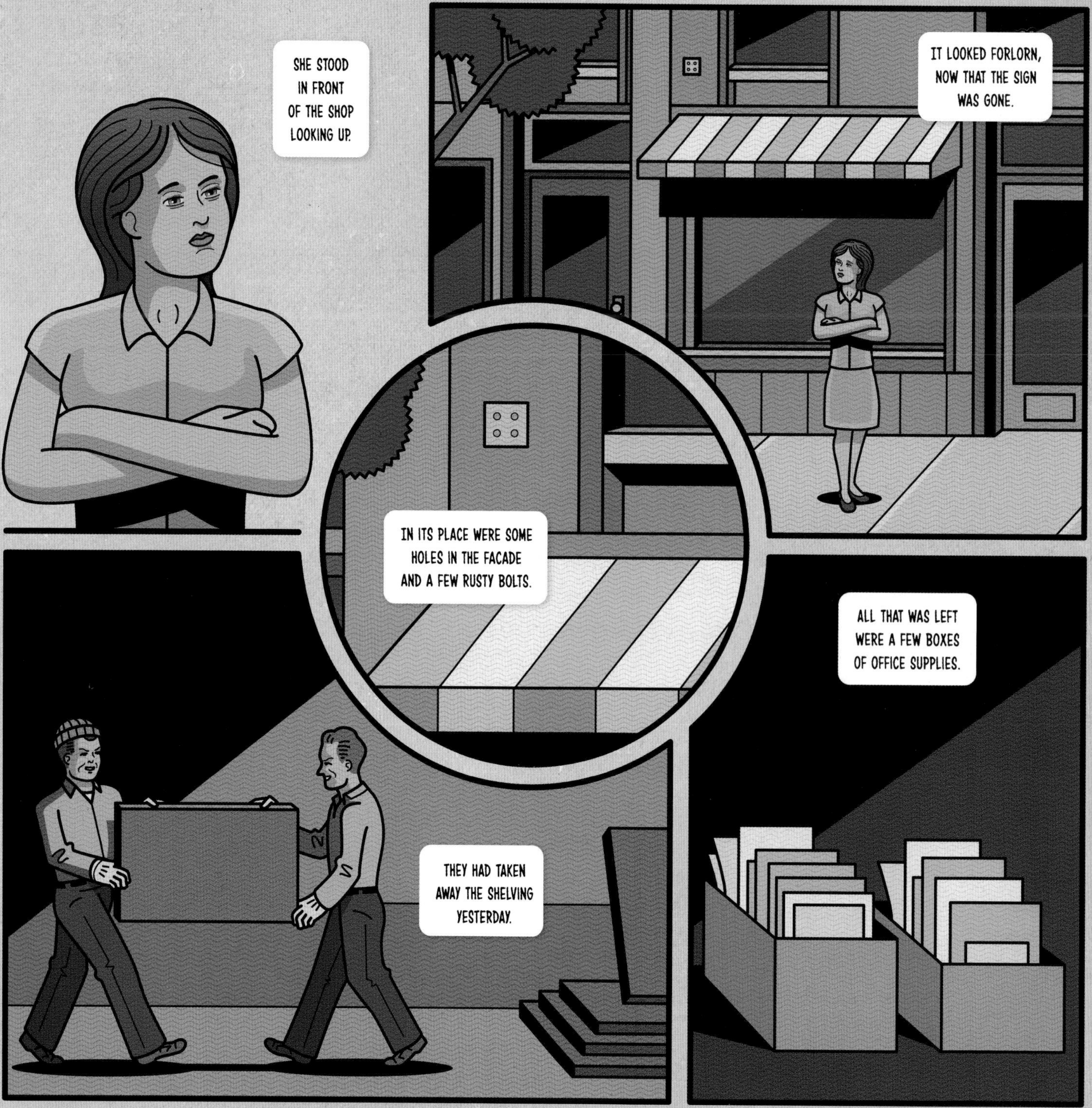
SHE STOOD IN FRONT OF THE SHOP LOOKING UP.
IT LOOKED FORLORN, NOW THAT THE SIGN WAS GONE.
IN ITS PLACE WERE SOME HOLES IN THE FACADE AND A FEW RUSTY BOLTS.
THEY HAD TAKEN AWAY THE SHELVING YESTERDAY.
ALL THAT WAS LEFT WERE A FEW BOXES OF OFFICE SUPPLIES.

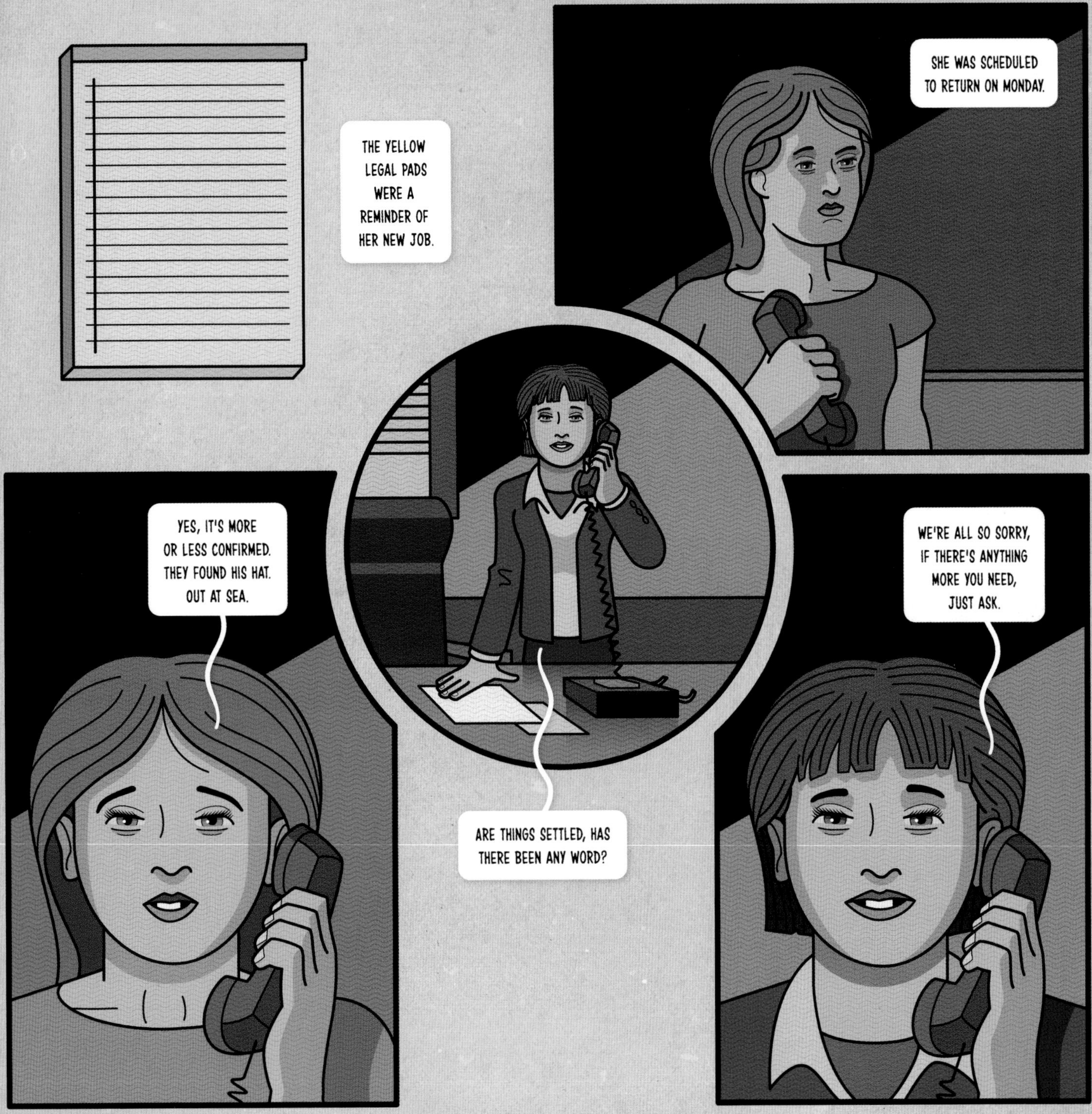
THE YELLOW LEGAL PADS WERE A REMINDER OF HER NEW JOB.
SHE WAS SCHEDULED TO RETURN ON MONDAY.
ARE THINGS SETTLED, HAS THERE BEEN ANY WORD?
YES, IT'S MORE OR LESS CONFIRMED. THEY FOUND HIS HAT. OUT AT SEA.
WE'RE ALL SO SORRY, IF THERE'S ANYTHING MORE YOU NEED, JUST ASK.

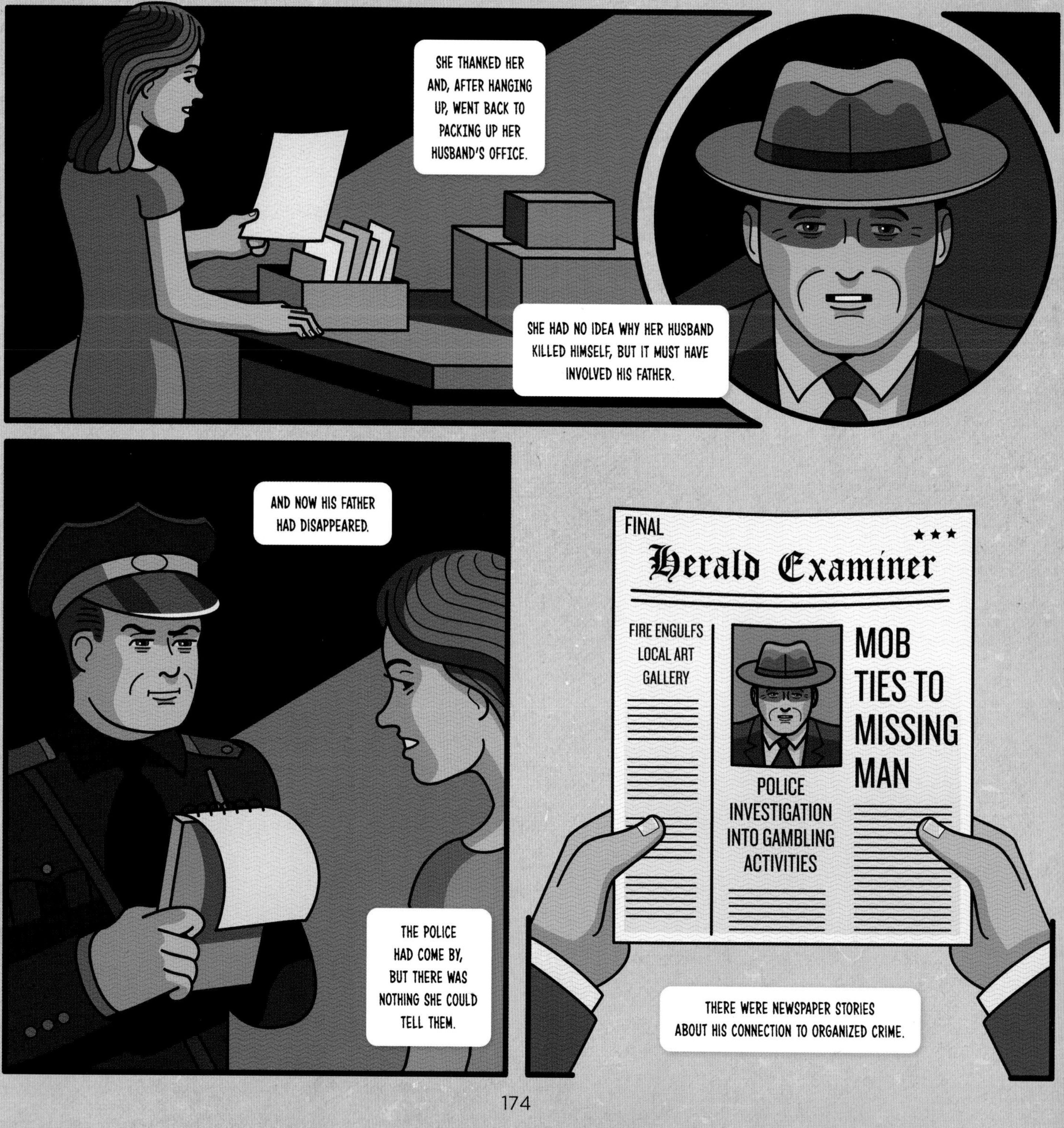
SHE THANKED HER AND, AFTER HANGING UP, WENT BACK TO PACKING UP HER HUSBAND'S OFFICE.
SHE HAD NO IDEA WHY HER HUSBAND KILLED HIMSELF, BUT IT MUST HAVE INVOLVED HIS FATHER.
AND NOW HIS FATHER HAD DISAPPEARED.
THE POLICE HAD COME BY, BUT THERE WAS NOTHING SHE COULD TELL THEM.
FINAL
Herald Examiner
FIRE ENGULFS LOCAL ART GALLERY
MOB TIES TO MISSING MAN
POLICE INVESTIGATION INTO GAMBLING ACTIVITIES
THERE WERE NEWSPAPER STORIES ABOUT HIS CONNECTION TO ORGANIZED CRIME.

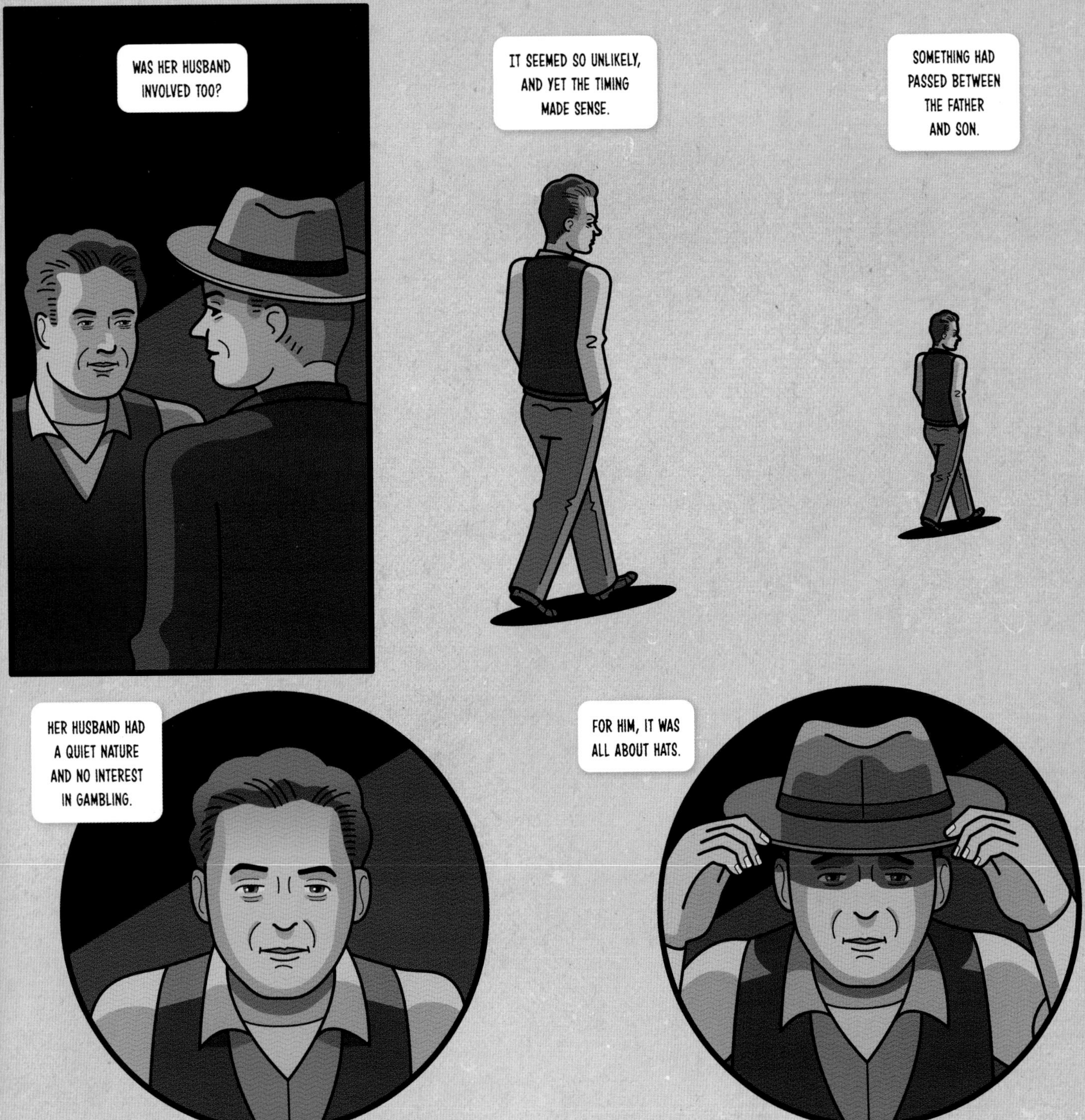
WAS HER HUSBAND INVOLVED TOO?
IT SEEMED SO UNLIKELY, AND YET THE TIMING MADE SENSE.
SOMETHING HAD PASSED BETWEEN THE FATHER AND SON.
HER HUSBAND HAD A QUIET NATURE AND NO INTEREST IN GAMBLING.
FOR HIM, IT WAS ALL ABOUT HATS.

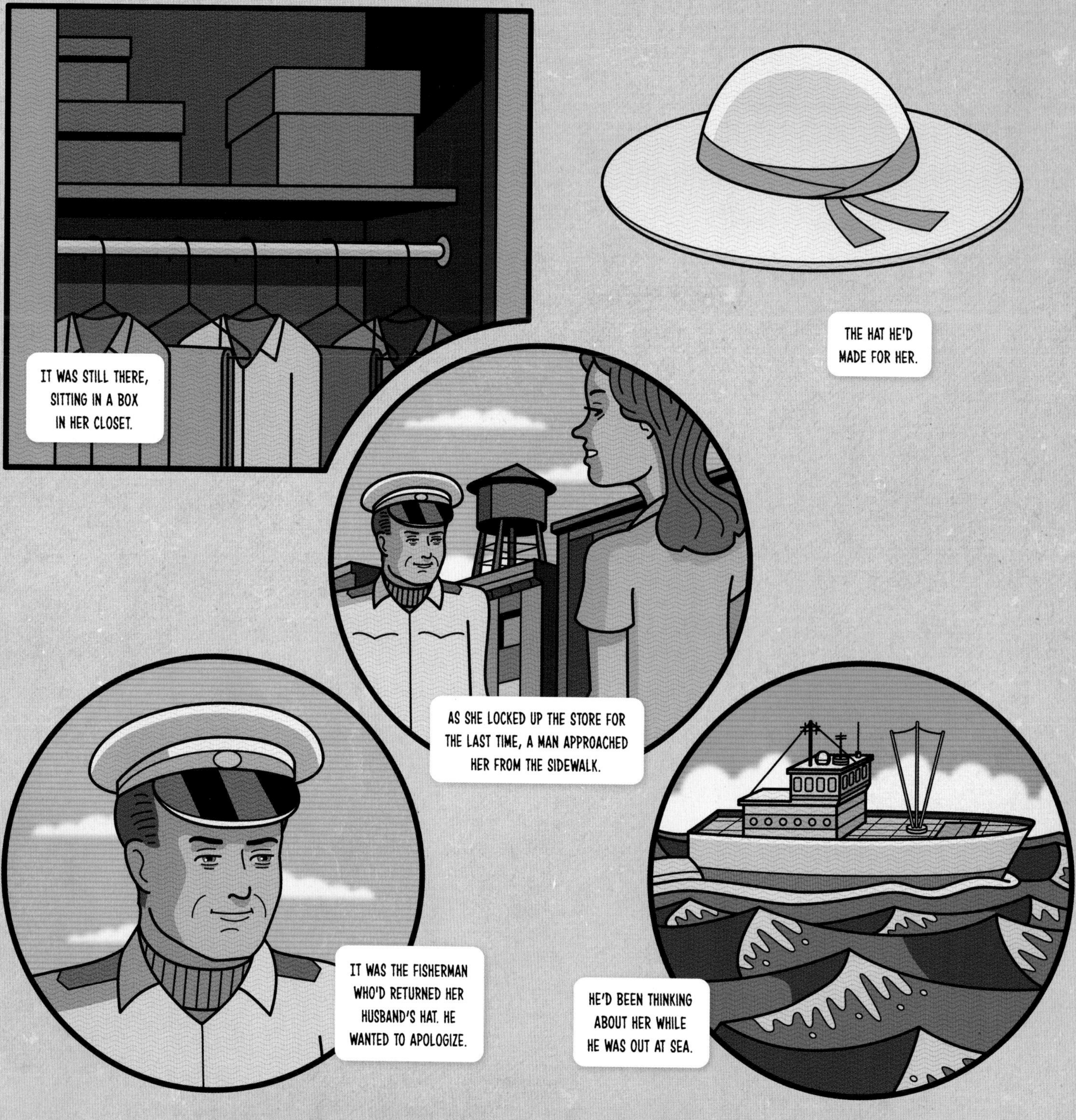
IT WAS STILL THERE, SITTING IN A BOX IN HER CLOSET.
THE HAT HE'D MADE FOR HER.
AS SHE LOCKED UP THE STORE FOR THE LAST TIME, A MAN APPROACHED HER FROM THE SIDEWALK.
IT WAS THE FISHERMAN WHO'D RETURNED HER HUSBAND'S HAT. HE WANTED TO APOLOGIZE.
HE'D BEEN THINKING ABOUT HER WHILE HE WAS OUT AT SEA.

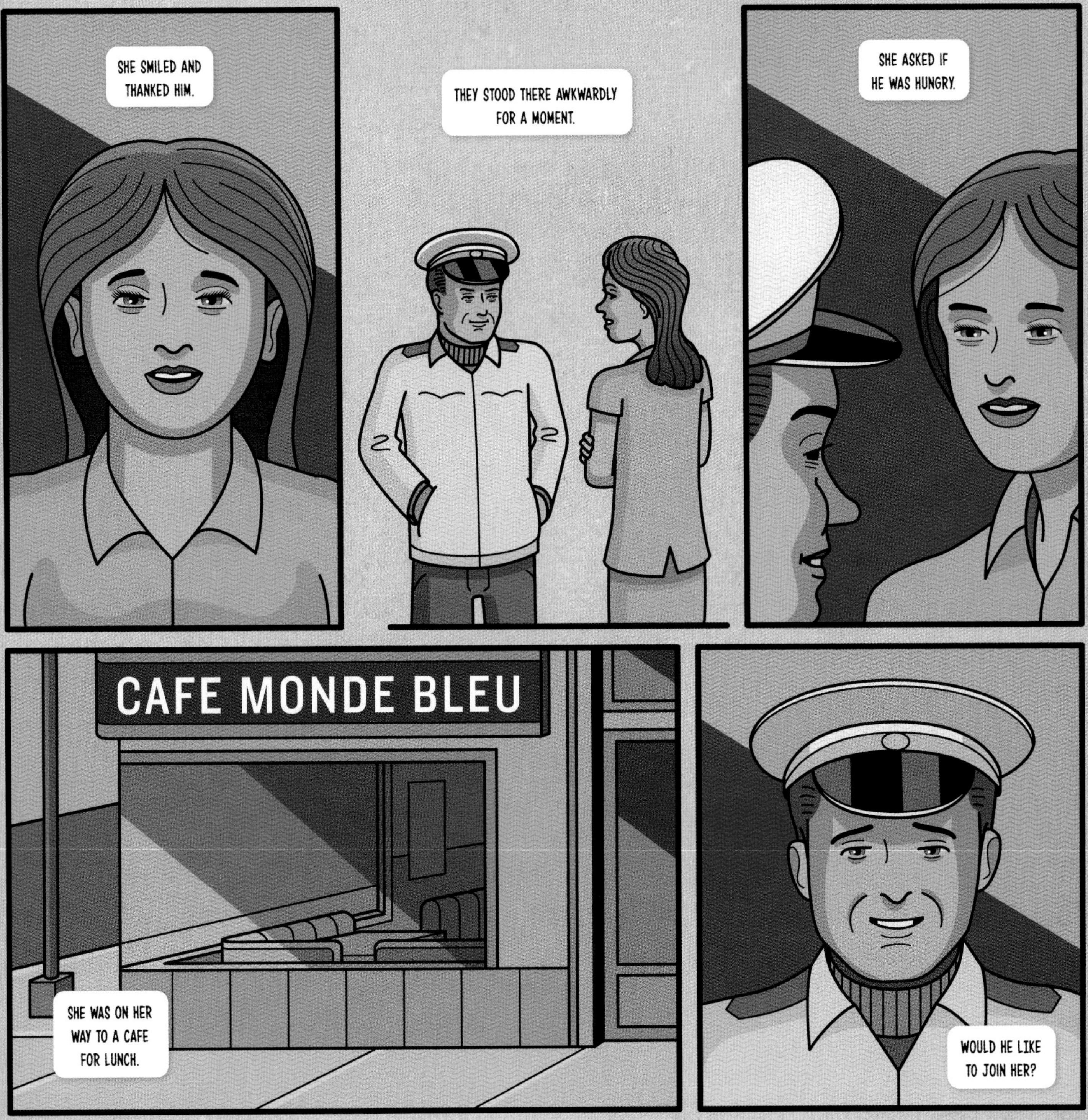

SHE SMILED AND THANKED HIM.
THEY STOOD THERE AWKWARDLY FOR A MOMENT.
SHE ASKED IF HE WAS HUNGRY.
CAFE MONDE BLEU
SHE WAS ON HER WAY TO A CAFE FOR LUNCH.
WOULD HE LIKE TO JOIN HER?

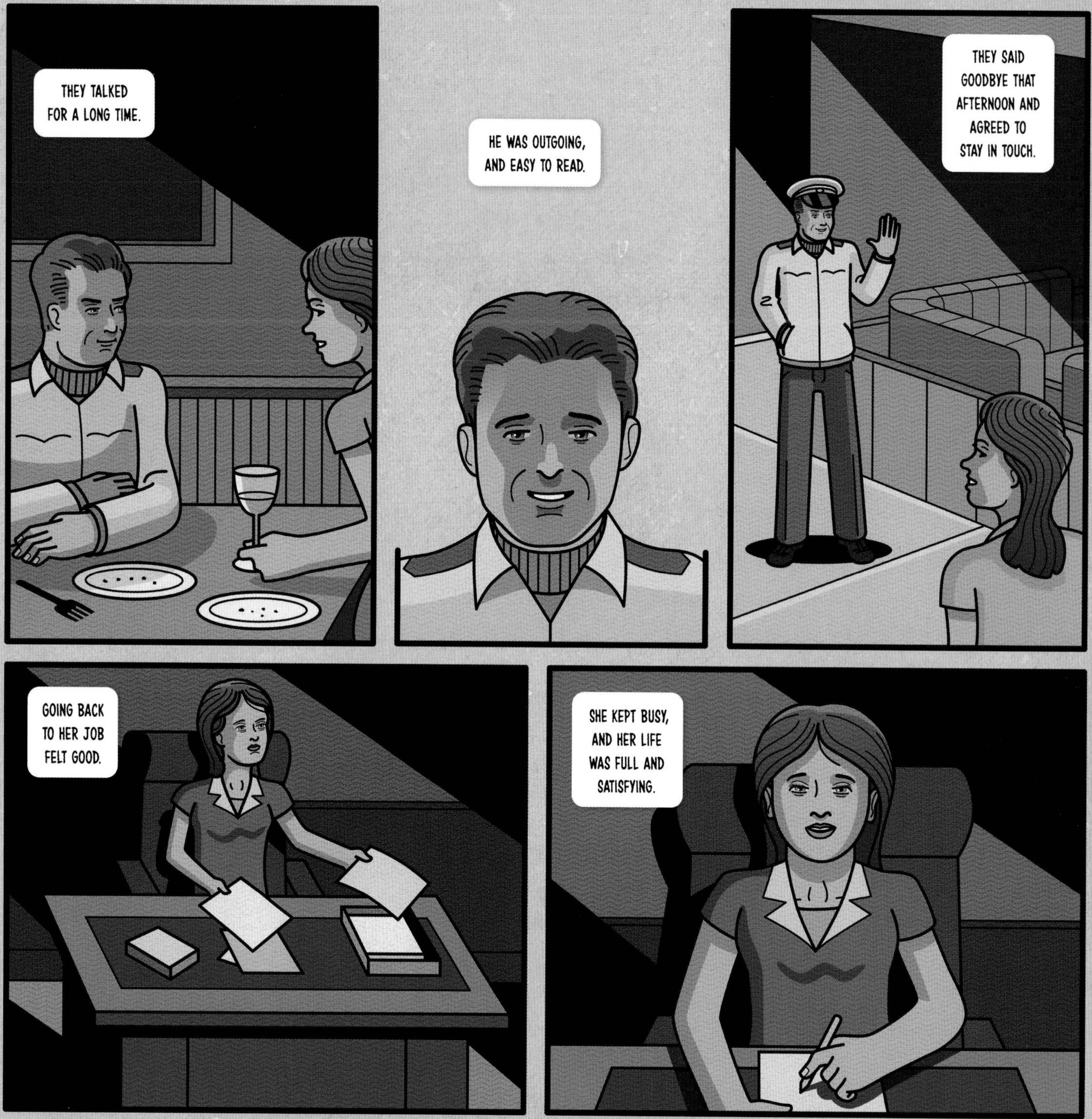
THEY TALKED FOR A LONG TIME.
HE WAS OUTGOING, AND EASY TO READ.
THEY SAID GOODBYE THAT AFTERNOON AND AGREED TO STAY IN TOUCH.
GOING BACK TO HER JOB FELT GOOD.
SHE KEPT BUSY, AND HER LIFE WAS FULL AND SATISFYING.

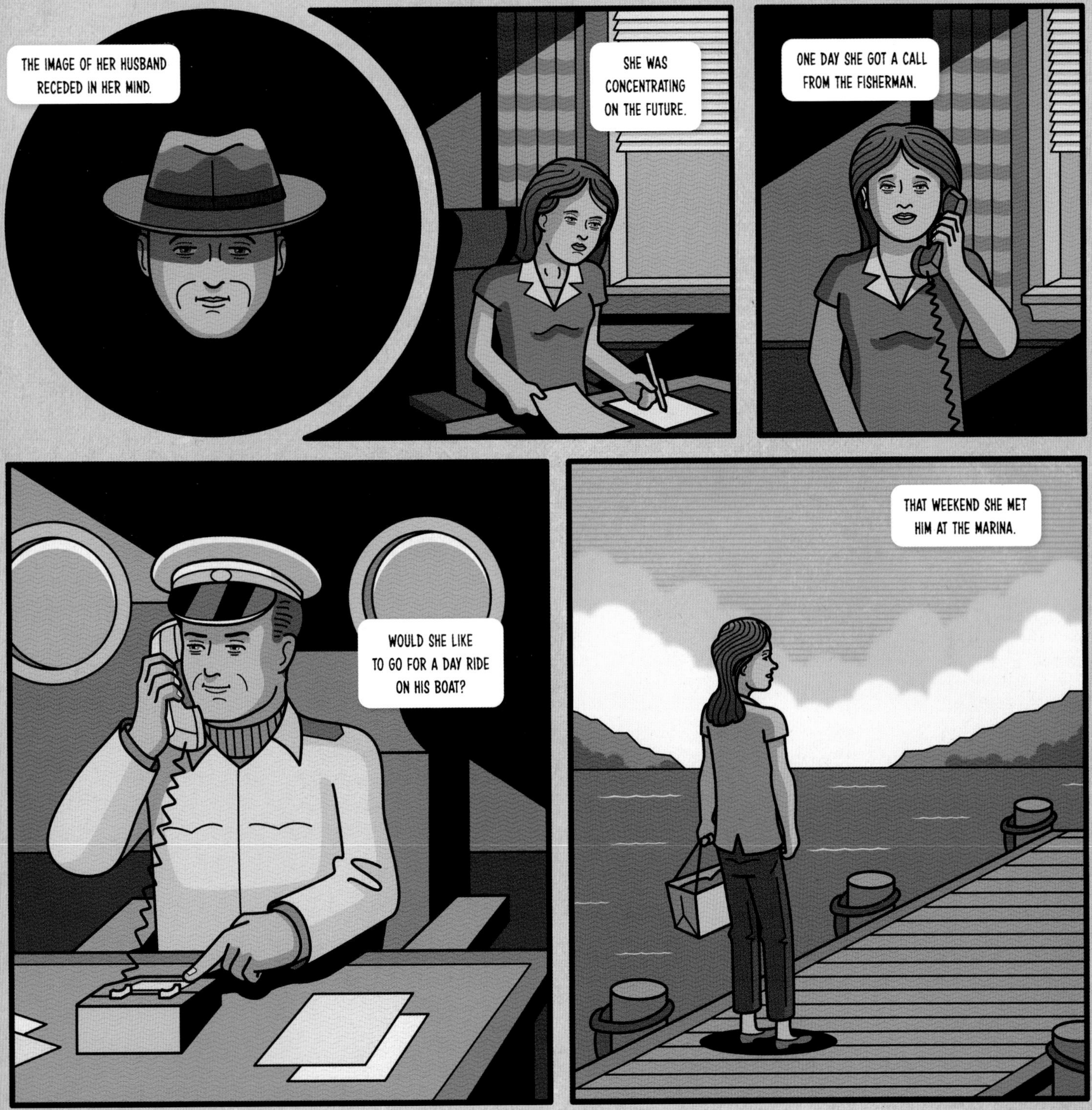
THE IMAGE OF HER HUSBAND RECEDED IN HER MIND.
SHE WAS CONCENTRATING ON THE FUTURE.
ONE DAY SHE GOT A CALL FROM THE FISHERMAN.
WOULD SHE LIKE TO GO FOR A DAY RIDE ON HIS BOAT?
THAT WEEKEND SHE MET HIM AT THE MARINA.

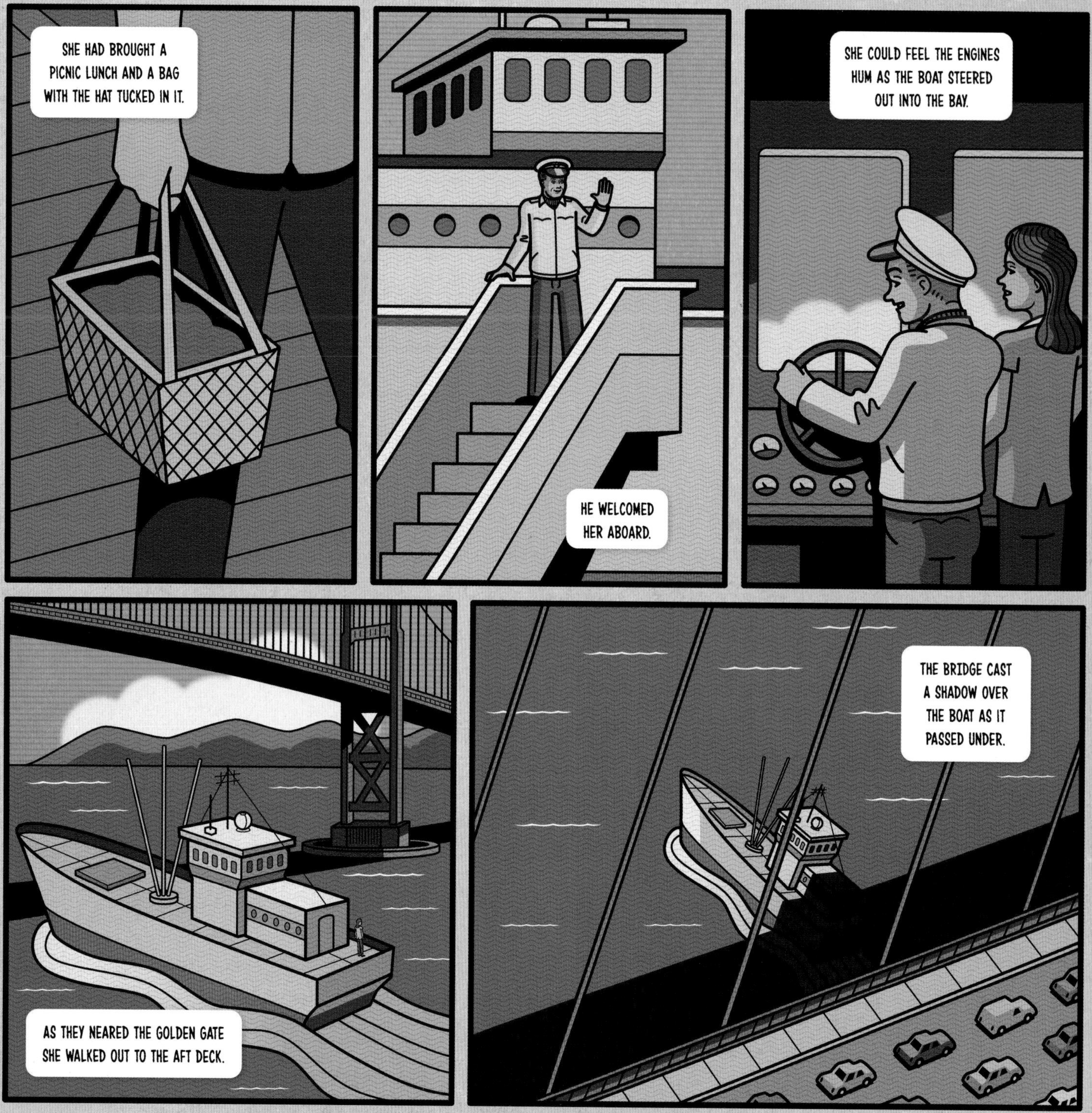
SHE HAD BROUGHT A PICNIC LUNCH AND A BAG WITH THE HAT TUCKED IN IT.
HE WELCOMED HER ABOARD.
SHE COULD FEEL THE ENGINES HUM AS THE BOAT STEERED OUT INTO THE BAY.
AS THEY NEARED THE GOLDEN GATE SHE WALKED OUT TO THE AFT DECK.
THE BRIDGE CAST A SHADOW OVER THE BOAT AS IT PASSED UNDER.

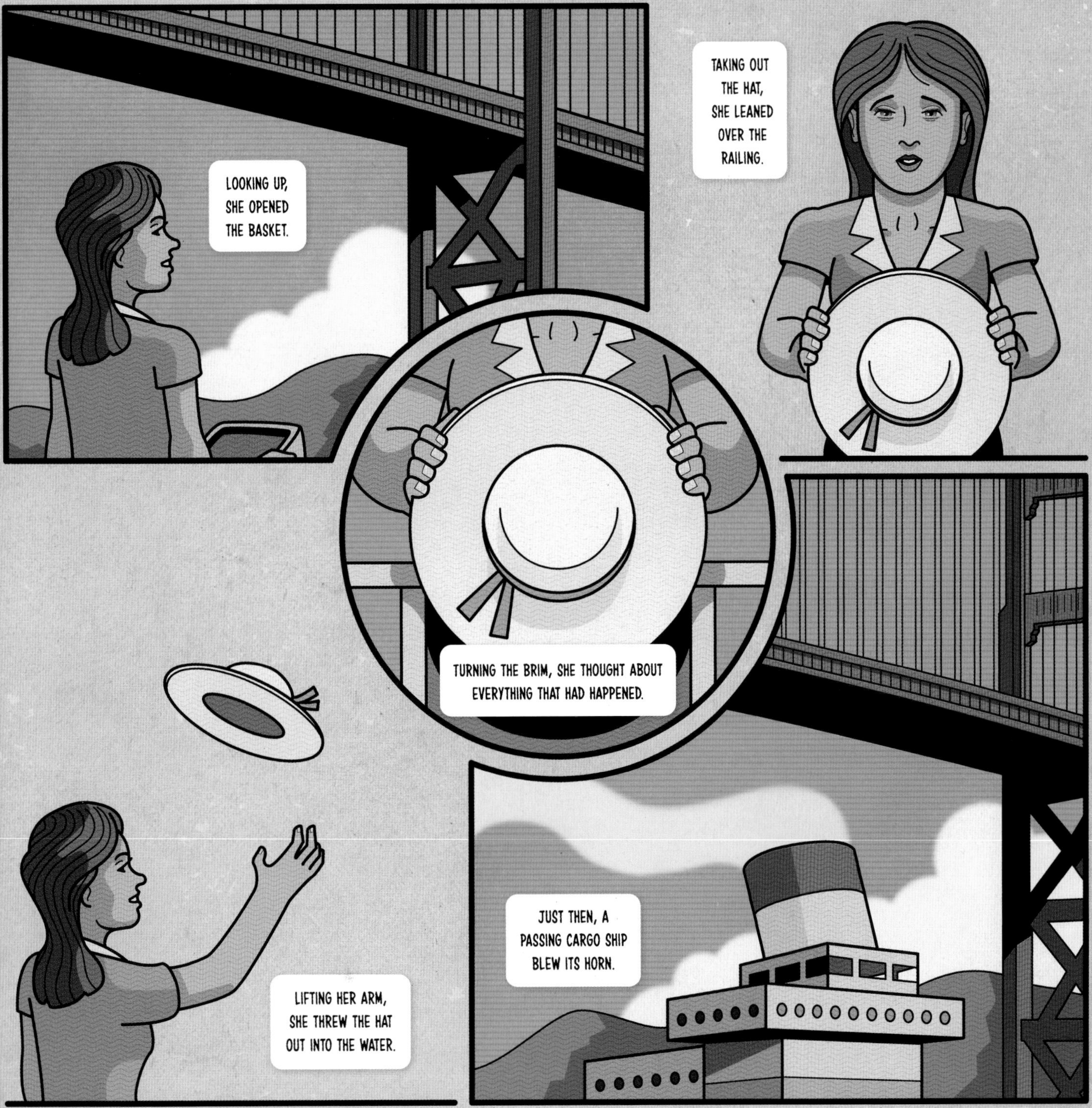
LOOKING UP, SHE OPENED THE BASKET.
TAKING OUT THE HAT, SHE LEANED OVER THE RAILING.
TURNING THE BRIM, SHE THOUGHT ABOUT EVERYTHING THAT HAD HAPPENED.
LIFTING HER ARM, SHE THREW THE HAT OUT INTO THE WATER.
JUST THEN, A PASSING CARGO SHIP BLEW ITS HORN.

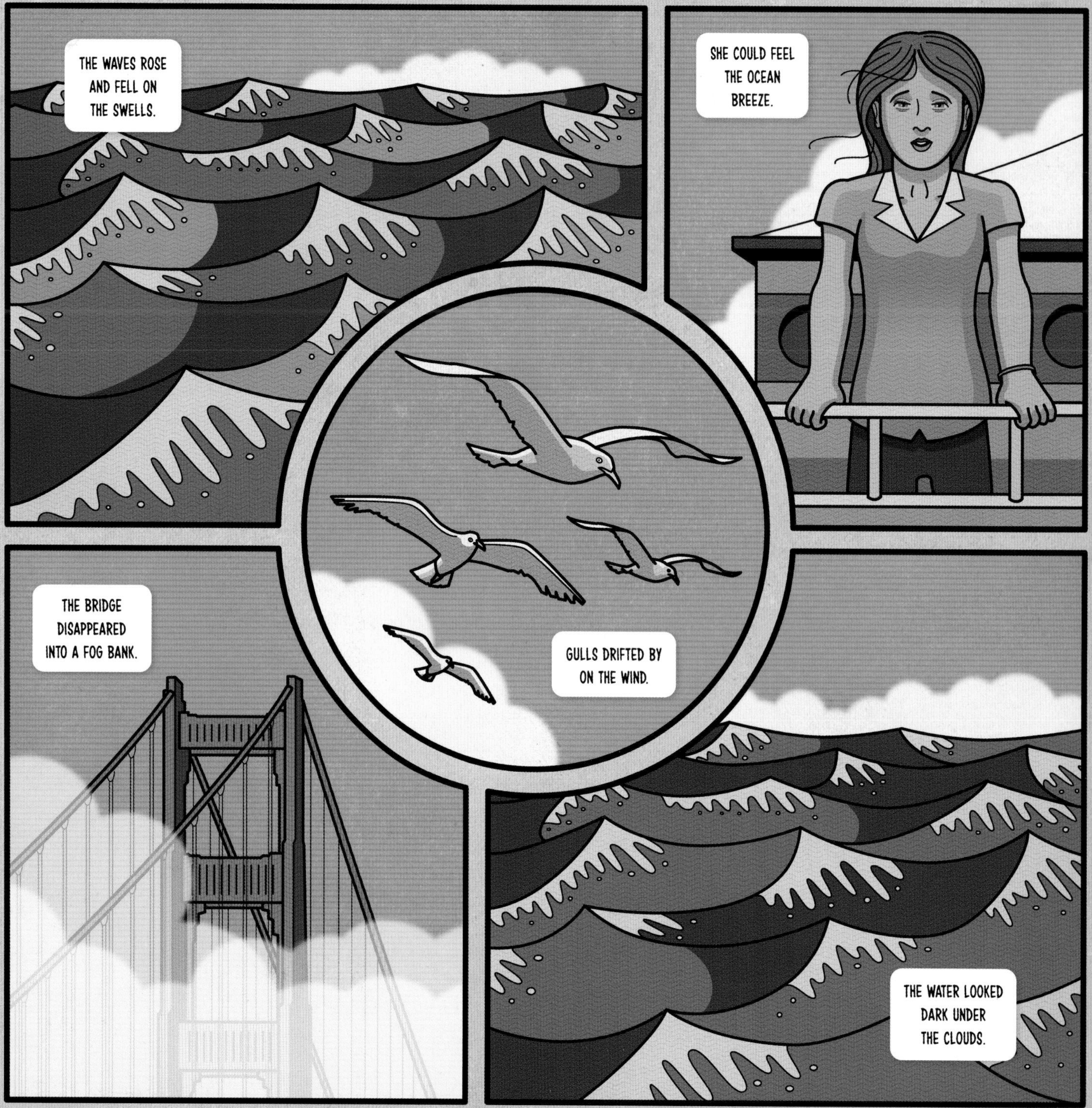
THE WAVES ROSE AND FELL ON THE SWELLS.
SHE COULD FEEL THE OCEAN BREEZE.
GULLS DRIFTED BY ON THE WIND.
THE BRIDGE DISAPPEARED INTO A FOG BANK.
THE WATER LOOKED DARK UNDER THE CLOUDS.

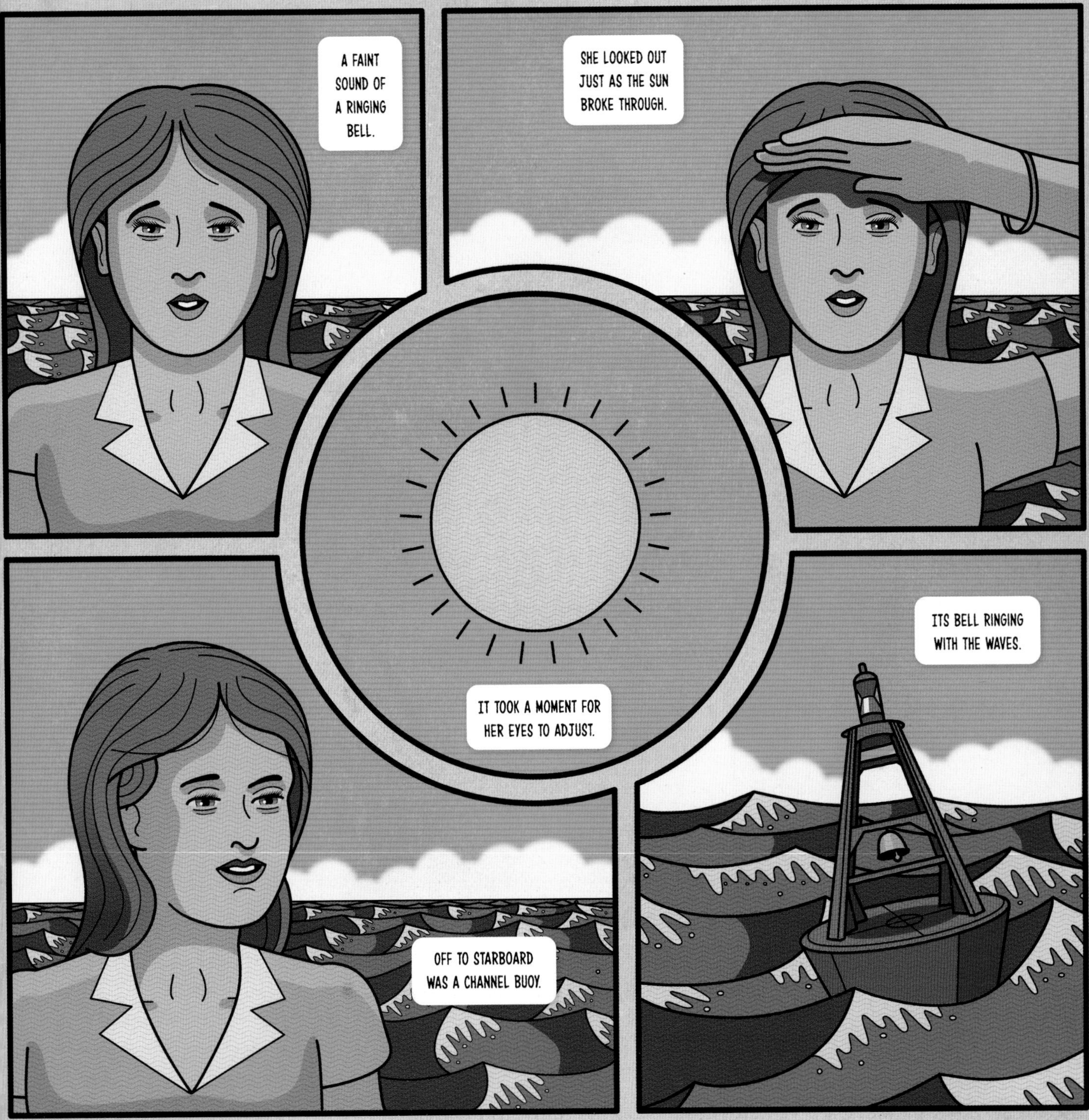
A FAINT SOUND OF A RINGING BELL.
SHE LOOKED OUT JUST AS THE SUN BROKE THROUGH.
IT TOOK A MOMENT FOR HER EYES TO ADJUST.
OFF TO STARBOARD WAS A CHANNEL BUOY.
ITS BELL RINGING WITH THE WAVES.

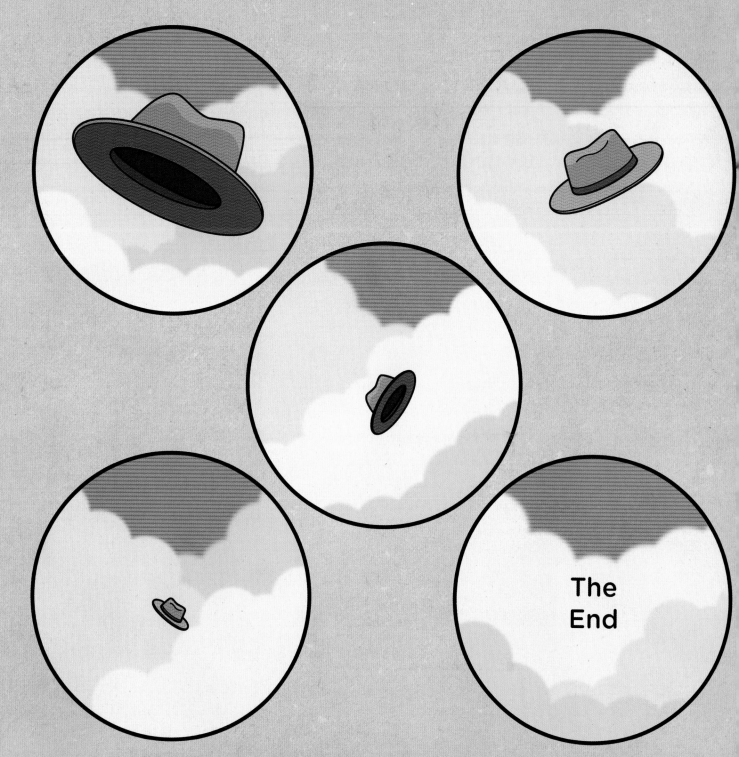

The
End